FORGET MY NAME

J.S. MONROE read English at Cambridge,
worked as a foreign correspondent in
Delhi and was *Weekend* editor of the *Daily
Telegraph* in London before becoming a
full-time writer. Monroe is the author of
six novels, including the international
bestseller *Find Me*.

Follow the author: @jsthrillers

By J.S. Monroe

Find Me
Forget My Name

FORGET MY NAME

J. S. MONROE

First published in the UK in 2018 by Head of Zeus Ltd

9 7 5 3 1 2 4 6 8

A catalogue record for this book is available from
the British Library.

ISBN (HB): 9781786698049
ISBN (XTPB): 9781786698056
ISBN (E): 9781786698032

Typeset by Divaddict Publishing Solutions Ltd

Printed and bound in Great Britain by
CPI Group (UK) Ltd, Croydon CR0 4YY

Head of Zeus Ltd
First Floor East
5–8 Hardwick Street
London EC1R 4RG

WWW.HEADOFZEUS.COM

In memory of
Len Heath

The other way of retention is the power to revive again in our minds those ideas which, after imprinting, have disappeared, or have been, as it were, laid aside out of sight... For the narrow mind of man, not being capable of having many ideas under view and consideration at once, it was necessary to have a repository, to lay up those ideas which, at another time, it might have use of.

—John Locke, writing on memory in *An Essay Concerning Humane Understanding* (1690)

DAY ONE

I

I can't remember my own name.

I repeat the words to myself like a mantra, struggling to stay calm, trying to comprehend their full meaning. Loosed from the moorings of my old life, I can only be guided by the present now.

I watch from the train window as the countryside slides by. Is the person opposite staring at me? I study his reflection in the glass. This must be what it feels like to lose your mind. From somewhere at the back of my skull a headache rolls in. Breathe. I can do this.

My legs start to tremble. I press my feet hard into the carriage floor, one at a time, focusing on the canal now running alongside the railway. I need to keep it together, be brave. How might a normal person behave in this situation? They would take time out, allow the brain to do its thing. Let the synapses fire. Half the people in this carriage have probably forgotten things: partners' birthdays, wedding anniversaries, pin numbers, their own names...

When we reach the station printed on my ticket, I step off the train, filling my lungs with fresh country air as I zigzag up the footpath to the road, following a column of weary commuters. Should I recognise any of them? Rush hour has only just begun. To my left, a river feels its way through a meadow, the shallow water sparkling in the summer sun. Sheep bleat in the distance, a cheer rises from the cricket pitch by the church. Beyond it, fields of rapeseed, the colour of English mustard. And then there's the canal, rows of brightly painted narrowboats tied up along the towpath.

The village is only an hour on the train from London, but it feels very rural. Pastoral. I walk over the railway bridge and head up the high street, past a letterbox, trying to think straight. I know I'm doing the right thing. When I tried to report my lost bag at the airport, the man at the desk said that temporary amnesia can be triggered by all sort of things, but work-related stress is one of the most common causes. In such circumstances home is the best place to be. Post on the doormat, letters with a name on the envelopes. And when he asked me if I could find my way home, I retrieved a train ticket from my pocket and we both agreed that it must be to where I live.

At the Slaughtered Lamb I turn right into a lane lined with old thatched houses. I should be relieved as I walk down towards the last building on the right, a small cottage with a teal-blue front door and dripping wisteria, but I'm not.

I'm terrified.

I try to imagine myself closing the front door behind me, flopping down on the sofa with a large glass of chilled Sauvignon Blanc and something trashy on the TV. Except that I don't have a key. Standing in front of the house, I glance up and down the street and hear a voice behind the front door. American. A chill runs through me. I step over to the window and peer in. Two people are moving about in the kitchen, silhouetted by low sunlight slanting in from the garden double doors behind them. I stare at the figures, barely able to breathe. My gaze settles on a man chopping salad at the kitchen island with a large steel knife that catches the light. I want to turn away, run down the street, but I force myself to watch as he cuts. Behind him, a woman stands at a Belfast sink, filling a saucepan with water.

I return to the front door, check the number. It's the right house. My fingers are shaking too much to press the front-door bell. Instead, I wrap both hands around the wrought-iron knocker and bang it, my head hanging forward like a supplicant in prayer. *Om mani padme hum.* No answer, so I knock again.

'I'll get it,' the man says.

I step backwards into the lane and almost lose my footing as the door opens.

'Can I help?' the man asks, with a faint, uneasy smile.

I feel dizzy. We stare at each other for a second, each scrutinising the other for something, an explanation, recognition. I realise I'm holding my breath. He glances down at my suitcase and then back at me. I look at him for as long as I can – one, two, three seconds – and then turn away.

I know I should say something at this point – *Who are you? What the hell are you doing in my house? Please tell me this isn't happening, not after all I've been through today –* but I remain silent. Speechless.

'We're not interested if you're selling anything,' he says, motioning to close the door. 'Sorry.' I recognise the accent: the cocksure, familiar sounds of New York. He throws another glance at my suitcase. He must think it's stuffed full of oven gloves and ironing-board covers, or whatever is hawked on doorsteps these days.

'Wait,' I say, grateful that I can remember how to speak. My voice startles him. Am I shouting? A high-pitched ringing has started up in my ears.

'Yes?' he says. His face is lean, alert, washed-blue eyes set deep, a neat goatee, hair tied in a ponytail. I sense it's not his natural response to close the door on a stranger.

'Who is it, darling?' a female voice calls out from behind him. English.

He breaks into a smile that's almost serene in its intensity. Fleur's face swims in front of my eyes, a fleeting smile on her lips too. I rest a finger against the tattoo on my wrist, hidden below my blouse sleeve. I know that we got one each: a beautiful lotus flower, purple, partially open. If only I could remember more.

'I live here,' I manage to say. 'I've been away on a business trip. This is my house.'

'Your house?' he asks, folding his arms and leaning back against the doorframe. He is well dressed – a floral-patterned shirt, buttoned up at the collar, thin charcoal-grey cardigan, designer jeans of some kind. He seems to find my suggestion more amusing than strange and glances up and down the street, perhaps checking for hidden TV cameras, a presenter clutching a microphone. Maybe he's just relieved that I'm not trying to sell him aloe vera.

'My front-door key was in my handbag, but it was lost at the airport, along with my passport, laptop, iPhone, purse…' My words tail off, the ringing in my ears now unbearable. 'I was about to get a key from the neighbours, and then I was going to call the police, report—'

The ground begins to rise up. I force myself to look at him again, but all I can see is Fleur in her apartment doorway, asking if I want to come in. I take a deep breath, visualise a bodhi tree, a figure in repose below its calming, sacred boughs. It's no good. Nothing's working. I thought I could cope, but I can't.

'Can I come in?' I ask, my body now swaying uncontrollably. 'Please?'

A hand on my elbow softens my fall.

2

'She's very beautiful.'

'I hadn't noticed.'

'Come on, she's stunning.'

'She needs help.'

'The surgery said they'd ring back in fifteen minutes.'

I lie there with my eyes closed, listening. They are in the kitchen, where I first saw them from the window, and I am in the small sitting room at the front of the house. His voice is confident, assured. Hers is more hesitant, softer. After fainting at the door, I came round on the sofa and chatted briefly with the woman, who is called Laura, reassuring her that I was OK and just needed to close my eyes for a few minutes until the dizziness passed. That was five minutes ago.

'Are you feeling better?' Laura says, coming into the sitting room.

'A little,' I reply, turning my head towards her. 'Thank you.' She's holding a large mug of fresh mint tea. I notice my blouse sleeve has rucked up, partially revealing the lotus tattoo.

'I brought you this,' she says, placing it on the low Indian table in front of the sofa. On one side of the mug is a drawing of a cat in a hero yoga pose. I involuntarily straighten my back.

'We've rung our local surgery, here in the village,' Laura continues, glancing at my wrist. 'The doctor's going to call back in a minute.'

'Thank you,' I say again, my voice weak.

'Still dizzy?'

'A bit.'

I reach forward for the tea. Laura is in her early thirties. She's wearing three-quarter-length leggings and a fluorescent sports top, as if she's about to go for a run, and she's in good shape: tall and manicured, hair pulled up into a bun, glowing skin. Almost too good to be true, apart from a pronounced darkness beneath her eyes.

'Tony says you thought this was your house,' she says, trying to make light of her words. I take a sip of the mint tea, hot and honey-sweet, hoping it might dispel the cold dread in my stomach. 'Said you were about to get a key. From our neighbours.'

She manages another short laugh and stops, turning away.

'It is my house,' I whisper, cradling the mug for warmth.

I can sense her bristle. Nothing obvious – she seems too kind for that – just the faintest recalibration. Tony, who must have been listening, comes to the doorway that links the sitting room with the kitchen.

'Thank you for the tea,' I say, keen to keep things cordial. 'And for ringing the surgery. I'm sure I'll be fine.'

'Not if you still think this is your house,' Tony says. He's smiling, but there's a hint of the territorial in his voice. My tattoo is still visible. After a few seconds, I casually pull down my sleeve to cover it.

I take another sip of the tea and look around the low-ceilinged room. Everything is immaculate, nothing's out of place. A wood-burning stove set in a large inglenook fireplace; to one side, a pile of logs, rounded like prayer rolls, neatly stacked; a collection of yoga and self-help books in a small bookcase, sorted by height; a wooden solitaire board, its marbles all in position. Even the reeds of a White Company 'Seychelles' room diffuser on the windowsill have been perfectly spaced. The contents might have changed, but the house's small proportions are familiar.

'I've come here because—' I pause, surprised by the emotion in my voice. 'I've been having a difficult time at work. Today, when I flew in from a conference, my handbag disappeared at the airport. I tried to report it, but I was unable to remember my own name.' I pause again.

'You can remember it now though?' Laura asks, turning to Tony. 'We all have our senior moments.'

Tony looks away.

I shake my head. *I can't remember my own name.*

'At the airport, all I could remember was where I lived. I thought if I could just get here, my house, this sanctuary, everything would be OK. And the one thing that wasn't lost was my train ticket home. I found it in a pocket.'

'You had your suitcase too,' Tony says, gesturing to the front door, where it is standing on end, handle still extended. 'Where was the conference?' he asks. Tony is more interested now, less defensive.

I can feel tears coming and do nothing to stop them. 'I don't know.'

'It's OK,' Laura says, sitting down next to me on the sofa. I realise I'm grateful for the arm she puts around my shoulders. It's been a difficult day.

'There should be a label on the handle,' Tony says, walking over to the suitcase.

'It got ripped off. Before I took the case from the carousel.'

He looks at me as my voice falters. I see myself in the arrivals hall, sitting down on the edge of an abandoned trolley, gazing at the same half-dozen suitcases going round and round. And then mine appeared, in front of a large, uneven parcel wrapped in black plastic and tape. An image of Fleur came and went, her body folded in on itself like a contortionist's, all elbows and knees.

'And you really can't recall where the conference was?' Tony asks.

'It may have been in Berlin.' Another image of Fleur floats up: dancing wildly, her eyes bright. I blink and she is gone, lost in the void.

'Berlin?' he repeats, unable to hide his surprise. 'That's a start. Airline?'

'I arrived at Terminal 5.'

'British Airways. Do you know what time?'

'This morning.'

'First thing?'

'I'm not sure. I'm sorry. I came straight here. Maybe late morning? Lunchtime?'

'And you can't recall your own name?'

'Tony,' Laura interjects.

I start to sob again, scared by how it all sounds when someone else is saying it. I need to stay strong, take this one step at a time. Laura gives me another hug.

'All I know is that this is my house,' I say, drying my eyes with the tissue she gives me. 'Right now that's all I can remember. My own home.'

'But you know that's impossible,' Tony says. 'I can show you the real-estate deeds.'

'It's OK,' Laura cuts in, glancing up at Tony again, who sits down on the other sofa, across from us. 'We should call the police,' she continues. 'Leave our number – in case someone hands your bag in at the airport.'

A shared silence as her words settle like dust in the room, absorbed by the ancient brickwork of the fireplace until there is nothing left of them.

'I guess there's no point, is there?' Tony says after a few seconds, his voice quieter now. 'Not if she still doesn't know her name.'

Another silence. I need to tell them everything that I know about this house, the details I can recall.

'My bedroom's upstairs on the left, the other one is across the landing, just large enough for a double bed,' I begin. 'It's next to the bathroom – shower cubicle in the corner, bath beneath the window. There's another small room beyond the bathroom, more of a storage space than a bedroom, and an attic above it.'

Laura looks across at Tony, who is staring at me in disbelief.

'At the bottom of the garden is a brick outbuilding, perfect for an office,' I continue. 'And there's a shower in the downstairs loo.'

I'm about to go on, tell them about the walk-in larder off the kitchen, but the phone rings.

'That'll be the surgery,' Laura says, picking up the receiver from the coffee table in front of us. I sense she's grateful for the interruption.

I sit in silence as Laura explains to the doctor about the woman who's just arrived on their doorstep claiming she lives in their house. Tony rubs the small of her back as she talks. I look away, close my eyes. This is all too much for me.

'Yes, she says she can't remember her name... where she's been... She says she lives here... I haven't asked.' She puts a hand over the receiver. 'She's asking for your date of birth?'

The expression on Laura's face suggests she knows already it's another pointless question. I shake my head.

'She doesn't know.' Laura listens for a while and then speaks again. 'She lost her passport at the airport, along with her bank cards, laptop' – a glance up at me – 'and all her other ID.' I nod. She listens again, this time for longer. I think she must know the doctor quite well, maybe as a friend.

'Thanks, Susie. Really appreciate it.'

She puts the phone down.

'Dr Patterson, one of the locum doctors, will see you this evening. A personal favour. She wanted you to go straight to A & E to check for any physical causes – head injury, stroke, that sort of thing – but I talked her out of it. We had a hellish time there last week, didn't we, darling?' She glances across at Tony, who nods sympathetically.

'Six hours,' he says.

I flinch at the thought of so long in a hospital.

'Because you're not registered at the practice, I'm taking you in on an appointment in my name.'

'Thank you,' I say.

'Maybe she is registered?' Tony says.

'I don't know,' I reply. 'I'm so sorry. Turning up here like this.'

'Have you heard of something called psychogenic amnesia?' Laura asks.

Tony looks up.

'Susie, Dr Patterson, she was just mentioning it. Major trauma or stress can cause temporary memory loss. A fugue state, I think she called it. I'll let her tell you more. It comes back, though, the memory. Over time. There's no need to worry.' She touches my hand.

'That's good,' I say. 'Can I use your loo?'

'Of course.'

'You know where the bathroom is,' Tony says, standing aside as I walk past him.

I don't answer. First left out of the kitchen.

3

When I re-enter the room, Tony is on the phone, waiting to be connected to someone. He turns his back the moment he sees me.

'Tony's calling the police station at Heathrow,' Laura says. 'To let them know about your missing bag. Tell them that you are here and are having problems with your memory. I'm sure Passport Control can run a check, see who's arrived from Berlin today, match your photo with their records.'

'I'm on hold for the "Heathrow Terminal 5 Safer Neighbourhoods Team",' Tony says, rolling his eyes, one hand over the phone. 'Doesn't exactly fill you with confidence, does it?'

His frustration seems to melt away when he looks at me. 'How you feeling?' he asks.

I smile weakly and sit next to Laura on the sofa. 'What time's the doctor's appointment?'

Laura glances at her watch, a purple Fitbit. 'Twenty minutes. I was thinking, is there anyone we can call? Your parents maybe? Friends? A partner?'

I look down, my lip starting to wobble.

'I'm sorry,' Laura says. 'It'll come back. You just need to let the mind settle.'

'About frickin' time,' Tony says, walking away into the kitchen with the phone. He glances back at Laura and smiles.

'He doesn't exactly like the police.' Laura turns from Tony to me, unable to suppress a giggle. 'Always catching him speeding.'

'I did have a friend,' I say. 'I kept a photo of her in my handbag.'

'Do you know where she lives?' Laura asks, encouraged. 'We could call her.'

'She died.'

I pause, trying to recall Fleur's face. And then I see her, knees up in the bath tub, crying. I grope for more, but the image dissolves into nothing.

'That's all I know,' I add.

'Oh.'

In the awkward silence that follows, we both listen to Tony talking on the phone in the kitchen. He explains about my missing handbag and my inability to recall my name and offers a brief description of me, glancing through the glass door in our direction. 'Short dark hair, late twenties? Business suit, a suitcase... We're going to look inside it now... She arrived at Terminal 5 late this morning, maybe lunchtime. BA flight from Berlin... Said she lost it, or it was stolen, at Arrivals.'

Again, hearing myself described by someone else makes me feels nauseous. Laura senses my discomfort and puts a hand on my forearm. She's very tactile. Her face is close to mine. Too close.

'Another tea?'

'I'm OK, thanks.'

'Shall we open your suitcase?'

I move to stand up, but Laura is already on her feet.

'I'll get it,' she says.

Laura wheels the suitcase into the room just as Tony comes off the phone.

'They've given me a website where all lost items at the airport are logged,' he says to us both, 'but don't hold your breath. It takes up to forty-eight hours for items to be registered.'

'What about her name? Are they going to check passenger records?' Laura asks.

'Better things to do. No one's in danger, there's no threat to the peace. Said it was more one for social services. Anything inside?'

Laura lets me unzip the suitcase.

'I think it's just clothes,' I say, lifting the lid as I kneel down on the floor. At the top are two pairs of black knickers, a cream camisole top and a black bra. Laura glances up at Tony, who stands back, keeping a respectful distance. I search through more clothes beneath: another black business suit, like the one I'm wearing, the jacket neatly folded on top of the skirt; three blouses, a pair of jeans, two T-shirts, another bra, one pair of heels, two paperbacks, a box of tampons, a washbag, some gym gear, a plastic bag full of dirty tights and a rolled-up yoga mat.

'You must have been away a while,' Laura says.

'Looks like it,' I say, searching more frantically. 'There must be something here that will tell me who I am.'

'Into your yoga?'

'I guess so,' I say, still rifling through my things. *Om mani padme hum.*

'I'm a teacher. Vinyasa. Maybe we could have a session together. It might help.'

'That would be nice.'

Laura is making me feel increasingly guilty. From the moment I arrived on her doorstep, she has been kindness personified. I sit back on my heels and flip the lid of the suitcase closed in a gesture of resignation.

'Don't worry,' she says, her hand on my forearm again.

'No diary?' Tony asks, joining Laura on the sofa. 'A hotel bill?'

'I think that was all in the handbag. Sorry.'

'It's not your fault,' Laura says.

'May I ask you something?' Tony glances at Laura. I get the impression she sometimes worries what he might say next. 'Can you remember anything about earlier today? Knocking on our door half an hour ago?'

I nod.

'Your journey here?'

'Yes.'

'But not your flight?'

'Tony?' Laura interrupts, a hand on his knee. He rests his hand on hers.

'It's OK,' I say.

Laura is being protective of me, which is good of her, but I also need to answer Tony's questions, however difficult I'm finding them.

'I think it happened when I went to the lost property office. Everything seemed to fall away at that point, when the assistant asked for my name and I couldn't tell him.'

'I'm not surprised,' Laura says. 'It must have been disorientating.'

'A nightmare,' Tony agrees, his tone more sympathetic.

'I can remember a few minutes earlier, when my suitcase arrived on the carousel, but... nothing before that.'

I begin to feel dizzy again.

'And you can't recall anything about your family?' Tony asks.

'I think we should leave it,' Laura says, standing up. 'Until she's been checked over by a doctor. It's time we went.'

'I'm OK, honestly.' I glance at Tony, who is studying me intently.

'And your name? Nothing?'

I shake my head.

'You look like a Jemma to me,' Tony continues, leaning back on the sofa. 'Definitely a Jemma.'

I shrug my shoulders. 'I don't know.'

'Jemma with a "J".' Laura looks from me to Tony. 'You can stay here if you like, in the spare room,' he adds. A flash of the serene smile he gave me earlier, when I was standing on the doorstep. 'For a few days, while you get yourself sorted. This can't be easy for you.'

'Absolutely,' Laura says. I sense she's been waiting for him to make the offer.

'No squatter's rights, though,' he adds. 'I've read about those.' I think he's joking.

A minute later, we are at the front door. I'm nervous about stepping outside, away from the house and into the world again. Laura senses my unease.

'It's OK, I'm coming with you,' she says.

'I'm sure the doctor will be able to help,' Tony adds. 'She's good. And will vouch for the fact that we live here.'

We open the door just as a man walks past.

'Evening,' the man says to Laura. 'Settling in OK?'

4

Tony moves fast once the front door has closed. He knows it's unnecessary, but Laura wants reassurance that it isn't them who are the crazy ones but the woman who's turned up on their doorstep today. Laura has done so well to beat her anxiety – all thanks to her yoga – but Tony's learnt it's best to address her worries quickly, before they gain currency.

Upstairs, he opens a stepladder on the landing and unlocks the hatch. The small loft is his space, his man cave, as Laura calls it. She doesn't come up here. Every square foot of the floor is covered with boxes, each one labelled with a year. Inside the boxes are sheet files of negatives from pre-digital days. Most of them are of weddings, but it's the row of boxes down the left-hand side of the loft that he's most proud of: his collection of daily images, 365 a year. A photo of Laura asleep; high, filigree clouds; shells on a beach.

Laura teases him that they're a sign of not wanting to move on, of failing to live in the moment, but it's not about that. It's about remembering. Not forgetting. Some people keep a diary; he takes a daily photo. No big deal. In recent years he's posted the images on Instagram rather than print them.

He leans forward, picks a box at random and pulls out a photograph: a tree heavy with late March snow, a few weeks before they got married. He can recall the day, the exact moment. Nothing wrong with his synapses; the neuronal traffic is still flowing freely. A few minutes after it was taken, he'd helped Laura sweep thick layers of snow off her VW Beetle. They had laughed, thrown snowballs. It was a month after another miscarriage and she was trying to be brave, but they had both known how happy the snow would have made a child, how happy a child would have made her.

He puts the photo away and turns to a box full of paperwork for the house: a real-estate survey, environmental report, property details and, finally, a copy of the deeds. All fine. Of course they are. What was she thinking? He takes a photo of them with his phone and texts it to her.

Laura suspects the woman he's calling Jemma might have lived here at some point in the past. She discussed the possibility with him while Jemma was in the bathroom, thought it might explain her unsettling knowledge of their house.

The previous owners gave Laura a bundle of historical documents, which are at the bottom of the box, and a list of the owners before them. Keen amateur property genealogists, they had traced the house right back to 1780, when it was built as an estate cottage. Tony finds the list of names and scrolls through them. No need to text a photo to Laura.

5

'We moved in a month ago,' Laura says as we walk down the road towards the pub. 'We rented in the village for a year, waiting for it to come on the market.'

'It's old, isn't it,' I say.

'Eighteenth century, I think. Tony's heart was set on the place – owning a slice of English history.'

We pass a young couple pushing a hi-tech pram, another child meandering behind them on a simple wooden pushbike with no pedals. The Slaughtered Lamb, on the corner of the high street, is busy, drinkers spilling out onto the pavement. Tony has stayed behind to cook dinner, which will be ready when we get back, if I want to eat with them.

'Do you know who lived in the house before you?' I ask.

'A young couple with a toddler. He worked for Vodafone and was relocated. She was a teacher at the primary school.'

'Not me, then,' I say, managing a faint smile.

'That's just what Tony and I were thinking. It would have made everything so much easier to understand.'

We arrive outside the village surgery, a shiny new

glass-fronted building with steps and an access ramp leading up to the main entrance. It can only be a medical centre, a place of doctors and disinfectant. Sharp instruments. My stomach tightens. My mind is like a bird, searching the open sea, occasionally alighting on tiny islands of memory.

'Perhaps you lived at the house when you were much younger?' Laura asks as we walk up the steps. 'You obviously feel some sort of connection with it.'

'I just knew I had to get back there,' I say, taking a seat in the waiting area.

'We've got a list of all the old owners in the attic. We can check your name against it – when you remember.'

I pick up a magazine while Laura enters her date of birth on the computer screen to let the surgery know she has arrived. It's an old copy of *Country Living*, full of tasteful cottages with roses around the door. I feel disorientated. Cut off. What am I doing here, sitting in a doctor's surgery in rural England?

'So sorry to trouble you...' a male voice says. His tone is tentative, uncertain.

I look up to see a man – late forties, maybe older – standing above me. He's in a cream linen suit with a white collarless shirt and no tie, and is wearing brown suede shoes. A tan courier bag is slung over one shoulder. I have never seen him before in my life – at least I don't think I have.

'Do we know each other?' he continues.

I shake my head, my confusion obvious. Is the guy chatting me up?

'Oh God, sorry,' the man says, looking at me with a mix of shock and embarrassment. 'I thought you were someone else.'

'Luke,' Laura says to the man, rushing over to join us.

'Laura, didn't see you there.' He gives her a kiss on both cheeks. 'I thought I recognised your friend.' He laughs nervously, but he seems to be finding our encounter anything but funny. 'From a long time ago,' he adds, his voice tailing off.

Laura looks at me, searching in vain for a flicker of recognition. I rack my brain desperately, but it's a blank. I don't recognise him at all.

'Sorry to disappoint,' I say. Despite his shock, Luke has a nice smile and for a fleeting moment I wish we did know each other.

'No need to apologise,' he says.

There's a pause as he waits for an introduction, glancing first at Laura and then back at me. His smile falls away as his eyes linger on mine. What's he thinking?

'My mistake,' he adds, quieter now, filling the silence. 'Funny thing, memory.'

Laura sits down next to me as Luke walks off.

'That was awkward,' I say, shifting uncomfortably in my seat.

'I couldn't introduce you because—'

'I know, it's OK.'

'For a moment I thought we'd solved the mystery. When he said he recognised you.'

'Me too,' I say, sitting back. 'Maybe I do know him? He seemed nice enough.'

'Luke? He's gorgeous.'

'Laura Masters?' a voice calls out from down the corridor.

'That's us,' she says, standing up. 'Luke's a journalist. Wrote an article about the local vicar banning my yoga classes from the church hall because they were "rooted in Hinduism".'

'Doesn't sound very Christian,' I say.

'There was an outcry. Apparently, the vicar didn't want to be seen supporting "an alternative world-view". No wonder no one goes to church any more.'

Just as we're walking away from the waiting area, Luke reappears by my side. 'Sorry, forgot to give you one of these,' he says, handing me a small business card.

'Thanks,' I say, disconcerted by his attention.

'You know, just in case.'

6

Laura's phone buzzes when we walk into Dr Susie Patterson's consulting room. She glances at it and shows me the screen as she sits down in one of two empty chairs. It's a text from Luke.

Who's the new woman in town? Weirdly familiar. x

We both smile, though in truth his interest makes me nervous. I sit down in the other chair. The room feels oppressively clean and I can feel my chest tightening already. There's a bed along one wall, covered in a roll of white paper. And on her desk, laid out like cutlery, the tools of Dr Patterson's medical trade. I glance away, pressing my hands together. In my mind I had prepared myself for an innocent consulting room. I force myself to look up.

'Thanks for seeing us so quickly, Susie,' Laura says.

'No problem,' Dr Patterson replies. She must be in her early fifties; confident manner, well-spoken rather than posh. No nonsense. She's wearing a fitted taupe cashmere jumper, a modest string of pearls at her neck. According to Laura, she's a locum who used to be a partner at a practice in Devizes. And they are good friends, as I suspected.

'Thank you,' I add.

'So tell me what happened, when you first realised you couldn't remember your own name.'

I take her through exactly what I told Laura and Tony.

'It's upsetting,' I say. 'Not knowing.'

'I can imagine,' Dr Patterson says.

'When I try to remember, there's just this void in my head.' I keep my voice steady, but my leg is shaking.

'Were you able to tell the lost property man anything at all?'

'Nothing.' I pause, thinking about the meeting with Luke in the surgery reception. Who does he think I am? 'It's easier if I'm called Jemma.'

'Jemma? Why Jemma?'

'I'm going to need a name and—'

'Tony thought she looked like a Jemma,' Laura says, laughing nervously. 'With a "J".'

'And you?' Dr Patterson asks. 'What do you think?'

'It's OK. For the time being.' I need to be called something.

'How are you feeling now?'

I take a deep breath. 'Disconnected. Isolated. Frightened.'

Dr Patterson sits back, glancing at the computer screen on her desk. On the wall behind her is a large map of the world, illustrating recommended injections for different countries. Southern India – diphtheria, hepatitis A, tetanus, typhoid – is partially obscured by her head.

'It's quite normal for someone in your position to feel these things,' she says. 'Your sense of disconnection may also turn into frustration and depression.'

'I'm not sure what I would have done if I hadn't met Laura,' I say, feeling another pang of guilt for the woman who doesn't know me and is being so kind.

She looks at Laura and then at me.

'We were talking on the phone earlier about the various different types of amnesia. In most cases, memory loss like this tends to pass quite quickly, sometimes in a matter of hours. If your condition persists, we will need to run some tests, establish if you've suffered any physical trauma to the brain. We also need to rule out other organic causes such as a stroke, a brain tumour, an epileptic episode, encephalitis or possible thyroid disorders, even vitamin B deficiency. Recreational drugs and alcohol can also be factors in memory loss. My guess, though, is that you're experiencing what we call psychogenic or dissociative amnesia – stress is one of the biggest causes.'

I sit up in my seat, aware of people passing on the pavement outside the window. It's disconcerting to hear myself being discussed in this medical way.

'Would you like some water?' Dr Patterson offers, sensing my discomfort.

I nod, watching as she fills a glass from a plastic bottle and passes it to me.

'I'm just going to take your blood pressure,' she says, getting up from her chair. 'Have a listen to your heart, check your breathing.'

She continues to talk as she wraps a sleeve around my arm, fastening it with Velcro before starting to inflate it. I try to relax, concentrate on my breath, the lower part of my lungs.

'Do you know today's date?' she asks. I shake my head. 'The month? Year?'

'I'm sorry,' I say. This is all so hard.

'Where we are?'

Another shake of the head. I hear Fleur's voice in my ear. Right now all I want to do is curl up in bed and cry.

'It's OK,' she says, undoing the Velcro. 'I'd also like to perform a brief neurological examination.'

My hands tense as she picks up a stethoscope from her desk. After listening to my heart, she conducts a series of tests, assessing my balance, eye movements and visual field, shining a torch into my pupils and checking facial and neck muscles. It's then that she reaches for her ophthalmoscope. An image of a white coat comes and goes.

'I just need to examine your retina,' she says, noticing me flinch. 'And look for raised intracranial pressure,' she continues, her cheek close to mine. 'All seems fine.'

She sits down again, putting the instrument back on her desk. My eyes linger on it for a second before I look away.

'Some people experience "anterograde amnesia", which is when you can't form new memories. They can recall the past, before the event that caused the amnesia, but nothing afterwards. Let's see what you can remember tomorrow, after a good night's sleep.'

'How do you mean?' I ask.

'It's possible you could forget everything that's happened today.'

She glances at Laura.

'The other main form of amnesia is retrograde, where you can't remember anything from before the event that caused the memory loss. Autobiographical details, your name, address, family, friends and so on. You are, though, able to form new memories. I suspect this is what you're currently suffering from.'

'But she will get better?' Laura asks.

'It's hard to say at this stage,' she says to me. 'I'd certainly recommend further examinations, maybe an MRI brain scan. If the amnesia is stress-induced, it should resolve but may take time. You might be experiencing what we call a dissociative fugue. A temporary loss of identity accompanied by unplanned travel, confusion and amnesia. Right now you just need to relax, perhaps do some yoga with Laura? I think she's already offered.'

Laura nods, smiling.

'I'd like that,' I say. Laura's kindness makes me want to cry.

'I don't think it's necessary for you to be admitted tonight – even if there were any beds available, which I'm afraid there aren't. The only other option is a night in an A & E corridor.'

'I'd rather not,' I interject.

'It was terrible up there last week,' Laura says.

'Your blood pressure's a little high,' Dr Patterson continues, ignoring her friend, 'which is to be expected, but your breathing is clear and I can find no evidence to suggest a stroke or infection.' She turns to Laura. 'Are you really OK for her to stay with you tonight?'

'Honestly not a problem,' Laura says.

However bad I feel about Laura, it's much better that I sleep in her house.

'Normally I'd like to exclude all organic causes first, but the community psychiatric nurse is in the village tomorrow. And we're in luck – there's been a cancellation at 9 a.m. Would that suit?'

I nod, glancing at Laura, who smiles back at me.

'In most cases like this, the semantic memory is unaffected. You should still be able to understand words, colours, how things work, general knowledge, that sort of thing. And I don't anticipate any other cognitive impairment. You aren't at any personal risk.'

'I knew what to do with my train ticket today,' I say, 'if that's what you mean.'

'If you've got time,' Dr Patterson continues, glancing at Laura, 'take a walk around the village together. Try to relax, let the dissociated mind reconnect. Often all our memory needs is a trigger, a familiar face, for everything to start coming back. Maybe go along to the pub quiz tonight. You never know, someone might recognise you. These things can resolve themselves very quickly.'

'She remembered the layout of our house,' Laura says, shifting the mood again.

'Really?'

'The upstairs rooms, a shower in the downstairs loo – before she saw any of it.'

Dr Patterson looks up at me and then back at her screen, deep in thought.

'We were wondering if she'd lived there before, a long time ago.'

'Normally with retrograde amnesia, those sort of episodic memories are lost,' Dr Patterson says, 'although sometimes patients can recall things from their very distant past.'

'Maybe that's it,' Laura says to me. 'Perhaps you lived in the house as a child.'

Dr Patterson either doesn't hear Laura's theory or chooses to ignore it. 'For what it's worth, we've got three Jemmas registered at the surgery, one with a "J"…' She pauses, turning from the screen to me.

Laura and I both look up, struck by the sudden change in Dr Patterson's expression. Her breezy manner falls away as she scrolls down the screen.

'What is it?' Laura asks.

I stare at Dr Patterson, scared of what she's about to say.

'Nothing,' she says, turning back to us, distracted, her mind clearly still processing what she's just read.

We both know she's lying.

7

'I suppose Jemma could be my name,' I say as we walk away from the surgery in the evening sunshine. 'Though I don't see how Tony would have guessed it.' Across the road, bell ringers are practising in the church, peals chasing each other down the scale.

'It suits you,' Laura says. 'And Tony's good at guessing names. Uncanny sometimes.'

'Do you ever do the pub quiz?'

'Not really my thing. Tony's obsessed with it. He's only forty but lives in fear of getting Alzheimer's – his father died of it. The quiz is his way of keeping his brain fit although he'll never admit as much. He doesn't like to talk about it.' Laura starts to giggle. 'Oh yes, he also likes to sing.'

'Sing?'

'They always wind down after the quiz with an open-mike session. The team who wins has to go first. Nobody can stop him, certainly not me. Singing's Tony's thing.'

'And you don't like it?' I'm smiling too now. 'His voice?'

'"Let there be spaces in your togetherness" and all that.'

'"And let the winds of heaven dance between you."' I look up at Laura, surprised. I completed the poem without even thinking.

'See – your memory's fine.' She pauses as we wait to cross the road by the church. 'Tony spent a large part of his early career taking photos of bands, hoping to sing in one himself. He used to sing to his dad too. In his dying days. Seemed to ease the Alzheimer's – if that's possible.'

We follow a path beside the graveyard and down through a water meadow to the railway, which runs parallel with the canal. A train is in the sidings, engines idling. After crossing the tracks, Laura shows me the slope where she and Tony went tobogganing on their first weekend in the village.

'Do you have any children?' I ask. I regret the question immediately. Behind us the church bells momentarily lose their rhythm, colliding awkwardly. There were no signs of kids in their immaculate house.

'We've tried,' Laura says.

'I'm sorry. I shouldn't have asked.'

'It's fine. We'll keep trying.'

We walk on down the canal, past a row of moored narrowboats, flowers tumbling down their sides like May queens' garlands.

'I know this sounds weird,' she asks, 'but do you think you have any kids?'

I pause to consider. 'I'm not sure how I'd know.'

'Tits heading south and a 24/7 state of tiredness and guilt?' she offers, laughing. 'At least, that's what the mums in my class say.'

Our conversation tails off after that as she shows me the draughty Scout Hut where she runs her yoga. I wonder if she's thinking about Susie Patterson, what the doctor saw on her computer screen. Something upset her, dented her professional calm. On our way back up the high street, we stop outside a café.

'This is Tony's place,' she says. 'His pride and joy. He's always dreamt of running his own New York-style vegan café and having somewhere to hang his pictures. We bought it a couple of months ago.'

I look up at a sign that reads: 'The Seahorse Gallery & Café'. There's a food counter with glass cabinets at the front and some tables and chairs at the back, where the walls are lined with big framed photos.

'It used to be the village shop,' Laura says.

'Are they his photos?' I ask, peering in through the window at the pictures hanging on the back wall.

'Tony loves seahorses.'

'Different,' I say, turning to walk on quickly. 'Was it always a shop?'

'It was once the village bakery – a long time ago. Is it ringing any bells?'

I shake my head. 'The only place I feel I've seen before is the pub.'

'And our house.'

'And your house,' I repeat quietly, stopping in the street to look around. 'I just wish I knew why I came here. Who I am.'

Laura touches my arm, managing a weak smile before she walks on ahead. This is difficult for me, but it's tough for her too. A stranger pitching up on her doorstep. As we turn into School Road, the adrenaline builds again as I remember the moment I knocked at the door. I look around for something to distract my mind. A thatcher is working on a roof up ahead, strands of straw lining the sides of the road.

'Are you sure it's OK for me to stay the night?' I ask. 'Tony seemed a bit—'

'Of course it's OK. He's keen to help you. We both are.'

'How long have you guys been together?'

'We got married last year. Six months after we met. Whirlwind romance.'

'White wedding?'

'Not quite.' She laughs. A group of people walk past us, on their way to the pub quiz, perhaps.

'I'm sorry, I shouldn't have asked.' Unable to discuss my own past, I seem to be obsessed with other people's.

'It's fine. We had a wonderful day. I always thought I wanted a white wedding, but he talked me out of it.'

'How come?'

'He's a wedding photographer – at least he was. Seen too many loveless white weddings to want a traditional one of his own. So he whisked me off to a field in Cornwall that overlooks Veryan Bay, near where I was born. It was so romantic. Twenty friends watched us get married in an old stone-built coastguard lookout – we spent the evening dancing and drinking among hay bales and new-born lambs as the sun set over the sea.'

I am surprised to find that Laura's memory causes a feeling of unbearable sadness to well up inside me. I swallow it down. 'Sounds like heaven,' I say. 'And at least the lambs were in white.'

Laura smiles as we reach the front door where I fainted. And then she stops.

'I saw your beautiful tattoo, by the way,' she says.

'Thank you.' I look down at it, as if seeing the tattoo for the first time.

'Why a lotus flower?' she asks, putting the key in the lock.

I blink, and Fleur smiles. 'I don't know.'

I wish I knew. Taking a deep breath, I follow Laura inside the house.

8

Tony is cooking dinner in the kitchen, where he has laid out three places around a small table beyond the island. A piano concerto is playing on a Bose sound system, scented candles burn and there's a Persian blue cat asleep on the sofa. A scene of domestic calm, but I'm nervous about being back in the house again. The plan is for an early meal and then Tony's off down to the pub for the quiz.

'How was it at the surgery?' he asks.

'Susie was very helpful,' Laura says, stepping in on my behalf again. She means well, but I need to speak for myself. My voice is not as loud or as confident as I'd wish.

'Apparently, I might be experiencing a dissociative fugue,' I say.

'Interesting.' Tony reaches for a porcelain jug of water shaped like a salmon dancing on its tail. He pours out three glasses through the fish's mouth. 'It might explain the travel. People in a fugue state have been known to travel hundreds of miles from their home. Adopt completely new identities. Can you still remember arriving here today?'

'At the moment, yes,' I reply, transfixed by the sound of the glugging jug.

'But Susie says it might be different tomorrow morning,' Laura says.

'How come?' His blue eyes are focused on mine and I have to look away.

'We'll know then if I can form new memories or not.'

'Anterograde amnesia,' Tony says.

'Tony's obsessed with not forgetting anything,' Laura says, by way of explanation. I notice she doesn't mention Tony's father, his Alzheimer's.

'Really?' I ask, my scalp suddenly tingling, but he chooses not to elaborate.

'I googled it while you were out,' he says, glancing at Laura. 'Shall we eat?'

Tony serves up fresh grilled sea bass with Jersey potatoes and a vine-tomato and avocado salad with fennel dressing. Laura seems happy to leave Tony to it in the kitchen.

'I didn't know whether you are a vegetarian or not so I compromised with fish,' he says, passing the plate of bass to me.

'I don't know either,' I whisper, serving myself.

'The village think Tony's a hardcore vegan, but he's a secret pescatarian at home,' Laura says. 'I can't live without my seafood.'

'That's love,' Tony jokes. 'I even ate steak on our wedding night.'

'You did not.' Laura laughs.

'I'm kidding.' He leans over to kiss her. 'Just don't tell my customers about the fish.'

'I won't,' I say.

Any reservations Tony might have had earlier about me seem to have evaporated. His whole manner is different, welcoming. I hope it stays that way.

'This must be so strange for you,' he says. He is sitting opposite me, Laura to my right.

'Leave it if you don't like it,' Laura says.

'They look delicious,' I reply, passing the plate of fish onto her.

'Where did you buy the bass, darling?' she asks.

'At the market, of course. Line caught from a single boat in Brixham. Only the best for you.'

I'm beginning to feel like a spare part at their not-so-white wedding.

'Going back to your memory,' Tony says, looking across at me. 'Why don't you come along to the quiz tonight? See if you know any of the answers.'

'I'd like that,' I find myself saying. I'm tired, but I want to see Luke again, establish if he knows anything about who I am.

'Just remember to leave before the singing,' Laura says.

'I'll sing now if you're not careful,' Tony replies.

'Dr Patterson said something might trigger my memory,' I say. 'A familiar face. Maybe I'll recognise someone at the pub – or they'll recognise me.'

'Exactly,' Tony says.

'Doctor's orders.' Laura smiles at me before turning to Tony. 'And she's agreed to call herself "Jemma".'

'Good call,' he says.

'I thought it would be easier for everyone,' I say.

'Didn't I tell you she was a Jemma?' he adds, but Laura is distracted by a text alert on her phone, which is lying flat on the table between us.

'Sorry, it's from Susie Patterson,' she says, glancing at the screen.

'I've tried telling her about not using her cell phone at the table,' Tony says with a mock sigh. 'Will she listen?'

'I better read it,' she says, casually swiping the phone screen.

I'm desperate to read it too, after the weird way things ended at the surgery. I try to look down at the phone without being obvious about it. It's a long message and all I can see is the beginning, but that's enough to make my stomach ball.

Be careful around your new friend. I think I know who she is.

Laura picks up her phone and glances at me. I've already turned away.

'What's up?' Tony asks.

I manage to smile at him, my mouth dry, and then at Laura. She doesn't reciprocate. It's as if someone has pulled a plug, draining all the kindness from her face, leaving only a cold hard stare.

9

It's a big mistake coming to the quiz. Laura's text message from Dr Patterson has left me feeling even more vulnerable than before. And I wasn't expecting the pub to be so noisy or for us to be received with such fanfare. Tony senses my unease. As we work our way towards the bar, greeted by everyone, he checks regularly to see that I'm OK.

I wonder if the locals know about me yet. The pub is old, all bricks and wooden floors, a blackboard on the wall above an open fire with a handwritten menu of homemade pizzas and pies. Today's special is 'Abdul's Pashtun lamb curry'. The only person I recognise is Luke, who catches my eye and turns away to another man at the bar.

Tony orders two Virgin Marys, one for me and one for himself, specifying the ingredients with forensic precision: three dashes of hot sauce, a pinch of celery salt, two squeezes of lemon.

'Is Laura OK tonight?' I say as he passes me my drink. My hand is shaking as I take it.

'Just tired. And a bit rumbled by your arrival.'

'What did Dr Patterson have to say?' I ask, narrowly avoiding my drink being spilled by the crush of people. I need to get out of here. It's too crowded. A flickering image of another crowded night, dancing with a thousand beautiful strangers, Fleur's arms swaying above her head to the thumping beats. 'Nothing about me, I hope,' I add, my head spinning with the memory, which vanishes as quickly as it came.

I remind myself I couldn't have stayed behind with Laura. After she read the text message, she rushed upstairs. Tony followed, but when he came back down again, it was as if nothing had happened. He was friendly and solicitous, keen to take me to the quiz, explaining that Laura just wanted an early night.

'Yoga wars,' Tony says. 'A new teacher's moved into the village. Laura being Laura, she's trying to help her out – and about to lose clients, according to Susie Patterson.'

Is Tony just being kind? Protecting me? Maybe I read the text wrongly.

'So Tony talked you into the quiz,' Luke says, coming over to join us with his friend. 'Sorry about earlier – at the surgery.'

Tony rests a hand on my shoulder. 'Back in a minute,' he says, turning to talk to a group behind him.

'Not a problem,' I say to Luke, but my mouth has gone dry.

'I'm usually good with faces,' Luke replies.

'Happens to the best of us,' the other man says, raising his pint in my direction.

'This is my Irish friend Sean,' Luke says. 'Screenwriter, collector of conspiracy theories and the best-read man in the village, which makes him annoyingly good at pub quizzes.'

43

Sean drinks deeply, tipping his head back until he's staring at the bottom of his empty glass, which he then smacks down on the bar. 'Sometimes I can't even remember my own feckin' name.'

I close my eyes and look away.

'That's because you're always in here,' Luke says, wincing an apology at me. He must know.

'As often as wallet and wife allow.'

'You're not even married,' Luke says.

'I'm sure she'll be very understanding.'

'My name's Jemma, by the way,' I interrupt, trying in vain to sound upbeat.

'Jemma,' Luke repeats. His eyes linger on me for a second before he shakes his head. 'I'm sorry, this is so weird, but you really do remind me of someone.'

'Who?' I ask nervously.

'His childhood sweetheart,' Sean chips in.

'It's not how it sounds,' Luke says, apologising again for his friend.

'It's OK,' I say.

'Freya,' Luke continues. 'Her name was Freya Lal.'

'Not Jemma then.'

He shakes his head slowly.

'It's just a name I've been given,' I say. 'By Tony. I don't know how much he's told you…'

'Laura rang me. After we met in the surgery. If there's anything I can do…?'

'I'm hoping I'll feel better in the morning.'

I watch Luke try to take it all in, process the implications.

'So it's not so daft, me thinking I recognise you,' he says, glancing at the tattoo on my wrist. 'I mean, perhaps you could be related to Freya in some way?'

He studies my face again, more serious now, still searching for a likeness. 'Nobody's heard of her since we all left school. Vanished into thin air.'

'Amelia Earhart – take two,' Sean says under his breath, gesturing to be served.

'And you're trying to find her?' I ask, ignoring the suspicious look that Sean gives me.

'I haven't thought about her for years.' He seems uneasy, glancing at Sean, now deep in conversation with the barman. 'Actually, that's not true,' he adds, his voice quieter. 'I broke up with my girlfriend last month.' He pauses. 'I'm not really sure why I'm telling you this. It sounds silly, but I've started to look for Freya online. You know, since the split.'

'Doesn't sound silly at all,' I say. I like Luke. His openness.

'Reconnecting with my roots or something. My childhood. Trying to get a bit of stability back into my life. I've been feeling adrift recently.'

'Know the feeling.'

'Of course you do. Much more than me. I'm sorry. This must all be so disorientating for you.'

'Hate to interrupt, guys,' Tony says, returning to our group, 'but the quiz is about to start.'

I follow Tony, Luke and Sean over to a large table in the bay window, where we are roundly heckled by our neighbours. It's all good-natured banter – Tony laps it up, gives as good as he gets – but it does nothing for my already fragile confidence.

'The local cricket team,' Luke tells me. 'Tony plays for them – at least he tries to. More of a baseball swing than a cover drive. But they've been winning every match since the Afghans joined them.'

'The Afghans?'

'Two brothers have been settled here in the village,' Luke says, taking a sheet of paper from the landlord, who is marching around the tables like a leafleting politician.

'The picture round,' Tony interrupts, taking the sheet from Luke.

'Both work in the kitchen,' Luke adds. 'Best Pashtun curries this side of Kabul.'

'Demon spinners too,' Sean says. 'You should see their googlies.'

Luke gives his friend a disapproving look. I have no idea what they're talking about and resist another urge to leave, run off into the night. I feel like an impostor, wasting kind people's time.

'Where do you think this one is?' Tony asks me, pointing at a picture. 'It's palaces around the world.'

I recognise the sloping, fortress-like walls immediately, which is a relief. I was worried that I might not be able to contribute anything tonight.

'The Potala Palace,' I say. 'Lhasa, in Tibet.'

He turns to me, pursing his lips in approval. 'Your semantic memory's working well enough.'

'How's your Russian history?' Luke asks. 'It's tonight's bonus round.'

'Jesus, Mary and Joseph help us,' Sean says.

'Lhasa, you say?' Tony asks. 'Impressive.'

I'm not sure if he means my powers of recall or the Tibetan architecture.

To everyone's surprise, including mine, I'm able to answer other questions too, particularly in the final, bonus round about Russia.

'Right spelling?' Luke asks me, as he writes down 'Dzerzhinsky Square'.

I glance at the sheet of paper, watched intently by Sean. 'Looks good to me.'

After the quiz is over, Luke checks through our answers with Tony and swaps them with another table for marking. Our team triumphs again – by a single point over the cricketers.

Luke and Sean head for the bar to celebrate, leaving me on my own with Tony. I'm not sure I can cope with the attention. I want Tony to like me, but it's a fine balance.

'You remind me of someone,' he says, looking me straight in the eye. 'I just can't remember who.'

'It must be catching,' I reply, managing a laugh before I have to turn away. I don't want to be here with Tony. In this pub. This village.

'It's not like me,' he continues. 'I don't forget a face. Don't forget anything.'

He pulls out a small camera, a Canon PowerShot, and takes a picture of me. I reel back at the flash. I didn't see that coming.

'Ask me in ten years' time about that picture and I'll be able to tell you everything about tonight. Who was here, who won the quiz and by how much.'

'I don't like my picture being taken,' I say quietly, struggling to regain my composure. I remember Laura's words, her theory about Tony's fear of Alzheimer's.

'I'm sorry,' he says, a hand on my shoulder. 'Shall I delete it?'

I shake my head. It's too late now.

'I hope it's helped, coming along tonight,' he continues, looking around the bar.

'It's been useful,' I lie.

'Are you worried you might forget everything that's happened today?'

'It terrifies me.' He has no idea how scared I am. No one does.

'Maybe you should write it all down. Leave a note to yourself.'

'I was going to, tonight. Just in case.' I look up at the bar, where the landlord is adjusting a mike stand. Once it's fixed, he raises a hand in our direction. 'Your big moment,' I say.

Tony acknowledges the landlord and reaches down for his guitar case. A cheer goes up.

'Fame beckons,' he says.

IO

Laura walks upstairs, pushes open the spare bedroom door and stares at Jemma's suitcase. For a moment she thinks about going over to it and emptying out the contents, but they went through it together earlier and there was nothing suspicious. She glances at the bed, where there's a trace of Jemma's figure on the duvet cover. She must have had a lie-down before dinner. The poor woman's tired, stressed out. Who wouldn't be after what she's been through today? Jemma needs sympathy, not her paranoia. Susie Patterson might have it all wrong.

Laura reaches out to the duvet, but before her fingers touch she hears something downstairs. Was it a click? The front door? She strains to hear another noise, but there's only silence. On the landing she stops to listen again. Nothing. She goes downstairs, satisfied that she must have imagined the sound, but the kitchen feels cooler, as if the front door has been left open, or a window, sluicing fresh air into the small house. She walks into the sitting room, opens the front door and looks both ways down the street. Empty.

Back inside, she goes through to the kitchen again, telling herself to relax, and then stops in her tracks, staring at the maple knife-block on the sideboard. One of the knives is missing. It's the biggest one – the 'man knife', as Tony calls it.

She turns to the wooden drying rack, looking for it. Calm, calm. She's overreacting. *Be careful around your new friend. I think I know who she is.* She breathes in and out deeply, trying to fog up an imaginary mirror. Slow ujjayi breathing is her go-to technique for anxiety, one of the reasons she took up yoga in the first place. She pulls open the kitchen drawers one by one, searching for the knife with mounting desperation. It's not in any of them. Breathing in deeply again, she rests her hands on the sideboard, head bowed between outstretched arms.

'Is everything OK?' a voice asks.

Laura spins round. 'Jesus, you scared me,' she says, looking up at Jemma, who has emerged from the downstairs bathroom.

'I'm sorry. Tony gave me the key, told me to let myself in, said you might be asleep already.'

'Asleep?' Laura repeats, unable to disguise a dry laugh. Nothing could be further from her mind.

'Have you lost something?' Jemma asks.

'I was just putting away the washing-up,' Laura says, keeping her back to the sideboard. She watches Jemma step into the room. The woman's movements are slow, hesitant. Both her hands are visible, but she might have hidden the knife somewhere. Instinctively, Laura glances across at the block, in case she needs to protect herself with another knife.

'Are you alright?' Jemma asks.

There's a look in her eyes that Laura hasn't seen before. A cold detachment, as if she's not fully present. She should just come out with it, ask her directly. 'Actually, I'm not OK,' she says, still watching Jemma like a hawk.

'What's the matter?'

'Jemma Huish,' she says.

'Jemma Huish?' Jemma repeats back at her.

'Is that who you are?'

'I've no idea, Laura. I don't even know if I'm called Jemma.'

'Susie, Dr Patterson, thinks that's who you might be.'

'And if I am?'

'She used to live here, in this house. A long time ago.'

Jemma nods slowly. Is she recalling something? Is it all coming back to her?

'Can you imagine what it's like,' she says, 'not knowing who you are? So far today I've been told that I might be related to Freya Lal, a long-lost school friend of some posh bloke called Luke I met in the surgery. Tony says I remind him of someone, but he can't remember who. And now I'm supposed to be Jemma Huish, a name I've never heard before. I don't even know if my name really is Jemma. I have no idea who any of these people are, Laura.'

She looks unsteady on her feet and slumps down at the kitchen table, holding her head in her hands. 'I'm sorry for coming here today, for walking into your life like this, your house, and I apologise if I've somehow upset you tonight.'

'It's me who should be sorry,' Laura says, spotting the missing knife on the other sideboard, where the letters are kept. She's been a fool. Tony must have used it to open this morning's post. She looks at Jemma again, her red-sore eyes. On impulse, she goes over and puts an arm around her shoulders. She can't help herself, despite Susie's warning, what she's read tonight about Jemma Huish. Too much empathy – isn't that what Tony is always teasing her about?

'I've left a towel out for you,' she says, standing back a little awkwardly. 'In the bathroom – you know where it is.' She manages a laugh, which prompts a small smile from Jemma.

'Thank you.'

'How was the quiz?' Laura asks.

'We won.'

'Yay,' Laura says quietly, raising both fists in faux celebration. Neither of them is convinced. 'Could you answer any of the questions?'

Jemma nods, wiping her nose. 'I seem to know a lot about Russia.'

'Who else was there? Luke? Sean?'

'Both of them. Does Sean always stare like that?'

'Always. Strange but harmless. Sizing up characters for his next screenplay.'

'Can I ask a favour? Another one?'

'Sure.' Laura wonders what she's going to say. *I always like to sleep with a knife under my pillow.*

'Do you have any paper?' Jemma asks. 'Tony suggested I should write down what's happened today. You know—'

'Of course. There's some over there.' She nods at the small sideboard, where there's a pad of lined paper beside the letter rack, and regrets it immediately.

Jemma walks over and tears off two sheets with a rasping noise that seems to fill the room. As she puts the pad down, she looks at the knife, picks it up and turns. Laura stares at her wide-eyed.

'Is this what you were looking for earlier?' Jemma asks.

Laura can't speak, fixated by the sight of Jemma holding the glistening blade. All she can think of is the online link Susie sent; the image of Jemma Huish, her vacant eyes.

'It belongs over there,' Laura manages to say. She takes the knife from her as quickly as she can and slides it back into the block with a sickening thud. 'You've got a pen?' she asks, failing to sound nonchalant. Jemma nods.

She turns to stack a couple of plates from the drying rack – anything to keep her mind occupied, her breathing steady. 'I'll be up in a minute,' she says. 'Sleep well.'

But when she turns around again, Jemma has already gone upstairs.

She hopes to God Tony will be home soon.

II

My bed is comfortable – white sheets that feel like expensive Egyptian cotton – and Laura has put a handful of freshly picked wild flowers in a miniature milk bottle on my painted bedside cupboard. The kindness of strangers. The room itself is just as I described it to Laura and Tony earlier. Perfect for a child, although the colours may be a bit muted.

Starting with my arrival at the airport, I begin to write down everything that I did: trying to report my lost handbag, travelling here by train, meeting Laura and Tony, visiting the surgery, going to the pub quiz tonight. I don't record anything personal about anyone, as I already feel like public property and have no doubt that whatever I write down will be read by others – doctors, police, mental-health staff. They all mean well, I'm sure, but I need to be careful. At the top of the paper I write: 'READ THIS WHEN YOU WAKE UP.'

Laura is still downstairs. She's behaving so strangely towards me. One moment wary, the next warm and tactile. We both saw the reaction of Dr Patterson at the end of our meeting at the surgery. Her shock was too obvious to miss.

Just like Laura's when she received the text at dinner. It was nothing about yoga. Who the hell is Jemma Huish?

I haven't heard Tony come back from the pub yet. He told me to leave the key under the flowerpot outside the front door. I was tempted to stay, just to see if his singing was as bad as Laura says, but I felt too tired.

I am desperate for sleep now, but I'm anxious about what the morning might bring. Can it be any worse, more stressful than today? I have to keep going but feel at the mercy of others, the medical profession, my own memory. Images of Fleur continue to come and go. The moment I see her, she's gone again.

If I close my eyes now, I can bring her up from the darkness. Here she is, sitting in bed in her apartment, her face obscured by the book she's reading: another account of Berlin's underground techno scene. 'Fleur,' I whisper, my eyes watering. She lowers the book and I gasp out loud. Her face is locked in a wide-mouthed scream.

The brain is a frightening thing, capable of remembering so much of what we want it to forget and forgetting the one thing that we most want it to remember. And then, years later, it chooses to work, operating like an autonomous neural state, summoning a nightmare from beyond the city walls, the badlands of amnesia.

12

Half an hour later, I read through all that I've written and reach to turn off the light. It's then that I hear them talking, downstairs in the kitchen. Their voices are muffled, too far away for them to be directly below me in the sitting room. I slip out of bed, wearing a pair of cotton pyjamas from my suitcase, and creep onto the landing, straining to hear. As far as I can tell, Tony seems to be fighting my corner, which is a relief, but Laura is keen for me to move out of the house as soon as possible.

'We can't just throw her onto the street, angel,' Tony says.

'Read this. Jemma Huish walks into A & E, warning that she wants to kill someone. She pleads with them to section her and take her in. The triage nurse refers her for psychiatric assessment, but while she's waiting to be seen, she strolls out onto the street. Why didn't anyone stop her?'

'I don't know, angel.'

'And look at this. Minutes before Jemma slits her friend's throat with a kitchen knife, she dials 999, warning again that she wants to harm someone and begging for help. The police arrived too late.'

I creep further down the landing, desperate to hear more.

'Susie just said to be careful,' Tony says. 'We've no way of knowing if it's her.'

'I've been speaking to her all evening. Jemma Huish would be thirty now. Jemma upstairs must be about that age. She was convicted of manslaughter twelve years ago, when she was a student in London.'

'Where is she meant to be now?'

'No one seems to know. Released back into the community. Susie also said that she used to live in this house. And that she was diagnosed with schizophrenia and amnesia.'

'I don't remember seeing a Huish on the list of owners in the attic.'

'Susie's not making this up, Tony. It's in her medical records. They keep them at the surgery for fifteen years.'

'It still doesn't mean that the woman who turned up today is her.'

'She told me earlier about a friend, that she'd died. That's good enough for me. And you didn't see her tonight – the way she was holding the kitchen knife.'

'Did she do anything with it? Threaten you in any way?'

'It felt like it. Look at this photo.'

Silence. 'It's so blurry,' Tony says. 'It might just be her, I suppose.'

'What about this court drawing?'

'Even harder to tell.'

'That woman is sleeping upstairs, in our house.'

I think I can hear Laura sobbing, but I'm not sure. It's a while before Tony speaks.

'It says she was an art student. Jemma was on a business trip in Berlin, arrived here in a suit. A professional woman...'

'What kind of professional has a tattoo of a lotus flower on her wrist? I'm going to sleep down here, on the sofa. Until we know for sure.'

'Come on, angel. There's no need for that.' Tony doesn't seem bothered by the tattoo.

'I'm just freaked out, that's all,' Laura says. 'You calling her Jemma, the text from Susie.'

I've heard enough and tiptoe back into my room, closing the door until it's just ajar. I don't want anyone to hear it click shut. Why does Laura think I'm Jemma Huish? And what were they reading? It would explain the look Laura gave me when I handed back the kitchen knife. She snatched at it as if she were disarming me. Jemma Huish slit her best friend's throat. I close my eyes. Could I do that? Kill another person with a knife? I try to imagine a piece of cold metal in my hand, the anger or fear I'd need to drive it home.

I get back into bed just as Tony begins to climb the stairs. The house is feeling more claustrophobic, smaller than I thought, the ceiling of my bedroom pressing down on me. Have I got time to close the door properly? Tony is already on the landing. I lie still in the darkness, my eyes shut, heart jumping, wishing I had pulled the door shut. Tony seems to be standing there, breathing hard after climbing the stairs. And then I hear a door being pushed open, just a few inches. Is it my door or his? Should I call out?

'Are you awake?' I hear him say at the doorway.

I say nothing, feign sleep, try to make my breathing more audible, but my lips are trembling too much. A tear rolls down my cheek as I face the wall.

'Welcome home,' he whispers.

I want to scream, but I can't move. What does he mean? I wish Laura would come upstairs. I'm trying to be brave, but I'm so fucking scared here.

I can't remember my own name.

13

Luke looks in on his elderly parents when he gets back to their house. They are watching a BBC Four documentary on digging the Crossrail tunnel under London, the third time they've seen it. After chatting briefly with them about Ada and Phyllis, their favourite pair of tunnel-boring machines, he heads out to his office in the garden. It's more of a summerhouse than an office, but it gives him some space to work when he's down here, away from the parental requests to recover lost emails, find car keys, order the weekly shop online. (The first time his mother tried to use the Waitrose website, eighteen shiny grapefruits turned up. Nothing more, nothing less.)

It's the least he can do considering all that they've done for him over the years, helping to bring up Milo. His fifteen-year-old son is over at a mate's house tonight. And Luke knows that's exactly where he is because Milo has forgotten he's friends with his old man on Snapchat and failed to turn off his location.

Luke fires up his desktop computer and searches for his old school photo on Facebook again. The girls are all sporting boaters, the boys silk skullcaps. He didn't want his parents to buy him one – they were too expensive and he'd never wear it again – but they'd insisted, saying it was important to mark the moment.

He zooms in on Freya Lal. Why had he confided so much in Jemma tonight? It had been unsettling, bumping into her in the surgery. Her voice had sounded so familiar and yet he couldn't place her. When he saw her in the pub again later, it was like being transported back to their schooldays. Her dark, expressive eyes, offset by pale skin, were identical to Freya's, but it wasn't so much an exact physical likeness as her manner. The way she tucked a loose strand of hair behind an ear, tilted her face upwards in conversation. The lilt of a faint Indian accent. Maybe it was all just wishful thinking, a symptom of his recent desire to find Freya.

He thinks again about Jemma, aware of a nagging idea in the back of his mind. If she's not connected in some way to Freya Lal, who is she? The mystery woman who turned up in their village today, unable to remember a single thing about her life. And that tattoo of a lotus flower. It would make a compelling story. Irresistible clickbait. He left that world behind long ago, but he still misses it, even if it has changed. The Fleet Street he once worked in, before the death of his wife, has all but gone, shoe-leather investigations replaced by big data leaks on the dark web, content providers taking over from reporters, drunken sub-editors sacked to make way for clean-living digital natives who clock on at 5 a.m. Milo has grown up not knowing a world without social media, or Google, or the internet.

The woman with no name and no memory. It's tempting. His phone buzzes. It's a text message from Laura.

Are you awake? Lx

He hesitates, glancing at the time. It's 12.50 a.m., late for a text by his generation's standards. He tries to rationalise the situation, his normal logic blurred by one too many pints with Sean after the quiz. Laura's a spice, as Milo would say. She's also married to Tony, blissfully so, it would seem. Luke had been very happy with his girlfriend, Chloe, but it wasn't right or fair that she'd been waiting for him to be ready to have children with her. He would never be ready. As he tried to explain to her, at fifty, ten years older than her, he is on to the next stage in life, with a teenager in tow.

He texts back.

Awake. Everything OK?

He pauses and then adds a kiss. Strict parity, no 'chirpsing', another Milo phrase. He can see his son rolling his eyes.

Google Jemma Huish + manslaughter.

He looks at her message, disappointed by the end of texting niceties, the cut to the chase. And then he searches Google. The first result is a brief story about a murder case, twelve years ago. He reads it through, taking in the sickening details, and looks at the woman in the fuzzy main photo. A sallow haunted face, beautiful in a deranged sort of way. Why's Laura asked him to google her?

His phone buzzes with another text.

Look familiar?

He glances at the photo again and sits up in his chair.
Christ.

You think it's Jemma?

He is still staring at the out-of-focus face. It's hard to tell
but it could just be her.

*Susie Patterson thought it might be. She used to live in our
house, before she moved to London.*

Where is she now?

Sleeping upstairs... :-O

Where are you?

On the sofa in the sitting room.

What does Tony think?

*That I'm an overanxious yoga teacher, which is probably
true. Susie says Jemma Huish has probably been rehabilitated
back into the community.*

Luke scrolls through the search results and clicks on a
longer article about the shortage of specialist-unit beds
and the dangers posed by psychiatric patients. In one NHS
trust alone, eighteen mental-health patients over the past
fifteen years have gone on to kill after being released into
the community. Jemma Huish, who lived in the village as
a child, long before his parents retired here, is cited as an

example of a potentially dangerous early release. After she was found guilty of manslaughter, it was ordered that she be held indefinitely in a high-security psychiatric hospital. First Broadmoor then Ashworth. No one seems to know where she is now.

Luke sighs, thinking back to his chat with the woman in the pub. She didn't seem like a psychotic killer. Far from it. He liked her. She struck him as a lost soul – a bit like him – and in need of help. No danger to anyone though. But then he's not sleeping in the same house as her.

He texts Laura back.

She was discharged because she was no longer considered a threat to society. Sure it's fine/not her.

He wants to add that he's a bit hurt by the suggestion as he thinks Jemma might be related to an old girlfriend, but he resists. For now he'll keep that theory to himself.

That's what Tony said. I'm taking Jemma to the surgery at 9 a.m. I'd rather stick hot needles in my eyes.

I'm sure you'll feel better in the morning. Sleep well.

Fat chance. Not sure why we let a stranger stay in our house.

Because you are kind, decent people. The kindest in the village. We're very lucky you moved here.

She sends a solitary kiss. He pauses and then sends one back.

DAY TWO

14

I stare at the ceiling, morning sun filtering through the blind. For a few seconds I wonder where I am. No fear yet, just confusion. Outside the window I can hear the sound of a train pulling away. Perhaps that's what woke me. I turn to reach the sheets of paper on the bedside table and sit up. 'READ THIS WHEN YOU WAKE UP' is written on the top sheet.

And then the feeling returns, like a lead cloak has been wrapped around my shoulders. The words shock me as I read them, a brutal reminder of what I am doing in this bedroom. Free of any sentiment, my short sentences are an unembellished record of all that's happened, like a child's diary. I lost my handbag. I took the train. I went to the pub quiz with Tony. I reach the end and read the last sentence again: 'Laura asks me if I'm someone called "Jemma Huish".'

Who is Jemma Huish? Why am I being mistaken for her?

I need to get ready for the day. A note's been slipped under the door in what I assume is Laura's handwriting:

If you want a shower, use the one in our bathroom (loo shower downstairs broken!). Turn on the switch outside the bathroom first. Lx

Friendly enough tone. The shower is perfect, just what I need. I tilt my head upwards, trying to focus on all that I need to do. But my body tenses as soon as I think of what might lie ahead. I let the water run over my face, allowing thoughts to come and go. I see a bodhi tree in a cleansing downpour, raindrops running off its heart-shaped leaves. I must stay strong.

Tony and Laura both look up when I walk into the kitchen for breakfast.

'How you feeling?' Tony says, making coffee at the sideboard. 'Sleep well?'

Laura is slicing a mango, dropping thick juicy pieces into a bowl of yoghurt at the table. The block of knives is nowhere to be seen.

'OK,' I say, turning to Laura. She avoids eye contact with me, maybe because hers are bloodshot. The truth is I feel sick. I summon what strength I have and begin to speak. Tentatively, quietly. 'I know that I'm calling myself Jemma,' I say, pausing. 'That I arrived at Heathrow Airport yesterday and lost my handbag, and that I then came out here to this village, where you two were good enough to look after me.'

Laura glances at Tony. 'That's great news,' she says, beaming.

'Is it?' Tony asks, looking at me and then at Laura. 'Did you find your notes from yesterday? By your bed?'

They both turn to me. I give the faintest acknowledgement, my cheeks reddening.

'So you didn't remember anything when you woke up?' Laura asks, unable to hide her disappointment.

'I knew it was my handwriting when I started to read the sheets, but it seemed like someone else's life.' I pause and look up at them both, struggling to continue. 'What's happening to me?'

'It's OK,' Laura says. She gets up from the table and walks over to me.

Tears start to come as she gives me a hug. I wish she wasn't so nice.

'We went to see a doctor at the surgery yesterday – Susie Patterson,' she says, standing back. 'Together, you and me. She said that if you woke up this morning unable to recall what happened yesterday, you might be suffering from something called anterograde amnesia.'

'I know,' I say quietly. 'I wrote that down in my notes too. I think I'm also suffering from the retrograde version.' I pause, wiping away my tears. 'I still don't know my own name.'

'Transient global amnesia,' Tony says, raising his eyebrows as if he's impressed. 'A rare dose of double forgetfulness.'

Laura looks at him. 'It will come back,' she says, turning to me. 'Don't worry.'

'The thing is, when I read the notes, I really tried to commit them to memory, imagine myself turning up here in the village, going to the surgery, but there's no feeling attached to any of the events I've written down. I can't remember what it actually felt like to knock on your door, see you open it.'

I stop and look up at them. 'Who's Jemma Huish?' They both flinch. 'It says in my notes you asked last night if I was her.'

'She suffered from amnesia,' Laura says, after a hesitation. 'Is that all?'

'And she once lived in this house. A long time ago. Which might explain how you know where everything is.'

I stare at her as she quickly scans the kitchen.

'And she looked a bit like you,' Tony says.

'Is that why you called me Jemma?' I ask.

'I had no idea,' he says. 'It was just a name.'

'But you both think I might be this woman?'

Laura glances across at Tony, checking with him before she speaks. 'I did, but I'm not sure any more. I'm taking you down to the surgery this morning – they'll know for certain.'

'Jemma Huish,' I repeat, watching Laura sit back down at the table. I wish I could put her mind at rest, but I can't.

'Would you like some breakfast?' she asks.

I sit down next to her. She moves her knife away from me before passing a plate of fruit.

'What did she do?' I ask, taking a dripping slice of mango. 'I really need to know.'

Laura hesitates before answering, exchanges another look with Tony. 'She killed her best friend.'

'What?' I whisper, unable to hide my shock.

'Twelve years ago. She was found guilty of manslaughter and sent to a secure psychiatric unit. Seven years later, she was released. No one's seen her since.'

'And she lived here? In this house?'

Laura nods. 'She was once registered at the surgery. A long time ago.'

'We really don't think it's you,' Tony says, glancing at Laura. 'But it's probably better that you're taken care of by the professionals from now on.' He clears his throat unnecessarily. 'I'm sorry, but you can't stay here any longer. With us.'

I hold Tony's gaze for a second, stunned by what he's just said.

'We're due at the surgery at nine,' Laura says.

There's an awkward silence. I'm not sure what to say. They've been very kind, taking me in for the night, and I know I should be grateful, but... I don't want to stay in a hospital.

'I'm guessing the surgery will know if I'm Jemma Huish,' I say, trying in vain to lighten the mood. 'If I'm not, maybe I could stay for—'

Another look between Laura and Tony. 'I'm sorry, Jemma,' he says. 'We've done our bit. Given you a bed for the night, shown you the village. It's over to them now. Laura didn't sleep too well.'

'Because you think I'm a murderer?'

'It sounds so silly now,' Laura says, getting up from the table to clear the breakfast plates. 'Crazy, in fact.'

She is almost in tears and keeps her back to me and Tony, who shrugs his shoulders. It's definitely not his call to kick me out, which is something. And then his blue eyes are on me again. I make myself return his smile before I look away. The house phone begins to ring.

Tony stands up to answer the call.

'Speaking,' he says, glancing first at Laura, who has turned around, and then at me.

I'm still sitting at the kitchen table. I watch Tony's demeanour change, his eyes lingering on me in a way that suggests I'm the subject of whatever conversation he's having. His smile has gone. And then he takes the phone out of the room, raising his eyebrows at Laura before he leaves. She follows him into the hall. I strain to hear them, but they are both talking in whispers. I think I hear Tony say the word 'police', but I can't be sure.

He comes back in on his own, which strikes me as odd, and replaces the phone on its base.

'That was the cops,' he says.

'Have they found my handbag?' I ask, tensing.

'Not exactly.' His manner is distant now, more objective. Any collusion between us has disappeared.

'What did they want?'

'They're sending over two detectives.'

'Did they say anything else?' I try to ignore the edge in his voice, the growing tightness in my chest.

'There's been a development,' he says, standing sentinel at the doorway.

'What? You need to tell me, Tony.'

He pauses before speaking. 'They're going to join you at the surgery.'

I hear the front door close and see Laura walk past, breaking into a run down the road. She is frightened and doesn't look in through the window. My stomach lurches.

'Jemma Huish seems to have got them interested.'

15

Detective Inspector Silas Hart glances across the water meadow, his gaze moving up to the hill that overlooks the village. Not for the first time in his career he senses that someone is out there, watching him go about his work. He dismisses the thought and tries to appreciate the view. England at its best, kept just this side of chocolate-box by the shifting tableau of canal boats and the Victorian grit of the Paddington to Penzance rail line. He takes a last drag on his cigarette and turns to walk back to the surgery with DC Strover, who is waiting for him by the road.

Strover is young and new but keeps him on his toes. She's also not afraid to take the initiative, one reason why he wanted her to work for him. Already this morning she's pulled the passenger lists for all BA flights from Berlin Tegel that arrived at Heathrow before 3 p.m. yesterday. And asked Border Force to check names against advanced passenger information and send over scanned passports. That way they get to see photos.

'Always meant to live in a place like this when I transferred out of the Met,' Silas says as they head for the surgery. 'Small village with a country pub, beer served from wooden kegs.'

Strover maintains a respectful silence.

'Not your thing?' Silas asks, glancing at her. Strover is from Bristol. More city and cocktails. She makes no attempt to disguise her Bristol accent, a pride he admires. Silas buried his Wiltshire intonations deep beneath an Estuary twang when he worked for the Met, worried about being branded a provincial carrot cruncher.

'Prefer somewhere a little livelier, sir.'

He just wishes she'd stop calling him 'sir'. In time, he hopes she'll come to call him 'guv' or 'boss'. Everyone used to call him 'guv' when he was working on homicides. Since his internal transfer from the Major Crime Investigation Team, a collaboration between local police forces, to Swindon CID – he tries not to think of it as a demotion – he's called 'sir' and spends his time investigating pop-up brothels.

Despite his rural aspirations, Silas has somehow ended up working in Swindon, reputedly the ugliest town in Britain, the place of his birth and boasting a roundabout as its main tourist attraction.

'How much do you know about the Jemma Huish case?' he asks.

'Just what I've read,' Strover says. 'She killed her flatmate and then rang the police.'

'Rang us before she killed her, that was the problem. Warned us what she was going to do. There was a Domestic Homicide Review – believe me, you really want to avoid those.'

On the plus side, a different DHR was how Silas had met Susie Patterson, while she was practising at her old surgery near Devizes. 'Early intervention', 'procedure and protocol assessments', 'inter-agency working' – he shivers at the memory. He's never been much of a corporate player.

'You think this case could be related?' Strover asks as they cross the road into the sunshine.

'Probably not.'

He knows she doesn't believe him. He dropped everything to be over here after Susie rang him late last night. Would he have come so quickly if someone else had called him?

'A mystery woman turning up in a village with no memory would normally be one for the local mental-health team,' he says, stopping to look at the small ads in the post office window. Bunk beds and babysitters mainly. His colleagues spend more than enough time doing 'uniform social work', picking up the pieces of a care-in-the-community policy that doesn't seem to allow for out-of-hours emergencies.

But Susie's call last night had been different. She'd mentioned Jemma Huish, a name he's not forgotten since his days as a sergeant in south London. A name he'll never forget. In uniform in those days, he was one of the first officers on the scene, a tiny room in Huish's university hall of residence. Her roommate was almost dead, but he stayed with her until the paramedics arrived. Huish was being restrained in the corridor outside, screaming how sorry she was, how it all could have been avoided if someone had just listened to her.

'As a precaution, I've got hold of Huish's old "This is me" file,' Silas says, pushing the memory of Huish's screams aside as they reach the surgery. 'Not that it helps much – the data is either out of date or wrong.'

'Did you see what the Japanese are doing with dementia sufferers?' Strover asks as a dog walker passes them on the pavement. 'Tagging them with QR codes.'

'They should do that here,' he whispers, entering the busy waiting room. The only useful piece of information in Huish's file is her DNA profile, taken at the time of her arrest.

Silas waits his turn and then walks up to the receptionist, who says that Dr Patterson will see him straight away.

'Join us in a couple of minutes?' he says, turning to Strover, unable to hide a sudden awkwardness. He doesn't mean to pull rank. He just has no wish to explain to a junior colleague that he fancies the arse off Dr Patterson and would like to spend a few minutes on his own with her. 'The old mags are always worth a flick through,' he adds, gesturing at the waiting room behind them. 'Only time my suits feel fashionable.'

Strover gives him a suspicious look as he turns to walk down the surgery corridor. She's not stupid.

16

'You're up early,' Luke says, surprised to see Sean walking past the train station with his dog, a tan-coloured whippet lurcher. Luke is queuing for the ticket machine, about to board the train to London.

'Not actually hit the sack yet,' Sean says. He looks rougher than usual in his baggy T-shirt and jeans. At odds with the quotidian uniformity of the assembled commuters. 'Trying to nail the third act. Staying in town?'

'Couple of nights.' Luke's looking forward to being submersed in the anonymity of London, far from the accountability of village life.

'Any news on our mystery amnesiac?' Sean asks.

'Haven't seen her today.' Luke thinks back to the texts last night from Laura, her suggestion that Jemma was a former psychiatric patient. He's sticking with his own theory, that she's somehow related to Freya Lal.

'Just saw a pair of plainclothes cops arrive in the village.'

'Where?'

'Up by the surgery.'

Luke instinctively glances in its direction even though the surgery can't be seen from the station. Several late-runners are heading for the train.

'How do you know?' he asks.

'Recognised one of them off the news. Salisbury.'

Sean doesn't miss much on the news. Doesn't miss much in the village.

'It's got me thinking,' he continues. 'Did you see the way she answered those Russian questions in the quiz last night? She even knew the address of the KGB headquarters.'

'And?' Luke glances at his watch and looks back down to the track. His train is nosing its way out of the siding onto the main line. He's fond of Sean but not in the mood right now for one of his wild conspiracy theories. Fidel Castro is Justin Trudeau's dad; Taylor Swift is a Satanist; Hunter S. Thompson was murdered. He's heard them all. As for the nerve-agent attack in Salisbury... where to start?

'2010 – ten Soviet sleeper agents rounded up by the FBI in America,' Sean says. 'They'd buried themselves deep within the fabric of suburban American society, waiting to be activated by Moscow. OK, so they were shite spies – the FBI had been bugging and following them for years – but my point is that they targeted ordinary America. These people lived in New Jersey, went to Colombia Business School, told everyone they'd been born in America.'

'You honestly want me to believe that Jemma might be a Russian sleeper?' Luke says over his shoulder, entering his details at the ticket machine. He reaches down to give Sean's dog a sympathetic rub behind the ears. Poor mutt has to listen to Sean's wild theories every day.

'After Salisbury, they've returned to basics. Had to. Moscow rules. Old school. This Jemma is confused, doesn't know who she is. Maybe she's been woken up too early, can't remember where her loyalties lie.'

'Write it all down, Sean – and file it under comedy.' Luke removes his tickets from the machine just as the train pulls up. 'Actually, make that farce.'

'Where was the third and final attempt made to poison Alexander Litvinenko?' Sean calls out as Luke steps into the carriage. 'Fourth floor, Millennium Hotel, Grosvenor Square. Who the hell knows that level of detail in a pub quiz, Luke? A former Russian sleeper, that's feckin' who.'

Luke shakes his head in disbelief as the train doors close behind him.

17

I stare at Tony as he makes his way into the hall. 'Do I look like I'm going to kill anyone?' I ask.

'They have to rule her out, that's all,' he says as he takes his house keys off the windowsill.

I try to think fast, my heart racing. Coming to this village was a mistake. If I can't tell anyone my own name, how can I convince them I'm not a killer?

'Can I pack my bag?' I ask.

Tony nods. 'Then I'll walk down with you to the surgery.'

'Where's Laura gone?' I'm haunted by the image of her running past the window like a fleeing animal.

'To see a friend.' He pauses. 'She's frightened.'

'Of me?' The idea sounds ridiculous when I say it out aloud.

Tony positions himself in front of the door as I walk past him and up the stairs, my legs heavy with adrenaline. I try to picture the bedroom where I slept, remembering the layout of the house outside, which is single storey at the rear. There's a sloping roof below the window, above the kitchen. Tiles and a central skylight.

I rush into the bedroom and look at my suitcase. There's nothing I need in there and I have no intention of taking it with me. Instead, I grab my handwritten notes from the bedside table, skim read them again and fold them into the back pocket of my jeans. My hands are shaking. Tony is still at the bottom of the stairs. I walk across the landing and stand by the bathroom door.

'Won't be a minute,' I call out.

I pull on the light cord and let it ping. Its handle is a carved wooden seahorse. I watch it whirl around for a second, feeling dizzy, and then I shut the bathroom door with its noisy farmhouse latch and tiptoe back to my room, closing the door behind me. The sash window opens more noisily than I expect and I slip one leg out onto the roof, desperate to get away.

'What the hell are you doing?'

I spin round to see Tony standing in the bedroom doorway, arms folded. I stare at him and then turn back to the window. A robin on a tree in their back garden looks at me as if I'm the most stupid human on earth.

'Running away isn't going to help anyone,' he says.

I don't move. He's right. I've made a mistake, thrown by the Jemma Huish development and the fact that she lived in this house. I just need to relax, trust the system.

'I'm worried they'll think I'm her,' I say.

'Listen, I dislike the cops more than most, but if you run now, you're guilty. Period.'

I pull my leg in from the window and drop back into the bedroom, leaning against the window ledge. I'm embarrassed by my attempt to escape. It was the wrong move. Even the robin has flown off in disgust.

'I'm sorry,' I say. 'I don't know what I was thinking.'

'It's OK. We've all run away. It never helps.'

The room suddenly feels airless, intimate. As I pass him at the top of the stairs, he steps into my way and wraps his arms around me.

'Here, let me give you a hug.'

I suppress my gut response to push him away and allow him to hold me. One, two, three seconds. And then I remove myself from his embrace. My breath shallowing, I follow him downstairs in silence and tell him I need the loo. After locking the door, I rest my forehead on the cold wall in front of me, close my eyes and try to think of the bodhi tree.

18

'Good to see you again,' Silas says, entering Dr Susie Patterson's consulting room. He waits until the door is closed before kissing her on both cheeks. 'Looking well.'

'You too,' she says, sitting down behind her desk. He remains standing, glancing around the room, the map of the world on the wall. He loves travelling. 'Slimmer,' she adds. 'A lot slimmer.'

He realises she's being kind, knows he has the gaunt look of someone who's lost weight too quickly. His skin, particularly around the face, is hanging off him like shredded wallpaper.

'I fast for a day and then trough like a pig,' he says. 'Now you see me,' he adds, arms held up either side of his head, 'now you don't.' He spins like a surrendering marionette to face her sideways on. 'Now you see me...' he repeats, spinning again, 'now you don't. Magic, eh?'

'You're wasted in the police,' she says.

He's going to enjoy his svelte new look while he can. Give him six months and he'll have put it all back on – and some.

'Still smoking?' she asks.

'When I can.' He takes a seat. In truth, he's trying to give up.

The last time they met, by chance at the bar of the Watermill Theatre in Newbury, she had openly flirted with Silas. He subsequently heard that she had separated from her husband soon afterwards. Is that why he's come here today?

'Are you happier?' he asks.

'Different person. It was long overdue.'

'Any kids?' he asks. 'I've forgotten.'

'One cross daughter. Angry about the divorce.'

'She'll come round.'

'And you?'

He falls quiet. 'Still just the one son.' Conor. He doesn't want to go into details.

'I'm assuming you haven't come all this way for a family chat,' Susie says, sensing his discomfort.

'Am I that shallow?'

'I really don't know if she is Jemma Huish. It's just a hunch.'

'I like hunches. A woman losing her memory is of no interest to us – mental-health services are welcome to her. But if the last time she lost her memory she slit her best friend's throat, your hunch becomes more interesting.'

'And you really don't remember her?' She knows Silas used to work in the Met – it was one of the reasons she called him last night – but had been unaware of his personal connection with the case. 'What she looked like?'

Silas shakes his head. 'I was more concerned with trying to save her friend's life.' He pauses. 'And I failed.'

'You tried. That's what matters.'

'If you say so.' He looks up at her and smiles. He knows that life has slipped through Susie's hands too.

'Couldn't you just check for her passport number?' she asks, changing the subject. 'See if she came through Heathrow yesterday?'

'Huish didn't have a passport when she committed her crime. Had never been out of Wiltshire before she moved to London, let alone travelled abroad.' It was silly, but he'd felt personally responsible in some way for what had happened with Huish. Maybe that's why he transferred out of the Met soon afterwards and moved back to Wiltshire. To try to do some good, set the record straight. 'All we've got is her last risk assessment, along with a physical description, family contacts, GP and financial details, and a mugshot. Not been updated since she left Ashworth five years ago.'

'Can I see the picture?'

'That's kind of why I came to see you.'

'There was I thinking you wanted to buy me lunch.'

He puts a grainy photo of Jemma Huish on her desk, keen to keep things professional. 'Is that her?' His own visual memories of Huish from twelve years ago have become too entangled with the subsequent media coverage of the case to be of any use.

'Not sure,' she says, moving the photo to take a closer look.

'Not a great image, I know,' he says. 'We've been trying to contact her last care coordinator this morning, as well as the shrink who saw her regularly. So far, no dice.'

'I tried too,' she says. 'Everyone's moved on.'

'We just need to bring someone down here who has worked relatively recently with Huish and get them to do a positive ID on her. A lot of the NHS files are also lost or missing. I don't know how you put up with it.'

'I gather Jemma Huish's fingerprints have gone missing too.'

'Touché,' he says, looking up at her from across the desk. His face is close to hers. 'We'll find them. In the meantime, we need to talk to Jemma.'

'She's next door. I'll take you through in a moment. Be gentle with her – she's very fragile.' She pauses. 'Do you really think she could be Jemma Huish?'

Silas sits back in his chair, glancing at the map on the wall behind her. India is somewhere he'd like to visit again. He's only been to the north – the golden triangle and then up to Ladakh. 'Whoever she is, she came to your village for a reason.' He pauses, his eyes on hers. 'Twelve years ago someone failed to act quickly enough on a 999 call made by Jemma Huish. She warned us and we were too slow to respond. I'm not going to let that happen again on my watch.'

A knock at the door and Strover appears. She glances from one to the other, as if checking for evidence of intimacy. 'Sorry to interrupt, but Jemma appears to have gone walkabout.'

19

I had to slip out of the surgery for the sake of my own sanity, if I ever had any, and I'm now in the graveyard across the road. It's as quiet as a library, each headstone like a book cover. Some are more emotional than others, passionate page-turners: 'Darling wife who died in the morning of her life'; others are more measured tomes: 'A much missed father and brother.'

I move among the stones, browsing, thinking. Ever since I woke up this morning I haven't felt in control; events are running ahead of me. The early morning call from the police, Laura racing down the street like that, Tony's erratic behaviour. Why did I agree to his suggestion that I call myself Jemma? None of this confusion with Jemma Huish would have happened if I'd been given a different name.

I'm now in front of a grave that reads: 'MARY HUISH, MUCH LOVED WIFE AND MOTHER.' A wave of emotion washes over me. I close my eyes and summon the bodhi tree again, listening to the sound of the warm wind in its leaves, whispering like a mantra. I take a deep breath. I hope I will see Mum again soon.

I should return to Dr Patterson. My absence will only cause more trouble, but I don't like the thought of meeting the police. They make me nervous. Like Tony did when he walked me down to the surgery. I tried not to think of him as my escort, but everything about his body language suggested that he'd been told to keep me under close supervision. I can't blame him, given I'd just tried to climb out of his upstairs window, but it's confusing. A few minutes earlier, he was giving me a hug on the landing.

I look up to see Dr Patterson standing over by the lychgate, a man and a woman next to her. The detectives, I guess. A minute later, she is by my side. The detectives are still at the gate, fifty yards away. She studies the Huish gravestone in front of us. 'Must be her mother,' she says, almost to herself.

I start to walk on through the old graves, many of them listing at different angles in the long grass, like masts in a rough sea.

'There's really nothing to worry about, you know,' she says, catching up with me. 'They just need to ask you a few questions. Take your fingerprints, do a DNA test. A simple medical swab from the inside of your mouth.'

My whole body tenses. Does she notice?

'They want to establish that there's no connection, that's all,' she continues, as if it's got nothing to do with her. 'Jemma Huish used to live in Tony and Laura's house.'

'Was it you who alerted them?' I ask quietly.

She stops and looks at me, surprised by my question. 'It was a precaution, nothing more,' she says.

'I've done nothing wrong,' I say, a new urgency in my voice. 'I'm not Jemma Huish. This is not my mother buried here.'

'I'm sure you're right.' There's growing concern in her eyes. 'But given your amnesia...'

'I may not know who I am, but I would never kill a friend. Never kill anyone.'

A red kite circles above us, its plaintive cry carrying on the light wind. We both look up.

'Of course you wouldn't,' she says.

I sense she's a kind woman, even if she did alert the police. My breathing has become fast and shallow. Could I take another's life, if it really came to it? Would I be able to slit someone's throat? I reach for my wrist and touch the tattoo.

'I don't want a DNA test,' I say, turning away from her.

A simple medical swab from the inside of your mouth.

'It might help to work out who you are, where you've come from,' Dr Patterson says.

'I desperately want to know that, but...' I falter.

I catch her signalling to the detectives – a raised palm, as if to tell them to wait, keep their distance.

'I've done nothing wrong,' I repeat.

'Let me talk to police. We need to find you a proper bed, in a specialist centre. Or up at the hospital.'

'Not the hospital,' I say quickly.

She looks up at me and notices my fingers still on my wrist. 'That's a pretty tattoo. What is it?' she asks.

'A lotus flower.'

'Can I see it?'

I hold up my wrist for her to inspect, like a child who has been caught drawing on herself in class. We both stare at the flower's nine purple petals.

'It's beautiful. When did you get it done?'

'I don't know,' I say, suddenly tearful. If only I could remember the details, why Fleur and I both chose a lotus, what happened afterwards. But it's like swimming in a dark sea. 'We both had one,' I add.

'We?'

'My friend and I.' I pause. 'She died.'

'I'm sorry,' Dr Patterson says, full of sympathy. 'When did this happen?' she asks, after a respectful silence.

I shake my head.

'Do you remember her name? It might be important.'

I need some strength right now and hope that saying her name out loud might help.

'Fleur. She was called Fleur,' I repeat, watching Dr Patterson write down her name.

We were matching flowers.

20

Tony is late to open up his café. A couple passing through the village on the canal are at the door, hoping for a coffee. He tells them to come back in ten minutes, once the Fracino Contempo is up and running. It's proving a little temperamental since he installed it – maybe why it was going cheap on eBay.

He could have done without having to take Jemma down to Dr Patterson, but Laura was in no state to accompany her after the police rang. She's reacted badly to Jemma's arrival. Very badly.

'How was it at the surgery?' she asks.

He turns round to see Laura standing in the café doorway. She's in her yoga clothes, no doubt on her way down to a class in the Scout Hut.

'The police want to take her DNA,' he says. 'I'm sure it'll all be sorted soon.'

'I hope so,' she says, stepping into the café. 'Do they think she's—'

'A psychotic killer? I didn't ask. It's not her, angel. Not in a million years.'

He takes a bowl of cinnamon quinoa and some jars of citrus granola parfait out of the fridge and places them in the display cabinet.

'How can you be so sure?' she asks.

He's not sure at all.

'I've spoken to the pub,' he says, pouring some decaffeinated coffee beans into the grinder. He's keen to change the subject. 'They're happy to put her up for a few days, until a bed is found for her. Susie seemed OK with that – thinks that out-of-area care wouldn't be appropriate right now. The village clearly holds some significance for her.'

'Too right it does. I don't think you quite realise who this woman is, Tony. She's ill.'

'And she's getting help,' Tony says. Laura doesn't often raise her voice and for the first time he notices that she's been crying. He walks around from behind the food counter. 'Susie's right on it,' he says quietly, squeezing her arm gently.

'I didn't sleep last night.' She turns away from him to look out onto the high street. 'Nor did you. You were calling out again.'

He hoped she hadn't heard. It must have been loud if it disturbed her on the sofa downstairs. Did Jemma hear too? He's been having more nightmares recently, ones where he wakes up only to discover that he's still dreaming. He wipes a tiny piece of food off a table using the tea towel that's draped over his shoulder. He hates dirty tables.

'And I'm not going to sleep any better tonight,' she continues, 'knowing she's just down the road.'

'I think you're overreacting,' he says, trying not to inflame the situation. They are not used to arguing, both of them preferring to avoid confrontation.

'Am I?' she says, spinning around to face him. 'So why did she choose our house? She could have knocked on any door in the village, but she came to ours, where she once lived. Doesn't that worry you? It fucking freaks me out, Tony, and you're doing nothing about it.'

A man on his way to the station stops at the open door. Damn Laura. They should be having this conversation at home.

'Open?' the man asks, glancing nervously at both of them. He must have heard the swearing. 'Need a bacon butty for the train.'

'Smoky-tempeh wrap with veganaise?' Tony offers in his politest voice, grateful for the distraction.

'OK,' the man replies hesitantly.

He steps back behind the counter and prepares the wrap for his customer, watched by Laura, still by the window, arms folded. He needs to get on. The locals are taking to his vegan food with impressive open-mindedness, given the place was once the village bakery. 'From Lardy Cakes to Falafel Wraps' – that's how the *Parish News* described it.

'I'm sorry, I've got food to prepare, customers to feed,' Tony says to Laura once the man has gone. He feels more comfortable with the food counter between them.

'You really don't care, do you?' she says, her voice more sad than angry.

'What?'

'About Jemma, what I think. My concerns.'

'Don't be ridiculous. Of course I care.' This time he decides not to go over and comfort her. Nothing he can say or do is going to help. He starts to polish some glass tumblers with the tea towel.

'It doesn't seem like it,' she says.

'It's been a stressful few weeks, the move and everything.' He holds up a glass to the light, checking for smears. He hates dirty glasses. 'And now this mysterious woman arriving on our doorstep. No wonder you're upset.'

She shakes her head in slow disbelief. 'Please don't patronise me,' she says, walking over to the door. 'There's nothing mysterious about her. It's pretty obvious who she is, isn't it?'

Tony places the last glass on the tray and flings the tea towel back over his shoulder. They stare across the café at each other for a moment. He needs to be careful with Laura, she's fragile. 'Maybe it's better if you take a short break, angel?' he says. 'You know, a visit to your mom? She hasn't seen you for a while.'

Laura nods her head sadly.

'You know, I might just do that,' she says and walks out of the café, slamming the door behind her.

21

As we continue along the path through the graveyard, towards the surgery beyond, Dr Patterson's phone rings. She drops behind to answer it. I wait for her, but she gestures for me to go on ahead.

'I'm coming,' she says.

I can't help feeling that the call is about me. She's already phoned one of the detectives – he's called Silas, I think – asking for some more time with me, and she's promised that she'll personally oversee my care. She's not going to send me to A & E. She senses my reluctance. Instead, she's put in another request to the Cavell Centre, a local specialist mental-health unit, where I'm now on a waiting list for a bed. I'm counting on it being a long one.

I walk on, checking behind me. Dr Patterson is following at a short distance. Up ahead, the detectives are nowhere to be seen, but there's a man entering the graveyard from the far end, a dog at his side. He disappears behind a large yew tree before I can see who it is.

I keep walking. The man should have emerged from the

other side of the tree by now. As I walk past, I can just see his dog, sitting on the ground, lean haunches trembling, but there's no sign of the man. It's as if he's hiding from me. And then a voice calls out in what sounds like Russian, although there's a strong hint of Irish too:

'*Ty skuchayesh' po zhizni v Moskve?*'

I stop, not sure whether to go around to the back of the tree or to keep walking.

'*Gde vashi loyal'nosti?*' the man continues.

I quicken my step. It's unnerving not being able to see the speaker. I'm almost at the lychgate when the voice calls out again – in English this time, but still with an Irish accent.

'Jemma, it's Sean, from the pub last night.'

I turn round to see Sean coming up to me, a smile twitching at his lips, dog by his side.

'Did you hear any weird voices back there?' he asks, looking around at the empty churchyard.

'No,' I say, wondering how long he plans to keep up this ridiculous charade.

'Funny – honest to God, I thought I heard someone speaking Russian.'

We both look across to the water meadow, where an intercity train speeds past. Beyond the track, on the wooded hillside, a flock of crows rises into the sky.

22

'I don't think she's up to being interviewed at the moment,'
Susie Patterson says, sitting down behind the desk in her
consulting room. 'That's all. I'm sorry.'

Silas gestures for Strover to take a seat and sits down in
the other chair. He's only got himself to blame. He should
have dispatched Strover and another junior detective
for a case like this, not driven over to the village himself.
Huish's name intrigued him when Susie called last night, but
in reality it was an excuse to see her again. A transparent
one. He can't be annoyed with her now if he's wasted
a morning.

'We just need to ask her a few questions, establish her
movements since she arrived at Heathrow,' he says. 'Strover
here is working on yesterday's passenger lists, but it would
help if we could narrow it down.'

Susie is not convinced and seems too embarrassed to look
at him. It's obvious what's going on here. She no longer
thinks the woman is Jemma Huish. Last night all the talk
was about her not making another big mistake in her career.

When Silas first met her, Susie was a partner at a practice near Devizes, but she left under a cloud, following a tragic misdiagnosis that was picked up by the national press. She told a mother her seven-year-old daughter was suffering from gastroenteritis and sent the girl home with instructions to drink lots of water. Two days later, she was dead from acute appendicitis.

'I know it was me who called you, raised the alarm,' she continues, keen to justify her change of mind, 'but I have to consider what's best for her – as a patient, her rights – and this morning she's too fragile to be interviewed. I'm sorry.'

Silas glances over at Strover, who is sitting impassively. She must think he's an idiot, coming here in person, only to be fobbed off.

'Perhaps you could take the DNA sample for us,' he suggests to Susie, trying to be more conciliatory. It was going so well earlier – before she started getting all Hippocratic with him. If she's so concerned about patients' rights, she shouldn't have called him last night about Jemma. He can only assume she's lost her nerve, worried that she might lose her job again if she doesn't play by the book.

'She doesn't want to give one,' Susie says. 'She's adamant.'

He knows Jemma doesn't have to agree to give a sample, not unless she's been arrested, and there aren't exactly grounds for that at the moment. Not on the basis of a GP's late-night hunch.

'That's a bit odd, don't you think?' Silas says. 'In her position, I'd do anything to establish my identity.'

Susie continues to avoid eye contact with him. 'There's something else going on – her blood pressure was very high when I saw her yesterday. Possibly white-coat hypertension, I'm not sure.'

'Fear of doctors?'

'"Iatrophobia". She's not exactly keen to go to hospital either.'

'Don't blame her.'

Silas often passes the Great Western Hospital on his way to the police station at Gablecross. Not his favourite building – his father died there last year.

'I'm currently working on the assumption that her amnesia is the result of anxiety, some sort of emotional trauma,' Susie continues. 'I thought it might be work-related stress, but maybe there was an actual event of some kind, some traumatic incident that triggered a dissociative fugue. She talked about a friend of hers who died.'

'Name?' Silas asks.

'Fleur – that's all she could remember. Didn't know when or where she died. This initial period is crucial as her brain begins to process what happened. It could be the key to unlocking other memories – establishing who she is. I don't want to do anything that might jeopardise that.'

'Maybe I could talk to her,' Strover offers. She doesn't look up at Silas either. The woman's touch. He's not proud. Whatever it takes.

Susie hesitates, glancing at her screen. 'Today's a mess,' she says. 'Jemma was meant to see the mental-health nurse at nine, but she's called in sick.'

'Where's Jemma now?' Silas asks.

'With a colleague next door. What she needs is to be admitted into a specialist unit, preferably the Cavell Centre, but they've got no beds. No one has. That's the problem. How long do you need with her?' she asks, pointedly addressing Strover.

'Ten minutes?'

'Sneak a photo if you can,' Silas says. A positive match with a passport that went through Border Force yesterday could sort this in no time.

'Not without the patient's consent,' Susie says, shooting a look at him. This is becoming awkward.

'I'll leave you women to it, then,' Silas says. He'd planned to invite Susie out to dinner this week, but his enthusiasm is waning.

Fifteen minutes later, Strover gets back into his car, where he's been waiting, making calls, feeling a fool. She has finished her brief interview with Jemma.

'Anything useful?' he asks, keying the ignition.

'I think she's hiding something.'

23

I sit down on the edge of the bed in my room. It's not much – a poky space in a former stable block at the back of the pub, up an old flight of wooden stairs. The ceiling is low and the room is an odd triangular shape with bare floorboards that are pockmarked with woodworm. There's one small window and a thin flowery curtain that will struggle to keep out the light in the morning. The only redeeming feature is an upright piano in the corner. It looks ancient, probably once used in the bar downstairs. I walk over, sit down on the threadbare stool and lift the lid. The keys are stained and several white ones are missing their covers, but it's still in tune. The notes come easily, which surprises me.

After a few minutes' playing, I stand up and walk over to the window, feeling calmer. I can see School Road below, including Tony and Laura's cottage at the far end. And then I see Laura walking down to the station on her own with a wheelie suitcase. She cuts a tragic, lonely figure. Did I look like that when I arrived? A part of me wants to rush down and tell her I'm sorry for everything that's happened. But I know that nothing I can say will reassure her. It will only make things worse.

I watch until Laura has disappeared out of sight then lie back on the bed. I'm tired to the core. The mattress is as hard as stone and I'm not convinced the sheets are clean. I lean over and sniff the pillow. It smells of fabric conditioner, which is something, I guess. It's a relief to be on my own. I've been asked too many questions this morning, prodded and probed like a criminal. First Dr Patterson, then Sean, talking Russian from behind a tree. What was that all about? And finally DC Strover, who saw me briefly with Dr Patterson. Routine questions, mostly about my arrival at Heathrow and what I think happened to my handbag. I wasn't able to tell her anything more than I'd told the others.

I need to write everything down. Dr Patterson, who walked me over here after the interview, has asked me to construct a timeline forwards from my arrival at Heathrow, using my written notes each night. She says my eventual goal is to extend the timeline backwards too, into the darkness of my previous life, building on the few things I appear to remember: my arrival at Heathrow Terminal 5, my flight from Berlin. No chance of that, not at the moment. I like Dr Patterson – she says she has a daughter my age – and don't want to disappoint her. I don't want to disappoint anyone, least of all Laura. One day I hope I'll be able to explain to her what happened in Germany, maybe even why I ended up here in this village, at her house.

24

Luke's glad he doesn't have to commute into London every day. His train is late to arrive and the Tube is crowded with dazed commuters, glazed eyes avoiding contact. Jemma would have been one of them, on her journey from Heathrow yesterday. He can't imagine how she must feel. No happy memories but no regrets either, just living in the present – 'in the moment', as Laura's always urging everyone.

He needs to find out who Jemma is. And if he discovers a bit more about himself along the way, so much the better. Ever since he's become single again, he's felt as if his life is at a crossroads. He's too embarrassed to talk to Sean about it. Mid-life crises are so boring for other people. His late wife once said that men either have an affair or run a marathon. He's done neither.

It was a bit of a wrench switching from national newspapers to a classic car monthly, but his working life had to change when she died, for the sake of Milo. He came to classic cars late, after his father-in-law left them a vintage 1926 Frazer Nash Boulogne in his will. A couple of years later, after her death, Luke had it restored in her memory. It's currently having its gear ratio changed in preparation for a hill climb at the weekend, otherwise he would have driven up to London in it today rather than taken the train.

His first task, on arrival at the magazine's dingy offices in Clapham South, is to take a call from a pompous reader who's upset that the magazine is always too hard on the Bentley Boys of the 1920s. The reader has rung in before and is usually fobbed off by the magazine's edgy young deputy, Archie, but this time he sounds persistent. Luke won't take the call as himself, though. He will become the magazine's fictitious editor-in-chief, listed on the masthead as Christopher Hilton. Whenever there's a difficult reader, the sulphorous Hilton is rolled out.

'Are you sure you want me to put you through to him?' Archie says as he looks across at his boss.

Luke rolls up his shirtsleeves, aware that Archie can't stall for much longer. The rest of the magazine's young staff gather to listen.

'I'm putting you through now, sir,' Archie says, 'but I must warn you that Mr Hilton is very busy and he's, well, he can be a bit of a nob.' He nods and connects the call.

'Hilton,' Luke says, deepening his voice and raising it at the same time. He listens as the reader struggles to find the right words. 'Come on, come on,' he urges, 'I've got Queen Margrethe of Denmark holding on the other line.'

A bit OTT, but it's the first thing that comes to mind. The magazine is running a feature next month on the seven-seat Rolls-Royce Silver Wraith favoured by the Danish royal family since 1958.

He has to gesture to his staff to keep down the sniggering as he listens for another couple of seconds to bleating about Woolf 'Babe' Barnato before he signs off with a loud 'Pleasure!'

'Send him some Skoda stickers,' he says.

Luke enjoys working at the magazine, nurturing the talented young staff. He glances at the Rolls-Royce spread, marks up a couple of changes and opens his emails. There's already been a response from a request he sent out on the train. After the thirtieth-anniversary school reunion last year, a bunch of his old friends set up a group email and Luke has used it to ask if anyone has had any further thoughts about Freya Lal's whereabouts.

The replies are mostly flippant ('Let her go', 'Thirty years – maybe time to move on, Luke?' and so on), but one of Freya's closest friends at school has emailed him privately. 'Please let me know if you find Freya,' she writes. 'I miss her.'

Luke looks up from his screen at the office and realises he misses her too. Perhaps he should jack in this job, buy a ticket for him and Milo and head off to India in search of her. He's about to look up ticket prices when he gets a text on his phone. It's from Laura.

Can you call me? Lxx

Two kisses. He tries not to read anything into it – Laura is blissfully married – but his heart skips a beat.

25

A knock on the door of my room in the pub. I sit up on the edge of my bed and check my clothes, pulling down my shirt at the front.

'Who is it?' I ask.

'I've brought you lamb curry, a dish from my home place in Kabul.'

'Thank you,' I say. 'Come in.'

A stocky, Asian-looking man puts a plate of steaming food down on the wooden bedside table. He rearranges a glass to make some space and then places a fork beside the plate.

'My name's Abdul,' he says, standing back, one arm diagonally across his chest.

'From the cricket team?'

He smiles proudly. 'They say you have problems with your memory,' he says, hovering at the open door.

'That's right,' I reply, wondering who 'they' are.

'Me also. There is much I want to forget. Sorry if I call out in the night. My brother says I am noisy in my sleep. We are just down the corridor.'

'Don't worry. And, hey, I won't remember anything in the morning, will I?'

He looks at me, not sure if I'm joking. After he's gone, I pull out yesterday's notes from my jeans pocket and read through them. The reverse of the second sheet is blank. I look around for a pen and find a plastic biro in the back of the drawer in the bedside cupboard. I'm not hungry, but I also don't want to offend Abdul. His curry is delicious – full of fruit and nuts – and I manage half of it. Putting the plate on the floor, I start to write, using the bedside cupboard as a desk. There is so much to cover. Will Laura ever return?

Someone is on the stairs. Another knock at the door.

'Come in,' I say for the second time in five minutes. No peace today. It's Tony.

'Jeez, you can't stay in this dump,' he says, stooping his head as he walks into the room. He's holding a brown paper grocery bag, like the sort you see in American movies.

'Why not?' I ask.

'Smells like a Karachi curry house for a start.'

'They brought me lunch. Abdul, the cricketer. From Afghanistan.' I gesture at the plate of curry on the floor.

'I brought you lunch too. Hummus-and-falafel wrap with coconut milk yoghurt and fresh mint.'

He passes me the bag.

'That's very kind,' I say, taking it. 'Thank you.'

'I was thinking, do you want to come over to the gallery? Help me hang some pictures? It doesn't seem so healthy, you sitting around in here all day.'

'It's not that bad.' I look inside the bag at the neatly prepared wrap and place the bag on the floor beside the plate of Abdul's curry.

'What is this?' he asks, holding the curtain in his hand. 'A shower drape? And you'll get splinters from this floor.'

'I haven't actually got much choice. Not until a bed comes free.'

'That's another reason I came round. You could stay at our house again, if you want. The spare room's still made up. I can sleep downstairs, on the sofa, if that makes things easier.'

'What about Laura?' I ask, watching him pace around my small room, stopping to scuff at an uneven floorboard with his shoe. I know Laura has left the village, but I want to hear it from him. 'I'm not sure she would be so keen on the idea.'

'Laura's a little loose in the saddle right now,' he says.

'Not because of me, I hope.' I'm being disingenuous. I must be the cause, given how she's reacted to me.

'She's gone to stay with her mom for a few days.' He walks over to the window and stares down at School Road, his back to me. Has Laura already caught her train?

'It will do her some good,' he continues, still with his back to me. 'A break from this place. Moving house can be very stressful. We're only just recovering.'

'She thinks I'm a killer, doesn't she? Jemma Huish.'

He turns around, looking me straight in the eye. 'I'll admit the cops turning up first thing unsettled her. Quite a heavy-handed response for a lost handbag.'

'What do you think?' I ask, managing to hold his gaze.

'I don't think you're about to slice my throat, if that's what you mean.' He laughs, turning back to look out the window, resting his hands on either of the wooden frame.

'Thank you – for trusting me,' I say. 'And for the offer of a bed tonight. I'm fine here, really. I've caused enough grief as it is.'

'Think about it,' he says, walking towards the door. 'And come over to the gallery for an English cup of tea. It's not all tofu and kale, you know.'

'Tofu sounds good. And kale.'

'Great.' He raps a knuckle on the ancient wattle-and-daub panel beside the door, as if he's testing it. The wall sounds thin and hollow. 'I could also do with some help hanging a new picture.'

'I might just do that. After I've had a rest.'

'Good luck with that,' he says, looking around the room again.

'It's nice of them to offer me a place at all.' I pause, watching him leave. I take a deep breath. 'What is it with the seahorses, by the way?'

He stops at the door and turns, his blue eyes locked onto mine.

'I've always liked them,' he says. 'My goal is to photograph all fifty-four species in the *Hippocampus* genus. Top half horse, lower half sea monster. There's a lot of cool mythology around them. And they're kind of memorable, don't you think?'

26

Luke looks around the small space – the 'writing room', as everyone calls it – and turns to the screen again. He hasn't called Laura back – there are limits to his chirpsing. If it's urgent, she'll call him. The writing room is off the main open-plan office, somewhere peaceful for staff to come to finish an article. Or to take a nap on the sofa after a heavy lunch. It was his idea. There used to be a similar room at his old newspaper until it was converted into a 'blue-sky breakout area' with high stools and nowhere to sleep.

He often comes to the writing room with his proofs, but he's here this afternoon to continue his search for Freya, away from his nosy secretary. After checking the price of flights to India, he decided it was cheaper to find her online. In recent weeks, following his break-up, his searches for Freya have been idle and random, like he's on some sort of uncommitted virtual rebound.

He types her name into Google Images and sifts through the photos he's come to know well. Freya Lal the cheerleader, Freya Lal the lawyer, Freya Lal the Australian porn star with pneumatic breasts and a 'mapatasi', none of them bearing any resemblance to his former girlfriend. No wonder he hasn't found her.

He needs to be more focused, systematic, but it's not easy searching the Punjab for a Lal. It's like looking for a Smith in Britain. And she's probably married, with a different surname. He tries to cast his mind back to the graduation ball thirty years ago, the last night he saw Freya, hoping for a clue that might narrow his search. They'd lurked in the shadows, away from the dancefloor where proud men were dad-dancing with their drunken daughters. She'd had tears in her eyes and seemed on the point of telling him something, but when he'd pressed her she said it was nothing and went to get a drink. She was flying back to the Punjab with her parents the next day, as she did every summer, and had given him an address to write to. He wasn't allowed to meet her parents that night. They didn't know she had a British boyfriend and she wasn't about to tell them. Instead, he'd watched them from afar, noticed how Western they looked, like Freya.

As they'd kissed goodbye in the early hours, out of sight of her parents, she'd held him long and tight. She'd given no indication that she wouldn't stay in touch, which had hurt in the months that followed, as he thought they were in love. He must have written more than thirty airmail letters but never heard back. By the time he got married a few years later, he'd almost forgotten Freya.

Maybe he had known deep down that he was never going to see her again. Or perhaps the address he wrote down had been wrong? He's sure that it was in Ludhiana, but that doesn't help much.

He searches for 'Freya Lal' and 'Ludhiana' again and scrolls through the familiar results. Then his eye is caught by a news story in the *Hindustan Times*: 'Ludhiana man kills daughter and her paramour in suspected case of honour killing'.

He skim reads it, shocked that women are still murdered for bringing 'shame' on their families. Could Freya have been killed? He shifts in his seat. Many reasons for Freya's silence have crossed his mind over the years but not this one. It seems inconceivable in this modern day and age. Besides, her father would have come after him – her 'paramour' – as well as Freya, wouldn't he? It seems so unlikely. Her parents were sufficiently liberal to send Freya to a mixed British boarding school. Maybe they discovered she had a boyfriend, had a row and told her to sever all contact with the school? No one else seems to have heard from her either in the thirty years since.

And then he acknowledges another thought that he's managed to ignore until now. What if she'd fallen pregnant? Was that what she'd been trying to tell him at the graduation ball? He glances at the door, trying to stop his mind from running away with itself. Freya didn't reply to his letters because she returned home to India pregnant. And he was responsible. They'd only had sex once, in the summer term on a weekend away in London. It was the first time for both of them and it had been a fumbling, tearful tryst. Not entirely protected either. Her family permitted her to keep the baby but insisted that she sever all ties with her school and Britain. Thirty years later, Freya's daughter returns to the UK in search of her biological father.

Or maybe she simply didn't want to stay in touch.

27

'You're working late,' I say, standing in the doorway of the Seahorse Gallery & Café. Tony has his back to me and doesn't turn around. He's holding one of his large framed photographs in both hands, trying to secure it to a picture rail. I take a deep breath and step inside.

'These are sons-of-bitches to hang,' he says. 'I'll be with you in a moment.'

'I'm sorry I couldn't come over earlier,' I say, glancing back onto the high street. A group of evening commuters is walking up from the train station. They look stunned after their day in London, their faces ashen with exhaustion.

'No problem,' he says, still trying to attach the picture.

I touch the tattoo beneath my shirt. 'Do you want a hand with that?' I ask. I need to be fearless, like Fleur. Whatever happened to her, I know she was brave.

'Thanks.'

I walk over and hold the picture while Tony attaches clear plastic threads to a metal runner bar on the ceiling. I can't bring myself to look at the image, which is inches from my face, and focus instead on a label on the wall. This picture is called '*Hippocampus denise*'.

'Your hands are shaking,' he says.

'It's heavy,' I joke, but we both know it's not. I try to change the subject. 'Strange name for a seahorse.'

'Denise Tackett was an inspirational underwater photographer. When she discovered this little critter in the Indo-Pacific region, they named it in her honour.'

'Maybe they'll name one after you.'

He turns around to look at me. 'Maybe.'

'I had a sleep,' I say, still holding the picture, keen to fill the awkward silence. My hands are still shaking, despite my best efforts. We are close to one another, close enough for me to smell his citrus scent. Clean. Almost antiseptic.

'There we go,' he says. The picture in place, Tony turns to walk back over to the food counter, leaving me in the gallery area.

'Have you heard from Laura?' I ask, lingering in front of the pictures. I still can't bring myself to look directly at them. 'Is she OK?'

He knocks out some old coffee grounds with a noise that startles me and begins to wipe down the machine, cleaning the steam nozzle again and again. 'She doesn't want to talk about it at the moment.'

'About me?'

'The whole thing. You turning up, my response.'

'They're beautiful,' I manage to say, finally forcing myself to look at the seahorses. I'm lying. I hate them with a passion. The bulging eyes, lizard-like tails, strange shrunken proportions.

'They do it for me,' he says. 'Time will tell if they do it for anyone else. I don't think this village could be further from the sea. Feels kind of landlocked here, don't you find?'

'Why do you like them so much?' I ask, walking over to join Tony in the bar area, where he is now wiping down tables with almost obsessive pride. I can't be in the presence of his seahorses any longer.

'Where to start? Because the male carries the offspring until term? Because they used to lead drowned sailors to the other side? Did you know that dried seahorses sell for up to $3,000 a kilo, more than the price of silver?'

'Don't they also have something to do with memory?' I ask.

'I wasn't going to mention that.' He stops wiping and looks up at me. 'But you're right: the part of our brain that encodes short-term memories into long-term ones is called the hippocampus because of its shape: it looks like a seahorse. Actually there are two of them, tucked into the inner surface of the temporal lobes, one either side of the brain. Particularly beautiful, intricate structures. Just like seahorses. They're also the first regions to be attacked by Alzheimer's.'

'You're really worried about that, aren't you?' I say tentatively. Laura said he didn't like to talk about it. I sit down at a table and glance at a copy of the *Evening Standard*, left by a returning commuter. The front-page story is on NHS cuts to mental-health care.

'Laura thinks so,' he says. 'I've just turned forty. Cognitive deterioration can begin at forty-five. Noxious brain changes in someone who goes on to develop Alzheimer's may start as early as thirty. My dad was dead at forty-one.'

I thought I was strong enough to talk to him about memory when I came into the gallery, but I'm not. Not yet.

'Are you coming?' he asks, moving to the door and flicking off the lights. 'You can bring the paper.'

I fold it up and follow Tony out of the gallery, watching as he pulls down the metal shutter and padlocks it.

'Can I cook you dinner?' he asks as we set off down the high street. 'Or are you going Afghan again?'

'Dinner would be nice,' I say, but my palms are sweating. *I can't remember my name.*

28

The one catch about the writing room is the memories. This is where Luke used to come with Chloe, ostensibly to talk about page layouts but mainly to flirt. It was a whole year before they came clean with colleagues, twelve exciting months of cryptic emails and stolen glances across the open-plan office. People must have known as no one was surprised when they made an announcement, which makes him feel foolish now.

Luke gets up from the computer and walks over to the window. Below him, people are cycling and walking home across Clapham Common, enjoying the evening sunshine. A lot of joggers too. He used to go running with Chloe.

He turns away and sits down at the desk again to resume his search. Think, think. What did Freya's parents do? It wasn't the sort of question people asked each other at school. And then he remembers Freya giving a beautiful burnt-amber pashmina to another girl, at the beginning of the Christmas term. He had secretly looked up the word 'pashmina' in the library and, hoping to impress Freya, went around explaining to anyone who would listen that the scarf was made from the fine wool taken from the underbelly of a Himalayan goat. Maybe her father worked in fabrics. In Ludhiana.

For the next two hours, when he should have been writing next month's 'Letter from the Editor', Luke scours LinkedIn for Lals working in fabrics in Ludhiana, cross-referencing to Facebook, Pinterest, Instagram, Twitter and Google Plus. He interrogates his old classmates on email, at least those who bothered to reply to his original enquiry, and confirms that Freya had once spoken about a family firm in Ludhiana. He scours every Punjabi newspaper site he can find, exceeds his free search quota on Indian People Directory and uses the Wayback Machine to look up archived pages of Friends Reunited.

For a long time it feels like a lost cause and he's haunted by the thought that she might have been the victim of an honour killing. And then, just as he's thinking of chucking it in for the day, a glimmer of hope: a wealthy Lal family based in Ludhiana who export pashminas to the UK and seem to have family connections here. Another breakthrough follows, via the school alumni office, which finally replies to an email he fired off earlier. It has no record of Freya's current whereabouts or contact details, but it does reveal that her family once made a donation to the arts department, where Freya had studied textiles. It was a long time ago, while Freya was a pupil at the school, but the lead takes him to a new website for benefactors and donors. And it's there that he finds a record of the donation, thirty-one years ago, and the name of the Lal family export business through which the donation was made (in return for an engraved brick in the arts building).

Thirty minutes later, as the office cleaner arrives, Luke is staring at a Mr Lal on LinkedIn who works for the same pashmina export business. He follows him onto Facebook, searches his friends and discovers a woman called Freya. Her surname is different, but she is listed as his niece. Bingo. Except that the account is private and annoyingly there is no picture of her, just a photo of a flower. He sits up and clicks on the image. A lotus flower – like the one he saw tattooed on Jemma's wrist in the pub.

Could it be Freya? There's only one way to find out. Fingers trembling, he begins to compose a long message request, praying that she is still alive. Why's he telling her his entire life story? He deletes it in favour of something simpler.

Hi, long time no see. Luke Lascelles here – is this really you?! It would be great to catch up. Please accept this request – I need to ask you something important. Maybe I can call you? Tomorrow?

He rereads the message – just the right blend of casual and a call to action – and presses send, tears coming. At times like this he realises how much he misses his old journalist's life. And then his phone buzzes. It's Sean, up in town and in need of a pint.

One of Luke's legs buckles as he stands to leave the writing room. He's not sure if it's cramp or nerves. He thinks again of Jemma, the woman who turned up in his village yesterday, her tattoo. Could she really be Freya's daughter? His daughter?

29

'I was convinced you were trying to sell us something when you were standing here yesterday,' Tony says as we hover outside his house on School Road in the evening sun. 'Almost told you to go to hell.'

'I don't remember,' I say, glancing at the door knocker. The sight of it makes me feel dizzy again.

'So you don't recall me saying how beautiful you were?' he adds, laughing.

I don't remember. There's more straw in the street, from the thatcher on the corner. Fleur was the beautiful one.

'Actually, that's a lie,' he says, opening the front door. 'It was Laura.'

'How long will she be away for?' I ask as we walk into the sitting room. Tony doesn't answer. I hope Laura's OK.

The house smells of cooking and homeliness, but I can't relax. Each time I walk through this door, I feel like I'm intruding. This is Laura's home, another woman's place, and I shouldn't be here. And yet I know I've come to this house for a reason. A purpose.

In my notes, I described how I sat on the sofa and drank sweet mint tea, brought to me by Laura in a mug with a yoga cat on it. The same mug, or a similar one, is on the low sitting-room table now, next to a printout of a news article from the internet. I manage to read the headline – 'Woman Who Slit Best Friend's Throat Found Guilty of Manslaughter' – before Tony snatches it up, like a teenager hiding porn.

'I already made dinner,' he says, walking through to the kitchen. 'Clam chowder, except I couldn't get any clams, so we're having scallops instead. Hand-dived from Devon. Hope that's OK.'

'But you didn't know I was coming.' I stay in the sitting room and perch on the sofa, trying to compose myself. My hands are still shaking and I've got no excuse now.

'I took a reckless gamble, based on the state of your prison cell at the pub and the Afghani food on your floor.'

I don't like him being rude about Abdul. 'The curry was delicious.'

'I'm sure it was.'

'Can I use your bathroom?' I ask, joining him in the kitchen.

'Go right ahead,' he says, starting to lay the table.

After locking the door, I sink down on the closed loo seat and shut my eyes. It was a mistake to come back here on my own. I'm not ready. And it's not fair on Laura. I should have stopped her when she was walking to the train, talked to her, but it would have been impossible. She's not listening, has a head full of her own theories. I look around the room and notice a small, framed photograph of a seahorse behind me. I breathe in deeply and walk out into the kitchen.

30

'You did what?' Luke says, gesturing to the barman for another drink.

'I flushed her out,' Sean says.

They are in the Windsor Castle in Westminster, one of Luke's favourite London watering holes. He loves its wooden panelling, the hand-etched glass partitions and the dumb waiter behind the bar that brings pies and chips up from the kitchen. The pub's also close to the flat in Pimlico where he's staying tonight, owned by friends of his parents. They are seated in a small sectioned-off area, away from the throng of office drinkers in the main bar, and Sean is trying once again to convince Luke that Jemma is a Russian sleeper.

'It stopped her dead in her tracks,' Sean says.

'What did?'

'When I spoke to Jemma in Russian. In the graveyard.'

'She must have been rather surprised.' Poor woman. She's got enough on her plate right now without mad Irish locals talking to her in Russian.

'She didn't know it was me,' he continues, spinning his beermat. Sean's body is as restless as his mind.

'How come?'

'I was hiding. Behind a yew tree. That's how these things are done.'

'You're losing me, Sean.' Luke looks up at the door. Two confused tourists have just entered, clutching guidebooks. The pub used to be called the Cardinal, a nod to nearby Westminster Cathedral. When he worked on a newspaper in Victoria, he spent his time directing tourists to the coach station.

'Covert exchanges in the field,' Sean continues. '*Tinker Tailor Soldier Spy,* chalk-marks in the park? I asked her if she was missing Moscow. In Russian. If she knew where her loyalties lay.'

'And she said...?' Luke is agog, trying to picture the scene. He's in a good mood tonight, buoyed by his earlier online sleuthing.

'She didn't. That's the point. She was rumbled.'

'The world must be such an exciting place seen through your eyes, Sean. And full of disappointment.'

Luke pays for two more pints of Guinness, served by a polite Polish barman, and turns to face his friend.

'I need you to understand something, Sean,' he says, trying to inject some gravitas into the proceedings. 'Jemma's not Russian, never was, never will be.'

'How can you be so sure?'

'Leave it, Sean. Please?'

They sit in silence for a few moments, unusual for them, and then Sean heads off to the loos in the basement. Luke knows that when he comes back he must get his friend onside about Freya Lal. He can't be certain that he's messaged the right person, but he's feeling optimistic. Providing she's still alive. No way would her father have killed her, even if she was pregnant. And he's got no evidence that she was.

'Actually, there's something important I need to tell you,' Luke says when Sean comes back.

'I'm all ears.' Sean glances around him as he sips the top off his Guinness. 'And so is Moscow, for sure.'

Luke can't help looking around the pub too, notices the selection of vodkas behind the bar. Maybe this place is on the Russians' radar.

'The reason I'm interested in Jemma is...' Luke falters, struggling to say the words out loud. 'If she is the daughter of my old girlfriend, Freya Lal, then...'

'What?' Sean asks.

He's not making this easy. Luke needs Sean's ebullient mind to quieten, just for a few seconds.

'Then I might be her father.'

'OK,' Sean says, more serious now. Almost respectful. 'That does kind of change things.'

'Will you help me find out if she is my daughter?'

'Sure.'

'And drop all the Russian shit?'

'That might be harder.'

'I did a lot of searching this afternoon. Think I might have managed to track Freya Lal down in India. The Punjab.'

'The land of five rivers,' Sean says. 'Breadbasket of India.'

But before Luke has time to reply, his phone vibrates in his pocket.

It's from Freya, replying to his message request. She wants him to call her tonight.

31

'It will come back, you know, your memory,' Tony says as we sit down for dinner. The lighting has been lowered and there's music playing: REM, I think. It's strange what I remember. The house is looking more spotless than ever, fresh flowers on the table, tea towel folded neatly on the oven rail. I mustn't let it upset me. I'm doing better now than I was earlier in the evening, managing the fear.

'That's what everyone keeps saying.' I watch him pour two glasses of water from the glugging jug. Where have I heard that sound before? 'I just want to find out what happened to me, who I am.'

'It's not Alzheimer's, I know the signs,' he says, passing me a glass.

'That's reassuring, thank you.'

'Are you going to write notes tonight?' he asks, starting to ladle chowder from an orange Le Creuset pot.

'Last night's notes have helped today. Saved me a lot of embarrassment. Dr Patterson says I should write notes every evening.'

'What are you going to say about today?' He looks up at me. 'This evening?'

'I must be careful.' I pause, looking down at the bowl of steaming chowder in front of me. 'A nice quiet dinner on my own in my room at the pub, I guess.'

He smiles conspiratorially and reaches for the bottle of Pouilly-Fumé. 'Do you want some wine?'

'No thanks. Dr Patterson says I should stay off the alcohol.'

'She's right. Bad for the brain. I might have a small glass.'

He talks further about his gallery café, how he's getting more passing cyclists and narrowboat tourists than he thought, and then there's a lacuna in our conversation. We've finished the chowder and I'm sipping on another mint tea, holding the mug with both hands in the hope that it prevents any more shaking.

'Can you describe how it feels?' he asks. 'To not remember?'

I think for a moment before I answer. I know I should talk to him about amnesia – it's important – but I'm finding this all so difficult.

'It's like I'm on a speedboat, racing across the open sea,' I begin. 'When I look back, expecting to see a wake behind me, there's just calm, empty water, stretching for miles and miles, no evidence that I've even been there. And what's really weird is that the water ahead looks empty too. It's almost as if I'm unable to imagine a future if I can't recall my past.'

'Are you frightened about tomorrow morning, having to start all over again?'

'When I read everything that's gone on today I won't believe that it all's happened to me, that it's my life.'

I begin to feel tearful, hearing myself summarise the day I've had. I've done well this evening to hold it together.

'The thing is, I'm starting to forget things myself,' he says. 'Little things.'

'Like what?'

He doesn't answer immediately and when he does, his voice is quieter, more thoughtful. 'It's not so much not being able to find the car keys but wondering for a split second what they're for when I do find them.'

'Does that worry you?'

'It terrifies me.' He pauses. 'Like a glimpse into old age.'

'My life has only just begun,' I say, managing a laugh. 'I'm two days old.'

He smiles, but I know his heart isn't in it, his mind elsewhere. He gets up from the table and starts to clear the dishes.

'I don't like the thought of you waking up on your own, in that poky old pub room,' he says, his back to me at the sink. 'You're welcome to stay here, you know. Down on the sofa, or up in the guest room. I just think you might need someone around in the morning.'

'Dinner was lovely. Delicious. But I need to go now.' I dab at my lips with a napkin. The shaking has started again. 'I'm tired. And I've got a lot to write up. To remember.'

'As you like,' he says, turning to me. He wipes his hands on the tea towel and folds it neatly.

'But thank you,' I say, getting up from the table. I need to be away from here. I head through to the sitting room.

'It's better you use the rear door,' he calls out after me. 'And at least let me walk you over to the pub.'

'I'm fine, honestly,' I say, trying not to panic. It's as if we've embarked on a frantic dance, manoeuvring around each other.

I manage to resist running out into the street and make myself return to the kitchen, where he has opened the back door. He puts a hand on my arm to stop me as I pass him. I know what's coming next, how our dance will end.

'Let's do this again,' he says, switching on that serene smile of his. He glances around and leans forward to kiss me on the lips.

I close my eyes and count – one, two, three, thinking of Fleur, my pulse racing – and step back into the garden, away from him.

We stare at each other for a moment and then I walk away, as fast as I can without running.

'Don't go putting that in your notes,' he calls out after me. 'We can have a first kiss all over again tomorrow.'

I think I'm going to be sick and then his mobile phone starts to ring. For some reason the sound makes me stop in my tracks, suppresses my nausea. I'm already at the bottom of the garden, fumbling for the latch on the wooden gate. I hope it's Laura, calling to say she's OK.

'I'm going to leave this here – in case you change your mind,' he says, taking a key out of his pocket and placing it under a small upturned pot, one of several by the back door.

'OK,' I say, watching him hide it, desperate to run.

'I need to talk to Laura now.'

32

Luke studies the message again, which is short and simple.

So good to hear from you! And after the last so many years! Please, call me tomorrow morning, 7 a.m. IST. 2.30 BST? I should be sleeping now... More tomorrow. Fx

He looks up and glances around the Windsor Castle, which is almost empty. He's been unable to stop smiling since he first read the message. Too many acronyms for his liking, but he can live with that. Now that he knows Freya exports pashminas for a living, he can see that hers is the language of international business. Sean has headed off to stay with his brother, leaving Luke on his own with another pint and his phone. He showed Sean the message before he went and they discussed it briefly, but Sean didn't share his excitement. He was tired – and a little aggrieved that the message appeared to prove that Jemma isn't a Russian sleeper.

He glances at his watch – another two hours before he can call her. Regardless of whether Jemma turns out to be their daughter or not, he's excited to have made contact with Freya, given how adrift he's been feeling. For the first time in years, he feels connected – tethered. His teenage years, at least the memory of them, feel a part of the person he is today, a reminder that he is a product of the decisions he made then. A reassuring line now runs back through his life that he wasn't aware of before.

It's only when he starts to read through Freya's Facebook page in detail that his heart sinks. He's not bothered that she's married or that her husband looks annoyingly nice in the photos. He's glad she's found happiness. It's the pictures of all the young people. They seem to adore her and he'd assumed they were her children, but each one turns out to be a nephew or a niece and none of them looks like Jemma.

He takes a deep draught of his Guinness. No children. He can't deny he's disappointed. He has been idly looking for her online ever since his split with Chloe, but the arrival of Jemma in the village has given his search a new urgency. Now, though, it doesn't seem so important. If Freya was pregnant – still a very big if – she most probably had an abortion, which means Jemma isn't their daughter.

Finishing his pint, he decides to head down to the river and walk to Battersea Park, where he will kill time before contacting Freya. It's almost 1 a.m. as he crosses south over Chelsea Bridge, but London feels alive. He feels alive. And young – far younger than his fifty years. At his parents' house in the village he would be asleep by now, lulled by the pure air and circadian rhythms of the countryside. He adjusts his Carhartt baseball cap, only worn in London (Milo gives him too much stick about it at home), and lengthens his stride.

The park shuts at 10.30 p.m., but there's a place on Queenstown Road, hidden by bushes, where he and Freya once climbed over, more than thirty years ago. He's confident that he can still scale the wrought-iron railings, but they look much higher than he remembers. He glances around and levers himself up without any difficulty. Pleased to have defied his years, he jumps down the other side, only for the bottom of his trouser leg to catch and rip. He falls to the ground with a grunt and lies there for a few seconds.

Freya will be up in an hour or so. Dusting himself down, he heads towards the Peace Pagoda overlooking the Thames. It was here that they sat and planned their future together, with all the optimism and naivety of teenagers. They talked and talked, first at the pagoda and then on long, looping walks around the park. When the attendants began closing up for the night, they hid in the bushes and talked some more before making love for the first and only time.

It seems an appropriate place, poetic even, to re-establish contact with Freya, but she doesn't need to know exactly where he is. He will only tell her if it seems right.

All he has to do now is wait.

33

'I hope it wasn't my mother's curry,' Abdul says as I come out of the shared bathroom at the end of the upstairs corridor in the pub.

'No,' I say. 'Your mother's curry was delicious.'

Unfortunately, I bumped into Abdul when I came back from dinner with Tony. He watched me run down the corridor to the bathroom and heard me throw up.

'Can I get you anything?' he asks, standing in the doorway of his room. He's wearing baggy shorts and an ill-fitting Bath Rugby Club shirt.

'I'm fine, thank you.' I feel better after cleaning my teeth. 'I'm sorry if I disturbed you.'

'I saw you walking to Tony's house this evening,' he says without accusation.

'We had dinner,' I say. 'He's been very helpful, his wife Laura too. I stayed there last night, when I arrived in the village.'

'My brother and me, we are teaching him how to play cricket.' Abdul gestures as if he's a caveman with a club and shakes his head despairingly.

'I must go to sleep – thank you again for the curry. It was very sweet of you.'

Back in my room, I lock the door and sit down to write about the day, beginning with reading my notes when I woke up at Tony and Laura's house and ending with dinner with Tony tonight. There seems little point pretending I was in the pub. Nothing goes unnoticed in this village. I wonder if Abdul saw me coming back from Tony's house too. My eyes start to close as I finish the day's entry. I lie back on the bed, still feeling sick.

An hour later, I wake to the sound of a piercing scream. Has Abdul been shouting in his sleep, having nightmares about overturned boats and bloated bodies in the sea? I lie there in the moonlit quiet of the village night, watching the breeze play with the curtain, and realise the scream was mine.

Am I asleep now? Or in that liminal state of waking? Fleur is lying supine, staring at me, fear in her eyes. I try again and this time I fall onto the floor, where I stay, looking into Fleur's bewildered, frightened eyes. Slowly, I crawl towards her on all fours, one hand in front of me in a hopeless attempt to reach out to her. But I collapse again, my body pressed flat against the floor until it is too late and Fleur's screams have died in the night.

There's a knock on the door.

'Hello?' I call out.

'Are you OK?' It's Abdul.

'I'm fine,' I say, propping myself up on one elbow. 'Bad dream, that's all. Thank you.'

'Me too.'

There's a pause. I'm glad Abdul is still there, standing on the other side of the locked door. I realise I'm shaking and drenched in sweat.

As his footsteps recede down the corridor, I turn to face the wall, waiting for sleep to take me again. I hope I will have forgotten my nightmare by morning.

34

The call comes at exactly 2.30 a.m. and wakes Luke from a light sleep. He is hunkered down in the corner of the pagoda and props himself up against the wall to answer it. Taking off his baseball cap and rearranging his hair, he holds the phone out at arm's length and up a bit to avoid a double chin. His hand is shaking as the call connects, even though it's a warm night.

'Oh my God,' Freya says, smiling at the camera, a dupatta draped loosely over her head. 'It really is you!'

She is sitting in what looks like an office, a ceiling fan stirring the air in the background.

'It's me,' he says, smiling, thrown by her beauty. She is exactly how he remembers her, particularly that lyrical voice. Just like Jemma's.

'How are you?' she asks.

'I'm fine.' God, can't he think of anything better to say? 'I'm so sorry for contacting you out of the blue like this,' he continues. 'You must think I'm some kind of weirdo Facebook stalker, but—'

'It's so great to hear from you, really,' she says, interrupting him. 'You haven't changed one jot.'

'Nor have you – in a good way, I mean.'

She blushes and looks around her. For the first time, Luke wonders if she's not alone. 'Where are you, by the way?' he asks.

'In my office. The family business. I came in early, to make this call.'

'I'm sorry if that was a problem.'

'Not at all. We often have to come in early, to talk to China, the Far East.'

'It sounds like it's all going well. The business.'

'It's good, yes,' she says, hesitation in her voice.

'Pashminas?'

'How did you know?'

'I'm a journalist. Well, I was. I am. Sort of. Used to work in newspapers, national ones. Now I look after a magazine for smelly old cars.'

'That sounds so great.'

'I changed career when my wife died,' he says. He feels he owes it to his wife to introduce her into the conversation, but inevitably it alters the tone.

'I was so sorry to hear about that,' she says, casting her eyes down respectfully.

'How did you know?'

'I googled you, of course. After you messaged me. You wrote an article about her once. It was very moving.'

He's still not sure whether that had been the right thing to do. To go public on something so private. But writing about his grief had undeniably helped him to move on.

'Where are you, by the way?' she asks. 'Some kind of temple?'

'I'm in the Peace Pagoda in Battersea Park.' It doesn't seem inappropriate to tell her, but he tenses as he waits for her reaction.

'No way.' She doesn't appear to be upset.

'You remember?'

'Of course I remember.' Her voice is quieter now, reflective.

'Happy days,' he says, more out of hope than anything.

'They were – so happy.'

'I'm sorry you had to leave at the end of term.'

'Me too.'

'I did write to you, many times.'

'I know. My father got your letters. Burnt them all.'

'Oh God, were they that bad?' Luke's tone is light, but his stomach lurches. It sounds as if he was right. Her family put pressure on her to cut all ties with her life in Britain and return to live in India. Was it because she was pregnant? With their child?

They both fall quiet, the first silence in their conversation. Luke glances across at the river, dark and fast flowing. He begins to feel more sad than vindicated, lost in a confusion of thoughts.

'I had to leave the UK,' she says quietly. 'That was the deal.'

'A deal with your parents?'

She nods, looking around her.

'Are you alone?' he asks.

'For the moment. The first workers will be arriving soon.'

'What was the deal?' he asks. He needs to know what happened, even though he appreciates it was her business. Her choice. It's a while before she speaks.

'Why did you contact me?' she asks. 'After all this time?'

'Someone turned up in our village yesterday, where I live. She looks just like you, when you were younger.'

'I haven't aged that badly, have I?'

'I don't mean it that way.' It's his turn to pause now. 'You look great. Fantastic, in fact.'

'Who is she then? This person who looks like me before I became old and wrinkly?'

'No one knows, that's the thing. Even she doesn't know who she is. She's suffering from amnesia – temporary, we all hope. But in the meantime, some of us are trying to establish who she is.'

'And you think she might be connected to me in some way?'

He takes a deep breath. 'Maybe related.'

'How old is she?' Her tone is serious now.

'She doesn't know. She's lost all her ID. Late twenties?'

Freya puts her hands together as if in prayer, pressing them to her lips, head bowed.

'Are you OK?' Luke asks.

'There's something I need to tell you,' she says, still looking down.

'I think I know,' he says eventually. 'If it makes things any easier. It's taken me thirty years, but I've finally worked it out. And it's OK. Of course it is. Whatever you decided.'

They both remain silent. He knows he's right.

'My father wanted me to have an abortion, but my mother talked him out of it, supported by my auntie,' she says, dabbing at her eyes with a tissue. 'They reached a deal: I could have the baby, in India, but it would be put up for adoption. And given that the baby's father was European, my father contacted an agency in Europe. They took her away at birth.'

'It was a girl?'

Luke is starting to cry now, his guilt tinged with a strange kind of joy, knowing he has a daughter, a half-sister for Milo.

'A beautiful girl,' she continues. 'I know I should have told you, but it was different in those days. So, so difficult. There were a few in our extended family who wanted me dead – for the shame I'd brought on everyone. But they were shouted down. We are a modern country now, you know.'

Luke closes his eyes, recalling the article he read about honour killings. 'It's OK. I'm just sorry for having asked you, made you revisit all this.'

'I feel much better now that we have spoken.'

'To be honest, I know very little about the woman who turned up in our village. She might not have anything to do with you.'

It's only his selfish desire to establish Jemma's identity that has made him get in touch with Freya, put her through this. It could all be for nothing.

'But a family likeness is there, you say? Do you have a photo?'

'It's more the way she talks,' Luke says, thinking back to when he first heard Jemma chatting to Laura in the surgery, his confusion, how he had momentarily mistaken her for a young Freya. 'Her manner.'

'Where is she living?' she asks.

'We don't know. She arrived in the UK on a flight from Berlin.'

'Berlin?'

'We think so. I don't have a photo.'

Freya dabs at her eyes again and then looks behind her. 'I must go. My colleagues are starting to arrive.' She glances around again before speaking. 'We were told nothing about the wealthy couple who took her away, nothing except their faith – she was a Baha'i – and their nationality.'

'And…?' Luke asks, but he already knows what she's going to say.

'They were a mixed-race couple living in Germany.'

DAY THREE

35

I wake early and listen to the birdsong outside the window, wondering why the day has already dawned so light, where I am in the world. My lower back is sore and I remain still, staring up at the stained ceiling. After a few seconds, I prop myself on one elbow, wincing at the pain, and look around the small room.

I can't remember my own name.

I see the sheets of paper on my bedside table and sink back onto the bed, the fear that had retreated in my sleep returning with a vengeance. I wish I wasn't in this village, lying on my own in a dingy back room of a pub, but I am here and I must deal with whatever lies ahead. I can only look forward.

I dress, grateful that there are several changes of clothes in my suitcase, and walk down the corridor. As I pass the room where Abdul and his brother are sleeping, I smile to myself, cheered by the sound of mighty, stentorious snoring. Abdul has been very kind to me.

I don't know how early it is when I head out onto the street. I want to take a walk around the village and see what's happening, but that could be problematic. As I wrote in my notes, my presence has upset Laura and there could be other people who might not be pleased to see me – pre-breakfast dog walkers, joggers.

I am about to set off up the hill, away from the train station, when I notice a light come on in Tony's café. The next moment he is on the street, putting out a wooden easel sign. He kneels down to write something on it, stands back to pull out his phone and takes a picture of it. After checking the image, he looks up and down the road, sees me and raises a hand in greeting. I reciprocate, cross the road and walk up to the café. It's important that we speak.

'You're an early riser,' he says, busy behind the food counter with the oven.

'You too,' I say.

'Did you see the sign outside? I'm trying something new. Targeting the early crowd. I'm figuring if I get myself down onto the platform in time for the 0545 with a tray of TLTs – smoky tempeh, lettuce, tomato and avocado served on sourdough wheat bread – a whole new unexploited market will be mine.'

'They'll just want a coffee, won't they?' I'm surprised by how early it must be.

'I'm taking a thermos too – what I need is a small bodega down there, an outstation of the gallery café with its own coffee machine. It will happen.'

'I'm sure it will.'

'You want a coffee, something to eat?' he says, glancing down at the display cabinet. 'I've only got the smoky tempeh on at the moment.'

'I'm fine, thanks.'

'How was it?' he asks. 'When you first woke up?' He turns to the oven, peering through the glass window.

'I read my notes,' I say.

'No change, then.' His manner is breezy, businesslike.

'It doesn't appear so.' I pause. 'Thanks for supper.'

'You included that?' He turns to look at me. 'I thought you weren't going—'

'Can we talk about what happened?'

'You wrote about that too?' He turns back to the oven.

I stay silent and watch him at work, regretting that I came into the café.

'It was out of order,' he says, opening the oven to remove a tray of baked tempeh. 'A mistake. You know, I was hoping you'd not made a note of it.'

I take a deep breath as he places the tray on the counter. 'So you could do it all over again tonight?' I ask.

He looks up at me and laughs unconvincingly. I can tell he's not sure which way I'm heading with this, whether I'm onside or not.

'I just didn't want you to misunderstand anything,' I continue. 'My reaction.'

'As I say, it was a mistake and I apologise.' He starts to slice the tempeh with a large knife.

Would I be able to kill someone with it? Would I choose a knife? 'I had a friend,' I say, mesmerised by his cutting, the flash of the blade in the early morning light.

'You mentioned her – when you first arrived. The one who died?'

'I think we were lovers.'

He stops cutting and looks up at me. 'You think?'

'I can't remember. She was my best friend.'

'That's cool by me.'

'But I was wondering... It might explain...' I pause, struggling to find the right words as he makes up a tray of rolls, carefully laying out the sliced tempeh into each one. 'It might explain if I was a little "neutral" last night.'

'Hey, if you're worried that my heterosexual pride was hurt because you didn't fling your arms around me, I appreciate your concern, but I would never be so presumptuous to think that you would.'

'You're also married.'

'As I say, I made a stupid mistake.' He looks up at me and then returns to the rolls. 'I spoke to Laura last night.'

'Did you tell her?' I ask. 'That I'd been over for supper?'

'As a matter of fact I didn't.'

'How is she?'

'Still mad at me, but we'll work through it. I've gotta go. Take these down to the station. Want to come?'

He has the tray of rolls in one hand. In the other he's holding a large thermos, with a stack of plastic cups tucked under his arm.

'I better stay up here,' I say, opening the café door for him. We both step outside onto the street.

'You're probably right. Just pull it closed. I'll be back in fifteen.'

'Can I see you later?' I ask as we set off in the direction of the station.

'I'll be in the café all day.'

'I have another appointment at the surgery at 9 a.m., with Dr Patterson. I'll know then if a bed has come free.'

A jogger runs up the other side of the street, lifting a hand in greeting. Tony nods and smiles, gesturing at his full hands. 'We'll miss you if you get one,' he says.

'Not everyone will.'

We are now outside the pub. 'I'm going back to my room,' I say. 'Thank you for your support yesterday. It seems from my notes that you did a lot for me.'

'We all need allies in this world,' he calls over his shoulder, walking on towards the station. 'Sorry – gotta go.'

'And, Tony...?' I call out after him. He stops and turns. 'Forgive and forget. Or in my case, forget and forgive.'

'Forget and forgive,' he repeats, smiling.

As he disappears out of sight, a police patrol car crests the brow of the railway bridge and drives up the high street. The driver slows and his female passenger glances across at me. I don't get a clear view, but I think I might have seen her before.

36

When Luke arrives at his office, there is a patchwork of yellow Post-it notes on his screen asking him to call Laura.

'She's rung quite a few times,' his secretary says, dumping the day's newspapers on his desk. 'Said your mobile's going straight to voicemail.'

'She's my yoga teacher,' Luke answers by way of a feeble explanation.

'Blocked chakras?' she asks, walking back to her desk.

He pulls out his phone. He left it in his jacket pocket all night and failed to put it on charge. FaceTiming Freya had drained it. Drained him too. He slept like a log afterwards, the best sleep he's had in years. He has a daughter.

'Chloe's not coming in again today,' she says. 'Still ill.'

Luke glances across the office at her desk, allowing his gaze to settle on her empty chair, the scarf draped over the back of it, a vintage Cinni fan in the corner.

The main office line rings. 'Your yoga friend again.'

He shakes his head and takes the call.

'Laura, hi, sorry, my mobile died.'

'I've been trying to reach you all morning. And last night.' She doesn't sound herself.

'Tell me.'

'Tony's been acting really strangely – ever since Jemma arrived.'

'In what way?' he asks, but he's not sure he wants to know the details. Other people's marital problems are a reminder that his own marriage was cut cruelly short. He'd give anything to be having difficulties if it meant his wife was still alive.

'I don't know. He just won't listen to me, to anyone. I'm scared she really might be Jemma Huish, but Tony thinks I'm overreacting. Susie Patterson's changed her tune too – and she was the one who called the police in the first place. Warned me about her.'

'The police?'

'They turned up yesterday to interview her, but she refused to give them a DNA sample. Why would she do that? It's really beginning to freak me out, Luke.'

'Where are you now?' he asks. He feels out of touch and needs to get back to the village. A lot has happened in his absence. Sean was right about having spotted a detective outside the surgery.

'Staying at my mum's for a few days.'

'In London?'

'I couldn't stay in the village another night with Jemma around.'

'Of course not,' Luke says, humouring her. He glances at his watch. After last night's conversation with Freya, the suggestion that Jemma is Jemma Huish seems less likely than ever. Distasteful too, given that she might be his daughter. How soon could he be back in the village? He suddenly feels very protective of Jemma.

Luke makes his excuses to Laura, hangs up and walks over to the window. Below him is the smokers' area, where the staff also park their cars. Several classic cars have just been delivered for a photoshoot, and in the corner of the yard stands the magazine's own staff vehicle, Hilton's Healey, named in honour of the fictitious editor-in-chief. A relatively rare 1967 Austin-Healey 3000 MK III.

'I've got to go out this morning, bit of an emergency back home,' he says to Archie, his deputy. They all know he looks after his elderly parents and for once he's prepared to use them as an excuse to leave. 'I'll take Hilton's Healey,' he adds. Trains back to the village are useless after rush hour.

Archie unhooks a set of keys from the wall behind them and throws them across to Luke.

Two minutes later, the three-litre, six-cylinder engine is revving. He turns to check behind him. The entire editorial team is at the window above to send him off. Do they know that there is something more serious at stake? Maybe they think he's off to see Chloe, to try to patch things up.

He waves, roars out of the yard and heads on down towards Wandsworth Common. It's just gone 9 a.m. Traffic permitting, he should be back at the village within two hours. The police clearly have no prima facie link between Jemma Huish and Jemma – not yet – but she could become very vulnerable.

37

I try to concentrate on Dr Patterson's questions, but the noise from the surgery reception is growing louder. At first, we both try to ignore it – Dr Patterson jokes that someone must be having a bad morning – but it sounds like a full-blown argument.

'I'm sorry about this, I'll tell them to keep it down,' she says, getting up from her desk.

'Do you think it's about me?' I ask. It's hard to make out individual words, but I think I hear someone mention Jemma Huish.

'You? Don't be silly.' She's not a good liar.

Dr Patterson was hoping to move me to the Cavell Centre today, but there are still no beds, which is a relief. Unfortunately, she has managed to get me an appointment with a psychiatrist tomorrow – at the hospital. I really don't need the extra stress.

I watch her walk over to the door, but before she reaches it someone knocks on the other side. 'Susie, could I have a quick word?' a voice says.

'Practice manager,' Dr Patterson whispers to me, rolling her eyes. 'I'm about to be told off.' She raises her voice. 'Come in.'

The manager opens the door enough for the noise in reception to swell, but he doesn't enter the room. Instead, he glances at me and then back down the corridor, before turning to Dr Patterson.

'A couple of minutes?'

'We were just finishing.'

'In private.'

'Your room?' she asks.

'Please.'

Dr Patterson doesn't look too happy about it. 'Are you OK to stay here?' she asks me. 'While we have a quick chat?'

'Sure,' I say. 'What's all the noise outside?'

The manager pauses before answering. 'Best you stay in here.'

I sit there on my own in her room, listening to the hum of conversation at the end of the corridor. They're definitely talking about Jemma Huish. After two minutes, I can bear it no longer. I need to be away from here, back in my room at the pub. I decide to run the gauntlet of whatever is going on and set off along the corridor.

'It's her,' I hear a female voice say. The conversation fades as I enter the reception area and a crowd of silent faces stares at me. There aren't as many people as I'd expected from the noise, maybe ten.

I lower my head and keep walking. They part for me as if I'm a pariah, standing further back than necessary, all eyes fixed on me. I should have stayed in the room, listened to Dr Patterson's advice. I walk on, my limbs heavy with adrenaline now, and breathe a sigh of relief when I'm out in the bright daylight. I don't look back, but I sense that some of them have come out to watch me walk away. I can feel their eyes on my back, narrowed in disapproval.

I cross the street, walk into the pub by the back entrance and head straight upstairs to my room. Closing the door, I sit down at the piano and play, trying to calm myself. The notes come easily until there's a knock on the door.

'It's me, Abdul.'

'Come in,' I say.

Abdul enters, staring sheepishly at his feet. He's wearing odd socks with his sandals.

'The village, they are saying things.'

'What do they say, Abdul?' I ask, but I already know the answer.

'Do you know Miss Huish?'

I shake my head, staring at him.

'Some people,' he continues, 'they say that you and her are the very same.'

I manage a dry laugh. 'Me?'

'I told them it was poppycock. They even showed me a photograph of this Huish woman. She doesn't look like you.'

'I know,' I say, sighing as I close the piano lid. 'But it was a long time ago and people have forgotten what she looks like.'

'The photo was also very blurred.'

'I'm not her, Abdul,' I say. I don't sound convincing. 'Don't worry.'

'That's what I told them. Balderdash.'

'Thank you,' I say, suddenly moved by his loyalty. I polish a smear on the wooden piano lid with the sleeve of my blouse.

'What music were you playing?' he asks.

'Philip Glass.' We stare at each other for a second. 'An American composer.'

'You haven't forgotten everything then.'

'It seems not.' I stand up from the stool. 'I need to get some rest. If anyone asks where I am, I'm not here.'

'Of course,' he says, still staring at me. 'I have not seen you.'

I close the door behind him and slump down onto the hard bed.

38

DI Silas Hart walks over to the window and looks out across Gablecross car park. It doesn't get much worse than Swindon in the rain. To be fair, Gablecross is not really in Swindon. A modern, three-storey police station, it's out on the eastern fringes – a problem for response colleagues who complain that it's too far from the 'action' of the town centre. Silas has other issues with the £22 million station. Like he doesn't have his own office any more. Instead he has to hot-desk in the open-plan Parade Room, the station's main operational hub, moving around the cluster of work stations with his laptop. 'Work is something you do, not a place you go to,' according to the latest HR missive. Not in Silas's book.

Jemma Huish shouldn't be occupying his time, particularly after his waste of a journey yesterday to see Susie Patterson, but he can't get Huish out of his head, even though he's double-checked that the friend she killed all those years ago wasn't called Fleur. That would have been too easy.

DC Strover's not letting it go either, not since her brief interview with Jemma. Something troubled her about the woman and she's been pursuing every lead as if her job depends on it. She even went back down to the village early this morning in a patrol car. He's asked her to track down everyone who used to care for Jemma Huish so they can try and get a positive ID. The only problem is that mental-health staff seem to come and go at an even faster rate than special constables. They've all either left or moved on.

Silas sits back down at his laptop and calls up the file on Jemma Huish. He and Strover have managed to piece together her medical-care history since the vicious knife assault on her friend, calling in old favours to bypass data confidentiality. (Susie is still being less than cooperative.) In addition to dissociative amnesia and paranoid schizophrenia, she was considered to have been suffering from violence ideation and command hallucinations in the months and weeks before the attack, confining herself to her hall-of-residence room and ringing friends, including the one she killed, as well as the police. She spoke to them all about hearing voices – usually in trees – and regularly warned them of approaching danger.

Five years ago, after being transferred to a low-security hospital in London, she was deemed fit for conditional discharge and was allowed to live in twenty-four-hour supported housing in Southwark. Two years later, following a gradual reduction of her anti-psychotic medication, a tribunal granted her an absolute discharge from sections 37 and 41 of the Mental Health Act, citing the patient's 'deep understanding of her own condition', which included occasional bouts of prolonged amnesia.

She was transferred to nearby 'move on' independent accommodation with 'floating support' – so floating, in fact, that it comprised little more than monthly outpatient appointments with a consultant psychiatrist and occasional home visits from her care coordinator. Within another year she was no longer receiving any care or medication at all and had moved away from London, possibly abroad.

Silas sits back. An example of textbook rehabilitation or is Jemma Huish a convicted killer on the loose, about to strike again? He looks up from his laptop. Strover has entered the far end of the Parade Room, where uniforms sit. He waves a hand and beckons her over to his corner, occupied by CID. Tribes will be tribes, even in the age of hot-desking.

'I've just spoken to one of her carers,' she says, an encouraging urgency in her voice.

'Sit down, sit down,' Silas says, watching her open up her laptop. All officers are now issued with 4G-enabled laptops and iPhones so that they can work anywhere, any time. *Work is not a place you go to…* They need a breakthrough, if only to justify the hours he's already spent on a case that he shouldn't be investigating.

'She cared for Huish when she was moved to supported housing,' Strover says, flicking back through her notebook.

'Quite recent then. Could she identity her?'

'She reckons so,' Strover says, her voice marginally less confident. She is impressively inscrutable – a good quality in a detective – but Silas is starting to read her better.

'What's the catch?' he asks.

'She's on holiday. Dubai. For another week.'

'Of course she bloody is.' Silas sits back, dropping his biro down on the desk. He glances at his emails. Still nothing from Border Force. He was hoping to have a file of scanned passports by now, every passenger who flew in to Heathrow Terminal 5 from Berlin on the day Jemma arrived.

'And she's no longer working in mental-health care,' Strover adds, glancing at her notepad again.

'It's a miracle anyone's left.' Silas thinks of Conor, his son, and pushes the thought away. He can't blame social services.

'She did say something else though,' Strover continues.

'Give me some good news.'

'Apparently Huish experienced "difficult feelings" around anniversaries, particularly her mother's death. They had to dial up her meds in the weeks before and after – every year.'

'What sort of difficult feelings?' Silas doesn't like where this is heading.

'Heightened violence ideation, bouts of amnesia. She also spoke of wanting to be with her mother. According to this carer, Huish should never have been granted an absolute discharge.'

'When did her mother die?' Silas asks, fearing the answer already.

'Eleven years ago next week.'

'Shit.' He sits up. 'Was the carer surprised when you told her no one knows where Huish is?'

'Shocked – worried what Huish might do if no one's overseeing her medication. Apparently, she has various mental strategies for coping – mindfulness, meditation – but they aren't enough around anniversaries.'

'No surprises there.' Silas tried mindfulness once, on the advice of HR, who were worried he was overtired from too much work. It wasn't a success – he kept falling asleep. 'Did her mother always live in the village?'

Strover nods. 'When I talked to Jemma yesterday, she told me she'd just seen a gravestone for Huish's mum.'

'As close as she can get to her.'

Silas remembers the graveyard in the village, watching Jemma and Susie from the lychgate. He calls Susie on her mobile.

'We've tracked down one of Jemma Huish's carers,' he says.

'And?' Susie asks defensively.

'We need to talk to Jemma again – urgently.'

'She's still very fragile.'

'That's why we need to see her.' He glances at his watch. 'We'll be rolling into the village in thirty minutes. No blues and twos. Just a nice quiet chat.'

39

My heart refuses to stop racing as I lie on the bed. I can't get over the looks I received in the surgery, the anger in everyone's eyes. They must have decided that I am Jemma Huish. It could become a major problem. None of this would have happened if I'd been given any another name by Tony. Why did I agree to Jemma? With a 'J'? And why did he choose it?

Should I talk to him now? He said he'd be in his café all day. I need to debrief with someone about the crowd in the surgery. Abdul's gone out – I heard him leave with his brother a few minutes ago.

I open my door and walk down the corridor. As I pass Abdul's room, someone comes rushing up the stairs.

'I came straight over,' Tony says, catching his breath on the landing.

'What's happened? I was about to come to the café.'

'Dr Patterson just called. She's looking for you. The cops want to interview you again.'

I let out a deep sigh. 'I don't know why. I can't tell them any more than what I said yesterday.'

'You need a lawyer, Jemma. Don't you see what's happening here? They're going to frame you. Jemma Huish has disappeared, dropped off the grid – that's embarrassing for everyone, the cops, the NHS. You're their only lead.'

'They'll ask me for a DNA sample again. I can't do it.'

A simple medical swab from the inside of your mouth.

'And you don't have to. Not unless they arrest you.'

'It will only make things worse if I keep refusing.'

'DNA testing is far from foolproof. And once you're on that database, you'll never get off it, no matter what they say. Your details could be used later for negative profiling.'

'What should I do?' I want him to take control of the situation.

'Head over to my house now.' He glances at his watch. It's almost 9.30 a.m. 'Walk back via the station. Linger there briefly. There's a westbound train due to leave any minute. The key's still under the flowerpot at the back of the house. I'll bring your bag. Your room's at the top of the stairs, on the right. It's where you slept on the first night, when you arrived.'

'Why are you doing this?' I ask. I need to know what's happening in his head, his motive, exactly why he's going the distance.

'Because I don't want to see you caught up in something you might not be able to get out of. They've no right talking to you like this. And no evidence against you. I've seen it before. A friendly chat without an attorney and bang, next thing you're being charged.'

'Upstairs in your house, you said running away never helps.'

'You're not running away. You're still a free citizen – you can go wherever you goddam like. They haven't charged you.

You appeared from nowhere and now you're disappearing again. End of story. It'll just be for a few days, until they find the real Jemma Huish. And once they've found her, all this will blow over and we can get back to focusing on that precious memory of yours.'

'Give me a minute to pack my case,' I say.

'Leave it by the door when you're done. I need to get back to the café.'

Once Tony's left, I move fast. I pack my clothes and make the bed – I'm not sure why. I look around the room, at the piano, the washbasin in the corner, and remember my toothbrush and toothpaste. My hairbrush is also on a shelf above the sink. I gather them all up and put them in the case, but then I take out the hairbrush and stare at myself in the mirror.

I can't remember my own name.

I brush my hair hard, still looking at my reflection, and walk over to the bed, my hairbrush in my hand. I kneel down and place it carefully on the floorboards under the bed, out of sight but easy enough to find.

40

Silas parks up outside the church and walks into the deserted graveyard with Strover. He wants to see the gravestone himself before calling on Susie Patterson. It doesn't take long to find it. Moss is marching across the stone, but the italic lettering is clear enough.

'No flowers,' Strover says.

Silas glances around him, across the water meadow and up to the woods. Again he wonders if someone is out there, watching, waiting.

'Still plenty of time,' he says, noting the date.

A distant boom rumbles across the countryside, shaking the summer air. For a moment he thinks it might be thunder before remembering the village is close to Salisbury Plain. The army must be out on the ranges today.

And then Strover is on her knees, scrabbling around in the long grass at the base of the gravestone. She holds up a small piece of cellophane-covered card.

'Can you read it?' Silas asks.

'It's rotten,' she says. 'Maybe "Mum"? Hard to tell. Definitely some kisses.'

Silas calls Susie Patterson on her mobile as they walk over to the car. There is no evidence yet to suggest that the woman who has arrived in this village is Jemma Huish, but the amnesia, her physical likeness, the way she apparently held a kitchen knife... They have all taken on a new significance since her old carer told them about the danger around her mother's anniversary. Jemma now needs to give a DNA sample in order to eliminate herself from their enquiries. The National DNA Database has confirmed they have Huish's profile and the lab is ready to fast-track for a match.

'Susie, it's me, Silas,' he says, looking down the road towards the surgery. 'We're ready to talk to your mystery woman.'

There's silence before Susie answers. A bad silence.

'Jemma's not with us right now,' she says.

'Not with you?' Silas is unable to hide the annoyance in his voice. He told her he was coming to talk with Jemma. He knows there's another reason for his anger too. She's pushed him back, rejected his unsubtle advances.

'She was with us five minutes ago,' Susie says.

'That's the second time she's disappeared,' he says for Strover's benefit, rolling his eyes at her.

'We're looking for her everywhere.' Susie sounds out of breath.

'Where are you now?' he asks.

'In the village – School Road.'

'I'll meet you at the surgery.'

He tells Strover to head off into the village to help look for Jemma. Silas would normally walk to the surgery – he likes to go on foot as much as he can these days, 10,000 steps a day, all part of his mid-life health crisis – but he takes the car the short distance. He has a feeling he might need it.

41

I check both ways, satisfied that no one is around, and walk onto the deserted station platform. A minute later, a westbound train pulls in. Nobody gets off. Everyone must be going on towards Exeter and beyond. I stand back as the doors close and the train pulls away, its driver glancing down the platform at me from his window. Once the train has gone, I swing round the back of the village to approach Tony's house from the far side.

The village feels quiet. The school run must be over, commuters gone for the day, leaving those who remain to settle into the rhythm of their rural lives. Tony will bring my suitcase in a few minutes. I walk up through a grid of bungalows behind the station and enter the back garden through a wooden gate. The key is under the flowerpot, just as he said it would be. Again I look around before I put the key in the door and step inside.

A faint smell of citrus in the house and the rumble of a washing machine. I walk into the kitchen and glance around. The knife-block is back on the sideboard, a full set of knives sticking out. I don't want to linger. The slatted wooden blinds are open and I can be seen from the street. I head upstairs and glance out of the back window of my room, from where I can see the station in the distance. I'm about to sit down on the bed when the front-door bell rings. Hasn't Tony got a key?

The bell rings again. I walk out to the landing. Pressing my face against the window, I can just see down into the street below. It's Dr Patterson. I hate to deceive her. I want to talk, tell her what I'm doing, but I know I can't. I watch in silence as she walks off down the street. Halfway towards the pub, she stops and chats to a person coming the other way. Dr Patterson points back down the street, looking around her. I can't hear any conversation, but I assume she's asking if she's seen me.

A noise downstairs, the back door being opened. I hope it's Tony. I stand at the top of the stairs and wait for him to call out, listening as he moves about the kitchen. I think I can hear my suitcase being wheeled in – the giveaway broken wheel.

'Jemma?' he calls softly from the sitting room.

'I'm up here,' I say.

'I've just seen the cops arrive.' He comes up the stairs with my suitcase. 'Unmarked car, but the big guy who got out might as well have had a blue light on his head. Outside the surgery.'

'I think I should just go and talk to them.'

'Trust me on this, Jemma,' he says, lifting my suitcase onto the bed. 'You need to stay low for a while, until they find the real Jemma Huish.'

'Dr Patterson rang the bell a few minutes ago,' I say, remaining on the landing. I don't want to be in my bedroom alone with him.

'Here?'

'I'm sure she was looking for me. I didn't answer.'

'You're certain no one saw you coming over?' he asks, walking over to the landing window. He glances up and down the street.

'Positive.'

He turns to look at me and then up at a panel in the ceiling. 'You're going to have to stay up in the attic.'

'The loft?' I look up at the ceiling too. The hatch is tiny and for a second I wonder if a human can get through it.

'With your suitcase. Just for a few hours.'

'Are you serious?' Discreetly, I reach for my tattoo.

'We can make it more comfortable,' he continues, lifting the suitcase back off my bed. 'Put some bedding up there, food and water. Anything's better than where you were staying.'

'I'm not sure I want to do this, Tony,' I say, pressing my fingers deeper into my wrist. I can feel my pulse, Fleur's beating heart inside me, strong and steady.

Tony holds me by both shoulders, looking into my face. 'I'll catch up with Dr Patterson, tell her I saw you heading towards the station, try to throw them off the scent, but they'll look everywhere for you.' And then he kisses me on the lips. 'Trust me, you really don't want them to find you.'

42

'I'm so sorry about this,' Susie Patterson says, as Silas walks
into her consulting room for the second day in a row. This is
what it must feel like to be a hypochondriac.

'How long ago was she here?' he asks, looking around.

'Fifteen minutes ago? Maybe less. I'm sorry, Silas.' At least
Susie is talking to him again, one good thing to have come
out of Jemma's disappearance. He's not going to make up
with her too quickly though.

'Tony, the American – he saw Jemma walking down towards
the station,' she continues. 'I went after her, but when I got to
the station, a train had just left.'

That's all Silas needs, but he restricts himself to an
exasperated shake of the head. Jemma's sudden departure is
starting to worry him.

'It's entirely my fault,' Susie says, watching Silas take out
his phone. He turns his back on her and puts a call through to
Strover, who's still looking for Jemma in the village.

'What are the next three stations up the line?' he says to
Susie, hand over his phone.

Susie tells him it was a rare westbound train. He asks Strover for police checks down the line. He's not hopeful. Force resources are already stretched in the region, but it's worth a shot.

'Did anyone get a photo of Jemma?' he asks.

Susie shakes her head. If she hadn't been so difficult yesterday, Strover could have sneaked one during her interview.

'There's CCTV in the surgery waiting room,' she says, brightening up. 'It was installed a few months back, after a bag was stolen. Patient confidentiality could be an issue,' she adds. 'The identities of other patients would need to be preserved.'

'Confidentiality, my arse. Who keeps the tapes?'

Two minutes later, Silas is in the practice manager's office, looking through CCTV footage of the surgery waiting room at 9 a.m. the day before. Susie and the manager are standing next to him. Silas has overridden any privacy concerns by explaining that disclosure is in the interests of public safety, but the manager seems to have similar objections, citing General Medical Council confidentiality guidelines. Data protection has become the bane of Silas's life.

'That's her,' Susie says, pointing at a woman and a man entering the surgery.

'Freeze it there,' Silas says to the manager. The woman in the image looks a bit like Jemma Huish, but it's hard to tell through the lens of cheap CCTV. 'Who's the bloke with her?'

'Tony, the American,' Susie says. 'He and his wife put Jemma up for the first night.'

'Where is he now?' Silas notices the man's body language, the way he is with Jemma, how close he's standing.

'He runs a café in the high street. I can take you there.'

'Get me a printout of that,' Silas says, peering at the screen again. 'And email the file to me at this address.' He gives the manager his card.

'I'll have to pixelate the other patients.'

'You can put flashing antlers on their heads for all I care. I'm only interested in her.'

It's not a great image, but there's enough of a likeness. Enough for Strover anyway. Unlike him, she's actually met Jemma in the flesh. The closest Silas has been to her is fifty yards away in the graveyard. He'll get the image circulated across the region – they can enhance it back at HQ.

'I don't know why she suddenly disappeared,' Susie says as she accompanies Silas down to the high street.

'Maybe she heard we were coming. Does Jemma have access to any money?'

Silas suddenly realises how hungry he is – and irritable. Yesterday was a fast day, which never helps.

'Not as far as I know,' Susie says.

'So she might not get far on the train.'

'They hardly ever check tickets at this time of the day.'

'Great,' he says, making no effort to conceal his frustration from Susie. He's going to milk this one for all it's worth. 'I need to speak to Tony,' he continues, increasing his pace. He's tall, with a long stride and Susie almost has to run to keep up. 'And his wife. They might know more if they put Jemma up for the night.'

'This is where he works,' Susie says, out of breath. They are standing outside the Seahorse Gallery & Café.

'Oh Christ,' Silas says, glancing at the board outside before going in. '"No bacon, no egg, no problem." It has to be a vegan café, doesn't it?' He didn't fast yesterday just so he can chew on a mung bean today. He walks up to the counter, where a man with a ponytail looks up at them.

'Tony, this is—' Susie begins.

'DI Hart,' Silas interrupts, showing Tony his ID. 'I'd like something edible,' he says, looking unhopefully around the counter, 'and a little chat.'

43

Tony made the attic as comfortable as he could before he left to go back to the café, but it still feels like a prison. Maybe it's the bare lightbulb hanging from the roof timbers. I've got a camping roll-mat spread out on the chipboard floor, some bottled water and fruit, a radio with headphones (Tony insisted) and a bucket for emergencies. It makes my room at the pub seem luxurious.

What worries me more is that I'm entirely reliant on Tony to let me out. The metal folding ladder can only be operated from the landing below as there's a small lock on the outside of the panel. I feel out of control again, but for the moment my options are limited and I am happier being out of sight, away from the police. Tony will come back later and let me know how long I need to be up here, once he's got a sense from the police where their investigations are heading.

I take a sip of water and glance around the attic. There are boxes everywhere, laid out neatly in a grid. Tony said they were his visual diary. Each box contains 365 photos, one for each day of the year. He told me I could look at them if I wanted – they're all on Instagram, the most recent ones anyway. It would be something to do while I'm up here, he said, but it's important I don't move around or make a noise if someone comes to the house.

He thinks the police might want to interview him, either at the café or at home, but if they ask to look around, he'll insist on a search warrant. He knows his rights. As a precaution, he's given me a basic mobile phone, one of Jemma's old 'brick' ones. They keep it as a spare, he said. All the numbers have been erased and it's got an unused pay-as-you-go SIM card in it. He'll warn me with an anonymous text if anyone is coming: something innocent and domestic, as if he's messaging Laura.

I listen to the stillness of the house. All I can hear is the distant rumble of a train, a solitary car accelerating up the high street. Satisfied that I'm on my own, I crawl on my hands and knees over to the boxes – the eaves are too low for me to stand up. The first box is the current year: A4-sized prints, some black and white, some colour, each one in a clear plastic slip with a date on it. I recognise one of the graveyard, a close-up of moss on the lychgate; another is looking down the canal at a beautiful arched bridge, a low mist rising off the water. I flick through some more photos, pausing at one of Laura. She is lying in bed, her naked body half covered by a sheet, eyes closed. Is she asleep? Did she know he took it?

I stop, guilty that I'm going through another person's private things, even if Tony said I could. And then I open an older box. Lots of the photos are of other women. Fashion-style shots in European cities – I recognise Paris and Rome, Amsterdam and Venice. Snow scenes in parks, sunny smiles to camera, nothing risqué. He likes a certain look in his women: short dark hair, big eyes. I flick through the images and stop at one of a woman in a beret. My heart flips. It looks like

Fleur. I look again and realise it's not her. I breathe deeply, the sheaf of photos shaking in my hand. The silence of the village feels eerie from up here, muffled. And then there's the distant cry of a red kite.

I move through the seasons in reverse, glancing at each image. Summer, spring. Photos of graffiti on a bridge wall, a complex matrix of train tracks stretching out behind. And then, in among images of cityscapes and rivers, a pair of seahorses. They are not alive like the ones in the café's framed pictures. These are small and shrunken, photographed against a white background, a table of some sort. I look more closely at them. The seahorses are shrivelled, as if they've been pickled. Or maybe they've been dried. Their distinctive tails are curved like a treble clef, but the long snouts have been damaged and are missing. Tony mentioned that dried seahorses fetch a lot of money, particularly those breeds that are popular in Chinese medicine. Were these some he bought, perhaps? Or sold for a large amount?

More than the price of silver.

I stare at the photo, holding it on one side and then the other. There's nothing to like about the images. I find them troubling, their almost prehistoric shape deeply unsettling.

I swallow hard and look away.

44

'When did you last see Jemma?' DI Silas Hart asks, wiping his mouth with a napkin. 'Surprisingly tasty.'

Tony has never liked cops and he dislikes the one sitting in his café more than most, but he knows he must talk to him, appear unflustered by his questions. Cooperate. So he has given him an extra portion of vegan mac-and-cheese balls, which he's dunking in buffalo sauce – anything to slow him down – and is now trying to appear helpful as they talk. Susie Patterson has left them to it, full of remorse, resuming what appears to be a village-wide search for Jemma.

'I was here in the café, serving breakfasts, when Dr Patterson called me, said she was searching for Jemma. I went outside, took a look around and saw her down the bottom of the street, turning off towards the station. I called out, but she was too far away to hear. I was about to head after her when a customer showed up.'

'What time was this?' Hart asks, pulling out a notepad from his jacket pocket.

'Fifteen, twenty minutes ago?'

'Why didn't you call Dr Patterson back?'

Because he's just made this up. He's always been a good liar.

'After the customer left, I went outside again and bumped into Dr Patterson,' he says, which is true. He'd caught up with her after leaving Jemma in the loft. 'She was looking for Jemma, so I explained that I'd just seen her heading in the direction of the station.'

The cop seems to buy his story, writing down a few short notes. 'Here's my number, in case she turns up,' he says, handing Tony a card.

'What's this about?' Tony asks.

'We just need to eliminate Jemma from our enquiries,' Hart says, giving nothing away. They always say that. And then the cop blindsides Tony with a surprising question. 'Why did you put her up on that first night?'

'Why?'

'Total stranger knocks on your door. "Come in, make yourself at home." Not very British.'

'I'm American. We don't bite.' The cop's caught him out. 'And it wasn't quite like that.'

'What was it like?' he asks.

Tony thinks back to the afternoon Jemma arrived, considers how much to tell.

'I'm just trying to build a picture in my mind of this mystery woman,' the cop adds. 'Seems to have caused quite a stir in the village.'

'She's a good-looking woman, if that's what you mean.'

'Did I mean that?' The cop stares at him. 'I've yet to meet her.'

'She also thought she lived in our house. Even knew the layout. She was clearly confused. Laura, my wife, and I... I guess we both felt sorry for her, gave her a cup of tea, took her down to the surgery.'

Hart writes in his notepad and then looks up at him. 'Your wife – is she around?'

'Right now she's staying at her mom's.'

The cop raises his eyebrows. 'Which is where?'

'London.'

He makes another note. 'Was she happy about Jemma staying?' he asks, still writing.

'For one night, yes.' Jeez, how much does this guy know? 'Then we felt it best the professionals took over. Jemma appears to be suffering from retrograde and anterograde amnesia.'

'You sound quite the professional yourself.'

Tony could do without the eyeballing. Hart's stare is unnerving. 'I take an interest in these things. My dad died young of Alzheimer's.'

The cop's phone starts to ring. 'Excuse me a moment,' he says, standing up from the table.

Tony involuntarily puffs out his cheeks once his interrogator's back is turned. And then he tries to catch what he can of the phone conversation.

'I want police units on all the main roads in and out of the village,' the cop says. 'And we'll need to do a door-to-door... Forensics too... I'll speak to Corporate Comms and Engagement about a public appeal.' He hangs up and turns to Tony. 'A colleague's just spoken to the train driver – apparently no one boarded the westbound train from here.'

45

I slip the photo back into the box, trying not to dwell on it too much. When will Tony be back? He hasn't sent any cryptic texts, so perhaps the police have lost interest in me. Their attention is becoming a big distraction, but I must deal with it. And then I see another box, away from the others, wedged under the eaves near the water tank. I crawl over and pull it out. Inside is a collection of newspaper articles, paper-clipped into separate bundles. Some of the newsprint is yellow and faded.

I check to listen and begin to leaf through them. Each one appears to be about amnesia: a migrant worker in Peterborough with no idea who he is; a British banker who walked into a New York police station saying he'd just woken on a subway train unaware of his own identity; several magazine articles about Henry Gustav Molaison, who underwent crude brain surgery in 1953 in an attempt to reduce the frequency of his seizures. Miraculously, the seizures stopped, but he was left unable to form new memories. And then Jemma Huish is staring up at me from a blurred photo, the student killer who slit her best friend's throat.

Is this what I look like to others? I skim through the article, the biro marks circling phrases such as 'dissociative amnesia', 'no recollection' and 'Wiltshire village'. I look at the photos, read the captions. It's this village, this house.

There are more annotated articles underneath it, many more, about the case, the trial, her obsession with the radio. She had to have it on whenever she was on her own, harming herself if she couldn't listen to it. And she reported hearing auditory commands that seemed to come from trees.

I am about to read further when I hear the front door open. Fumbling with the articles, I put them back into the box, wedge it under the eaves again and return to my mat just as the loft hatch opens.

'We've got to go,' Tony says, his head appearing. 'Everything OK?'

'Fine,' I say, trying to compose myself. 'What's happened?'

'Get your stuff,' he says, looking around the attic from the hatch.

'Where are we going?'

'Away from here – out of the village.' He starts to descend the ladder, disappearing from sight. 'The cops know you didn't get on a train,' he says, louder so I can hear. 'They're about to lock down the whole place.'

'Tony,' I call out, 'I think we should—'

Silence. And then his head reappears at the hatch opening. 'Do you remember what we ate for dinner last night?' he asks, his voice cold and baleful.

I look at him, scared by his question, the tone of it, and shake my head.

'You're vulnerable, Jemma,' he says, descending again. 'The cops are panicking about Jemma Huish – they're under pressure to arrest someone. It's not going to be you.'

I gather up my things and lower my suitcase down to Tony, who is now on the landing below.

'Where are we going?' I repeat, once we're by the back door.

'I know a place in the forest,' he says, grabbing a bottle of water from the fridge. 'It's not much, but it's dry. Used to be an ammunition shelter in World War Two.'

I follow him out into the garden. 'You'll have to hide in the car trunk, with your stuff,' he says, locking the back door. My heart's beating too fast. Tony looks around and opens the boot of his old BMW. We both stare at the cramped space. There's an empty green plastic petrol can in the corner, next to a folded-up high-vis jacket.

'Trust me,' he says, sensing my reluctance. 'We need to go now.'

He checks both ways again as I climb into the boot clutching the sleeping bag for comfort. Is this the right decision? Judging when to run is critical. I got it wrong once, when Tony found me climbing out of the window. He wedges the suitcase in next, by my feet, followed by my roll-mat, the radio and finally the bottle of water.

'It's going to be OK,' he says, one hand above him, ready to close the boot door. He manages a smile that I am unable to return. My legs are tucked up into the foetal position. 'Only for a few hours, maybe a day or two.'

A click and my world turns black.

46

Luke remembers the day he arrived in the village with Milo as if it was yesterday. His wife had died six months earlier and he'd chucked in his job on a national newspaper to bring up their four-year-old son in the country with his parents. It had felt like a new beginning, which helped to numb the sadness. Selling the house in East Dulwich had been difficult, but he couldn't stay in it after she died. He'd found her on the kitchen floor. A brain aneurysm, out of the blue. At least Milo had been at playgroup when it happened.

Over the years his parents have suggested sending Milo away to boarding school, but Luke has always resisted, signing him up for the village primary and then the nearby state academy. Luke's father was an army officer and Luke was sent away to board when he was eight. His parents had wanted stability for him as his father moved from one posting to another, sometimes abroad. Maybe Milo will board next year, when he's in the sixth form, if only for the food. Milo's eating them out of house and home.

Now, as he comes over the hill and down into the village, working the gears of the Austin-Healey, he feels nothing but dread. He's already been overtaken by two police cars, lights flashing. Up ahead, another police car has parked in a lay-by and two uniformed officers are erecting signs on the other side of the road. Beyond them an old silver BMW is driving up the hill, away from the village and towards the police. It looks like Tony and Laura's car. Luke watches as it slows to pass the officers, who are now starting to put out cones. One officer looks up at the BMW and the driver waves a hand in acknowledgement.

Luke's sure it's Tony, checks no one's behind him and brings the Austin-Healey to a halt, waving down the BMW as it approaches. Tony stops too, lowering his window.

'Nice set of wheels,' Tony says, turning down his car radio.

'Office car,' Luke says. 'Laura still with her mum?'

'And still mad at me.'

Luke feels guilty about Laura. When she rang the office this morning, he sensed she was wanting him to talk to Tony, find out what's going on, ask why he's so keen on helping Jemma. But Luke hasn't rushed to the village to save their marriage. He wants to talk to Jemma, check she's OK.

'Have you seen Jemma around?' he asks.

'Are you kidding? Everyone's looking for her,' Tony says, nodding at the police behind them. 'They're about to cordon off the whole village. She disappeared this morning apparently.'

'Not staying with you then?' Luke asks, cursing himself for having been in London last night.

'Took a room in the pub. Laura wasn't happy with her being at ours.'

'I can't understand why Laura's so convinced she's Jemma Huish,' Luke says, watching as the policemen further down the road stop a car.

'Search me.'

'I mean, why would she come back to the village?'

'I thought you stayed in town in the week anyway?' Tony asks, ignoring his question. He seems distracted today.

'I need to talk to Jemma – about her mother.'

'Her mother? She doesn't know who she is, let alone her mom.'

'No change?'

Tony shakes his head. 'Still can't tell us her own name. What's with the mom anyway?'

'I think we might have been at school together.' Luke pauses. 'Did Jemma take that DNA test in the end?'

'Last I heard, she'd refused. Don't blame her. You guys have the biggest DNA database per capita in the world. Steer well clear of it, I say – a threat to all our civil liberties.'

Luke glances in his wing mirror. Another car is coming down the hill behind him.

'Maybe she should do one,' he says. He doesn't want to tell Tony why, that it might be the only way to establish his paternity.

'Better get going,' Tony says, noticing the approaching car. 'Before the cops arrest me.'

'Problem?'

Tony grins, tapping the steering wheel. 'Car's not taxed.'

47

I can't catch all the words, but I know that Tony has stopped to talk to Luke. There's a faint smell of petrol and stale milk in the boot. As I listen to the two men, a part of me wants to smash my fists against the side of the car, shout and scream, but I know I must stay silent.

It sounds like Luke has come down from London specially to see me. He's talking about how he thinks he was at school with my mother. I want to see him on his own again, but it's not possible now.

Tony accelerates away after he's finished chatting and we drive for another five minutes. It's hard to be sure, but I'm guessing we're on small roads. Lots of twists and turns, and very few other cars seem to pass us.

When we stop, Tony doesn't let me out immediately. He just sits in the driver's seat, turns up the radio and listens. I can't hear any other noise except for the menacing call of distant crows. Maybe he's checking that no one is around. The high sun dazzles my eyes when he finally opens the boot. He looks at me for a moment – in pity, perhaps – before he speaks.

'We got out of the village just in time.'

'Is that why we stopped?' I ask, uncurling myself. 'The police?' He holds my arm as I jump to the ground. We have come off the road and driven down a narrow track. All around us is dripping-wet woodland, mostly beech, washed leaves glistening in the sun. It must have just rained, a short summer shower. Beyond the trees are fields dotted with sheep.

'They waved us through – still setting up the roadblock. Another minute and you'd have been caught. I stopped to talk to Luke. He's driven down from London in some old car – surprised he made it.'

I decide not to let Tony know that I heard most of their conversation.

'I thought he worked in London during the week,' I say as he takes my suitcase and radio out of the boot. He leaves me to lift out the roll-mat and sleeping bag.

'You remember that?' he asks, pausing before he snaps shut the boot door.

'It's what it says in my notes.' I've still got them with me, in the back pocket of my jeans.

'His father's unwell. He's come down to check on him.'

I know Tony's lying. It's good for me to see how he behaves when he's not telling the truth. He's an accomplished deceiver.

'The shelter's about a hundred yards in there,' he says, nodding.

We both stand still, taking in the ancient woodland. I feel so vulnerable out here with him on my own, but I know there's no choice. The solitary bark of a deer does nothing to quell my fear.

'Are you staying with me?' I ask as we start to walk down a faint footpath.

'I've got to head back to the café,' he says.

I'm relieved. At least I won't be out here on my own with him for long. I'm not ready. Not yet. We veer off the footpath and head deeper into the woods, stepping through thick brambles. I can see the shelter up ahead, a small mound covered in grass and nettles. The entrance is overgrown. How many people know about this place? I follow him down a set of graffiti-covered concrete steps. At the bottom, twelve feet underground, he kicks away a crushed can of lager and an old packet of cigarettes. The litter of teenagers, lovers.

'You won't be here long,' he says, holding up the light on his phone to show me the dingy space. He must sense my fear. The shelter is about five yards long and two yards wide. Like a cell. The far end is illuminated by a pool of sunlight streaming in through a hole in the roof. Some old leaves and twigs have fallen through it, but otherwise the concrete floor is clear. It's dry, but that's about all this place has got going for it.

'When were you here?' I ask.

'Last Sunday. The village history society organised a walk. I was the honorary Yank. US forces stationed here in the war used it to store ammunition, preparing for the Normandy landings.'

'So it's quite well known?'

'Not this one,' he says. 'Everyone goes to another shelter, near the memorial. 'You'll be fine here. You've got the radio. And I'll bring some food later. Coffee too?'

'Tea would be great. Anything herbal.'

'Look, it's not ideal, I know, but you need to be out of the village.' He puts an arm around me as if we are newlyweds surveying our first home. I try not to flinch, but I want him to go now. I need to get my head around everything, work out where I am, what happens next.

'Can I call you?' I ask, peeling away to climb back up the steps. 'If someone arrives.'

'No one's going to come out here,' he says, following me up to the surface. 'Trust me. And if anyone does, maybe a dog walker, just stay low until they've gone. Text is better – if you're worried. Just don't call me. I might be with the cops again.'

'How far is it to the road?' I ask, looking over to where the car is parked.

'A mile, perhaps a bit more. It's remote.'

Without warning, Tony turns to face me, holding both my shoulders. There's a chill in his eyes and his grip is firmer, more aggressive than before, his body pressed close to mine. I start to panic, unable to reach for my wrist, but I'm spared by the sound of a ringtone. He steps back and removes his mobile from his pocket, looking at the caller ID.

'Unknown,' he says, raising his eyebrows at me. 'That'll be the cops then.' He becomes more serious as he takes the call and listens. 'I'll be at the café in fifteen.'

He hangs up and turns to me again, the same look in his eyes. 'DI Silas Hart wants some more mac-and-cheese balls,' he says, his voice heavy with sarcasm. 'I need to head back to the village.'

He smiles at me for a second, his hands on my shoulders again. 'I'll return as soon as I can.' And then he kisses me hard on the lips. I think of Fleur, try to recall her face, praying for him to be quick. I was prepared for a kiss, but he wants more this time, his hands searching under my shirt, squeezing my thigh. Fleur was never like this. Her touch was gentle, mutual.

'Later,' I say, trying to push him away, frightened by his strength. 'The police are waiting for you.'

'Fuck the cops,' he whispers, starting to rip at my shirt.

'Please, Tony,' I say, louder now. 'I'm not ready.'

Reluctantly he stops and looks at me, his eyes heavy with lust and something more frightening. And then he turns and sets off through the brambles towards the car.

'Text me,' I force myself to call after him. 'And thank you. For everything.'

His silence is scaring me. 'Did we bring any paper?' I ask, trying to bring things back to the everyday, the mundane. 'A pen? I've got a lot to write up.'

He stops in his tracks. It's a while before he speaks and when he does his voice sends a shiver down my spine. 'Maybe it's best you don't write down anything today.'

48

Luke is in the pub, having a swift midday pint with Sean. He's looked everywhere for Jemma, walked the canal towpath, skirted the woods on top of the hill that overlooks the village, scoured the allotments, the station, the church, but he knows it's a lost cause. If the police can't find her, he's got no chance. Officers seem to be everywhere, conducting door-to-door enquiries, checking every car that drives in and out of the village, making appeals in the media.

The mood among locals has changed since Luke was here yesterday morning. Gossip has given way to sadness and maybe a touch of shame as the quiet village finds itself in the public glare.

'When I spoke to Freya Lal, she said the woman in Germany who adopted her was a Baha'i,' Luke says.

'Interesting religion,' Sean replies.

'I know,' Luke says. 'I've been doing some research.'

'Practised by the chemical-weapons inspector Dr David Kelly, of course. He of the sexed-up Saddam Hussein dossier.'

'You're incredible, Sean.'

'Murdered, for sure.'

'I thought he took his own life?'

'Suicide is forbidden by Baha'is. How long have you got? There's a theory that—'

'Sean, Jemma has a tattoo on her arm. I don't know if you noticed.'

'I'd be lying if I said I did.'

'It's a lotus flower. The Baha'i temple in Delhi is shaped like a lotus.'

'It's also a Buddhist symbol. The eight petals of the mystical purple lotus represent the noble eightfold path taught by the Buddha. Kind of an important flower for Hindus too. And Jains and Sikhs. I'll need to check about the Russian Orthodox Church.'

Now's not the time for more of Sean's Soviet conspiracies. 'If Jemma's adopted mother was a Baha'i,' Luke says, 'there's a good chance she might be too.'

Sean seems to notice his change of tone. 'You really want to find this woman, don't you?'

Luke nods, drinking deeply from his beer. 'She just seems to have vanished into thin air.'

'A well-known Russian speciality.'

Luke glances up to see a crime-scene investigator pass through the pub into the old stable block at the back, where Jemma stayed. He's wearing a white oversuit, mask and purple gloves.

'What's going on there?' Luke asks the barman.

'They're searching the room where the woman stayed.'

'Forensics?'

'Full works.'

'I need to speak to them,' Luke says to Sean, slipping off his bar stool and heading for the back door.

49

Jemma turns up the radio and listens. She's early – it's the weather forecast. Her watch must be running fast. She walks up the flight of steps and looks around. Dark woodland, afternoon light slanting through fir trees. She's lucky to be in a place like this, with only muntjacs for company. It really doesn't look as though it's been used for years. So close to the village and yet so far. She misses it more than she thought she would: the security of an enclosed rural community, the friendliness of the people. Most of them.

She hears the hourly pips down below and returns for the news bulletin. A tit-for-tat expulsion of spies from Moscow and London; new powers of arrest for the police; a manhunt in a Wiltshire village...

Her blood runs cold as she listens. Police are searching for a former mental-health patient who has not been seen for a year. There are fears that she may be dangerous and the public is warned not to approach her. 'We ask that anyone with information about Ms Huish contact us immediately,' a detective is saying. His name is familiar.

Jemma closes her eyes. She can feel the memories coming back, like a flash flood, sweeping down the barren mountain of her past, restoring it to life. She suddenly feels vulnerable, out here in the woods on her own. Angry too. Anger like she hasn't felt for a long time.

She walks over to her bag, rifles through her clothes and finds what she's looking for. Her hand is shaking too much to hold up the kitchen knife for long. She drops it back into the bag and sinks to the floor, where she cradles her knees and starts to sob, rocking backwards and forwards. More memories. Nightmares. She has a routine for this, a strategy to restore order, but this is way too big, swatting away the years of therapy and medication as if they never happened.

She puts her hands over her ears, trying to shut out the voices, but it's no good. Panicking now, she goes back outside to breathe in the peace of the forest. Nature is her last hope. The trees here are untroubled by news reports. At first she hears nothing, but then a faint whisper from high up in the canopy of the forest begins to speak, quietly encouraging her to call. Give warning.

She looks away, ignoring the voices, and returns inside to pick up the knife.

50

Silas Hart is in the middle of interviewing Tony in his café again when he gets a call to go over to the pub. It's been a busy few hours, no time to eat. He'd rather die than admit it, but he was looking forward to trying some more of Tony's vegan food, maybe one of his black bean and chipotle veggie patties. It will have to wait.

'Stay here,' he says to the American as he stands up from the table.

'Is that an order?'

'A polite request. And if we don't get anywhere with Jemma's room at the pub, we'll want to search your house.'

'You'll need a warrant for that,' Tony says, retreating behind the food counter.

'We'll get one, don't worry.'

Silas walks out of the café door with Strover. Tony is beginning to get on his tits. They won't need a warrant if they arrest him.

'Run that clown through the PNC,' he says, crossing the road to head up to the pub. Strover has many skills, including an ability to return sarcasm with interest, but she's also one of the best when it comes to searching the Police National Computer, cross-referencing intel with the newer Police National Database. Good at anything to do with computers. And social media. A digital native, according to HR. Whatever that is.

'Has his wife left him then?' Strover asks.

'Gone away for a break with her mum, according to the good doctor.'

There's no point hiding anything from Strover. She knows that he still fancies Dr Patterson, even if she did hamper their investigation. Female intuition.

'Jemma's a fit-looking woman,' Strover says.

'You said it, not me. And she went back to Tony's for dinner last night, according to Abdul the Afghani.' Silas had caught up with Abdul earlier, had a nice chat in the pub kitchen, promised to try one of his lamb curries.

'You think Tony knows where she is?' Strover asks.

'Not sure,' Silas says as they arrive outside the pub. 'We might be wasting our time anyway. CSI have found something.'

51

I couldn't stay in the shelter for a second longer, not after hearing the news on the radio. The next few hours will be critical. Have I left it too late? The hairbrush should buy me some time, but I will also need a slice of luck for what lies ahead.

I've left my suitcase behind – I've got everything that I need. Up ahead I can see the grass track that leads to the lane. There's no traffic around, but I must be careful. If I'm right, the lane runs one way to the village, the other up to the main road out of the valley. A mile, Tony said. Maybe a bit further. I stop and listen. All I can hear is the sound of the summer breeze rippling the beech trees high above me.

Tony hasn't texted or called since he left. I've not contacted him either. He must be with the police again, answering their questions, trying to keep up appearances, denying that he knows my whereabouts. I will text him later.

I take one last look around me and set off down the lane, breaking into a run.

52

Silas walks through the bar, pushing the thought of a pint and some peanuts to the back of his mind. Later. Much later. When this is all sorted. The public appeal should throw up something. They usually do. He's also upgraded Jemma Huish's risk assessment from low to high and flagged it up with the UK Missing Persons Bureau, who have redistributed her file, including her DNA profile, to all UK forces and reclassified her as 'missing' rather than 'absent'.

He walks around to the stable block, where CSI are searching the room that Jemma stayed in last night.

'I thought you should see this,' the CSI manager says, coming out to meet Silas and Strover.

'What is it?'

'We've found a hairbrush. Under the bed.'

'Jemma's?'

'We think so. An initial dust analysis suggests it's recent, sometime this morning.'

'Roots?' Silas learnt on day one of being a detective that a strand of hair is no good to anyone unless the root is attached.

'That's what's strange,' the CSI manager says. 'Lots of roots. Fresh ones. Someone brushed their hair very hard with this. Much harder than necessary. And then there's the position we found the brush in.'

'Under the bed,' Silas says, wondering where the manager's going with this.

'If it fell to the floor and was accidentally knocked under there – kicked, for example – you would expect it to have picked up some dust, or at least left a trace where it skidded across the floorboards. It's a very dusty room.'

Why do CSI managers always talk in riddles? 'Are you suggesting it was deliberately placed under the bed?' Silas asks.

'After the user had used it to comb their hair excessively hard.'

'To ensure there were enough hairs with roots attached?'

The CSI manager nods.

'Could I possibly have a word?'

Silas looks up to see a tall man, early fifties, standing in the doorway. He can smell the beer on his breath. Drunk *and* posh.

'How did you get up here?' Silas asks the man.

'The stairs?' he offers.

Silas thought an officer had been posted below to keep people away. The last thing he needs is drunks staggering up from the pub.

Strover moves towards the man.

'I'm a journalist, used to be,' the man says. 'Worked with you guys on the Swindon Strangler case.'

Silas is more interested now. Strover senses as much and drops back. The press and police cooperated closely on that case – a rare exercise in mutual benefit. Back then, Silas was a key player in the Major Crime Investigation Team that solved it.

'What's your name?' he asks.

'Luke Lascelles. I live in the village. Got something that may be of interest. About Jemma.'

'Go on.' His name sounds familiar.

'I don't think she's Jemma Huish,' Luke says.

'She's a Russian mole,' another voice calls out from down below. Strover struggles not to laugh. Drunk *and* Irish this time.

Luke turns to remonstrate with the Irishman, who has now appeared at the top of the stairs.

'Can you talk to these two gentlemen in the bar,' Silas says to Strover. 'Find out if they've got anything useful to say.'

Plenty of inebriated locals have provided Silas with useful intel over the years. He just doesn't want to be the one to extract it today. Once they have returned downstairs, escorted by Strover, he turns back to the CSI manager.

'What you're saying is that the hairbrush was meant to be found,' Silas says, for his own clarification.

'That's not my job to say, but yes, I'd conclude that it was deliberately placed under the bed.'

Why would Jemma do that? Why would she want the police to extract her DNA from the brush within hours of refusing a test? Silas puts a call through to his office. 'Get me a search warrant for Tony Masters' house.'

53

'I know it's weird,' Luke says, looking at DC Strover before he turns away, 'but when I first saw Jemma, down at the surgery, I could have sworn I was looking at Freya thirty years ago.'

They are sitting in a quiet corner of the pub, which is empty apart from Sean, who is sulking over a pint at the bar. He'd wanted to be interviewed first, can't understand why, given the Novichok poisoning in Salisbury, his Russian theory isn't being taken more seriously.

'So let me get this straight,' Strover says, glancing at her notepad on the table. 'You think Jemma is your daughter?'

'The likeness was uncanny,' Luke says, frustrated with himself, the emotion in his voice. He's sounding like a guest on *The Jeremy Kyle Show*. He has already explained to Strover how late last night he FaceTimed Freya, an old flame who now lives in India and who once looked like Jemma. They had a child together, but she was given away at birth to a mixed-race couple living in Germany, one of whom practises the Baha'i faith…

Strover stares at him impassively.

'Everyone else says she looks like Jemma Huish,' she says, folding over a sheet of her notepad. She's got small, tidy writing. Everything about her is neat, controlled.

'What's your opinion?' Luke asks.

'I don't have one,' she says. 'Just a boss who wants this sorted.'

Luke feels like he's wasting police time. 'It's not like she's the spitting image of Freya, but...' He pauses. 'You just know when you see someone that they're related. The way they talk. Their posture, gait. Their mien.'

She stares at him. Her silent manner is making him talk more than usual, fill in the gaps. A standard police tactic, no doubt.

'When someone turns up in a village like this, it can be unsettling,' Strover says, wrong-footing him with a more sympathetic tone. 'People project their own theories. Is there anything else apart from her "mien"' – she exaggerates the word in her Bristol accent – 'that might link Jemma to your old girlfriend's daughter?'

'Like hard evidence, you mean?' he asks.

For the first time in their conversation, she smiles at him. 'That would be useful.'

'Jemma's got a tattoo on her wrist – a lotus.' Strover nods. He's got her attention now. 'It's an important flower for Baha'is, a minority religion practised by Freya's... our daughter's adoptive mother.'

Strover makes a note, he assumes about the tattoo. Her writing is too small to be read upside down. Another police trick.

'I know how it must sound,' Luke continues, fiddling with a beermat. 'But if she's not Jemma Huish, then who the hell is she? She has to be someone, must have come here for a reason.'

'I thought the Kremlin sent her,' she says, nodding towards Sean at the bar. Luke laughs drily.

'Will you let me know, when you find her, about her DNA?' he asks, more serious now.

'You know I can't do that.'

'I just mean where she's from in the world. Asia, Africa, North America.'

'How well do you know Tony, the American who runs the café?' she asks, ignoring his question.

'He's been living in the village for a year or so. Decent bloke, community-minded.' Luke likes Tony – they're quiz pals, village mates – but how well does he know him? Well enough to pop round to his house after he's finished here and tell him that the police have been asking questions.

'Happily married?' she asks.

Luke pauses, looking at Strover. He was never able to do that as a journalist: slip in a personal question without batting an eyelid.

'As far as I know, yes,' he says, remembering what Laura told him on the phone, how Tony had started to behave strangely.

'He cooked Jemma dinner on the second night. At his house. After his wife had gone to London.'

Luke's phone rings, saving him from having to comment any further on the state of Tony and Laura's marriage. 'Do you mind if I take this? It's actually Laura.'

Strover nods. 'We've been trying to speak to her.'

Luke glances up at Strover as he takes the call. Can she hear their conversation? Laura sounds increasingly agitated, talking quickly. She's seen the police news reports and is glad that someone is finally sharing her concerns about Jemma.

'She's on her way back to the village,' Luke says, checking his watch as he hangs up. 'In half an hour. I'm meeting her off the train.'

'Mind if I join you?'

54

The knife is tucked up inside Jemma's right sleeve, the handle gripped firmly in her hand. She was carrying it down by her side until a minute ago, when she thought she heard someone up ahead. It was nothing more than a twig snapping, but it sounded heavier than an animal.

She listens again and then she sees her, diagonally to the right: a woman running through the trees. Jemma watches, transfixed. The woman is like a gazelle, her stride long and light. Soon she's crossing the path that Jemma is on, two hundred yards up ahead. The woman stops, breathing heavily, and looks back down the track. The two of them stare at each other, like reflections. And then she is gone, racing away through the forest.

Jemma turns and heads for the hill she used to climb as a teenager, on nights when the anger could no longer be contained. She is out of breath by the time she reaches the top. More memories come flooding back. Up here, by the solitary, windswept tree, its branches thrown out to one side as if dancing at a rave, she used to rail at the sky. Not today though. Not any more. The village is spread out far beneath her, the valley dissected by the canal and railway line. She can just make out School Road, running down from the pub; the surgery and the train station. And there's the church, surrounded by its graveyard.

Jemma sets off down the hill, breaking into a run.

55

Luke stands outside Tony and Laura's front door, waiting for it to open. It sounds like there are a lot of people inside.

'What's going on?' he asks, following Tony into the sitting room. Two CSIs in white oversuits are coming down the stairs.

'I invited the cops round for tea,' Tony says, tracking the CSIs as they go past them into the hall. 'You know me. Don't slam the door,' he shouts, his voice full of sarcasm. He shakes his head and sits down on the sofa, gesturing for Luke to do the same. Tony is flustered.

'I've just been interviewed by DC Strover,' Luke says.

'Lucky you. I got the fat guy.'

Luke waits until the door has closed – they don't slam it – before he speaks.

'They were asking about Jemma, said you cooked dinner for her last night.'

'So I cooked Jemma dinner. Big frickin' deal. Clam chowder. Mussels, actually. She stayed here the previous night. That's why the cops are upstairs, searching her bed for some DNA to stitch her up with.'

'They wanted to know about Laura too, said she left yesterday to stay with her mum in London.' He looks up as another CSI talks past from the kitchen and heads upstairs.

'She's coming back,' Tony says. 'Just called.'

'She called me too. The police want to meet her off the train.'

'Good luck to them. She doesn't want to meet me, that's for sure.'

Tony stands up and walks over to the bottom of the stairs. 'Careful with those pictures on the landing,' he shouts out. 'They're Picassos.'

He comes back to sit on the sofa, smiling. 'Assholes,' he says, his leg bouncing nervously.

Luke's never seen Tony like this before. He realises how little he does know him. Their village friendship has been forged in the pub, on the cricket pitch, and has its limits. They've never talked about marriage, for example, or love or death. It's the same with Sean. Drinking pals.

He takes a deep breath. 'I got the impression that the police think there might be something going on between you and Jemma.'

Tony laughs. 'Is that what they said?'

Strover hadn't actually used those words, but it had been obvious to Luke that she was implying as much. 'Well, is there?' he asks, charting new waters.

'Of course there isn't. I'm a married man. What's it to you anyway?'

'I was just wondering.'

'Well don't.' Tony says, heading off into the kitchen.

Luke watches him fill the kettle, wipe down the sideboard unnecessarily. He knows why he hasn't asked Tony about such things before. 'Have you seen Jemma recently?' he asks, keen to move things on. 'Everyone seems to be looking for her.'

'Have they sent you?' Tony says, coming to the kitchen doorway. 'Is that it?'

'Of course not,' Luke replies, struggling to understand Tony's behaviour, where he's coming from. Another CSI walks through the kitchen, watched by Tony. Is this all an act for their benefit?

'I've told the cops everything I know,' Tony continues, still in the kitchen. 'I last saw her heading down towards the train station this morning.'

Luke's phone buzzes. It's from Laura:

Got off the train early, want to walk canal path to clear my head. Can we meet? Welcome a chat. Keen to make up with Tony, but he's refusing to see me. ☹ Lx

'I'm sorry,' Tony says, coming back into the sitting room. 'You know how much I love cops.'

Luke doesn't know what to think any more. He just wants to get out of here, meet Laura.

'My dad just texted,' he lies, putting away his phone. 'Their Wi-Fi's playing up. I ought to head over there and sort it.'

56

Laura walks along the towpath, a heron lifting forlornly from the water in front of her to settle further down the canal. She was feeling fine about returning to the village, happy to give a statement to the police and catch up with Susie, who's not been returning her calls, but she lost her nerve one station before the final stop. The police appeal for information about Jemma Huish has given her a certain grim satisfaction, making her own paranoia that first night seem less irrational, but it's been tempered by Tony's worrying behaviour, how protective of Jemma he has become. She can't help feeling that he's connected in some way with her disappearance.

Her phone rings. It's Luke. He texted earlier to say he would come out to find her on the towpath.

'Where are you now?' he asks.

'Near the Blue Pool,' she says. It's somewhere she hopes to visit often one day. A mile out of the village, it's an old millpond where the local kids come to swim and play, swinging off a rope from a high branch and launching themselves into the water. One day.

'I'll be there in a minute,' he says. 'Have you tried Tony again?'

'He won't pick up.' After failing to speak to him, she sent a text asking to meet, but he hasn't replied.

She hangs up and walks on towards the Blue Pool, which she can see up ahead. It's a hazy summer's day, but the canal is not busy except for a couple of fishermen, seated far apart from each other on the opposite bank. There's a place along here where she and Tony first came when they moved to the village. Set back from the towpath, it's meant to be the site of a holy well, although the water has long since dried up. A wishing tree marks the spot, covered in brightly coloured ribbons and trinkets with messages written by people describing their hopes and dreams. She and Tony wished for a child and tied their card to a high branch, away from prying eyes. She wants to see if it's still there, maybe write another one.

She turns off the towpath and heads down through the undergrowth towards the well, following a faint track. Most wishes are made in spring, when there's a steady stream of people coming down here. As she draws near, she hears something up ahead: a woman starting to talk. Her voice is strained, desperate. Laura's never heard such anguish before. She walks closer, treading quietly, holding her breath.

'I really need to speak to the police,' the voice says.

Laura's first instinct is to turn and run, but she's transfixed by the woman's pleading tone.

'I'm scared what I might do, you know?' the voice continues. 'Please... It was hearing my name on the radio that stirred it all up. Why are they suddenly looking for me?' Laura can hardly bring herself to move. 'I need help here. I've tried everything, but nothing's working. I'm telling you, I need fucking help. They want me to kill the first person I see.'

Laura manages to turn around and walk back to the towpath, where she calls Luke. Why isn't she ringing Tony? Up until a few days ago, she would have done – he's her husband, the love of her life – but everything's changed now. And so quickly. She can't trust him any more, which breaks her heart.

'Are you near?' she says, her voice barely a whisper.

'You OK?' Luke asks.

'She's here. By the wishing tree. The well.'

'Who is? I can hardly hear you, Laura.'

She stops talking and looks up. The woman has come down the footpath from the well and is standing ten yards away, a large kitchen knife in her hand.

'Laura?' Luke asks again. 'Are you there? Laura?'

She doesn't want to say or do anything. Her eyes are fixed on the woman, who is standing motionless, staring back at her, pain in her eyes.

'Please come,' she manages to whisper before the phone slips from her hand to the ground.

57

Tony queues at the police roadblock, waiting to leave the village. Window open, he taps impatiently on the roof of his old BMW. It's done 162,000 miles and counting. He hopes they're checking for people rather than for car tax. It's been a while since he's paid any. He's tried ringing Jemma on the cell phone he gave her, but it went straight to voicemail.

She has no idea how close the cops are to arresting her. They will recover more than enough DNA in the bed she slept in. She can't stay in the forest any longer. The cops will widen their search until they find her: officers, sniffer dogs, choppers.

He's next in line to be checked at the roadblock now. Two young cops, looking for a woman who's right under their noses. The car ahead has a roof box, which the jackasses insist on being opened. He watches, happy to see them waste their time.

It was soon after Jemma arrived, after she revealed a knowledge of their house's layout, that he first began to wonder. Was Jemma Huish returning to her childhood home? He'd recognised the name of the village when Laura originally found it during their early house-hunting days, knew he'd read about it somewhere. He dug out his old newspaper cuttings, the ones on amnesiacs, and came across a big bundle of stories about Jemma Huish, her court case and mental condition, the house where she grew up.

Unfortunately, the house wasn't for sale, not yet, but they both loved the village, so they rented a bungalow for a year. Tony made enquiries and was told by the house's elderly owner that he would soon be moving into a retirement home. The house would be theirs when he was ready. Laura liked the place, even if it was smaller than she'd wanted. There was no need to tell her that 'Huish' was on the list of previous owners. In the meantime, the village stores came up for sale and Tony converted it into a café and gallery. They still had enough money left to buy the house, but it conveniently prevented them from purchasing anywhere bigger, as Laura was secretly hoping. Tony couldn't wait to move in, intrigued by the possibility, however slight, that Jemma Huish had once lived there and might one day come back. She hadn't been seen for years, whereabouts unknown.

And she ticked all the right boxes.

Then, a month later, a mysterious woman turns up on their doorstep out of the blue. Tony couldn't believe his luck. Didn't dare. She looks just like Jemma Huish, suffers from amnesia, and is even more beautiful than in the newspaper reports. He suggests her name might be Jemma – with a 'J'. A crude attempt to trigger something, to dispel the fog of forgetfulness. And he encourages her not to give a DNA sample – as soon as the police have a match with Huish, they will take her away. He isn't going to let that happen.

It's his turn at the checkpoint. The cops search the trunk, ask him where he's going (food shopping for the café – he's had a bunch of greedy cops to feed all morning). They wave him through with no grief. Unusual for him. Laura's the only complication. He wishes she was staying at her mom's for longer, but the cops want her to give a statement. She's rung him several times, but he's got no desire to talk to her. Not yet.

He senses something's wrong as soon as he pulls up at the ammunition shelter. It's too quiet, even for this remote corner of the forest. He steps out of the car, checks that no one is around and walks through the brambles to the entrance.

'Jemma? It's me. Tony.'

No answer. She might be sleeping. He walks down the steps and shines his phone inside. Her suitcase is next to one wall, lid still open, clothes spilling out. The roll-mat and sleeping bag are curled up next to it, alongside his radio, which is on quietly. Maybe she's gone out for a walk.

'Jemma?' he calls up the steps, louder this time. 'Jemma? We need to go.'

More silence. He walks back into the shelter and squats down next to the suitcase. Holding a blouse up to his nose, he breathes in her scent as he searches through the rest of the clothes. What's he looking for? He closes the lid and notices two zipped compartments on the outside. The larger one is already open. Sliding his hand in, he finds a leaflet for the Excess Baggage Company. She must have picked it up at Heathrow, when she was looking for her handbag.

He reaches for his cell phone to try Jemma again but stops to listen. Cutting through the silence of the forest is the sound of an approaching car.

58

Silas pulls up next to Tony's old BMW and waits. Strover is sitting next to him. She was meant to be meeting Laura, Tony's wife, off the train, but she was a no-show and is not answering her phone.

'He's got to have heard us coming,' Silas says, staring ahead, hands still gripping the steering wheel. He's never liked this forest, not since he found his son sleeping rough in it once. Where others see peace and tranquillity, he sees only loss and isolation. At least it's not a pine forest. They're the worst: dark, lifeless places.

'Why do you think Tony was lying?' Strover asks.

'Where to begin?' Silas likes the fact that Strover is keen to learn. Flattered too. 'Unnaturally calm, speech too slow, telltale stillness in the body language.'

After the interview in the café, Silas sent out Tony's BMW registration number to all the village checkpoints with instructions to conduct a particularly thorough car search if they saw him – long enough for Silas to be called. In the event, he got a message saying that Tony's car had been spotted waiting to be searched. By the time Tony was making idle chat at the checkpoint, Silas had joined the back of the queue and was waved through at the appropriate moment, following Tony up the hill at a discreet distance. He's convinced that Tony has led them to Jemma. He just hopes to God she's still alive.

'What's his motive?' Strover asks.

'Other than taking sexual advantage of a confused and vulnerable woman, you mean?' He turns to look at Strover, who is calm, focused. 'I don't know yet. It depends on who Jemma turns out to be, doesn't it?'

'Do you think she's Jemma Huish?'

'You're the one who saw her.'

Strover doesn't reply. Silas is still annoyed that Susie blocked him from talking to Jemma. It could have saved a lot of time. They'll just have to wait for the fast-track DNA results on the hairbrush and bedroom samples, due back in a couple of hours. Whatever the findings, Tony has perverted the course of justice by concealing the woman's whereabouts. And he could be holding an individual against her will. His excellent vegan mac-and-cheese balls aside, he's also a deeply irritating individual.

'OK, let's go,' he says to Strover. 'Walk round the back in case he tries it on, but I'm expecting him to come quietly.'

Tony's head appears above the shelter as they push through the brambles. When he sees them approaching, he pauses for a moment and then continues up the steps, both arms held above him. Christ, this isn't Compton, USA. Silas hates the force's increased use of guns, what it's already done to community policing in Britain.

'She's not here,' Tony calls out. 'I thought she was, but she's gone. Left all her stuff.'

It's not what Silas is expecting.

'Did you bring her out here?' he asks as he starts to frisk Tony. It must be catching. The guy's not under arrest, not yet. And Silas doesn't suppose he's carrying a gun, even if he is from New York.

'She ran off from the pub,' Tony says as Strover heads down into the shelter. He's lying again. 'Called me up, asked me to come out here.'

'I didn't know she had a phone.'

'We lent her one of our old ones.'

'That was good of you.'

Tony smirks as Silas sees Strover coming up the steps behind them.

'There's a roll-mat, sleeping bag and a suitcase full of female clothing,' she says, walking over to join them.

'No sign of Jemma?' Silas asks.

She shakes her head. It's enough for Silas. Tony doesn't look the cross-dressing type.

'Tony Masters, I'm arresting you on suspicion of conspiracy to pervert the course of justice by obstructing a police investigation,' he says, trying not to savour the words too much. He nods at Strover, who produces a set of handcuffs and clips them onto Tony's wrists while Silas reads him his rights.

'This is some kind of joke, right?' Tony says as they walk over to the car. 'I mean, what exactly have I done wrong here?'

'How long have you got?' Silas is about to elaborate when his phone rings. It's the force control room. He hangs back to answer as Strover bundles Tony into the car.

'We have an immediate commitment in your area. A white female threatening to kill a woman she's holding at knifepoint. Armed response are on their way. The boss thought you might want to know – she's calling herself Jemma Huish.'

59

Luke can see the Blue Pool up ahead and forces himself to keep running, despite a growing tightness in his chest. He should have gone on more runs with Chloe. He hopes she's OK. After the call from Laura, urging him to come quickly, he dialled 999, explaining that his friend, Laura Masters, had just phoned him from the canal towpath and sounded in trouble. He was worried that he might be wasting police time, but they took his call seriously, explaining that they'd already had reports of an ongoing incident in the area. They wouldn't elaborate, which worried Luke even more, made him run faster.

It's as he gets close to the Blue Pool that he spots two figures away from the towpath to his right, on the way down to the wishing tree. He stops in his tracks, breathing hard. One of the people he recognises at once as Laura, the other looks like Jemma. At first he thinks she is hugging Laura from behind, both arms around her upper body, but then he sees that in one hand she is holding a large knife. It's pressed against Laura's throat.

'Stay back,' Laura says to Luke. 'Don't do anything. It's OK.'

The other woman nods.

Luke is still a hundred yards from them. He wants to call the police again because Laura looks far from OK. But both women are watching him and he daren't do anything that might inflame the situation.

'Shall I phone someone?' he calls out, careful not to mention the police.

'Jemma's already dialled 999,' Laura says.

She's talking more quietly now and Luke can barely hear her from where he's standing. He glances behind him to see if anyone's coming. The towpath is empty. The canal is deserted too. And then he hears the distant sound of a police siren.

He tries again to get a better look at Jemma, but it's hard from this distance and she's partially concealed behind Laura. There's a new wildness about her, as if she's been living rough, not like the quietly spoken woman he met in the pub on the first night. Where has she been? He feels helpless just standing there. He wants to walk up to them both, remove the knife from her grip, but the sight of the blade at Laura's throat checks any impulse to act.

'Stay away, please, Luke,' Laura begs, as if reading his thoughts. 'She'll kill me if you come any closer.'

A moment later, four armed police officers arrive seemingly out of nowhere. Three fan out and take up positions around Laura and Jemma, keeping their distance, a fourth officer runs down towards Luke, dropping to one knee in front of him and raising his gun to his shoulder.

'Get back,' the officer barks at Luke, signalling furiously with his hand.

There's an authority in his voice that Luke finds hard to ignore. He starts to retreat but not before he sees DI Hart arrive on the far side of the towpath. Luke looks again at Jemma, the knife still at Laura's throat, the hope of proving that she is his daughter slipping away with every second.

60

Silas knows at once from Jemma's body language that she's not bluffing. She's locked the other woman from behind in a firm hold and the knife is tucked under her chin. A smear of red suggests she might have already drawn blood – nothing more than a nick, he hopes.

Four authorised firearms officers have arrived already, dispersing around the target. He passed their BMW X5s on the towpath, just down from the train station. They are from Tri-Force Specialist Operations, a collaborative unit made up of police officers from Wiltshire, Gloucestershire, and Avon and Somerset. Silas has never seen these particular officers before. Patrolling the region 24/7 in their armed-response vehicles, AFOs don't have enough firearms work to keep them busy, so they regularly attend routine enquiries if they're in the area, Glock 17 pistols at the ready. So much for gun-free community policing. These four have dipped into the steel gun-boxes in the boots of their BMWs and come down the towpath with their 'long guns': Heckler & Koch MP5s. Their presence now feels way too heavy-handed, an inappropriate show of strength for a woman in a fragile mental state, even if she has got form with a knife.

'Jesus, what a mess,' Silas says under his breath.

The woman being held is Laura, Tony's wife, according to Luke the journalist, who dialled 999 after receiving a distressed call from her. Silas recognises him standing further down the canal, the only other person in the vicinity. One witness and he has to be a bloody journalist. Tony is still in the car up at the train station with Strover, who is briefing uniforms. Silas thought about bringing Tony along, but he's not sure where the American's loyalties would lie if it came to the crunch – with Jemma or with his wife?

'Stay away from me,' the woman with the knife shouts at the AFOs. If only Silas had got here before them.

He walks over to the senior AFO, a sergeant, keeping an eye on Jemma.

'Let me talk to her first,' Silas says. 'DI Hart, force negotiator.'

'She's right on the edge,' the sergeant replies nervously. It must be catching. This is Silas's manor, his case, no place for outsiders. Or inter-force collaboration. Where's the sergeant from? The Somerset bloody Levels? Silas moves towards the two women, trying to concentrate on the scene in front of him, the protocols he must adhere to in a spontaneous firearms incident.

He hasn't got much time. As soon as the call from the control room came through in the forest, he asked to speak to the force incident manager. He and Silas go way back, hence the tipoff about Jemma Huish. The FIM authorised the initial armed deployment, but he won't be running the show for much longer. Tri-Force duty tactical advisors, intelligence liaison and God knows who else will have been contacted already and a tactical firearms commander will soon assume control.

Until then, Silas has a window in which to try and bring this to a peaceful close. It's been too long since his last refresher course as a force negotiator, but no one needs to know that.

'Tell your officers to pull back,' he says to the sergeant.

The sergeant reluctantly signals for his colleagues to retreat. 'My boss will be taking over in five minutes,' he says as Silas approaches Jemma.

Silas and the sergeant's boss go way back too, but they are definitely not old mates.

'And until she does, you let me negotiate,' Silas says, still looking ahead.

It's obvious the sergeant resents having to answer to plainclothes. And Silas knows he shouldn't be blurring the lines between commanders and negotiators, but the situation is dynamic and decisions must be made quickly. No one is better qualified. He is the one who knows about Jemma Huish, saw what she did with a knife twelve years ago. He's not going to let that happen again. That day changed his life, prompted him to move back to Wiltshire, try to be a better cop. A better dad. He glances across at Jemma again. He won't tell her they've met before, in case it starts something no one can stop.

'Keep away,' Jemma shouts, picking up on the tension between the two men. Her voice is frayed with fear.

Silas puts both arms out in front of him, trying to calm her, calm everyone, his eyes locked onto hers. He's transfixed by the sight of the woman he hasn't seen for twelve years. Where was she living before turning up here in the village? Off grid. Uncared for. She looks frightened, terrified, unrecognisable as the person in the news reports, the young woman he saw being led away in handcuffs, sobbing at what she had just done, her best friend lying dead in his blood-soaked arms. The system's let her down. Washed its hands of her. He needs to give her a way out, remove the blame for what she's doing now, holding a knife to an innocent person's throat.

'Where's home?' he asks, glancing at Laura, who looks even more scared. 'Since you were discharged?'

'What's it to you?' Jemma fires back.

'Just curious. You've done well. Model recovery. You don't want to ruin all that.'

She seems to respond to the flattery, her taut face slackening around her mouth. 'You have no idea what it's like,' she says. 'How hard it is. The voices.'

'Oh I don't know.' He pauses, taking a deep breath. 'My son Conor, he was twenty-one last week. Spent his birthday in the Fleming Way multi-storey car park in Swindon. Super-strength skunk didn't agree with him at uni. Now he's homeless. Won't take his meds either.' His close colleagues know about Conor – he's been brought into the station enough times – but it will be news to the AFOs. A gift to the sergeant. 'Why did you come back?' he asks. 'To the village?'

She looks at Silas and then at the AFOs kneeling down behind him, the barrels of their MP5s lowered grudgingly to the ground. By telling them to retreat, he's calmed everyone down, but he's also put Jemma beyond the twenty-five-feet range of a Taser. He glances around. More uniforms have arrived. One of them, a woman, he recognises as the tactical firearms commander, here to take over. Just his luck she's decided to turn up in person. She would normally assume command from the comfort of the control room.

He needs more time. Is Jemma about to act? Listen to the

voices? Repeat what she did twelve years ago to her friend at uni? He must keep her talking.

'I was doing OK until I heard it on the radio,' Jemma says. 'Not great, but doing OK, you know?'

'Heard what?' he asks.

'Why didn't they leave me be? I've come here before. To see Mum.'

Jemma is shaking now, barely able to keep the knife at Laura's throat. She must have listened to his press conference, heard the public appeal for information about her.

'Please don't,' Laura whispers, just loud enough for Silas to hear.

'Guv, my boss is here,' the sergeant says behind him, unable to conceal the urgency in his voice. '"Firearms Silver" has been transferred to her with immediate effect.'

Silas closes his eyes in defeat. Another five minutes and he would have defused the situation. Jemma seems to clock the change in his manner. He hasn't retreated, but he can't disguise the look of resignation, of apology, in his eyes. Laura's noticed the change too. There's nothing more he can do here, for either of the women.

'Please, no,' Laura whimpers as Jemma adjusts the position of the knife at her neck. Silas holds up his own hands again in one last attempt to placate her.

'Guv, I must ask you to step back,' the sergeant repeats, one hand to an earpiece, listening to orders. Silas has been bypassed, not for the first time in his career.

Jemma stares back at Silas. He's never seen such sadness before, not even in Conor's bloodshot eyes. At first he used to pick his son up off the streets himself, bring him home at 2 a.m. But the social workers said it wasn't helping, told Silas to show some tough love.

'I think you'd like Conor,' he says. 'Maybe you could even help him, share your story, tell him how to beat his demons. You've beaten yours, haven't you? I mean, for twelve years you've been OK, done your time, lived your life, no danger to others, to yourself. Weaned yourself off meds, been rehabilitated back into the community. That's pretty impressive, isn't it? You could help others, not just Conor.'

He's beginning to sound like a social worker. At least Jemma's still listening.

'It hasn't always been easy,' Jemma says.

'Of course it hasn't.'

'Sometimes I forget everything. Who I am. Then it all comes back and I remember the things I want to forget.' She pauses. 'Anniversaries are the hardest.'

'Anniversaries?' Her carer was right.

'My mum's death. I always like to be near then, somewhere in the area. This time it was different – when I heard you talking about me on the news. That's when the voices started.'

Christ, she recognises him. After all these years. He stares at her again, thinking back to that fateful day. 'What did the voices say?' he asks, worried what he might have triggered in her.

'Told me to come back into the village.' She looks around her and then stares at him. 'To kill again.'

Silas stares back. He must keep her talking if he's to prevent another death.

'Will you at least meet Conor?' he asks. 'Promise me that?'

'Guv,' the sergeant says again, even greater urgency in his voice.

A smile breaks across Jemma's face. 'I'm not so good with boys.'

'I know you'd like him, see through to the nice lad underneath. My boy, who worked hard at school, had good friends, scored lots of goals – until I walked out on his mother. He never got over that. Never forgave me.'

'Maybe you didn't listen to him,' Jemma says, shifting her footing. She adjusts the grip on the knife, as if bracing herself to strike.

Silas feels a surge of adrenaline run through him. Has he said something wrong? Gone too far? He won't be able to live with himself if she kills again.

A gust of warm air whips down the canal. Jemma looks up at the swaying treetops. Silas looks up too, listening to the plangent sound of the branches bending in the wind, like the roar of a distant sea. What's Jemma hearing?

A moment later, she drops the knife – at the same time as two gunshots ring out through the warm summer air.

Jemma slumps to the ground, felled by the impact of the bullets striking her torso. Her blank eyes stare up at the trees. Laura stands there, stunned, as if waiting for the pain, but she hasn't been hit. The next moment she rushes towards him.

Silas folds Laura into his arms but his eyes are on Jemma's limp body, his thoughts elsewhere, twelve years ago, the different paths that have led them both from south London to a canalside in Wiltshire. She was on the road to recovery, preferring to live in the shadows, away from help, doing it her way. Is this his fault? He launches a nationwide manhunt and tips her over the edge. He closes his eyes. Did he cause this? They didn't have to shoot her. He was winning, talking her around. Finally, someone was listening to her.

Silas peels his arms gently from Laura, who is shaking uncontrollably, and looks around for a female officer. At the same time, the sergeant signals to one of his colleagues, who moves forward, MP5 trained on Jemma's still body, until he reaches the knife. He puts a foot on the blade in the grass.

'She'd dropped it,' Silas says over his shoulder to the sergeant, as he escorts Laura away. 'She'd bloody dropped it.'

61

Luke stands there in silence, trying to understand what he's just witnessed. The armed police officer had ordered him back down the towpath so that he was more than a hundred yards away when the shots were fired, but he still had a clear view of everything that happened. He heard what was said too, enough to know that the woman who turned up in the village three days ago was Jemma Huish.

It's just as Laura feared. And Jemma's been shot dead in front of him, while holding a knife to Laura's throat. He assumes she's dead. Jemma's body is lying in the long grass, off to one side of the towpath, surrounded by police officers and an ambulance crew, one of whom has begun to unfold a blanket. He half expects Jemma to get up and dust herself down as a director shouts 'Cut!'. But there are no cameras, none of the bustle of a film set. Just the afternoon stillness of the canal, the sound of gunfire already a distant memory.

Jemma wasn't his daughter, wasn't a Baha'i from Berlin, wasn't adopted by German parents in India. She was Jemma Huish, a disturbed woman who came home after many years of being away. He feels foolish, embarrassed. What was he thinking? Laura had been right all along. Right to be worried that night when Jemma returned from the pub and one of the kitchen knives was missing. And then, two days later, here on the towpath in the clear light of day, her worst fears were confirmed.

He knows he can't leave the scene. The police will want a statement, not least because he's the only public witness. The journalist in him is already asking if it was necessary to shoot her. He sees Jemma drop to the ground again, hears the shots ring out. DI Hart was talking to her right up until the last moment, seemed to be making progress.

Tears prick his eyes as he walks over to where Laura is being comforted by a female officer. She is still in shock. The officer is about to tell him to stand back when Laura sees him and rushes over, throwing her arms around him.

'It's OK,' he says, her sobs rocking both their bodies. 'You're safe now.'

They stand like that for a minute or two before Luke speaks again. 'I'm so sorry, we should have listened to you.'

Slowly her sobbing starts to ease and then stops altogether.

'You knew from the start, when she first arrived, and none of us believed you,' he continues.

Laura extracts herself from Luke and looks at him, puzzled by his words.

'What did you say?' she whispers.

'We should have listened to you. When you thought it was Jemma Huish. The woman who came to your house.'

'It's not her,' she says, her voice growing stronger.

'Not who?'

'It's not the same woman.'

'How do you mean?'

Luke knows at once what she's saying, but he doesn't dare to believe it.

Laura glances behind her at the body, which is now covered in a red blanket. DI Hart has overheard their conversation and is walking across to them.

'She's not the same Jemma who came to our village,' Laura says, louder now, as if for the detective's benefit. 'Who turned up on our doorstep.'

'How do you know?' Luke asks.

'I'm sorry, I know this is difficult,' Hart says, interrupting her, 'but I'm going to need you to make a full statement. You too,' he adds, turning to Luke.

Luke's happy to oblige, to do anything that might confirm what Laura has just said. He feels guilty for how happy he suddenly feels inside, sick with guilt, given a woman's dead body is still cooling in the summer grass barely twenty feet away from them, but he can't deny the joy in his heart that his daughter might still be alive and well and somewhere nearby.

62

'I'd like you to make an identification,' Silas says, leaning in through the open rear door of his car, where Tony, still handcuffed, is sitting. Strover is outside the car, chatting to a uniform.

Tony doesn't say anything. He stares ahead, sullen, subdued, all his former resistance gone. Silas told him earlier that the incident on the canal path involved Jemma Huish. He must have heard the gunshots.

'I could have talked her out of it, whatever she was doing,' Tony says quietly.

'I tried, believe me,' Silas says. 'She was holding a woman at knifepoint.'

Tony looks up. 'Who was it?'

Silas pauses. He hasn't told Tony everything. 'Your wife.'

'Laura?' Tony seems genuinely surprised, concerned. 'Is she OK?'

'She's fine,' Silas says. 'Shocked but unharmed.'

'Can I see her?' Tony asks.

Maybe Silas has got this all wrong. Maybe Tony loves his

wife and wasn't hiding Jemma. 'She's with the medics right now,' he says. 'And then she's got to give a statement.'

'What do you want from me?'

Silas gestures for Tony to get out of the car. 'We can't be certain who was holding your wife at knifepoint,' he says, taking Tony by one arm. 'As you know, we think it was Jemma Huish.'

'Is she dead?' Tony looks around at the busy scene. A police helicopter passes low overheard.

Silas nods. 'We just need to establish if she's the same woman who arrived in the village three days ago.'

Silas could ask Strover, but she only interviewed Jemma briefly at the surgery. He needs more certainty. Laura is too distraught, although he overheard her saying it wasn't the same woman. He also wants to observe Tony's reaction.

Five minutes later, Silas is standing with Tony on the towpath, looking down on the unmistakeable contours of a body beneath a medic's red blanket. He has attended plenty of formal IDs in his time, but it never gets any easier. Perhaps it's because one day he expects to see Conor's face staring back up at him. He bends down, shutting the thought away, and lifts the blanket from the woman's face.

'That's not her,' Tony says at once. Is there a hint of relief in his voice? They both look down at the body.

'Not who?' Silas asks, his eyes drawn to Jemma's, cast sideways in an abject look of shock. Someone could at least have closed them. He covers her face up again.

'The woman who came to my house three days ago.'

'She told us that she was Jemma Huish,' Silas says, walking back towards his car with Tony. 'When she dialled 999. Warned us that she wanted to kill someone. Like she did twelve years ago. This time we believed her. She certainly looks like the file photos we have of Ms Huish.'

'Then it must be her.'

'So who's the woman who came to the village?'

'Does it really matter any more?' Tony asks. 'After what's happened here?'

The American might be right. She was technically only a threat to the public while everyone thought she was Jemma Huish. Social services will pick up the case again if she reappears. The shooting will now become everyone's main priority. There will be a long and time-consuming investigation by the Independent Office for Police Conduct. The role of Tri-Force Specialist Operations will also be queried amid more talk of budget cuts and the lack of interdepartmental communication.

In particular, questions will be asked about his own initial decision to order the AFOs to retreat out of Taser range, but he knows that the order to shoot was given too quickly. She dropped the knife before the shots were fired. That's how he remembers it anyway. No doubt pressure will be brought to bear on him to recall the sequence of events differently – in return for overlooking his decision to pull back the AFOs – but he won't play the game. He never does. No wonder he's still only a DI.

'Everyone thought she was Jemma Huish,' Tony says.

'Did you?'

'I didn't know who she was.' He's lying again. Silas is also starting to doubt Tony's insouciant attitude to the other Jemma. He invited her around for dinner when his wife was in London, which was beyond the call of neighbourly duty. This is a woman he cared about. And he's sure there was relief in his voice when he first saw the dead body.

'So where is she now?' Silas asks. 'The other Jemma?'

'As I said, I don't know. She disappeared and then she called me from the forest.'

'Were you hiding her?' Silas asks, increasingly certain that Tony is lying.

'No.'

'But you did advise her not to take a DNA test?'

'She was worried about being mistaken for Jemma Huish. Frickin' good call in the circumstances, I'd say.' Tony glances back in the direction of the dead body. 'Am I still under arrest?'

Silas hasn't had time to consider Tony's situation. All he knows is that his relationship with the other Jemma, if that's really her name, is troubling him more and more. She's a vulnerable single woman suffering from amnesia. Did Tony take advantage of her? It seems unlikely that she could have set up home in the woods on her own, given Susie's assessment of her fragile mental state.

They are now at his car, where a uniform is still chatting with Strover, no doubt discussing her boss's failure to defuse the situation, his poor career prospects, whether she should jump ship.

'DC Strover, take Tony Masters back to the station and interview him,' Silas says, tossing her the keys to his car. He will need to be on site for several more hours and can get a lift back later. They've got less than twenty-four hours to charge Tony, which now seems unlikely, but there's something about the American that won't go away. 'And get forensics to search his house again – properly this time.'

63

'Funny thing is, I never felt I was going to die,' Laura says, sitting with Luke on a bench on the towpath. They are up near the train station, waiting to be interviewed by the police. A female officer is standing at a distance, keeping a kind eye on her.

Laura knows she is still in shock, speaking too fast. 'Of course it was terrifying,' she says to Luke. 'Jemma told me quite clearly that someone was ordering her to kill me, but she also said that she would listen to the treetops instead. We just had to wait for the wind to blow, to drown out the voices in her head. I believed her. I think the detective did too. The one who was talking to her, who wants to talk to us. And then the wind did blow, ruffling the leaves high up above us. I've never heard such a beautiful sound in all my life.'

She stops talking and the tears come, hot and burning. Luke puts his arm around her and she rests her head on his shoulder. The female officer approaches.

'Are you OK, madam?' she asks.

Laura looks up and nods, wiping the tears away. 'Thank you,' she says, trying to be strong.

She's grateful Luke is with her. It should be Tony, but they've just seen him being driven away in handcuffs. There was no time to talk and she's not sure what they would have said. She shakes her head, watching a mother duck and her ducklings on the canal. Above them, a red kite soars and circles on the summer currents.

Four days ago, life was so simple. The yoga classes were going well, she was optimistic about her chances of getting pregnant, her marriage seemed good. How things change. Out of the blue a stranger turns up on her doorstep and they argue like never before. Tony just didn't seem to care what she thought; her worries about the new woman in their house. And now this. She puts a hand to her neck, thinking again about the cold blade that was pressed against her throat, the firecrack of the police guns, the way Jemma's grip loosened, her body falling away. She shivers, closing her eyes.

'You're safe now,' Luke says, putting an arm around her again.

'Am I?' she asks, sighing. 'She's still out there, Luke.'

'I'm sure the police are looking for her.'

She turns to watch another police car pull up in the station car park, joining a row of others. 'How long will they hold Tony for?' she asks.

'Normally they have twenty-four hours to charge someone. It depends what he's been arrested for.'

Laura shakes her head, thinking of Tony, the empty look she gave him just now as he was being led away. How can love disappear so quickly? Maybe it doesn't and just gets transferred elsewhere. Redistributed.

'Do you think he was hiding her?' she asks.

'Why would Tony do that?'

She doesn't know the answer herself, not yet, why her loving husband placed a stranger's needs above his wife's. 'You saw her. A beautiful woman.' The tears come again.

'And it definitely wasn't her?' Luke asks. 'Just now.'

'Absolutely not.' It would have been so much simpler if it had been. If the woman who knocked on their door had been Jemma Huish and was now lying dead by the canal. But she's alive and out there somewhere, circling her husband like the red kite above them.

64

I don't know if I've made a mistake by hitchhiking, but my options are very limited without any money. I must keep moving, get myself away from the woods. Away from the police. It terrifies me that I've been mistaken for Jemma Huish. Why didn't I see that coming? Why didn't I guess that Tony is living in her village, in her old house?

He must have thought I was Jemma Huish from the moment I turned up on his doorstep. She's just his type: short dark hair, suffering from amnesia. It explains why he called me 'Jemma', the radio, why he made sure I had one in the loft and in the forest. Apparently Jemma Huish could never be without one if she was on her own. I hope I've done enough to convince the police that I'm not her. They will find the hairbrush soon enough, test it for DNA. I just pray that Tony won't give up on me now. I'll call him from Heathrow.

The guy driving seems sweet enough. He's called Mungo, on his way up from Falmouth, where he's been DJing, and has to be back in London for college tomorrow. That's if his battered old Golf lasts the distance. The other problem is that motorways make him nervous and I'm beginning to feel sick on the smaller roads. I can't complain, though. He's agreed to drop me off at Terminal 5, which is so nice of him, particularly as I'm not sure he's bought my story. And he's playing a top line in funk music. Takes me back.

'I don't get it,' Mungo says, glancing across at me. He's got a shaved head and a beautiful smile. Twenty-one, maybe a bit younger. 'You say you weren't on a bender, but you couldn't remember a thing about the previous three days. Come on, you must have taken something. And I'd like to know what it was.'

'Honestly,' I say, 'I didn't take anything.'

'Maybe your drink was spiked? On the plane?'

An image of Fleur comes and goes. Carefree, happy, dancing at the bar, Long Island Iced Tea in one hand, mine in the other.

'No chance.'

He glances across at me, but I stare ahead, determined to keep the tears at bay. We both fall quiet.

'What was the last thing you could remember, then?' he says, relentlessly cheery, nodding to the music.

'Arriving at Heathrow Terminal 5 from Germany.'

'And that's where you lost everything,' he says, glancing at me. I wish he'd keep his eyes on the road. 'Passport, bank cards, the lot.'

'All gone.'

'Nuts.' Another glance at me, his hands tapping to Sly Stone on the steering wheel. 'Did you ring the police?'

'What would I have said? I didn't know my name, so how could I report it?'

'Mental. And you're sure your name is Maddie?'

Maddie.

I do a double-take. I told Mungo my real name as soon as I got into his car, but it still feels strange after three days of being called Jemma.

'I'm sure,' I say, smiling properly for the first time in a while. I have already explained how I turned up at the village using a train ticket I found in my pocket and how a kind couple looked after me. I didn't tell him why I left, that I feared I was about to be mistaken for a psychotic murderer called Jemma Huish. Instead, I told him a lie, that I woke up this morning feeling different, memory restored after three days of amnesia, and decided it was better for everyone if I just slipped away, much like I had arrived.

If only it was that simple.

Mungo shakes his head. 'And they've definitely got your handbag? With everything in it?'

'Absolutely,' I say, telling another lie, smaller this time. 'I rang the lost property office at Heathrow this morning, as soon as I recalled my name. Seems like it was handed in a few minutes after it disappeared from my trolley in Arrivals. Takes a while to be processed.'

'Don't expect to find any cash. OK if I listen to the news?' he asks.

'Fine by me.'

'There's been a big police shooting.'

My whole body tenses. 'Where?'

'Somewhere near here, I think.'

65

'Why don't you stay round my place tonight?' Susie Patterson asks, resting a hand on Laura's arm. They are sitting on the sofa in Laura's sitting room. DI Hart had insisted on her being checked over by a doctor and Laura was pleased – and surprised – that it was Susie. She hadn't been replying to her texts or calls.

'What exactly have they been looking for?' Susie asks quietly, nodding towards the kitchen.

'Tony might have been hiding her,' Laura says. It had been a shock to discover a team of forensics in the house, but most of them have gone now. Only one, a woman, is still there, sitting at the kitchen table with Tony's laptop, and she's about to leave.

'At least, that's what the detective said,' Laura says. 'He kept asking me if I thought Jemma was "Tony's type".'

'Are they still looking for her?'

Laura nods. 'They think she could be in danger. I'm not sure why they care, to be honest.'

'Because she's unwell,' Susie says. 'Not herself. Possibly in a fugue state.'

'She can rot in hell for all I care.' Laura is struggling to hold back the tears.

'If you want me to prescribe you something, to help you sleep tonight—'

'I'm OK,' she says, in between sobs. 'Thanks for being here.'

'Don't be silly.'

'I was beginning to wonder where your loyalties lay.'

'I had a duty of care to her as a patient. That's all. I should never have texted you that first night. Particularly as I was wrong about her.'

If she isn't Jemma Huish, who is she, and why did she target her house? Her marriage? That's what worries Laura. And where is she now? 'You should have seen Tony, the way he behaved around her,' Laura says. 'He apparently cooked dinner for her while I was up in London. In our fucking house.'

'I'm sure he was just trying to be helpful,' Susie says, without much conviction.

Laura laughs drily as the CSI walks through from the kitchen. 'All done,' she says.

Laura gets up to open the door but feels dizzy and hesitates.

'I'll let myself out, don't worry,' the CSI says, smiling. 'Are you OK?'

'She's fine,' Susie interrupts, helping Laura to sit down again.

'I've seen it in him before,' Laura says, once the CSI has closed the front door behind her.

'Seen what?'

'There was something about Jemma that fascinated him. Her condition, the whole amnesia thing. You know how much he worries about Alzheimer's, losing his own memory.'

'Because of his dad?'

Laura nods.

'He came to see me in the surgery about it once, wanted to know the early signs,' Susie says. 'Knew more about it than I did.'

'Do you want another tea?' Laura asks, getting up slowly.

'Thanks,' Susie says, watching her. 'You OK?'

'I'm fine.'

Laura puts the kettle on in the kitchen, slips peppermint teabags into two mugs and stirs a spoonful of honey into hers. She never has honey.

'I don't think it was a coincidence that we ended up buying this place,' she calls out to Susie, looking around the kitchen. The knife-block is on the sideboard, her iPad on its stand. 'The house where Jemma Huish grew up.'

Tony would hate to see it now. CSI have tried and failed to put everything back in exactly the right place. A part of her wants to pull the house to pieces, rip out all the books, throw the cushions on the floor.

'How do you mean?' Susie says from the sitting room.

'Tony decided to call her "Jemma" long before we came to see you. It was just after she turned up at our door. Jemma with a "J". Why that name? He told me later that Huish wasn't on the list of previous owners – we've got a record of them all in the attic.'

'Did you check it?'

Laura shakes her head, knows she's been a fool. 'Tony did.'

Two minutes later, she is making her way up the wobbly stepladder into the attic, gripping the sides, trying to control her dizziness. Susie said she would climb up instead, but Laura knows what she's looking for. She crawls into the narrow space and looks around at all Tony's boxes. She pulls out a photo at random: her smiling at the camera, love in her eyes, soon after they moved to the village. Were they happy? She's sure they were. CSI were up here earlier, looking for traces of Jemma's DNA. They suspect this is where he kept her. Could he really have done that? Her Tony?

'You alright up there?' Susie calls from below.

'I'm fine,' she says. Wiping away a tear, she crawls across the wooden floor to a box below the eaves and opens it. She glances at the latest property deeds – her name and Tony's, their first married home – and digs around for the list of owners. It takes her a split second to find 'Huish', four down from the top. Tony lied to her. He thought she was Jemma Huish from the moment she turned up at their door and chose to do nothing about it, even when his own wife was too terrified to sleep in the same house. It doesn't make any sense.

And then she sees another box, wedged under the water tank. She crawls over and opens it, leafs through a series of old newspaper articles. They are all about Jemma Huish, her amnesia, the Wiltshire village where she lived, the day she killed her best friend. And each one is covered in Tony's handwritten notes.

'Maybe I will stay at yours tonight,' she says, calling out to Susie below.

66

'Could we pull over?' I ask.

'Are you OK?' Mungo turns to look at me. It's 3 p.m. and we're still an hour from Heathrow.

'Feel a bit sick actually.' I can't believe what I've just heard on the radio.

'My driving, sorry. Makes my girlfriend throw up too.'

'It's not your driving.'

He stops in a lay-by and I step out into the fresh air. Mungo gets out too and comes round to stand beside me. He leans against the car, looking across the fields as he rolls a cigarette. A police car drives past, lights on, siren sounding.

'Heavy stuff, that shooting,' he says, watching the police car as it disappears around the corner.

'Terrible,' I whisper.

'Not exactly a terrorist, was she? You'd have thought they'd have learnt their lesson after the Duggan shooting in London – not that they'd be expecting a riot around here.'

There's a gap in the traffic and the surrounding countryside feels more silent than ever.

'I think I might have seen her,' I say.

'The one who was shot?'

I take a drag of his cigarette. I haven't smoked for years and it catches at the back of my throat. 'Jemma Huish. She was in the woods, running. We stopped and looked at each other.'

'Shit. Like, shouldn't you tell someone?'

'No point now, is there?' I look at him, envious of his youth. He turns away, drawing heavily on his cigarette. I don't want to involve him in my world, no more than I have to.

'Why was she running?' he asks.

'I don't know. I had no idea who she was, that she was even alive.'

I think back to the moment this morning when I saw a figure in the trees. We stared at each other for a few seconds. She wasn't out jogging and didn't appear to have a dog with her. Two women in a hurry. Was she coming back to her village, like everyone said she would? Rushing back to kill again?

'Here, there's a picture of her,' Mungo says. He looks at his phone and then hands it over apologetically. 'Looks a bit like you actually.'

I stare at the woman in the photo.

'You think so?'

'Maybe not.'

I still can't see any likeness. It's an old image, from the original court case, the same as the one used in the newspaper cuttings in Tony's loft. The story is still breaking, but there's a brief report below the photo, giving details about her past.

'Poor woman,' I say, passing back his phone. 'She must have been unwell.'

'It says she killed someone at uni – twelve years ago,' Mungo says, reading from the story. 'Slit her throat with a kitchen knife. Jesus, maybe they were right to shoot her. They could have used a Taser, I guess.'

I'm not listening. My mind is thinking back to my first night in the village, when I had no idea that Jemma Huish had once lived in Tony's house. I could so easily have been arrested that evening. Laura snatched the knife away from me as if I was a murderer after I came back from the pub. Christ, I could have been shot! Poor Jemma. Poor Laura. I feel sorry for them both. Laura must think she's jinxed. Two Jemmas brandishing knives in front of her.

'Shall we go?' I ask.

'Anything you say, Maddie,' he replies, smiling.

It feels good to be Maddie again. One less lie to tell myself.

I can't remember my own name.

67

Silas sits at a desk in the major incident mobile command vehicle parked up at the train station near the canal. He's writing notes for his post-incident procedure (PIP) statement about what happened while it's still clear in his mind, although he doubts he'll ever forget any of it, particularly the final look of surprise on Jemma Huish's face.

'Fancy a quick chat? To compare notes.'

Silas glances up to see the tactical firearms commander standing in front of the desk.

'I'm alright,' Silas says, returning to his statement.

'Shame you pulled the AFOs out of Taser range,' she says.

'I can live with that.' Silas continues writing. He thinks about saying that it would have been impossible for the Taser's barbs to have attached themselves to either side of Jemma's torso, given the way she was holding Laura in front of her, but he'll save that for his statement.

'Let's see if the IOPC can,' she says, starting to walk off. 'And how they respond when they discover you've not been on a negotiator refresher course for—'

'She'd been clean for twelve years,' Silas calls out after her. Other officers in the van look up.

'And she was holding a knife to a member of the public's throat,' she says. 'Last time that happened, she severed the person's carotid arteries. Not sure I could live with that.'

Silas hasn't got the energy to argue right now. Or the inclination to confer with other officers, which is now strictly forbidden. He never has. Jemma Huish rejected a hallucinatory command to kill Laura, releasing the knife moments before she was shot dead. End of story.

Outside the van, he looks around for a lift back to the station at Gablecross. It's 4 p.m., almost three hours since the shooting, and the area is still busy with forensics taking measurements, marking out the positions of key personnel in the grass, where the relevant MP5s, now unloaded, have also been placed. He's about to approach an officer he recognises, but the man looks away. Is he a pariah already, not someone to be seen with? His phone rings. It's Strover, who's back at Gablecross.

'The lab's just been on,' she says. 'Results are in on the hairbrush.'

'And...?'

'It's not Jemma Huish.'

The news comes as no surprise, given that Laura and Tony have both now given formal statements saying that the woman who was shot was not the same person who turned up in the village with no memory.

'Any idea who she is?' Silas asks, looking around for another lift.

'They've got no record of her, or anything on the database that might be a family match. The hairbrush sample matches the one from her bed at Tony's house and at the pub.'

'Fingerprints?'

'Nothing.'

'A true mystery woman.'

Silas makes no attempt to disguise the irony in his voice. She shouldn't be his problem any more – he's got the IOPC to worry about – but he won't rest until he's found her safe.

'It gets worse,' Strover says, deadpan. 'They match hair samples found in Tony's loft – forensics has just confirmed. Looks like Tony was hiding her there this morning when we were looking for her. He must have taken her out to the forest before the roadblocks went up. They're checking the boot of his Beamer now.'

Silas closes his eyes. It's the last thing he needs after the shooting. Was Tony holding her against her will? And if he was, what's he done with her?

'We're running a trace on the phone Tony gave her,' she continues.

'We haven't got the resources right now to search the forest. Not with what's kicked off over here,' Silas says, looking around the busy canal scene. 'Tell the lab we're sending over Jemma Huish's DNA for fast-track confirmation.' He pauses. 'And, Strover?'

'Yes, sir?'

'Couldn't come and pick me up, could you?'

68

Mungo pulls up at the departures drop-off area of Heathrow Terminal 5. Two armed police officers glance across at us, eyeing the old Golf with suspicion. Mungo must get a lot of that.

'It's free here,' he says to me. 'They charge you everywhere else.'

'You fly often?' I ask, trying to hide the surprise in my voice.

'Went to Berlin last summer,' he says.

'Berlin?'

'Brilliant city. Saw Jeff Mills from Detroit play Tresor.'

'The Wizard?'

'You know him?' He almost chokes with amazement. Do I really look that old?

'It was a long time ago,' I say.

'My plan is to move out to Berlin when I've finished my studies in London. Only place to be if you want to cut it as a DJ. You know the city, then?'

'I do, yes.' I pause. 'But my memory of it isn't so good.'

'As in you've got bad memories or you can't remember it?'

One of the policemen knocks on the car window, gesturing for Mungo to drive on and saving me from having to answer Mungo's question.

'You better go,' he says. 'Nice knowing you, Maddie.'

'You too. Thanks for the lift.' I give him a peck on the cheek. 'Maybe see you again one of these days.'

'DJ Raman, that's my club name,' he says as I get out of the car.

'I'll look out for it. Sounds Indian. Short for Ramachandran.'

'If you say so.'

I stand and watch as he accelerates away in a puff of black exhaust.

I need to move quickly now. I assume that the police are no longer looking for me in connection with Jemma Huish, but they will have almost certainly discovered that Tony was hiding me in his loft and at the ammunition shelter in the forest. In which case he will be in trouble and there might be concerns for my welfare. I walk past the policeman who knocked on Mungo's car window, trying not to catch his eye. I'll call Tony in a minute.

I take the lift to the arrivals hall on the ground floor. It feels strange to be back at Heathrow again. A lot has happened in the three days since I turned up on a flight from Berlin. So much has gone right, a lot has gone wrong too. I look around and head for the women's loos. Once inside a cubicle, I slip a hand into my bra and retrieve my ticket for the Excess Baggage Company. It's a little crumpled but should still do the trick.

Back outside in the main hall, I walk past a sign for the Lost Property Office where I had visited on my arrival.

'Unless you tell me who you are, I am unable to register your handbag,' the man in the airless office had said, glancing down at the form in front of him. His tone had been routine, just this side of polite. Unsuspecting.

I can't remember my own name.

At the Excess Baggage Company desk, I have to queue for several minutes while a family in front of me deposits a fleet of bulging suitcases. Each one has to be scanned before it can be stored.

And then it's my turn.

I hand over my ticket and wait, glancing around the hall. There's no reason why the police would still be looking for me, not unless they believe I was being held under duress by Tony.

'Here we go,' the member of staff says, passing me my handbag.

'Thanks.'

We both know it's an unusual item of luggage to have left for three days, but he doesn't comment. I take it, check that my passport, phone and bank cards are inside, and head upstairs to Departures, trying to suppress a smile of satisfaction.

I'm back on track with the plan.

69

'I haven't got time for this,' Silas says. He is in an interview room in the custody suite at the back of Gablecross police station. Tony is sitting across the table from him.

'Then let me go,' Tony says. 'I've done nothing wrong.'

Silas glances up at the big clock on the bare wall. It's 5 p.m. He wants to rule out any possibility of there having been an abduction or worse before downgrading the search for the mystery woman. He went to see his boss earlier, keen to voice his concerns about Tony. The shooting is bad enough for the force. The last thing it needs is another major incident. His boss reluctantly agreed, reminding him that he's with Swindon CID now and not the Major Crime Investigation Team.

'You wilfully obstructed a police investigation – perverted the course of justice,' Silas says. 'We have samples of the woman's DNA in your loft, the boot of your car and at the ammunition shelter in the woods. Why were you hiding this woman when you knew we were trying to find her?'

'I was concerned for her safety,' Tony says, quieter now, less bullish.

Progress. Last time Silas talked to him, down at the canal, Tony denied everything. He's not stupid. The mounting forensic evidence is hard to dispute.

'Were you physically attracted to her?' Silas asks.

'What kind of question's that?'

'She's a good-looking woman.' Tony doesn't need to know that he's only seen Jemma from a distance, in the graveyard. 'And I'm trying to understand why you were protecting her from the police.'

'Isn't that obvious? After what happened at the canal? I thought that sort of gun shit only went down in America. Or so your media's always telling us. She was worried that she would be wrongly arrested as Jemma Huish. So was I. Neither of us had any idea she was at risk of being frickin' gunned down by two trigger-happy cops.'

Silas ignores the rant. It's not up to him to apologise for Tri-Force's armed response. 'And you didn't personally believe that she was Ms Huish?'

'No, I didn't.' Another lie. Tony's body has closed in on itself, the faintest turning of a shoulder.

'So why did you call her Jemma?' Laura, his wife, explained in her interview earlier that the name was Tony's idea.

'Because she looked like one.'

'With a "J"? The less common spelling.'

'An uncommon woman.'

Thirty million search results for 'Gemma'; half as many for 'Jemma'. Silas googled it before the interview.

'She was a bit out of the ordinary, you know?' Tony continues.

'Were you aware that Jemma Huish once lived in your house?'

'I'd no idea. Not until Dr Patterson told us. Can I go now?'

Silas really doesn't like Tony, but he's learnt to put personal prejudices to one side, not let them cloud his judgement. 'What's the hurry?' he asks.

'Like, I have customers wondering why my café is closed.'

'Really? Never knew vegan food was so popular.' It was tasty though, he can't deny it.

'And a wife who wants to see me.'

'She must be very forgiving.'

Tony sits back in his chair. 'I don't have to explain my personal life to anyone except my wife, but for the record there was nothing going on between Jemma and me. OK, so I was intrigued by her mental condition. I happen to take an interest in such things, have done ever since my father died young of Alzheimer's. And I didn't want to see her caught up in the Jemma Huish case. But that's as far as it went.'

His story matches what Laura told Silas of Tony's obsession with memory. 'So she wasn't being kept against her will?'

'Absolutely not.'

'There was a lock on the outside of the loft hatch in your house. She couldn't have got out if she'd wanted to.'

'I gave her a cell phone.'

'And a bucket – that was decent of you. It's what we do in prisons. Slopping out.' Silas doubts the American even knows what the phrase means.

'You're making it sound way worse than it was. And she was only in the loft for a couple of hours, before I took her out to the forest.'

'In your car boot. Not very comfortable. Hogtied, was she? You can see how it looks. That you've hidden her somewhere. Deeper in the woods, perhaps?'

'Of course I frickin' haven't. I've as much idea as you where she is now.'

Both men look up as Strover comes into the room.

'Sorry to interrupt, sir, but we've got a location for Jemma's mobile phone. She's just turned it on.'

'And…?' Silas says. At least she's not dead.

'She's at Heathrow – Terminal 5.'

Tony seems as surprised as Silas. Maybe he knows less about the woman than they thought.

'Get Tony's phone from the duty sergeant,' Silas says. 'Tony here can give her a call. See how she is. And we can all listen.'

70

The Slaughtered Lamb is packed when Luke walks in. He's meant to be having a quiet early-evening pint with Sean, but it takes a while to reach him at the bar. Everyone is talking about the shooting by the canal and Luke, as the sole witness, is the person they all want to discuss it with. He hates to disappoint, but DI Hart has warned him against talking about the incident while it's under investigation. He's had his phone off and told his parents not to answer the door to reporters.

'Sorry I'm late,' he says, standing next to Sean.

'You OK?' his friend asks.

'Better after a pint.'

Luke glances around as Sean beckons the barman. Most of the assembled drinkers are locals, drawn out of their houses by the need to discuss the dreadful events of earlier. Luke fears the village will never be the same again. There are a few media types in too. Broadcasters rather than hacks, drinking in the corner. He will avoid the temptation to go over and chat with them, much as he'd like to.

'I know this doesn't sound so good,' Sean says. Seems like he's had a few already. 'But you know, at least it wasn't the Jemma we all met. The one who came to the pub quiz. She was a fine thing.'

'It was a tragedy, Sean. Whoever it was.'

'Someone said your friend DI Hart was talking her out of it when the cops opened up with their Heckler & Kochs.'

'You know I can't say anything. And I'm not sure DI Hart's my friend.'

He's got Luke's respect, though. The detective was still negotiating right up until the end. Luke wishes he could tell Sean more. He needs to talk to someone. An image of the detective's outstretched hands comes and goes. Luke gave a detailed witness statement earlier, which was a useful start, and he'll take up the offer of a session with a police counsellor. Talking to a professional helped when his wife died, allowed him to make her sudden death less surreal. He still can't believe what he saw today.

'Any news on Tony?' Sean asks.

'They've got until tomorrow lunchtime to charge him,' Luke replies, grateful for the change of subject. 'Depends what he says. You know Tony, how much he loves the police. If he manages to behave, they might release him without charge.'

Luke now knows that Tony hid the woman in his loft, the woman who could be his daughter. Everyone in the village knows. The hideaway in the woods is also common knowledge, after a dog walker saw Tony being arrested beside an old ammunition dump. Nothing goes unnoticed around here. But the emerging consensus is that the mystery woman had every reason to be concerned for her own safety, given the police's eagerness to track down Jemma Huish. What's less clear is why Tony took it upon himself personally to protect her.

'People are saying their marriage is over,' Sean says. Luke's inclined to agree, after his last awkward meeting with Tony at his house. 'Did you know that Laura legged it up to London?' Sean continues. 'They'd rowed about Jemma, apparently.'

'And she came back down to patch things up with him.'

Luke dislikes the thought of Laura being the subject of so much village gossip. Or that Tony has no desire to see her. Luke's been trying to ring her, ask if he can help in any way.

'So have you been in touch with your old flame Freya again?' Sean asks.

'Not since we FaceTimed in the park. Why?'

'I've been thinking,' Sean says, more serious than Luke's heard him for a while. 'If I was adopted and I'd been having a tough time in life, you know, a bit of a cultural-identity crisis, I might want to get back to my biological roots. She was suffering from amnesia, didn't know who she was. Maybe her subconscious was kicking in and that's what drove her here.'

'But how would she know who I was? Where to find me?' Luke's grateful for his friend's support. Up until now, Sean has been more interested in his own crazy Russian theories.

'You tracked down Freya easily enough. The internet's made the world a smaller place. Maybe she knew where her old man lived, but that was as far as it went. She just had to get herself here, to the village, in the hope that you would recognise her.'

'Which I did,' Luke says. Where's Sean heading with this?

'Exactly.' He pauses, drinking deeply from his pint. 'On the other hand, her sudden disappearance from the village bears all the hallmarks of a textbook Kremlin exfiltration.'

'Jesus, Sean.' He knew it was too good to last.

'The way she seduced Tony to get out of the village – typical "swallow" behaviour.'

'"Swallow"?' He mustn't encourage Sean, but it's an intriguing thought. Not the Russian stuff, but the use of seduction for a different end.

'It's what the Russians call a female operative who uses her sexual charm to manipulate the enemy. If you or I did that, we'd be known as ravens. My guess is she's being debriefed over blinis in Moscow Centre as we speak.'

'Come on, Tony's hardly the enemy.'

'He's American, Luke. The Cold War's back, remember?'

Before Luke can reply, his phone buzzes. He pulls it out, in case his parents are trying to contact him, and opens up Facebook Messenger.

Hi Luke, please call me urgently.

It's from Freya Lal.

71

Tony dials the number of Laura's old cell phone and waits, watched by Strover and Hart. God how he hates cops.

'Place the phone on the table and switch it to speaker,' Hart says.

Tony does what he's told. He wants to get out of this lousy interview room as soon as he can. He also wants to know why 'Jemma' is now at Heathrow. He's been through every emotion today. Sadness when he heard that Jemma Huish had been gunned down at the canal; joy when he discovered that it wasn't the woman who'd turned up on his doorstep.

'Hello?' she answers.

It's so damn good to hear her voice again. 'It's Tony. Are you OK?'

'I'm fine,' Jemma says. 'I was about to call you.'

Hart told him not to reveal that they know she's at Heathrow. Tony's not sure why. Either the cops don't have permission to track her phone or they hope to establish more by asking questions they already know the answers to. Oldest cop trick in the book. Hart nods at him.

'Where are you now?' Tony asks.

'Heathrow. I'm sorry, had to run. I was worried about the police.'

Tony glances up at Hart, who holds a finger to his lips. He's not a child, but it works. Tony was about to tell 'Jemma' that the cops are listening.

'Have you heard what happened?' she continues.

'At the canal?' Too right he heard. He'll never forget the sickening feeling in his stomach when the shots rang out.

'Poor woman,' she says.

'I thought it was you.' Tony throws another look at Hart, whose eyes narrow. If he plays this carefully, she can help him get out of here without being charged. 'Now you understand why I was trying to protect you,' he says, still looking at Hart.

'I know.' She pauses. Come on. Just say the words. 'Thank you for all you did,' she continues. 'You know, for hiding me, getting me out of the village in time.'

Good girl.

'I'm not sure what I'd have done without you,' she adds.

Tony's unable to resist a look of triumph. Surely that must be enough.

'What are you doing at Heathrow?' he asks.

'After you left me at the ammunition dump, I went for a walk. Not far, just down the lane. It was there that it suddenly came back to me, who I am.'

'Everything?'

'Just my name.'

Tony closes his eyes, trying to conceal his relief. He has come to terms with the fact that she's not Jemma Huish, that she wasn't returning to her childhood home, but it would be too much to bear if she was no longer amnesic.

'Enough for me to come here and ask at Lost Property. Seems like my bag was handed in the day I lost it.'

'And everything was still in it?'

'Passport, bank cards, phone, even some cash. When I gave the man my name but couldn't produce any ID, he called his supervisor, who checked me against the photo in my passport and handed it all back.'

'That's great.' Tony knows what everyone in the room is waiting for him to ask. 'And what is your real name?'

There's a pause. 'Maddie. I'm called Maddie.'

'Not Jemma then.'

'Not Jemma.' Another pause. 'Did you really think I was her? Jemma Huish?'

Tony wants to be honest with her, but he can't. Not here. He's told the cops a different story and the last thing he needs is for them to get interested in him again.

'I just thought you looked like a Jemma.'

'With a "J".'

'With a "J",' he repeats, allowing himself a small laugh.

'Tony? Are you on your own now?' she asks.

If only. Her tone is different, more intimate. Does she suspect he's with the cops? Know that he's been arrested? She must mean is Laura is with him. He glances around the interview room. The two cops are still watching him, Hart's arms folded across his spreading stomach. 'It's just me,' he says, more quietly now. 'Why?'

'I'd like to see you again.'

'I'd like that too.' Screw the cops. They can't stop him. He's in the clear now anyway. No one listening can believe that she was being kept by him against her will.

'I've been reading my notes,' she continues, 'about all you've done for me, the dinner we had together. And I can still remember today at the shelter, in the woods.'

'Maybe I was a little forward.' Jesus, he'd wanted her badly this morning. He adjusts his position on the chair, aroused at the thought. He wants to see her again now, savour her amnesia, the synaptic imbalance that exists between them. Own her mind. Her memories.

'And maybe I was a little shy.' She pauses. 'The thing is, I've been through all my contacts on my phone. I don't recognise any of the names.'

Hart leans forward with a piece of paper. Tony has almost forgotten the detective's there. On the paper, it says: 'Ask if there are any family numbers on the phone – Mum, Dad, etc.'

'Perhaps you've got some family contacts on there,' Tony duly says. 'Mom? Dad?'

'I've been through them all. Nothing.' She sounds tearful. 'I've got a name now, but I still don't know who I am.'

Tony knows it would be sensible at this point to suggest to Maddie – he likes the name, he's not fussy – that she call one of the contacts in the phone. Maybe a number she's recently dialled, ask their name, explain to them what's happened, that she's suffering from amnesia. But he doesn't. He wants to see what she says next.

'I was thinking, this might be too much, but... would you consider coming back with me to Berlin?' she asks.

'Berlin?' He is unable to hide his surprise, the shock. He looks up, relieved to see that the cops seem equally wrong-footed by the suggestion.

'To help me sort my life out, find out who I am. I thought I was coming back to Heathrow from a work conference, but it seems my home might be in Berlin. There's a return plane ticket in my bag.'

Berlin?

He can think of nothing better, but he's still under arrest for perverting the course of justice. He glances up at DI Hart, whose face offers no clues. Surely she's said enough for the charges against him to be dropped?

'I'm asking too much, I'm sorry,' Maddie continues. 'I think that's where I must live, that's all. And there's a set of house keys in my bag too.'

'For our house?'

Maddie laughs. 'I still don't know why I came to the village, why I had a train ticket.'

'And knew the layout of our home.'

'I'd forgotten that.'

Tony will never forget. That surge of excitement when she described the layout of their home on that first day, a growing sense that she might be Jemma Huish.

'You must have lived there once,' he says. He doesn't give a damn now. He just needs to get to Berlin with her.

'It's going to be quite disorientating, when I get back,' she continues. 'I'd really appreciate having you there, someone to show me around Berlin.'

What did she just say? There's a commotion of some sort on the line, maybe a person coming into her room. Tony swallows, replaying her words. *Someone to show me around Berlin.* What's she implying? That he knows the place? He's never told anyone about Berlin. No one, not even Laura. It's his secret. City of memories, forbidden fruits. It's been a while since he's been there. Too long. He closes his eyes. Was it just a casual remark, a confused mistake? Or does Maddie know something? He was careful not to betray any knowledge of the city when she told them she'd flown in from a business trip in Berlin. Very careful.

Hart slips Tony another piece of paper: 'Ask her what her surname is.'

Tony has to read it twice, unable to concentrate, too distracted by the thought of Berlin, what she's just said.

'I've got to go,' Maddie says. 'Call me later. I'm staying near the airport tonight.'

Hart gestures for him to ask her, but it's already too late. The line is dead.

72

I look at the phone for a second before putting it away. Tony definitely had company – it sounded like I was on speakerphone. Did I say enough? Lay it on too thickly? I turn down the TV and glance around the room where I'm staying, in a hotel close to Terminal 5. Sitting on the end of the bed, I run through the most likely sequence of events again.

The police find my hairbrush under the bed in the pub, check its DNA and confirm that I'm not Jemma Huish. (Given the subsequent shooting, I left that a bit late.) As part of a village-wide search for me, the police interview Tony and establish that his wife Laura has left for London after a row. Suspicions aroused, they follow him, possibly out to the ammunition dump in the forest, where they find my things. Tony's now in the frame for obstructing a police enquiry.

Should I call the police, explain that I'm OK? I could even find a police station near here, present my passport, tell them I'm fine. The last thing I need is for Tony to be charged. The police were only interested in me because they thought I was Jemma Huish. Now that she's dead, I assume that I'm no longer their concern. But going to the police is too much of a risk.

I google the main number of the village surgery on my phone and call it.

'Can I speak to Dr Patterson, please?'

'Who's calling?'

'Tell her it's Jemma, a patient of hers. I was with her this morning but had to leave.'

I am put on hold and then Dr Patterson comes on the line. I don't like involving her again, but I can see no alternative.

'Jemma?' she asks tentatively.

'I'm sorry for running off this morning,' I say.

'Where are you now?' she asks.

I picture her consulting room and shiver at the memory, the instruments. It was so tough going there, but it was unavoidable. 'I'm at the airport, Heathrow. Long story, but I got my bag back from Lost Property. My real name's Maddie. I just wanted to let you know. And to say thank you. I'm flying to Germany tomorrow.'

'Are you feeling better?' she asks, clearly surprised by my manner.

'I know my own name now, which is a start. And I think I live in Berlin. The rest is still a bit of a blur, to be honest.'

'Will you be able to get help there?' she asks. Dr Patterson is a good woman.

'I hope so.'

'Have you spoken to the police? DI Hart?'

'Not yet.' He was listening when I spoke to Tony, though. And it's important Dr Patterson relays this conversation back to him too. 'I'm so sorry about what happened by the canal.'

'We all are.' Her voice is suddenly full of emotion.

'Thanks – you know, for everything you've done for me. I've been reading my notes this evening.'

'I'm not sure I did much.' She pauses. 'For the record, I did change my mind, I no longer thought you were Jemma Huish, not after we met on the second day.'

'I hope I haven't caused you too many problems. Professionally.'

She laughs sarcastically. 'You shouldn't have disappeared from the surgery like that. The police were looking for you everywhere.'

'That's why I had to run off.' I think again of the looks I got in the surgery waiting room. 'I didn't want to be mistaken for Jemma Huish. Poor woman. I'm really sorry.'

'Look after yourself then.' Dr Patterson's tone has become perfunctory. She's understandably hurt.

I am about to hang up – I've said all that I need to – but I need to ask one more thing. 'Is Laura OK?'

'Laura? She's far from OK actually. After everything that's happened. She's staying with me tonight.'

It's a mistake to have asked. 'Please tell her I'm sorry,' I say.

I hang up, pressing my lips together until they hurt. I hope I said enough, reassured her that I'm OK. Safe. And that I'm not completely heartless. Dr Patterson will contact the police, let them know that I've called. She can then close the case, shift her attention to more needy people. I've wasted enough of her time already.

I'm shattered after the day's events. I'll get something to eat in the hotel restaurant downstairs and turn in early, watch the news again. The shooting has been dominating the headlines all evening. My plan is to stay here until Tony can join me, hopefully tomorrow morning. Then we will fly to Berlin together.

I pray that Laura will one day forgive me. For what I've done and what lies ahead.

73

'One more?' Milo asks, turning to Luke on the sofa.

'Shouldn't you be revising?' Luke asks, regretting the question immediately.

'Fine,' Milo says, walking off to his bedroom.

And it had all been going so well. As part of his ongoing effort to bond more, Luke had watched back-to-back episodes of *This Country*, his son's favourite TV show, a mockumentary set in a Wiltshire village not dissimilar to their own. They'd laughed like drains, eating pizza on their laps. In between episodes, they'd had a more serious chat, talking about the shooting. Milo knew all about it from social media but hadn't realised his dad had been by the canal at the time. Luke spared him the details.

Back in the kitchen, he clears away their plates. He'd taken his eye off Milo while he was with Chloe, let a distance grow between them. Sometimes parenthood feels like a long guilt trip, particularly if there's only one parent. Upstairs, he pops his head round Milo's bedroom door. Milo is at his desk, revising hard. His GCSEs start in a week.

'We'll watch some more tomorrow,' Luke says. Milo smiles briefly back at him. 'Mucklowes look after Mucklowes, eh?' Luke adds, quoting a line from the show.

Another mistake. Milo returns to his work, shaking his head in disbelief.

Luke retreats downstairs and tries Freya's number in India again. This time the number connects. It would be wonderful if Milo could meet his older sister. Some female influence on his life.

'Luke?' Freya asks.

'It's me. Is everything OK?' He glances at his watch: 2 a.m. in the Punjab. She told him to ring at any time. It's good to hear her voice again, makes him feel a little more grounded.

'After we spoke, I made some enquiries,' she begins. 'Not to my parents but to my auntie, who's always been my ally in the family. She was involved in the adoption, handing our daughter over and so forth.' Freya pauses, clearly struggling to contain her emotion. 'Auntie told the couple to get in touch with her if there was ever a problem, or if she wanted to make contact with her biological mother when she was older.'

Luke's struggling too now, thrown by the reference to 'our daughter', anxious to know where Freya is going with this. He switches on the dishwasher and walks down to the French windows, staring out into the dark garden.

'It turns out her adoptive parents got in touch with Auntie ten years back,' Freya continues. 'She'd gone missing. Disappeared. They thought maybe she'd travelled to India – they'd explained a lot to her about her background and whatnot when she turned eighteen. Auntie never told me all this time, didn't want to upset me. She let me know just now when I explained about your call.'

'Is she still missing?' Luke asks.

'It seems so. But what is missing? She's an adult – twenty-nine years old now. Why not? As the police said at the time, she's free to live her life.' Freya pauses. Luke can tell she's trying to put a brave face on Freya's disappearance. 'The parents say it wasn't like her to run off,' she adds quietly. 'Not for so long. She was a good girl, home-loving and all.'

'Did they tell you her name?' Luke asks, glancing up at the ceiling. Milo has started to play loud music.

'No. But Auntie...' She takes a deep breath. 'When she handed our baby over, she asked if they might call her Freya. None of us know if they did.'

Our baby. Luke suddenly feels overwhelmed. It's been a long day.

'Thank you for telling me,' he says.

'I'm not sure it helps. I just wanted you to know. Maybe there's a slim chance she is the same woman who came to your village, if some likeness is there. Is she still with you?'

'She's disappeared.'

He hesitates, looking up at the ceiling again, thinking of Milo. 'Just like our daughter.'

74

'The good news is that the boss is happy we've released Tony Masters,' Silas says, walking back into the Parade Room with Strover after a meeting upstairs. He notices two uniforms discreetly eyeing her up and gives them a stare normally reserved for murderers.

'The bad news—' He sits down at a free desk with Strover.

'Is that you're not happy?' She's getting to know him better. Has even started to call him 'boss'.

'Correct,' he says. 'Far from it.'

Silas hopes Strover hasn't made any plans for the evening. It's going to be another late one. His own date with Susie Patterson tonight bit the dust long ago. He'll call her later. She rang earlier to tell him about a phone call she took from Maddie at Heathrow. Her tone was conciliatory and on impulse Silas made the mistake of asking her out to dinner. He's been in this game long enough not to be booking restaurants.

'I want you to find out everything you can about Tony,' he

says, opening his laptop. Despite what his boss said, he's not going to let Tony drop off the grid that easily.

After listening again to a recording of Tony's phone call with Maddie at Heathrow, Silas had no option but to release him without charge. If Tony did brief her in advance, she deserves an Oscar. Maddie's subsequent call to Susie Patterson seemed to confirm it was the correct decision. Susie said that Maddie sounded better, now that she knew her real name. Hardly a kept woman. But Tony lies. Silas knows it.

He is learning to read the American, understand his poker tells, the pauses. His denial that he knew Jemma Huish had lived in his house as a child is particularly troubling. Laura Masters had already called Silas to tell him she'd found the Huishes on a list of previous owners. Why would Tony deny that? She also found a sheaf of newspaper cuttings on amnesia, including a number of articles about Jemma Huish. And it seems Tony likes to take a photo a day. Strover's been going through his Instagram posts. Rather her than him.

'We need to know more about Maddie too,' he says. 'A surname would be nice.'

'While you were upstairs I got back a list of scanned passports from Border Force at Heathrow.'

'About bloody time.' Silas leans across as Strover angles her own laptop for him to see.

'We've been cross-referencing them with the passenger information lists from all Berlin flights that day,' she says.

'And...?'

'There were only two Maddies who arrived from Berlin, including this one, who appears to be our woman.' She pulls up an image of a passport page.

'"Maddie Thurloe",' Silas says, reading from the screen.

'I ran a quick check on her,' Strover continues. Silas is starting to like those words. They mean Strover's got the bit between her teeth, trawling social media and accessing digital sources he's too late in his career to learn about. 'Daughter of the well-known Irish travel writer James Thurloe,' she adds.

'Had his own TV series in the 1990s,' Silas says. He used to watch it with his dad, who wanted to travel but could never afford it.

'Bit before my time, boss,' Strover says.

'You're not suggesting I'm old, I hope?'

Strover ignores him and starts to read out from her computer. 'According to Wiki, Thurloe drank himself to death ten years ago, shortly after his divorce from Maddie's Indian mother. She renounced her UK citizenship and moved back to live in India after the marriage broke up.'

'And Maddie?'

'She must be a nun. No Facebook, LinkedIn, Instagram.'

'Or just trying not to waste her life.' Silas has refused to embrace social media, personally or professionally, much to the despair of the force's Comms and Engagement team. Some of his colleagues spend more time tweeting than policing.

'The only thing I can find is a travel blog from ten years ago,' Strover says. 'Nothing in it except a title.'

'Which is?'

'"Berlin".' Strover pauses. 'She flew into the city last week on an Emirates flight from Cochin.'

'Kochi.'

Strover glances up at him.

'Cochin's now called Kochi,' Silas says. He went to Kerala once, stayed on a houseboat. One good thing about living and working in Swindon is that it encourages global travel, a desire to get as far away from the town as possible. 'Like Madras is called Chennai?' he continues.

'Still called Chicken Madras at my local takeaway,' Strover says, not looking up. 'Maddie was travelling on an Indian passport with visas, which suggests she's been living in India. I've checked with the Passport Office – she renounced her UK citizenship nine years ago, a year after her mother, and also became an Indian citizen.'

'Not living in Germany then.' She told Susie and Tony that she thought she lived in Berlin. 'We know more about her than she does.'

'I wish we could say the same about Tony.'

Strover's initial search of the Police National Computer revealed nothing. Not like Strover at all. No criminal record, never been the subject of a police enquiry. Just three speeding charges.

'There is one thing,' Strover continues. 'I spoke to a friend in forensics, the digital investigator who looked through Tony's laptop at his house. Seems like there were some hidden files on there.'

'Did he open them?' Silas asks. Vegan porn probably. The joy of ceps.

'There wasn't time, but *she* made a copy of the hard drive.'

Strover throws her boss a look that he ignores. He's all for women doing jobs that were once only done by men, he's just not used to it.

'Now that Tony's been cleared of all charges,' she continues, 'she's meant to delete it.'

'But she hasn't?' Silas asks, raising his eyebrows.

'Not yet. Offered to take a closer look in her own time. The files were deliberately hidden.'

'Let me know what she finds,' Silas says, impressed. Strover is learning fast. A little rule-bending never hurt anyone. 'Are we sure Tony's a British citizen?'

'He took up dual citizenship a year ago, when he married Laura. Hasn't lived in America for twenty years.'

'Where was he living before he met Laura?' Silas asks, looking at scans of the old newspaper articles that Laura found in the attic. They predate their marriage by years.

'Europe, we think. Photographing DJs in France, Germany, Italy. I found a cache of his old website – no contact address.'

Strover's phone starts to vibrate. They both hear the sound, but she doesn't take the call.

'Answer it,' he says.

He watches as she puts the phone to her ear, embarrassed to be taking a call in her boss's presence.

'Thanks,' she says, after listening for a few seconds. She hangs up and turns to Silas. 'Something interesting's just shown up on Tony's computer.'

75

'Where are you?' I ask. Tony has rung me on Laura's old brick phone.

'Swindon,' he says. 'The cops have released me without charge.'

'That's fantastic,' I say, turning down the TV in my hotel room. Another news item about the shooting.

'I'm buying a ticket for the 11 a.m. flight. Can you transfer yours?'

'I'll try.'

I can hear heavy traffic in the background.

'How are you feeling?' he asks. I know it's a loaded question.

'I thought I'd start to remember more...' I hesitate, unable to resist toying with him, his expectations.

'But?'

'Still only my name.'

I can hear a sigh of relief down the phone – or maybe I'm imagining it.

'It's important you don't write any notes tonight,' he says.

'Just leave yourself a message for the morning, explaining that you're going to Berlin because you think you live there, you're currently suffering from amnesia and I'm going to help you sort everything out.'

'Nothing else?'

'Just that.'

I pause, judging how much to protest, looking at an image of Jemma Huish on the TV.

'It's important that we establish the ongoing extent of your amnesia,' he continues. 'See if you can recall more than your name.'

An understandable test, but it's going to make things much harder. 'My notes, they're really important to me,' I begin. 'I don't think I'll manage if—'

'I know. It won't be easy. You've just got to trust me on this one.'

I flick off the TV. And he will have to trust me.

76

Luke looks in on his parents, keen not to chat with them for too long. He might be fifty, but he feels like a teenager returning late from a party when he gets back from the pub and they're still up.

'Milo's awake.' His dad nods at the ceiling. The sound of thumping music is dull but persistent.

'You should tell him to turn it down,' Luke says.

'We just turn up the TV,' his mother says.

Luke glances at the screen. They are watching a documentary about the Flying Scotsman. He's sure they've seen it before. Several times.

Upstairs, Luke stands outside Milo's bedroom, listening to the music. It's been a while since he's recognised anything his son plays, not that Milo would know. He pulls out his phone, opens up the Shazam app and holds his phone towards Milo's door. After a few seconds, the track and artist are displayed. Luke knocks and enters. Milo is at his digital mixing decks, headphones on, dancing with his back to him. Luke flicks the lights off and on to let him know he's there.

'Hey, Dad,' he says, spinning around, lifting one headphone off an ear.

'Nice track,' Luke says, pausing for a necessary second or two. '"Tru Dancing" is definitely O'Flynn's finest tune.'

Milo stares at him. 'My man, Dad,' he says, mock-punching him on the shoulder. He turns down the music. 'Heard more about the shooting – sounds peak.'

'Actually it was pretty bad,' Luke says, welling up.

'You OK?'

'I'm fine.' He nods at the decks. 'Keep it down, hey? They're just below.'

'They love it,' Milo says, taking off his headphones. 'Saw them dancing to Jaydee the other night.'

Luke watches his son, the way he moves so effortlessly to the music, just like his wife did. 'Your mum liked a dance,' he says. He tries to talk about her as much as he can, keep her memory alive, although he knows Milo can't remember much.

'Must have got it from her mum and dad,' Milo says.

Luke leans against the doorway. 'She would have loved to have had a bigger family, you know. Given you a sibling. Maybe a sister – how would that have been?'

'Good way to meet girls.' Milo turns off the decks. 'Think I might get an early one.'

Why do those words always fill Luke with such suspicion? He considers going down to his garden office but realises he's in need of an early night too. First, though, he must make a call. He's not drunk but still feels guilty as he walks into his bedroom and dials DC Strover's office number. Police always have that effect on him. Strover handed him her card after they chatted in the pub and he needs to discuss the woman who might be his daughter.

'It's Luke the journalist, from the village,' he says. Is he slurring his words? He's only had two pints with Sean.

'Late to be calling,' Strover says, her voice more frosty than he remembers.

'Late to be working,' he replies.

'We never stop, haven't you heard?'

'I just needed to talk to you about the other Jemma.'

'She's not called Jemma,' Strover says, pausing. 'Her name's Maddie.'

'Maddie?' he repeats. 'How do you know?'

'I work for Wiltshire Police, Luke. Swindon CID, remember? It's my job to know. That's what we do. How can I help?'

Luke tries to take in the new information, thrown by the name change. Not Freya, then. She could have been given it as a middle name. 'I've been speaking to my old girlfriend in India, the one I told you about in the pub.'

'You still think Maddie might be your daughter?'

Strover likes to cut to the chase. He ignores her question, knowing it will make him too emotional. 'Apparently our daughter went missing a while ago,' he says, 'when she discovered she was adopted.'

'I can't help you, Luke. All we know about this woman is that she's called Maddie.'

'Do you have a surname?'

There's a pause before she replies.

'Maddie Thurloe.'

'How are you spelling that?' It's a good name to search for online. Can't be too many Maddie Thurloes around.

Strover spells it out for him. He always keeps a pad beside his bed, next to a framed photo of his late wife. He turns the frame away to face the wall as he writes.

'Officially we're off the case now,' Strover says. 'Far more important things to be investigating in Wiltshire – like hare coursing. And barn fires.'

Luke hasn't got the measure of her yet, when she's being serious.

'I took a look at your stories on the Swindon Strangler,' she continues. 'You should've joined the force.'

'I'll take that as a compliment. Is Maddie OK?'

'She's fine. Heading back to Berlin.'

'So she wasn't being kept by anyone in the village?' He's careful not to mention Tony by name.

'My boss just needs to know a bit more about her. Seems to have lived an unnaturally quiet life for the past ten years, we think in India. Indian mother, English father – the late travel writer James Thurloe.'

Luke's read one of his books. At least Maddie's parents are mixed race. Whether they lived in Germany thirty years ago and adopted a baby girl from India is another matter.

77

Tony checks the moonlit street either way and lets himself into the house. The place is empty. No sign of Laura. No sign of forensics either. He knows they were here earlier. DI Hart told him. Everything appears to be in its place – except his laptop on the kitchen sideboard, near the knife-block. His heart sinks. He's sure he left it in the garden office.

He walks over and flicks it open, trying not to acknowledge a rising panic. His sole concern is the hidden files. He looks at the metadata for one of them, checks when it was last modified. Not recently, but they could have copied the entire hard drive. It's just a question of how quickly they can open the files. They contain no proof of any wrongdoing – he wouldn't be that stupid. But there is evidence on there of a past life that he'd rather keep hidden.

Frickin' cops. It depends what they were looking for. How much they know. He smacks his hand down on the sideboard, cursing himself for not updating his encryption software. It's well past its sell-by date, been nagging him for months with dumb pop-up reminders in the corner of his screen.

He makes his way upstairs with the laptop, looking in on the spare room where Maddie slept that first night. They will be together again tomorrow. In Berlin. He lies down on her bed and closes his eyes, troubled by what Maddie said on the phone today. *Someone to show me around Berlin.* He's reading too much into her words. Most people have been to Berlin, haven't they? Know their way around? In her case, she just can't remember, needs someone to help her.

And yet… suppose she does know more about him than she's letting on? Even more reason to go with her to Berlin, establish the extent of her knowledge. It's why he asked her not to write any notes tonight. At present she can recall her name, nothing more. What worries him is that it's unlikely to be an isolated neural network that's been reactivated. Time will tell.

He gets up from the bed and walks over to the window. The sodium lights of the train station are burning brightly, casting an orange glow over the deserted platforms. He smiles at the memory of Maddie trying to escape out of the window yesterday morning. She was right to be afraid of the cops, given what happened to Jemma Huish today. Too frickin' right. And he'd been right to protect her, even though it had almost cost him his freedom.

A click downstairs. He turns away from the window and listens. Someone has come into the house through the back door. It must be Laura. Or the cops, back to sniff around again. Maybe they meant to take the laptop with them and forgot? The cops have caused him enough trouble for one day.

He walks over to the doorway and listens, glancing at his laptop on the bedside table. Somebody is coming up the stairs. He retreats into the shadows and waits.

'Thought you'd be staying round at Susie's tonight,' he says as Laura reaches the top step.

'Jesus, Tony,' she says, spinning round.

He stays where he is, half hidden in the darkness of the spare room, keeping his distance.

'They've released you then,' she says, unable to hide her disappointment.

'It would seem so.' He holds out his arms as if to confirm he exists. 'No charges either.'

'I'm not staying.' She walks into their bedroom. 'I've just come to get my things.'

He watches her gather up her washbag and a nightie and walk back out onto the landing. Head down, avoiding eye contact.

'Wait,' he says, grabbing her arm.

'Get off me,' she says, shaking her arm free.

'I owe you an explanation,' he says.

'It's too late for that.' She moves to walk downstairs, but he steps in front of her. When she tries to push past, he grabs her by the arm again, harder this time.

'At least hear me out,' he says quietly, staring into her eyes. He's never seen her frightened of him before.

'You're hurting me.' They are face to face now and he can smell alcohol on her lips. He lets go of her arm. 'There's nothing to say,' she continues. 'I saw Huish's name on the list of owners, Tony.' She nods at the attic hatch above them. 'Found all your articles on her.'

'You shouldn't have gone up there,' he says.

'Jemma did.'

'Her name's Maddie.'

'You called her Jemma when she arrived – Jemma Huish. I can't believe you'd been waiting for her all this time, hoping she'd come home – is that why we bought this fucking place?'

'One reason.' He's struggling to think of another.

She shakes her head in disbelief. 'You're sick, Tony.'

'Intrigued, not sick. Not yet. Give me time. You know how it is with the cerebral cortex. She had an unusual form of amnesia. Dissociative. I was curious.'

'And you put your curiosity before your wife's safety. I can never forgive you for that.'

He watches her go down the stairs, wondering if he'll ever see her again, if he cares. The front door slams, followed by the sound of fading steps in the street. Running steps.

Forgiveness is not something he's ever sought in his life.

78

'What have you got for me?' Silas asks, looking up at the digital forensics investigator who has just walked into the Parade Room. She's wearing noticeably casual clothing and has a laptop tucked under one arm.

'I was just taking a look at the hard drive we copied off Tony Masters' laptop,' she says, glancing nervously at Strover from under a blunt, jet-black fringe.

'It's OK,' Silas says, keen to put her at ease. 'I know the score.'

He pulls up a chair and the three of them look at her laptop, now open on Silas's desk. The Parade Room is empty except for a few uniforms at the far end.

'The files were hidden,' the investigator says.

'Well hidden?'

'Third-party freeware, nothing too clever,' she says, coming alive, 'but deliberately concealed – using the standard functionality of the operating system to make certain files and folders invisible.'

Strover glances at Silas, who nods. He understands all

about invisible files. More confusing is talking to two computer-savvy women. All the digital forensics investigators he's ever worked with have been men. Shy, socially dysfunctional men, not confident women who look you in the eye when they're talking about operating systems and freeware.

'Easy enough to find, but he's also encrypted them using a symmetric-key block cipher, Triple DES,' the investigator continues.

'Triple data encryption algorithm,' Strover says.

'Thank you,' Silas snaps.

'A bit outdated these days,' the investigator says. 'Key length of 168 bits, but with an effective security of only eighty, making it susceptible to chosen-plaintext attacks.'

'She means it's easy to break,' Strover says.

'Relatively easy,' the investigator adds, glancing at Strover.

'And what did you find in the files?' Silas asks, keen to move things on. He reminds himself that his dad used to bang on about the importance of surrounding yourself with good people.

The investigator pulls up an image and adjusts the laptop so Silas has a better view.

'It's a verified petition, filed in a district court in New Mexico twenty years ago, applying to change a name,' the investigator says.

Silas looks closer at the two names on the document: 'Tony Masters', formerly known as 'Tony de Staal'. He's back on safer ground now, what he does best: dealing with real people, establishing motives.

'There's also a copy of the notice published in a local weekly newspaper, giving details of the name change.'

'By state law, he has to publish it twice,' Strover adds. 'And there's an order of the court, signed by a judge, allowing the petitioner to take a new name and accepting his reasons for the change.'

'Which were?'

The investigator turns to Strover.

'It's an unusual surname – de Staal,' Strover says. 'There was a lot of publicity surrounding his father's death – he was one of the youngest people in the States ever to die of Alzheimer's. Tony Masters argued that he might be prejudiced against by the association.'

'Meaning insurers might not give him cover, assume it was hereditary?'

Strover nods at her boss.

'Are we buying that?' he asks.

'The judge did,' Strover says. 'Tony could have had another motive, though. I ran a quick search.' More music to Silas's ears. 'There was a Tony de Staal who was suspended indefinitely from the University of New Mexico School of Medicine a year earlier.'

Strover pulls up a local story from the website of the *Santa Fe New Mexican*, a daily state newspaper. 'They've put every edition up online as far back as 1868,' Strover says. 'All searchable – for a fee.'

'Just keep the receipts.'

Silas reads the story, recognising a young Tony Masters, captioned as 'Tony de Staal', in a photo. He'd been suspended as a first-year medical student for showing disrespect to a cadaver in a dissection class, including taking Polaroid photos of himself holding a brain and later trying to remove a part of it – the hippocampus – from the lab.

'Tony de Staal,' Silas says, mulling over the name.

'It got a bit of coverage at the time,' Strover says. 'But it was twenty years ago, so no social media. Otherwise it would have gone viral.'

'I don't suppose his wife knows.' Silas pauses. 'So he drops out of medical school, changes his name and moves to Europe to become a photographer – swapping corpses for nightclubs.'

'And seahorses.'

Silas remembers the framed pictures in Tony's gallery and glances at the story on the screen again. 'What is the hippocampus when it's at home anyway?'

He watches Strover work her laptop, fast fingers touch-typing. 'It's located in the medial temporal lobe,' she says, half reading out loud, half summarising. 'We've got one each side of the brain and it's often referred to as a "gateway through which new memories must pass" before being stored permanently in other parts of the brain. "Hippocampal damage can result in anterograde amnesia – the inability to form new memories."'

'What our friend Maddie suffers from,' Silas says, unable to stop himself reading ahead.

'Hippocampus derives from the Greek words for "horse" and "sea monster",' Strover continues. '"Part of the brain's limbic system, the hippocampus owes its name to its distinctive curved shape, which represents a seahorse."'

'Call up an image of a seahorse and a human hippocampus,' Silas says.

They both stare at the photograph of the two side by side. They look almost identical.

'Jesus,' Silas whispers.

Alzheimer's, hippocampi, seahorses, amnesia – Silas is missing something here, another connection between Tony and Maddie. 'How long has he traded under the name "Seahorse Photography"?' he asks.

Strover calls up another file on her laptop. 'He used it when he was photographing DJs in Europe,' she says, 'but he seems to have dropped the name when he moved to the UK five years ago and set up shop as a wedding photographer in Surrey.' She scrolls down her screen. 'After that goes bust, a "Seahorse Photography" picture credit starts to show up on various Wiltshire newspaper sites. He recently took some photos of a group of Buddhist monks who visited the village.'

'To pay the bills, I guess,' Silas says. 'Can't be making any money from that vegan food.'

'Thought you liked it, boss?' Strover says, looking up at him.

'I'd been fasting the day before.' Silas gives her a withering look. 'We need to get back into Tony's gallery first thing, take a look at those pictures again. And see what else you can find tonight on Tony de Staal.'

79

'Are you asleep?' Tony asks.

I sit up in bed and look around the room, remembering where I am, who I'm meant to be. My name is Maddie and I'm in a hotel at Heathrow.

'Not yet,' I lie, adjusting the phone, trying to wake up quickly. Is this Tony testing me? If I tell him that I've been asleep, he will expect me to have forgotten everything.

'We need to catch an earlier flight,' he says.

'OK,' I say. He sounds tense. I want to ask him why, but I can't risk it, in case I slip up, recall too much.

'I'll be at the hotel as early as I can tomorrow,' he adds.

I try to think of what he might expect to hear. 'I haven't written any notes – just a message, that we're going to Berlin together.'

'That's good,' he says. 'I'm looking forward to it. Showing you around.'

I close my eyes. 'Me too.' I open them again with a start. Why did he say that?

'And, Maddie...?'

'Yes?' I say, dreading his question. Have I made a mistake?

'Don't go checking out of that room of yours too early.'

80

Luke's slipping into sleep when the text comes through. His phone should be charging on the landing, given that he insists Milo puts his phone out at night. The text is short and cryptic and from his new best friend, DC Strover:

Tony de Staal.

What does she mean? There is only one Tony they both know. The search-junkie in him likes the surname already.

He's spent most of this evening trying in vain to discover more about Maddie Thurloe. He can find plenty on her father, but the man seems to have kept his wife and only daughter out of the media. Certainly nothing on adopting a child from India. Or the Baha'i faith. Just one article about Delhi in which he mentions the Lotus Temple. All he can find is an aborted travel blog in Berlin she started ten years ago. Too much literary expectation, perhaps, for the daughter of a famous travel writer. It's still odd though for someone her age not to have left any kind of digital trail.

He reaches for his laptop and has just started searching for 'Tony de Staal' when he hears music. Milo's still awake. He was meant to be having an early night. Luke listens again. It's only the two of them up here in the old, eighteenth-century part of the house. His parents are in a self-contained ground-floor flat. He walks down the landing to his son's room, pushing aside the Jamaican rainbow drapes now hanging in the doorway. Another eBay purchase.

Milo is fast asleep, his music still playing quietly. He's done well in the circumstances, steered a sensible course through the maze of modern teenage life, but Luke can't help thinking how different Milo would be if his mother were still here. How much happier. He hopes a sister will help. He's getting ahead of himself. He turns off the music and rests a hand on his son's shoulder, leaving it there for a while, envying the stillness of his sleep.

Back in his bedroom, Luke resumes his search for 'Tony de Staal' and comes across an archived story about a medical student in New Mexico. It's on a local newspaper site and an access fee is required. He switches to searching for images, and a photo of a young Tony stares back at him. An extended picture caption reads: 'Tony de Staal, a first-year medical student at the University of New Mexico School of Medicine, was suspended for showing disrespect to a cadaver during a dissection class.'

Luke stares at the image, taken twenty years ago. *For showing disrespect to a cadaver.* Everyone has secrets, but Luke is shocked. It might have been just a student prank, but it's still sick. Does Laura know her husband changed his name? That he has a dodgy past in America? So much for his New York accent. It looks like he's from New Mexico.

Luke glances at his watch, realising how little he knows about the couple. It's almost 1 a.m. Tony's medical background would explain his obsession with Alzheimer's. Why did Strover send him the text? Earlier, she'd asked him to share anything he discovered about Maddie Thurloe. What's the connection? Is Tony with Maddie now? He was released without charge, but no one's seen him back in the village. And Luke's got no desire to go around there, not after their last meeting.

He searches through the contacts on his phone until he finds his old university friend Nathan. There was no reason why their paths should have crossed at Cambridge – Luke studied classics, Nathan medicine – but they were in the same college and rowed together in their first year, since when they've been good if absent friends. Nathan used to help him out with occasional NHS stories in his early days as a journalist, until he moved with his family to America twenty years ago. Like all medics, he's a heroic gossip. He might just know something about Tony de Staal's medical indiscretions, given they made news at the time.

Luke texts him a message, asking first after his family (Luke's an errant godfather to Nathan's eldest son) and then explaining that he's writing a story about medics who post disrespectful cadaver photos on Facebook. Does he happen to know anything about a Tony de Staal from New Mexico? Details of his former misdemeanours twenty years ago, which made headlines at the time, would be particularly appreciated. He signs off by telling him to call him soonest with any news – even if it's the middle of the night.

81

I can't sleep, not after Tony's last call. He suspects something. I get out of bed and walk over to the sideboard, where there is a pill in a plastic bag. The guy outside the nightclub in Berlin called them 'xany bars' when I bought one off him before my flight to Heathrow. That took me back. Two milligrams of alprazolam, a potent, fast-acting benzodiazepine anxiolytic – a tranquilliser, in other words.

I'd put it in my purse and was relieved to find it was still there when I collected my handbag earlier from the Excess Baggage Company. In the old days, Fleur and I used to parachute our pills, grinding them up and wrapping them in a sheet of one-ply tissue paper before chasing them down with vodka. But never Xanax or other benzos. Not with alcohol.

I sit down on the chair, take the pill out of the bag and start to grind it up – tricky with a knife and spoon – until it is eventually a fine powder. I was going to do this in the morning, but it feels better to have got it out the way now. I pray that it will have the desired effect: amnesia, incapacity, compliance.

I glance across at the powder, telling myself that everything will be OK. Maybe I need to practise some yoga now, but I'm too tired. Instead, I close my eyes and think of the bodhi tree in blossom, hoping it will clear my mind of all the deceit.

82

Silas waits until Strover has left for the night before he rings Susie Patterson. He knows it's too late. He promised he'd ring her earlier, but work, as ever, has got in the way. The shooting and now Tony de Staal. He has a feeling about him that he can't let go. The woman, Maddie Thurloe, is harder to read. She has an Indian passport and flew into Germany from south India last week, but she said to Tony that she thinks she might live in Berlin.

'It's me,' Silas says, glancing out the Parade Room window as a patrol car accelerates away from the station yard, lights blazing. He tries to imagine where Susie is. In bed? That would be nice.

'What time is it?' she asks, her voice heavy with sleep.

'It's late – I'm sorry.' He shouldn't have rung her. 'Shall I call back tomorrow?'

'It's fine.' He imagines her sitting up in bed, pushing hair out of her eyes. 'How's your day been?'

'Busy,' he says, spinning a biro on his hand. He does it more when he's trying to quit smoking. 'Sorry about supper.'

'Another time.'

Silas knows he shouldn't bring work into their conversation, but he can't help it. Not tonight. 'What did you make of Maddie?' he asks. 'The mystery woman?'

'I thought you were ringing to wish me goodnight.'

'I was.' Sometimes Silas hates himself with a passion. Or is it his job he doesn't like? How it makes him behave.

'I'm not sure I'm the best person to ask,' Susie says. 'As you know, I thought she was Jemma Huish when she first arrived.'

'Everyone did.'

'Then I changed my mind.'

Tell him about it. She made Silas's life more difficult than it already was, prevented him from interviewing Maddie, but he's forgiven Susie already. It's a weakness of his.

'If you are asking me if she's going to be OK, I would say probably,' Susie continues. 'Her manner on the phone today was quite different, more together.'

'Too together?'

'How do you mean?' she asks, suddenly defensive.

Silas spins his biro again. He needs a cigarette. 'Could she have faked it? Her amnesia?'

It's a longshot but the only explanation that Silas can come up with that might explain Maddie's behaviour.

'I doubt it,' Susie says. 'I saw her in the surgery on that first night, just after she turned up in the village. She cut a tragic figure. I mean, it does sometimes happen – people looking for attention – but she wasn't doing that. I'm almost certain she was suffering from a dissociative fugue.'

Silas has been reading up on fugues since Susie first mentioned the condition, discovered that one of his favourite film characters, Jason Bourne, was based on a real-life nineteenth-century preacher and amnesiac called Ansel Bourne.

'It's just strange, that's all, given Tony's interests,' he says.

'What sort of interests?'

'Memory. Amnesia.'

'He's certainly obsessed with Alzheimer's – came to see me about it once. His father died very young of the disease.'

Silas pauses, weighing up what Susie has said, how much to tell her. 'Tony's going with her to Berlin,' he says. 'Tomorrow.'

'Oh Christ, really? Laura's already in a bad way.'

Silas had forgotten about Laura, the effect this must be having on her, that she's friends with Susie. 'Have you seen her tonight?' he asks.

'She's here, sleeping in the spare room.'

'I think Maddie might be driving this.'

'How do you mean?'

He hasn't shared this theory with anyone else yet, not even Strover. Silas reminds himself how Maddie sounded on the speakerphone. It was definitely Maddie who asked Tony to come away with her to Berlin.

'Why did she knock on his door and not someone else's when she arrived in the village?' he asks. 'Now that we know she's not Jemma Huish.'

'I can't answer that, Silas. All I know is that it's late.' She pauses. 'You know it won't look good for me if it does turn out she was faking it.'

A part of him hopes he's got this all wrong. That Maddie is suffering from a fugue. If he's right, he's not sure how Susie will cope with another professional misdiagnosis. High profile too. The media have already got wind of 'the other Jemma', the woman everyone thought had been shot.

'Can we try for dinner tomorrow?' he asks, keen to change the subject. He has no desire to remind her of the past. Everyone makes mistakes.

'I can't do tomorrow,' she says, her enthusiasm waning. 'Maybe next week.'

'I've quit smoking.'

'You should get some sleep,' she says, hanging up.

Silas nods at the handful of uniforms at he walks out of the Parade Room, trying not to feel resentful. They get enhanced rates of pay for their whole night shift, unlike detectives, who get much less for working late. Clothing allowance has been cut for detectives too. And they wonder why no one wants to join the CID any more.

Five minutes later, Silas is driving out of the car park at Gablecross. He shouldn't have called, shouldn't have mentioned Maddie, implied that Susie might have messed up again.

On impulse, he decides to take a different route back to his flat in Old Town and drives down Fleming Way. He turns into Princes Street and then into Islington Street, past the Crown and County Court building, where he's spent too much of his life. The old police station used to be here, a covered walkway connecting it with the courts. He slows beside the multi-storey car park, looking up at the corrugated structure. Conor is in there somewhere, usually in the lift lobby on the fourth floor, surrounded by the detritus of drugs.

Silas brings his car to a halt in the street below and sits in the darkness, still holding the steering wheel. Should he go up there, remove Conor from that world, tuck him up in bed at home? He failed to save Jemma Huish's life by the canal. If he doesn't do something soon, Conor will be dead too. What can he do? He's removed him from here before, but it never works. Last time a fight broke out as he tried to drag him away. Two uniforms turned up. Not his finest hour.

Wiping his eyes with the back of his hand, he drives off into the Swindon night, glancing up at the car park again, thinking of Jemma Huish's face as the shots rang out. Too many wasted lives.

83

Luke answers the phone after one ring. He's always been a light sleeper, a result of years of being on solo night duty for Milo.

'You did say to call any time,' Nathan says.

Luke turns on the light and glances at his clock radio: 2.30 a.m.

'It's fine,' he says, sitting up in bed, trying to orientate himself. 'No problem.'

'Bitchin' good to hear your voice, buddy,' Nathan says. 'Been way too long.'

Is Luke still asleep? Dreaming? Each time they speak, Nathan sounds less like an English medic and more like a Californian surfer. Or a caricature of one. He's always been a good mimic, could have gone on the stage, but medicine called. Nathan is now a professor of cardiothoracic surgery at Stanford School of Medicine and by far the most successful of all Luke's university friends. They talk family for a couple of minutes – Nathan's wife, also a doctor, recently got made a professor of anaesthesiology; looks like all three of their children will go into medicine too – and then Nathan turns to the subject of Tony de Staal.

'I've put in a call to an old colleague over in Santa Fe,' he says. 'Turns out your friend Tony—'

'He's not my friend.'

'I'm kinda glad you said that – I was beginning to worry for you. By all accounts, this Tony was one sleazefuck of a freshman.'

'What did he do?' Luke asks. 'Apart from trying to walk out the lab with a brain in his back pocket?'

'You know about that?'

'I read an old news story online.' Luke thinks again of the article about Tony being kicked out of medical school. *For showing disrespect to a cadaver.*

'We've got the right guy then. I wanted to check before hitting the phones – my colleague gave me a whole list of people who might know more. It might take some time.'

'Is it a problem?' Luke asks, grateful for his old friend's help. Nathan never did do things by halves. 'Don't go out your way.'

'Hey, I'm intrigued – and I owe you one, remember? Speak later.'

Luke had forgotten. A year ago, he'd arranged for his godson to work for a week on an English newspaper. The experience persuaded him to ditch journalism forever and follow his delighted father into medicine.

DAY FOUR

84

Tony wakes early after a night of fitful rest and dark dreams of Berlin. He's sure he called out in his sleep again, maybe even screamed, but no one was at home to hear him. Laura didn't return again after she'd taken her things, which makes matters simpler now. He dreamt of his old photographic studio (he must remember to take the keys), locked up for five years, empty and unloved. And he dreamt of Maddie, of what must happen to her if she knows anything about his life in Berlin.

It was then that he had screamed, he remembers now. But was it out of guilt for what he has done to others? Or was it fear for what is happening to his atrophying brain? In between nightmares he lay awake, thinking about the files, how much the cops might discover. How quickly. Damn the cops.

His plan is for them to catch the earliest flight they can out of Heathrow. Right now though he needs to sort the café. It's important to give the impression to others – the police – that he might return from Berlin to the village, even though he knows his future now lies in his past. The teenage daughter of the pub landlord sometimes covers for him in the café at weekends. He rang her last night and she's agreed to come in today and run the show. No early-morning TLTs on the station platform, just the basics.

Taking a small overnight bag with him, he heads down the road in the dawn light. Sunrises are good. It's when the sun sets that Tony feels vulnerable. He becomes confused and disorientated. Restless. They call it sundown syndrome, associated with the early to middle stages of Alzheimer's.

The teenager is waiting bleary eyed and barely awake when Tony arrives outside the café. He glances at his watch: 5 a.m. He lets her in and hands over the keys, briefing her about today's specials and to be nice to any passing cops. If people ask where he is, she's to explain that he's gone up to a food show in London.

She looks suspiciously at his suitcase.

'How long are you going for?' she asks, pushing a strand of hair away from her eyes.

'Couple of days,' he says, stepping behind the counter to turn on the coffee machine. 'Sure you're OK for tomorrow?'

'I'll have to close early.'

'That's fine.' He checks the fridge. 'Just keep the place clean.' There's enough baba ganoush and dolma for the Middle Eastern platter to stay on today. He'll miss the café. Maybe he'll open another one in Berlin.

'What about the pictures?' she asks.

He looks up at her. 'What about them?'

'If someone wants to buy one.'

He laughs, glancing over to the photos hanging on the wall. He's never thought through what would happen if someone actually bought one. That would be interesting. 'There's twenty per cent commission on every sale.'

'Really?' she asks, her sleepy eyes brightening.

'Don't get your hopes up.' He pauses at the door to take one last look around the café. He'll get the pictures sent out to Germany, back where they belong. 'Text me if any cops do drop by, will you?'

'Are they likely to?' she asks, suddenly alarmed.

'I was wrongfully arrested yesterday, released last night without charge. You know what they're like,' he adds, winking at her.

85

At 5.30 a.m., Nathan calls Luke again. This time Luke is in a deep sleep and he wonders how long the phone has been ringing before he answers it.

'Turns out your man Tony de Staal had quite a reputation at college,' Nathan says, as if they'd been talking only a couple of minutes ago. 'A lot of people still remember him in Santa Fe.'

'Reputation for what?' Luke asks, hoping to buy some time while he opens his notebook. He's struggling to wake up.

'He was obsessed with the work of a neurosurgeon called William Beecher Scoville – crazy dude from Connecticut who performed lobotomies in the fifties, mainly on asylum patients. It was the era of "psychosurgery" – when parts of the brain tissue were either destroyed or removed in the hope of curing mental disorders.'

'Do they still do that?' Luke asks, writing down 'William Beecher Scoville' in his notebook.

'Banned in most countries. These days it's more about deep brain stimulation. Anyway, this guy Scoville, he liked to, shall we say, experiment. His most famous operation was on an epilepsy sufferer called Henry Molaison – both medial temporal lobes were resected, including the hippocampi.'

'Resected?' Luke asks, fearing the worst.

'Surgically removed. The operation cleared up the epilepsy, but it also wiped the poor man's memory.'

'That's awful,' Luke says, thinking back to what Laura told him of Maddie's amnesia. The void in her head.

'Forming new memories was impossible for Molaison,' Nathan continues. 'He lost most of his old memories too. He lived in a permanent present tense, telling the same stories over and over. Couldn't even remember if he'd just eaten and had to carry a note around in his wallet explaining that his father was dead and his mother was in a nursing home.'

'And you said his name was Henry Molaison?' Luke asks, checking his notebook. His handwriting is bad enough when he's awake.

'Known to all as "H.M.", he became a bit of a celebrity, particularly among cognitive neuropsychologists. After his death, his brain got even more famous. Cut up into 2,400 slices and now on display at the University of California in San Diego. You can even go online and watch the video of it being sliced.'

'Thanks.' It's the last thing Luke wants to do. He's never had a strong stomach.

'Tony de Staal was big into drugs too, benzos mainly. Seems like the authorities tried to be sympathetic at first. His dad died of Alzheimer's ridiculously young, just before Tony's first fall semester – quite a famous case over here. Reading between the lines, I'd say Tony got kicked out of medical school not for disrespecting cadavers but for date rape. Hushed up by the victim's parents, apparently. No one's heard of him for years.'

86

I stare at the ceiling of my room, listening to the sterile sounds of the hotel: the hum of air conditioning, traffic outside. The transience of airports. I've woken early, troubled by the thought of Tony's imminent arrival.

It's 6 a.m. and he'll be here soon. I need to be in control today, but I feel disconcerted by the earlier flight, his desire to test my amnesia by asking me not to write any notes for yesterday. Sitting up in bed, I look at the simple message I wrote to myself on the table. How could I forget that I'm going with Tony to Berlin today?

I've been planning this for weeks.

My phone, the one Tony gave me, buzzes with a text. No explanation, just a brief message that his coach is not far from Heathrow and he hopes to be at the hotel in half an hour. I am about to reply when I check myself. There are no numbers stored on the phone and the text is anonymous. It's obviously from Tony, but is he testing me again? I glance at the simple note he asked me to write to myself last night and text back.

Who is this?

I'm not taking any chances. I need to forget everything again. Wipe the slate clean. *I can't remember my own name.*
He replies straight away:

It's Tony – read the note by your bed. xxx

I shower and dress, wearing new clothes that I bought at the airport yesterday. After looking around the hotel room one last time, I walk out the door with my handbag. Tony didn't want me to check out, but I'm not falling for that one. I'll tell him I've forgotten.

I feel scared as I wait for the lift to reception and wish Fleur was with me. What happens next is not about me but about her. And all the others.

87

Silas walks into the Seahorse Gallery & Café with Strover, surprised that it's open so early. He should be back at Gablecross, dealing with the fallout from yesterday's shooting: writing up his PIP, briefing the Comms and Engagement team from Devizes. He's left a message for his boss, keen to explain his continuing concerns about the woman who wasn't shot and his related worries about Tony, but he hasn't heard back.

Tony is nowhere to be seen. He's probably at the airport already, on his way to Berlin with Maddie. Silas can't stop him, not without hard evidence. He's not in the mood for a fresh fruit chia pudding, tofu scramble or anything else on the blackboard – what was he thinking yesterday? – and just nods at the young woman behind the counter as he walks through to the gallery area at the rear. Strover hangs back, ordering a takeaway soya mocha.

'"*Hippocampus denise*",' Silas says, standing in front of the first framed picture of a solitary orange seahorse. He glances up at Strover as she walks over to him, but his attention is caught by the woman behind the counter. She's sending a text.

'Also known as "Denise's pygmy",' Strover says, reading from her phone. '"One of the world's smallest seahorses, native to the western Pacific. And a master of camouflage."'

'Hiding in plain sight,' Silas says, noticing the way the seahorse matches the colour of the orange coral behind it. It looks new-born and old at the same time, almost alien.

They move on to the next picture like two art students in a gallery. There are eight pictures in total. Swindon's got artistic ambitions apparently. A local philanthropist wants to make it the cultural centre of Britain. The man must like a challenge.

'"*Hippocampus florence*",' Silas says, looking at the picture. This one is of a pair of seahorses. 'Italian presumably. Can't see it hanging in the Uffizi.'

'There are fifty-four known species of seahorse in total,' Strover says, scrolling down her phone. '*Hippocampus fisheri, Hippocampus fuscus*...' She pauses, glancing up at the label again. Her voice is more serious when she speaks. 'No *Hippocampus florence*.'

Silas picks up on her tone and leans in closer to the image. He fancies himself as a photographer, travel pictures mainly, not this sort of stuff. Unlike '*Hippocampus denise*', there's something about the bodies of these two seahorses that doesn't look quite right, as if a second photo has been superimposed on top of each one. He's not sure if the images are untreated or Photoshopped. The colours have definitely been saturated to highlight the seahorses' tones and the texture of the coral.

He moves on to the next picture, glancing back at the café area. The woman at the counter turns with a takeaway cup in one hand. Who was she texting? Tony?

'Your soya mocha's ready,' Silas says to Strover, relishing the words.

She goes over to the counter to collect it. 'What?' she says as she walks back.

'Nothing.'

Truth is, her coffee smells damn good, but he can't order one, not now. He turns to face the picture in front of him. It's called '*Hippocampus alwyn*'. Welsh seahorses, presumably.

And then it hits him. *Hiding in plain sight.* Silas's stomach lurches, like it did the first time Conor was brought into the station, unrecognisable, almost unconscious.

'Remember what Susie said to us in the surgery?' he asks. 'About Maddie having a friend who'd died?'

Strover nods. 'She told me about her too, when I interviewed her.'

'And what was the name of her friend?'

His question is rhetorical, but he doesn't stop Strover from pulling out her notebook. As she flicks through her notes, he walks back to stand in front of the first picture again, reading the label: '*Hippocampus florence*'. This is the moment he lives for in his working life, the moment he also dreads, when the adrenaline rush of a breakthrough is tempered by the imminent discovery of victims.

'Fleur,' Strover says, looking up from her notebook. 'Her friend who died was called Fleur.'

He leans in closer to the picture, studying the seahorse's reptilian features. 'Another name for Florence,' he says.

'*Hippocampus florence*' has got nothing to do with Italy.

88

I spot Tony before he sees me. There must be no sense of recognition, no familiarity. I am at a table in the far corner of the hotel's reception lobby, clutching my handbag on my lap, last night's note to myself in one hand.

'Maddie,' he says, approaching me.

I look up at him, one stranger to another. Just like I did that first day when I turned up on his doorstep.

'It's Tony. You got my text?'

I nod and manage a tentative smile, noncommittal.

He glances at the note in my hand. 'We're going to Berlin today,' he says, leaning forward to kiss me on the lips. Instinctively, I turn away and his lips brush my cheek.

'I'm sorry,' he says quietly, sitting down next to me.

Is that OK? What someone in my position would do?

'Rushing ahead. You found the message then?' He looks at the note in my hand again.

'I read it this morning. I really don't know what's going on.'

Tony rests a hand on my knee. I choose not to disguise the anxiety in my eyes.

'Everything's going to be OK,' he says. 'Trust me.' He pulls out his phone and leans into me to take a selfie of us. 'Today's photo.'

I look at him with confusion.

'You just need to read your notes,' he says. 'They'll be in there, I'm sure.' He nods at my handbag.

I search inside, as if I don't know what I'll find, and pull out three A4 pages of writing.

'Won't be anything for yesterday,' he continues, watching me start to read. 'You had a difficult day. The other days should explain everything. We're going to Berlin together – to get you well again. Have you got your ticket? We need to change to an earlier flight.'

He orders a coffee for himself and a peppermint tea for me and for the next few minutes we chat intermittently as I read through the diary of my first few days in the village. I'm impressed by how thorough I was.

'Making more sense now?' he asks. 'You and me, being here together?'

'You've been very kind,' I say.

'Not sure my wife would agree.'

I flinch again at the reference to Laura and keep reading. 'Did the police find Jemma Huish?'

'Yeah, they found her.'

'Why did I leave the village?'

'Because you feared the cops might mistake you for Jemma. Good call. Have you checked out?'

I nod, still reading.

'I told you not to.'

I look up, the sudden change in his tone taking me by surprise.

'Last night.'

'I don't remember,' I say.

He turns away, frustrated. 'It's OK. My mistake. I should have told you to write it down.' He pauses. 'Have they cleaned the room yet?'

'I don't know.'

But Tony isn't interested in my answer. He's already walking away to the reception desk. What's he doing? I watch him chat to the woman, who glances over in my direction. Tony then beckons for me to come over.

'I was just explaining that you've accidentally left your bag in the room,' he says, looking from me to the receptionist. I turn to him for an explanation, but he doesn't offer one. 'That you forgot it. That you're forgetting a lot of things at the moment.'

There's no need to fake my concern. I now know exactly what he's doing. The woman behind the desk gives me the key to my room, the one I handed in to her half an hour ago, despite my pleading eyes. It feels like female betrayal, but I can't be angry with her.

Two minutes later, we are back in my hotel room.

'Nice enough,' he says, glancing around the confined space. 'I don't care how small a room is as long as it's clean.' He runs a finger along the sideboard, checking for dust and nodding with approval.

'Why are we up here?' I say.

He turns to face me, holding my shoulders like he did in the forest. 'You don't remember anything, do you, baby? What we did yesterday?'

'What did we do?' I can't bear to look into his eyes.

He lets me go, removes his jacket and places it on the back of the chair. I try to suppress a rising nausea. This wasn't part of the plan.

'Don't we have a flight to catch?' I ask.

He leans forward and kisses me on the mouth, pushing me back down onto the bed, a hand already making its way into the front of my jeans. One, two, three. I think fast, desperately working through my limited options, unable to reach my tattoo. This is a nightmare, why I checked out of the room, why I have to get Tony back to Berlin.

'I just need the bathroom,' he says, leaving me lying on the bed. 'Wait here.'

'Don't be long,' I say, letting go of his lingering hand as he walks over to the bathroom door. Thank God for his obsession with cleanliness. He closes the door.

Too nervous to breathe, I rifle through my handbag and pull out a small bottle of perfume. A quick look around the room. There's a smoke detector by the main door, above the wardrobe. It's my only chance. I stand on tiptoe and spray the perfume through the plastic grille, hoping the fine particles will trigger it. Nothing. I try again, glancing at the bathroom door. I hear him flush the loo and I spray the perfume again. Come on. A moment later the room is resonating to the sound of a piercing alarm. I rush over to the bed, drop the perfume back into my handbag and slip off my top.

'Jesus, what's going on?' he says, coming out of the bathroom. He's naked except for a white hotel robe, too loosely tied at the front.

'Just a practice, I hope,' I lie, trying to look keen, unflustered.

'I can't even think straight,' he says, eyeing my breasts. The sound is deafening, music to my ears, his passion wilting in front of me.

The phone rings as he comes over to the bed. Tony snatches at the receiver.

'There's no frickin' fire here,' he snarls. 'No smoke, no flames, nothing...' He listens for a moment, eyes locked onto me. 'There can't be any steam because we haven't used the goddam shower yet.' He slams down the phone just as there's a knock on the door.

'I'll get it,' I say, pulling on my top. I'm keen to get off the bed and to avoid him walking through the fog of my perfume by the door. He must have smelt it by now. Hopefully he'll think I was getting myself ready for him. Fat chance.

'I just need to check the room,' the uniformed man says.

'Sure,' I say, stepping aside, never so happy to see someone at my door.

89

Luke tries speaking to Strover for the third time this morning and gets her answerphone again. He leaves another message, asking her to call him as soon as possible as he has information about Tony de Staal. He couldn't get back to sleep after the second call from Nathan in California, troubled by 'H. M.' and William Beecher Scoville, the neurosurgeon from Connecticut. He made the mistake of looking up Scoville's experiment on H.M.–not a good idea before breakfast.

His phone rings. It's Strover.

'What have you got for me?' she asks.

'I've been calling you all morning,' Luke says, unable to hide his frustration.

'I've been busy. Proper job, being a detective, you know.'

What's she implying? He's got a proper job too.

'When Tony was using his old name, de Staal, the one you sent me—'

'I didn't send you anything,' Strover interrupts, more curt than usual.

Luke checks himself. 'I was forgetting. It's been a while. Tony Masters, who runs the café, used to be called Tony de Staal.'

'We know.'

'Before he left America twenty years ago, he was a medical student in Santa Fe, where he was in trouble for disrespecting cadavers.'

'Tell me something I can't find on Google. What did Luke the award-winning journalist discover? Something that the police are too busy to find out for themselves because a boss wants their limited resources directed elsewhere. Like farm fuel thefts. And cock fighting.'

Luke pauses. He likes Strover, now that he's getting the measure of her. 'I spoke to an old friend in America, a senior doctor on the West Coast.'

'Better.'

'Tony was obsessed with a famous neurosurgeon from the 1950s called Scoville. He once operated on an epilepsy sufferer known as H. M. – removed both his hippocampi with a hand crank and drill saw and wiped his memory. Oh yes, and Tony was kicked out of medical school for date rape.'

'Are you sure?'

He has Strover's attention now, knows she's taking notes. He's forgotten that feeling of getting ahead of the police in an investigation. 'I think that's why he changed his name,' he adds.

'Where are you now?'

He doesn't want to tell her. It would only confirm her worst suspicions. After cooking breakfast for Milo, he went back to bed with his laptop.

'At my parents' house, in the village.'

'Isn't it time you flew the nest?'

'Long story.'

'We're just outside Tony's café. Meet here in five?'

Luke's surprised to hear that Strover is in the village. There is still a lot of activity on the canal, mainly police investigators, but he assumed Strover and her boss, DI Hart, would be buried beneath paperwork back at the office. The shooting's still making headlines on the TV news this morning.

Five minutes later, he's down by the café. Strover is nowhere to be seen. Then he spots an unmarked car across the street. Strover lowers the front passenger window.

'Get in,' she calls, nodding at the seat behind her.

Luke walks over and climbs into the car. On the seat next to him is a framed picture sealed in Bubble Wrap. Strover acknowledges him in the rear-view mirror, unlike DI Hart, who sits impassively in the driver's seat, hands resting on the steering wheel.

'You don't publish anything until we say so,' Hart says, staring ahead.

Luke doesn't like being told what to do. He turns away, glancing at the picture next to him. A sticker on it says 'Seahorse Photography'. He feels uncomfortable sitting in the rear of a police car, even if it is unmarked. The last time he found himself in one he was breathalysed. Nudging 45 mph in a 30 mph area at 7 a.m. on Christmas Eve, collecting a turkey from the local butcher's.

'I'm not on a story,' he says. 'The only thing I've written recently is my witness statement about the shooting. And for the record, you did everything to disarm her.'

Strover glances at her boss, watching to see how he reacts to Luke's comment.

'You're a journalist,' Hart says, still looking forwards.

'And the sole witness,' Luke adds, keen to remind Hart. 'I've left that world behind. I just want to find out if Maddie is adopted. If she's my daughter.'

Hart seems to believe him. 'Did Maddie ever tell you anything about a friend of hers called Fleur?' he asks, more engaged now, fingers tapping the steering wheel.

'Not that I can remember.' He wishes he had talked more with Maddie, he'd felt that there was a real bond between them. Or is that wishful thinking again? She'd been a good listener when he had confided in her at the quiz, seemed to understand why he had started to look for Freya online since his split with Chloe. 'Has she arrived in Berlin?' he asks.

'We last spoke to her yesterday evening at Heathrow,' Silas says.

'And Tony's with her?'

'We assume so. She asked him to accompany her and he's free to do so.'

'Shouldn't you be more concerned? Given Tony's history?'

Hart pauses, his eyes fixed on Luke in the mirror. 'At the moment we're speculating.'

'Tony was done for date-rape at university.' Luke was shocked when Nathan had told him on the phone.

'How much do you know about the brain and memory?' Hart asks.

'Enough to know that a part called the hippocampus, which looks like a seahorse, plays a crucial role in storing and processing memories,' Luke says. 'The part that Tony de Staal tried to lift from a lab in New Mexico twenty years ago. The same part that a surgeon called Scoville removed from a patient called H. M., leaving him amnesic.'

If Hart is impressed with how much he knows, he's not showing it. 'Take a look at this,' he says, nodding at Strover, who passes Luke a printout of a photo.

'Seahorse on the left, hippocampus on the right,' Strover says.

'Could just as easily be the other way round, though, couldn't it?' Hart adds, still watching Luke in the rear-view mirror.

Luke stares at the photo, his eyes drawn to the hippocampus. He's never seen one on its own before. All the images he's looked at show the hippocampi in context, one either side of the brain.

'We're getting one of Tony's seahorse pictures analysed,' Hart says, 'but we need more. Unless we find the "Mona Lisa" underneath, it still won't be enough to issue a warrant for his arrest.'

'What exactly are you looking for?' Luke asks, his mouth beginning to dry.

'Seems like each seahorse has been overlaid with another image – of a human hippocampus.'

Luke involuntarily tightens his grip on the photo, creasing its sides. He needs to get himself to Berlin too.

90

I try to concentrate on the flight attendant as she takes passengers through the safety procedure, but my mind is elsewhere. Tony is sitting next to me, his hand on mine. He has persuaded the person originally beside him to swap with me.

The fire alarm was eventually switched off, by which time the hotel's entire maintenance staff had gathered in our room. Tony smelt the perfume when we walked out but said nothing. None of the staff commented either, but I think they knew something was amiss from the looks they gave me. I flinch at the memory of Tony pressing me down on the bed.

'Are you OK?' he asks, patting my hand. 'You feel tense.'

'I don't seem to like being in an aeroplane.'

I close my eyes and sit back. This is even harder than I thought it would be. No notes for yesterday means I have to tread more carefully, make no reference to anything that's happened in the past twenty-four hours: the ammunition shelter in the wood, hitch-hiking with Mungo, being reunited with my cards and passport. When I made mistakes in the village, remembered things that I shouldn't have, I was able to cover them up by using my notes as an excuse. I don't have that safety net any more.

Another flight attendant walks past, handing out newspapers. Tony takes one, glancing at the front page. He starts to read it, making no attempt to hide the headline from me. It's about the canal shooting. I lean into him, resting a hand on his knee. It's important we look like just another loved-up couple going on a European break.

'What's all that about?' I ask, trying to keep my voice as neutral as I can.

He looks at me. Is he searching for signs of recovery? Of synaptic connections? A smile breaks across his lips.

'Another good reason for going to Germany,' he says. 'A woman was shot dead beside a canal in Wiltshire. Not in downtown New York but in rural Britain. Seems like she had a history of mental illness.'

'That's terrible.'

'Could have happened to any of us,' he says, folding the newspaper away. Another test, I'm sure of it. He looks at me again. It still terrifies me that I might have been shot, but I manage not to show it. 'Cops, eh?' he adds.

I think I've passed.

I had expected us to be stopped by the police as we entered Terminal 5, but there were no problems at the airline desk, where we managed to switch to an earlier flight, nor as we moved through Departures. My only worry now is about when we arrive in Berlin. There shouldn't be an issue. All charges have been dropped against Tony and I'm free to do as I wish, travelling on a valid Indian passport with all the necessary tourist visas. I tell myself that I've done nothing wrong apart from waste good people's time in an English village. And broken up a marriage.

'Hold tight,' Tony says, taking my hand again as the plane accelerates down the runway.

'A drink might calm my nerves,' I say.

He glances at his watch.

'They're an hour ahead in Germany,' I say, a coy smile on my lips.

'You're right. Time to celebrate.'

91

It's almost twenty minutes into the flight before drinks are served. Just in time. Maddie is becoming increasingly anxious. Tony hasn't seen her like this before. The flight attendant is one row in front of them with the trolley. He waits for her to finish serving a passenger and then she's beaming at him, asking what he'd like to drink. Nice eyes but not his type. He pays for the champagne on his card, hoping there's some credit left, and passes the opened bottle and two glasses to Maddie. She has lowered her table in readiness. Patience. He frightened her in the hotel room, got ahead of himself. There will be plenty of opportunities in Berlin. Memorable opportunities – at least for him.

Maddie's amnesia seems to be holding up well – she's still only able to remember her name. And he's beginning to think that yesterday's comment about him showing her around Berlin might have been a casual remark, nothing more. If anything was going to stimulate the synapses, rebuild the degraded networks, it would have been the newspaper headline about yesterday's shooting, but she appeared utterly unmoved when he showed her the story before take-off.

'Shall I pour it now?' Maddie says, holding the bottle.

'You go right ahead. I just need the bathroom.'

Tony walks down the aisle. His hands are dirty from all the travel. The champagne should help her to relax. He can't imagine what it's like to be afraid of flying. He's done so much over the years, criss-crossing between Europe's capitals. Maddie is unable to remember being on a plane and yet she has a fear of flying. Like experiencing pain in a phantom limb. Where does that fear reside if not in her memory?

He steps into the tiny cubicle, slide-locks the door and starts to rinse his hands, adding more soap as he rubs his fingers together. After he's satisfied his hands are clean (they can never be completely clean), he looks at himself in the mirror. Without memory, Maddie is nothing and he is everything. When she wakes each morning, their shared experiences of the day before, the previous night, reside only with him. Her life is his.

For now, at least.

He leans closer to the mirror, turning his head to one side and then the other. It's his medial temporal lobes that are starting to deteriorate, furring up with the rust of Alzheimer's. He's had the test, volunteered for a trial. They gave him a PET scan and injected his veins with a low-level radioactive glucose tracer that measured levels of amyloid plaques and protein tangles in his brain, the hallmark abnormalities of Alzheimer's.

His brain lit up like a Christmas tree.

92

I pour out the champagne while Tony is still in the loo. My hand is shaking so much that I spill a few drops. I need to move quickly. Checking that the passenger next to me isn't looking, I tip the crushed Xanax into one of the glasses. I'd stashed the tiny bag of powder in my bra. Thank God the smoke alarm went off before I had to remove it in the hotel room. I stir the glass with a biro and wait for him to return, hoping the champagne will mask the taste of the Xanax – like chalk, apparently. Not that I can remember. And bitter. All the powder seems to have dissolved.

A minute later, he's back in his seat, beaming at the sight of the two glasses on my tray. I pass one to him.

'Berlin,' he says, clinking glasses.

'Berlin,' I say, and we down our champagne in one.

93

Silas has long got over the fact that his boss, Detective Superintendent Ward, is ten years younger than him. He's also accepted that Ward's rocketing career is on a trajectory that is widely assumed will only level out at chief constable level. Unlike his, which he sometimes feels has yet to leave the launchpad.

'How's Conor?' Ward asks, turning to a printout of the report Silas has just emailed him. They are in a meeting room upstairs, which he had to book. Even Ward doesn't have his own office, has to hot-desk with the rest of them in the Parade Room.

'No better,' Silas says, watching him digest the report, a summary of his concerns about Tony de Staal and Maddie Thurloe.

'If you need time off—'

'It's OK.'

Silas doesn't like talking about his son with Ward. His boss's genuine sympathy always makes him tear up. He's about to change the subject when his phone vibrates. Strover said she'd text him in his meeting only if something important came up. Silas glances at his boss, who is still reading, and sneaks a look at his phone.

'I gave you half a day when I shouldn't have done,' Ward says, looking up at him.

'And I think we're onto something,' Silas says, trying to process the contents of Strover's text.

'This woman, Maddie Thurloe,' Ward continues. 'She's not even a British citizen any more. And Tony Masters, Tony de Staal, he's a dual US citizen.'

'And...?' Silas is struggling to concentrate.

'We have to prioritise, you know how it is, Silas. I've also got the chief's office on the phone every half hour, asking about yesterday's shooting—'

'I'm working on my PIP—'

'Asking why you hadn't been on your negotiator's refresher course.'

Silas knows he should have done the course. Just like he should have done his expenses. And his 360-degree appraisal. In between solving crimes on a rapidly diminishing budget.

'If your dots do join up, and that's a big if, what exactly are we looking at here?' Ward asks. 'Tony hasn't committed an offence by changing his name or by making art from photos of body parts.'

Silas weighs up his options. Should he cut to the chase and share the contents of Strover's text or stick to his plan to win Ward over with some wider context? The boss appreciates context, likes it when cases break out of routine police work and extend into other spheres, the more esoteric the better. Everyone knows he studied theology at Oxford.

'As I'm sure you know, sir, in medieval Christian art, European painters liked to paint memento mori – images of death, skulls and so on,' Silas begins.

'"Remember that you must die",' Ward says, sitting up. For the first time in their meeting he seems interested. 'Not just medieval, of course. The photographer Joel-Peter Witkin uses real body parts in strikingly macabre tableaux.'

Silas regrets his decision to go wide, already feels ignorant. Always has done in the company of graduates. His father was an advocate of the 'university of life'. He used to tell him that there was no better education than a career in a British police force, preferably the Wiltshire Constabulary. Silas's only act of rebellion had been to apply to the Met. And now all new police officers will need a degree.

'Exactly,' Silas continues. 'I think that's what Tony's doing in his pictures, except that death is not so explicit. Most people who look at them wouldn't get the message.'

'And that message is...?'

'He's showing off, sir. By including a part of the brain, the hippocampus, that deals with memory, he's being ironic. Clever. Remember you are mortal – that's if you *can* still remember.'

'Last time I checked, irony wasn't a crime.'

'It depends whose hippocampus it is.' Silas thinks again about the text.

'I assume the ones he tried to steal from medical college in the States had been donated to science.' Ward glances at a photo Silas included in his report. The lab has managed to separate Tony's images into the original seahorse and a hippocampus. 'He probably found these online.'

'We've got digital matches for all the seahorses – they're not his photos, he lifted them from various marine photography websites – but we can't find anything for the hippocampi.'

'Dark web?'

'DC Strover's checking now. Assuming these hippocampi have been taken from real people, they're either walking around with no memories like zombies, or they're dead.'

'I guess it depends who removed them,' Ward says, sitting back, hands behind his head, displaying an annoyingly lean midriff. Silas could look like that one day. Quit the fags, vegan diet, 10,000 steps.

'What do you want from me, Silas?' he asks.

'One more day. Let me liaise with Interpol, check against international misper lists.'

'That's quite a long list.'

'We start with mispers in Berlin – we've got first names of seven people from the pictures, excluding Denise, which I think is a diversion. There's actually a real seahorse called that – and there's no hippocampus overlay in that photo. Maybe that's what gave him the idea. I reckon these people are either English or North American – English speakers – and they're not all common names: we've got an Alwyn and a Florence, which should make searching easier, even if we include variations.'

'And why's this Maddie at risk?' Ward asks.

Silas takes a deep breath. 'We've just found some picture files on Tony's computer,' he says.

'Of hippocampi?' Ward picks up the report from his desk. 'You didn't mention that in here.'

'Of seahorses. The computer file names match the pictures in his café. All except one, recently created.'

'And…?'

Silas thinks again of Maddie, prays that she's still alive. 'It's called "*Hippocampus madeleine*".'

94

I don't know exactly how long it will take for the Xanax to kick in. It's a fast-acting benzo, so anything between fifteen and thirty minutes – well before we touch down in Berlin. Two milligrams is large for a single dose, according to the guy outside the club. The maximum you can get in one pill of quick-release Xanax. I haven't noticed the telltale signs of drowsiness yet, but we've both just had a second glass of champagne, which will only help to speed things up, magnifying the effects of the alcohol and benzo to a potentially lethal level. Later, the amnesia will cast its long shadow back to at least half an hour before the powder was ingested. Maybe longer.

'Are you feeling more relaxed?' Tony asks quietly, his hand on mine again.

'Much better,' I say, but I don't like the new tone in his voice.

'Funny thing, fear,' he says.

'How do you mean?'

'You started to relax before we drank the champagne.'

'Did I?' My stomach tightens.

'As soon as I returned from the restroom. Your whole face was different, less tense.'

I shift in my seat as he grips my hand a little tighter, pressing it into the armrest.

'I was pleased to see you again,' I say. 'You were in there a while. I got stuck in one once,' I add, trying to defuse the tension with a light laugh. 'Terrifying.'

My laugh evaporates. I've made a mistake. Has he noticed too? I've never been stuck in an aeroplane loo and even if I had, how would I be able to remember?

'You weren't scared to climb into the trunk of my car,' he says.

I sigh inwardly with relief. He didn't notice. 'That was different,' I say, smiling at him.

He doesn't smile back. Instead, he fixes me with his blue eyes and all I can see is anger. Anger and disappointment. Another mistake and this time there's no reprieve.

'That was yesterday,' he says, letting go of my hand. 'You didn't write any notes for yesterday, did you?'

I shake my head. 'You told me not to,' I say quietly. My mouth is almost too dry to talk.

'What did you put in my champagne?' he asks.

'Nothing.' The Xanax will kick in soon.

He holds up a hand and catches the attention of a passing flight attendant.

'Two large black coffees. Strong as you've got.' He's starting to slur his words.

'I don't drink coffee,' I say.

'They're both for me.'

Tony watches the attendant pour out two coffees and place them on his tray. Then he turns to face me, a heavy drowsiness weighing down his eyelids, his voice barely a whisper.

'I don't know who you are or what game you're playing.' He pauses, sipping at one of the coffees. 'But you won't win.'

95

Luke is booked on to the first flight to Berlin he could get. He has no idea what flight Maddie and Tony took, or how he will find them. All he knows is that he has to get himself to Berlin. Is it the journalist in him, hunting down a good story? He's confident it's not. Does he still believe that Maddie might be his daughter? Enough for him to feel protective towards her, with a force that's shocked him. Hart's haunting words in the police car won't go away: *Seems like each seahorse has been overlaid with another image – of a human hippocampus.*

He's also found evidence online of a stronger connection between Maddie's father and the Baha'is, a talk he once gave to a group of Iranian Baha'i exiles living in Cheltenham. Freya said it was their daughter's adoptive mother who is the Baha'i, but at least it's something. He needs to talk to Maddie again but she's now in Berlin, where her life is potentially at risk. Strover and Hart assured him that they would be contacting Interpol, sharing what they know, but the police are busy people, as Strover's always reminding him, with other priorities. Like explaining how Jemma Huish was shot dead by the canal on a sunny afternoon in Wiltshire.

He drove to Heathrow in the Austin-Healey, leaving it in the short-stay car park, where it looked out of place sandwiched between two shiny SUVs. As he passed through the airport's security checks, he tried to picture Maddie and Tony before him. Was Maddie in charge? The swallow – isn't that what Sean called her?

He sits back in his seat, drawing comfort from the fact that she can now remember her name and has been reunited with her handbag and passport. Maybe it's just a simple affair and he's stalking a couple on a romantic break in Berlin. That would be weird. He feels bad he didn't contact Laura before he left. The last he saw of her was when he walked her back along the canal to the surgery, after they'd both given their statements to the police.

Luke keeps his phone on during take-off in case Strover contacts him. He's about to switch it off when a message appears, from an international number. The dialling code is 91, which he knows from his calls with Freya is India.

Can you come to Berlin? Today? I need to tell you my story.
Maddie x

Luke stares at the message. What story does she want to tell him? About her life? How she was adopted? And how did she get his number? Then he remembers he gave her his card that first day, when he saw her in the surgery. She must have kept it. Again, it feels good to be ahead of the game. Did she somehow know he would come to Berlin anyway, in search of his daughter? The message doesn't sound panicky. Maddie seems in control.

He's about to text a reply when a flight attendant asks him to turn off his phone. Luke protests, but the attendant is insistent. He glances at his phone again. The signal has gone. It's two hours before touchdown in Berlin.

96

'He suffers from acute fear of flying,' I say to the flight attendant. 'Always gets anxious in aeroplanes, ever since he was a kid.'

The attendant glances back down the aisle to where Tony is slumped in his seat, semi-conscious.

'It's happened before – I'm sorry, I thought the therapy was helping,' I continue. 'We wouldn't have had a drink if I'd known he'd taken medication.'

'Does he need medical attention when we land?' the attendant asks, casting her eye across the sea of upturned passenger faces. 'We could also ask if there's a doctor on board today. There often is.'

'No, it's fine,' I say, keen to snuff out that idea as quickly as possible. 'I just need a wheelchair at the other end – and maybe a bit of help getting him down the aisle,' I add.

'I'll see what we can do. Normally we require forty-eight hours' notice. You're sure he's OK?'

'He's fine. I'm just sorry for the other person in our row. My husband can snore for Britain.'

The flight attendant smiles at me sympathetically, wondering perhaps why I'm with an older man who passes out on planes and snores. I return to my seat. I'd hoped to book a wheelchair for Berlin when I rescheduled my flight at Heathrow, but it proved impossible as Tony was with me and insisted on doing all the talking. Hence plan B and arranging what I can on the plane.

I squeeze past Tony's legs and sit down in my seat. He's unconscious now. I breathe out and look around, acknowledging the man next to me, who is taking off his headphones.

'Likes to knock himself out completely,' I say by way of explanation. 'Can't stand flying,' I add. The man smiles nervously.

'That's all fine,' the attendant says, appearing by my side and saving me from further embarrassment. 'A wheelchair will be ready for your husband at disembarkation.'

'Thank you so much,' I say.

For the first time in a while I can relax, at least for a few minutes. Plan B seems to have worked out well. I've had to do a lot of planning in recent weeks. Ever since I saw the photo of the monks. Ever since I started to remember.

I glance across at Tony again, slumped beside me. Amnesia was my bait when I turned up on his doorstep: anterograde, retrograde, a hint of distant childhood memories. I had done my research, knew how to reel him in.

I can't remember my own name.

And now we are about to land in the city where it all started. I reach down under the seat for my bag and pull out a crumpled photo of Fleur, her cheek pressed close to mine. We look so similar, like twin sisters. Same haircut, matching clothes. A fatal likeness. Tony's type, both of us. She's smiling at the camera, laughter in her eyes. Fleur was my name for her. Everyone else called her Flo, apart from her mother, who apparently called her Florence.

I will phone my own mother in India when this is all over, explain what I've done and why. And I must make contact with Luke again. I messaged him from Heathrow, asking him to fly to Berlin. He hasn't replied, but I hope he will come. I liked him when we met at the pub quiz and he talked about Freya Lal, how he'd started to search for her again. It was moving to hear him talk in that way, rare to encounter such openness in a man. He feels like someone I can trust. When we land I will send him another text. And when we finally meet, I will explain why I came to his village. Tell him my story.

97

Silas stares at a printout of the latest list of Berlin mispers on his laptop, sent through by his colleagues in the Bundeskriminalamt (BKA), the federal investigative police agency in Germany. Its head office in Wiesbaden also acts as Interpol's central bureau for the country, which is why Silas went there first for help.

Ward's not going to like this. Silas doesn't like it. He looks around the Parade Room, which is busy today, full of response officers. Why aren't they out on the street? *Work is what you do, not a place you go to.* Word's got round that he's on a potentially big case and people have been throwing glances in his direction all morning.

'Are you sure they're all here?' he asks Strover, who is scrolling through the list on her laptop too. She's already diced and sliced the data (her phrase, not his), searching for people who have disappeared in Berlin and have a first name that matches the labels on Tony's pictures in the gallery.

'All seven of them – three males, four females. Four of them are British. Two Americans, one German. No one's over thirty. And they all disappeared from Berlin between five and ten years ago.'

Silas should be pleased with the breakthrough, but the implications fill him with dread. A network of loss and pain, spreading out from a small village in Wiltshire. Each person's file includes their name, age, country of birth and place of disappearance. The more detailed ones also list parents' names, language spoken and distinguishing marks. Lacerated wrists come up too often for his liking. Conor cut his wrists once.

It could all be coincidence, of course, but Florence and Alwyn aren't the most common names. Alwyn turns out to be a man from the UK (Holyhead). The file for Florence says that she goes by the name of Flo. Although there's no mention of Fleur, Silas is convinced she's Maddie's friend.

'She looks like Maddie too, don't you think?' he asks, glancing at Strover's laptop.

Strover is deep in concentration, studying the screen. 'Flo's identifying marks include a lotus-flower tattoo on her wrist,' she says. 'Exactly what Maddie had.'

'Did you see the tattoo?'

'Luke told me about it. He thought it might be linked to a religion connected with his daughter. Long story.'

'It's definitely Fleur,' Silas says, thinking aloud.

'There was a lot of social media activity around all of them when they first went missing,' Strover says. 'MySpace, Bebo, DontStayIn. Facebook and WhatsApp for the later ones.'

Silas looks up at her. Conor's mother once tried to persuade him to join a WhatsApp group with Conor, but he refused.

'Appeals for information,' Strover continues. 'Twenty-four-hour hotlines in case of sightings. The ones I've checked all seemed to like clubbing, according to their profiles. It's what a lot of young people go to Berlin for.'

'I'll take your word for it.'

Silas went to Berlin once, for the currywurst and Checkpoint Charlie, both of which had disappointed. The Topography of Terror, on the site of the former SS and Gestapo headquarters, had left him reeling.

'And Tony used to take photos of DJs,' he adds, remembering the American's old website.

Strover looks up at him. 'Alwyn and Flo both listed GrünesTal in their music likes,' she says. 'It was a nightclub, techno mainly, on Revaler Strasse in what was once East Berlin. Closed down now.'

'Complaints from the neighbours?'

'Unlikely. It was a run-down part of town. Lots of old warehouses, abandoned factories. The club was in a former railway yard.'

'We need to get an image of Maddie over to Interpol in Wiesbaden – use the one from her Indian passport,' Silas says, standing up from his desk to stretch his long legs. He's been sitting down all morning. 'They'll forward it to the BKA office in Berlin. Ward also wants us to establish contact with Maddie.'

A couple of response officers by the window look over at him, chatting. No doubt they think he's trying to get back onto the Major Crime Investigation Team. He misses the big cases and fancy ID passes – they featured silhouettes of Sherlock Holmes and Swindon legend Isambard Kingdom Brunel – but not the collaboration with other forces. He joined Wiltshire Police to investigate local crime.

'The phone Tony rang her on from the interview room was his wife's old one,' Strover says, keen to get her boss's attention again. 'He'd lent it to her. We've checked the number – it hasn't been turned on since.'

'She must be using her own phone now,' Silas says. 'The one she got back from Lost Property.'

'Luke might have the number.'

Silas still feels uncomfortable about Strover's relationship with Luke. He's proved useful so far, but he's clearly got his own agenda and hasn't flown all the way to Berlin just because he thinks Maddie is his daughter. Once a journalist, always a journalist. At least he let them know he was going to Berlin. And he seems to be onside about the shooting.

'He's still in the air,' Strover continues. 'I've sent a text asking him to call us as soon as he lands.'

'About what?'

Strover pauses. 'I came across a misper in the Berlin list called Freya. She's Indian-looking and—'

'And...?'

'Luke's former girlfriend was called Freya. It might be his daughter...'

'Stay focused, Strover,' Silas snaps. 'Ask him if he's got a number for Maddie. That's all we're interested in. If her phone's switched on, Wiesbaden can locate it.'

He looks at the list on his laptop again, feeling a pang of guilt. Strover's working hard, no need to bite her head off. The list is too long, each one a personal tragedy. One day he fears it might include Conor. At least he knows where his son is. Some of these people will be found by the police or other agencies and will choose not to let their loved ones know their whereabouts, that they are OK. Their right but a cruel one. Others will never be found.

Silas might soon have answers for the families of seven of them. Just not the news they've been waiting for.

98

Tony is semi-conscious as we enter the passport-control hall, still slumped in his wheelchair like a drunkard. The member of airport staff who met us at the aeroplane door is pushing him. He doesn't speak English and I have forgotten what little German I once knew. When we reach the front of the Non-EU queue, the passport official beckons for us all to come forward together.

'He's asleep,' I say by way of explanation. 'Doesn't like flying – his way of coping.'

I pass both our passports to the official, who looks at Tony, now stirring enough to open his eyes. He probably thinks Tony is just another city-break tourist who's consumed too many in-flight drinks. He examines his British passport and then my Indian one.

'How long are you planning to stay in Germany?' he asks, glancing again at Tony, whose eyes have closed.

'A week? Then back to India.'

'And him?' He nods at Tony.

'I hope he'll come with me.' I contemplate how much

more to elaborate. 'He still needs persuading,' I add with a smile.

He stamps my Indian passport and returns them both to me without comment.

We walk on, the man still pushing Tony. I texted Luke when we landed, telling him I'll give instructions soon about where to meet, and then I turned my phone off as the batteries are low. Two officials in the far corner of the passport hall scrutinise us as we head out towards the baggage-reclaim area. I try not to panic.

The carousels are full of luggage, passengers swarming towards them like sales shoppers in search of a bargain. The man pushing Tony gestures towards the nearest carousel, but I shake my head. Neither of us has any hold luggage, just my handbag and Tony's small suitcase, which is on his lap.

I'm worried that Tony might have built up a tolerance to Xanax over the years. He also managed to drink both black coffees on the plane. The caffeine can heighten Xanax's toxicity, but it can also nullify the benzo's sedative effects. He knew what he was doing, which suggests he might be a user – or maybe just proficient at administering it to others.

We find a taxi and the airport assistant helps me ease Tony into the backseat. I tip him twenty euros, hoping it will prevent him from saying anything unhelpful to the driver. He's been eyeing me suspiciously ever since he met us off the plane.

'Revaler Strasse, *bitte*,' I say to the driver once we're in. 'Via Potsdamer Platz, Kreuzberg?'

'*Stadtring?*' he asks, looking at me in his mirror.

Tony and I are in the back together. Tony is lapsing in and out of consciousness, still unaware of where we are.

'*Nein,*' I say. I want to go through the parts of town where Fleur and I once hung out rather than take the ringroad. I need to stay focused, remember why I'm here. I also need to text Luke.

Twenty minutes later, we are at the Bundestag and its glass-domed roof, and then we are crossing the green expanse of Tiergarten, the Brandenburg Gate to our left. Fleur and I came here once in the early days, soon after we first met. It was important to see the historical sights, I insisted, and walked around like a wide-eyed tourist until Fleur showed me a better life out east.

I checked out of my hostel by the Hauptbahnhof and moved into Fleur's flat in Friedrichshain, where she was living on a shoestring. I was on my gap year and Fleur was studying for an art degree. At least that's what she said. I don't remember seeing her doing any work but I might not have noticed. I was in awe, wanted to be just like her. Within days I had got the same hairstyle – a short pixie cut with tiny bangs – and we both wore black from head to toe. We even had matching bumbags and chokers. She took me clubbing at Tresor and Club der Visionaere in Kreuzberg and showed me the sights: the Stasi museum in Lichtenberg and the mural of Honecker and Brezhnev's full-on kiss at the East Side Gallery.

It took me six attempts to get past the bouncers at the legendary Berghain, a club that left me wide-eyed for different reasons. I was eighteen and had never seen naked men having sex on a dancefloor or met anyone as wild as Fleur, who smiled at me when strangers in studded leather masks came up and licked her ears. Looking back, I realise we were both rebelling against our upbringings. She had fallen out with her parents and I had just witnessed the messy end of my own parents' unhappy marriage. My mother had moved back to India and my father was drowning his sorrows in too much Irish whiskey.

And then of course there was our fatal trip to GrünesTal, the club where we are heading now. It was on the way there that we must have got our matching lotus tattoos, a sign that our relationship was becoming more serious. If only I could remember the details, but my amnesia that night leached into the before as well as the after. Did we make promises to each other as the lotuses blossomed into life on our wrists? Did I vow to love and look after her forever? If I did, I failed on the very first night.

I stare out the taxi window, not wanting Tony to see my tears. Pulling up my sleeve, I look at the purple lotus again, tracing the edges of the delicate flower with my finger, drawing strength from its purple petals.

Nine of them.

Tony is unconscious again. We drive on through Kreuzberg and north over the River Spree, past Warschauer Strasse station. To our right, a lattice of train lines heading east towards Ostkreuz and beyond. The first time I got off at that station, there was a beggar on Warschauer bridge with four plastic cups spread out in front of him on the pavement, each one labelled with the drug he was collecting for: 'Speed', 'LSD', 'Weed' and 'GHB'. A far cry from my sheltered life back in north London, where I'd worked hard at school and steered clear of the cool set.

'Turn just up here, please,' I say to the driver as we proceed down Revaler Strasse, past RAW, a sprawling industrial site of former railway workshops, now a mix of nightclubs, steampunk art galleries and skate parks. I signal with my hand too. Where we are heading is a vast abandoned workshop beyond RAW, set back from the road and away from the tourists. The site of GrünesTal, a dub-techno nightclub that was closed down two years ago.

'Finish,' the driver says in a heavy German accent as we drive along the potholed track to the front of the building. 'Over.'

'I know,' I say. 'No problem. Thank you. My friend here, he wants to visit it one last time.'

The driver can't understand me, but it's important that I convey a sense of purpose. It's not the sort of place people ask to be driven to by taxi.

'Here?' he asks again, clearly feeling uneasy about our destination.

'Perfect,' I say, glancing up at the old workshop that was once GrünesTal. The sight of it sends a shiver through me. I get out of the car and go round to open the door on Tony's side.

'We've arrived,' I say to Tony, whose eyes are now open.

I help him out of his seat. He still looks punch drunk and continues to be compliant, but I have no idea for how long. The effects of Xanax can last for twelve hours. If Tony's built up a tolerance, it could be much less, particularly with all that caffeine in his system.

The driver is a lot happier when I tip him generously. '*Danke,*' I say again.

Tony sways next to me as we watch the taxi turn around and drive back up to Revaler Strasse.

'Remember here?' I ask, looking at the old workshop, its high walls covered in graffiti.

He smiles helplessly and I have to stop him from falling backwards. Xanax is a muscle relaxant and his movements are heavy.

I lock my arm through his and march him around to the back of the building.

He won't be smiling for much longer.

99

Luke stares at his phone, reading the message from DC Strover. His plane has just touched down. Strover has been going through Interpol's Berlin missing persons list and has come across someone called Freya who apparently matches Maddie's age. Unfortunately, her surname is Schmidt, which is not Indian or Irish.

His phone vibrates with another message. It's from Maddie on her own phone, the Indian number.

Are you coming to Berlin? Will text soon with details where to meet. x

Luke replies immediately, worried by her tone.

In Berlin already – just landed. Where are you? All OK?

He waits for her response, glancing out the window at Tegel Airport's terminal buildings. People have started to retrieve their bags from the overhead lockers. He delays until it's time to leave the plane, checking his phone constantly, but she doesn't reply.

Once he's passed through Arrivals, Luke looks around. Should he head into the centre of Berlin? Stay here? He still hasn't heard back from Maddie. And then his phone rings. It's Strover.

'Did you get my text?' she asks. Her tone is urgent.

'I've only just landed.' Why does he feel he needs to make excuses?

'Are you with Maddie?'

'Not yet.'

'But you know where she is.'

Luke shifts from foot to foot, unsettled by her rapid-fire questions. 'She just sent me a text, asking if I was coming to Berlin. Is everything OK?'

'From her own phone?' Strover asks.

'Her Indian one, why?'

'Give me the number. We need to alert the German police of her whereabouts.'

Luke is liking the conversation less and less. He hoped Strover might be calling with news about Freya Schmidt. He scribbles the number down and reads it out.

'When did she last text you?' she asks.

'When I was in the air. Could have been up to two hours ago.'

'Have you replied?'

'About fifteen minutes ago. I haven't heard anything back.' Maddie's silence is beginning to feel ominous. 'She said she'd tell me soon where to meet.'

'Keep me updated. The German police will try to trace the number.'

'Thanks – you know, for the message about Freya Schmidt.'

'I have to go.'

'Can't you tell me anything else about her?'

There's a pause before she speaks, her voice quieter than usual, as if she doesn't want to be overheard. 'She's a German national, twenty-nine years old. Speaks English as well as German. And she looks...'

'Looks what?'

Strover is clearly unable to speak freely. DI Hart's probably on her case. 'Looks Indian – a little like Maddie.'

'A little?'

'I have to go.'

Freya Schmidt. Luke decides to get a coffee, wait there until he hears more from Maddie. *Twenty-nine years old. Speaks English as well as German. And she looks... a little like Maddie.* It was good of Strover to tell him. Could Freya Schmidt have come to England under a different name? Using someone else's passport? Maddie Thurloe's? Her age and looks, if Strover's right, match Maddie's. But what was she doing coming to his village? And what story does she now want to tell?

100

Tony looks like a prisoner behind the metal bars, slumped on the concrete floor, his back against a brick wall.

'Remember here?' I ask.

'Here?' he says, confused. His voice is sluggish and seems to have dropped an octave. I walk over to the bars and grip them, looking at him. His drunken smile of earlier has been replaced by a vacant look in his eyes. Emotionless.

'We're going on a trip together,' I say.

'A trip?' he asks after a long pause, but he doesn't sound engaged or interested.

'Back to the past. Ten years ago, GrünesTal. You, me and my best friend Fleur.'

Tony stares ahead. I'm not sure he's heard me, taken in what I've just said.

After the taxi left us, I marched him around to the rear entrance of the building, away from prying eyes, not that anyone comes past this patch of industrial wasteland very often. I chose it well when I was in Berlin a week ago, before leaving for England.

We are in the basement of the oldest railway workshop, separate from the others that have become increasingly popular with tourists and clubbers. I looked up Revaler Strasse after I came out here for a recce. The area was originally known as the Royal Prussian Railroad Workshop and was only renamed Reichsbahnausbesserungswerk – RAW for short – after World War One. I wasn't interested in its history when Fleur and I used to come here. We just knew it as GrünesTal, part of the city's subversive underground scene, although even then there was talk of private investors hiking up rents, a nostalgia for the area's more edgy past.

The metal caging in the basement was originally installed to protect mechanics from the workshop's power units. When it became a nightclub, the old equipment was ripped out and the DJs moved in, setting up their decks behind bars, safe from the mayhem of the dancefloor. It was the same when we visited Tresor, down the road in the basement vaults of a former department store. The iron grilles that had once protected the safeboxes were used as DJ cages.

It seems almost unnecessary to lock the cage door. Tony doesn't look like he's going anywhere in a hurry. But the Xanax will wear off and he will try to escape. I have planned for this moment, like I planned everything else. Last week I came down here with a heavy-duty padlock and hid it behind some old car tyres in one of the building's many alcoves. I glance at Tony and walk over to retrieve it.

I know at once that the padlock has gone. The tyres have been moved around. I glance back at Tony. He is still staring into space. I search again. Nothing.

I try to remain calm as I embark on a wider search, walking around the vast industrial space, the bare brick walls and steel girders that once echoed to the unforgiving sounds of techno. Relax. I had a plan, bought a padlock, but the best-laid plans of mice and men... I mustn't panic. The padlock will be somewhere. I have come this far, overcome other problems, like being mistaken for Jemma Huish. I will find it. And if I can't, I will wedge some heavy objects against the cage door. Tony has been physically weakened by the Xanax. Emasculated. There is plenty of time to sort this.

I stand on what was once the main dancefloor, where Fleur's lithe body swayed to the heavy beats. I am certain now that it was here where we met Tony. GrünesTal was our favourite club. Fleur knew her music, liked her techno. I try to work out where the main drinking area was. The bar itself used to be supported by a kitsch marble sculpture of naked men with gargantuan erections. It's where Fleur first kissed me.

'I reckon this is where you bought our cocktails,' I call across to Tony. 'One for me, one for Fleur.'

Can he hear me? His eyes are still open. I will deal with the padlock in a minute.

'We were naive, didn't suspect a thing. Broke, too, happy to be bought Long Island Ice Teas by a nice American man who thought we were twins and said we should be models and did we want our photos taken? At least I'm guessing that's what you said. You see, I've struggled for years to remember anything about how we met.'

I walk back over to Tony and squat down next to him, our faces separated by the iron bars. His pale temples are beading with sweat.

'We woke up in Fleur's flat eighteen hours later,' I continue. 'Splitting headaches, sore between our legs. Neither of us could remember anything about the previous night, where we'd been, who we'd met. Do you have any idea how terrifying that feels? We lay in bed, staring at our fresh, matching tattoos, scared by our love for each other, its intensity. A sudden uneasiness started to grow between us. What had we done to each other? But it wasn't Fleur, was it? I know that now. She was always so gentle with me. Did you bathe us both afterwards? Wash away your sins? I keep picturing a bathroom, you see: flashes of Fleur shivering on a cold tiled floor, knees clutched to her chest, dead-eyed, begging me for help. That's now, though. For ten years there was only darkness. An episode erased from our lives by whatever it was you slipped into our drinks.'

I walk away from Tony towards the entrance and step outside for some fresh air, surprised by my strength, the bright sunshine. I was worried I wouldn't be able to confront him, wrong-footed by the missing padlock, but I feel empowered, able to cope with anything. Beyond the graffiti-covered wall, trains rattle past on their noisy way to Ostkreuz. Somewhere in the distance a police siren wails. Tony won't remember what I've told him, being brought here, but I've been preparing my speech for a long time. I go back inside, feeling more sorted, and spot a pile of cement sacks in the far corner of the building, beyond the old bar area. I saw some building works where we turned off the main road. Maybe a contractor is keeping their materials in here. There's a lot of rubble around.

'Fleur disappeared the next day, in the afternoon,' I continue, gripping the bars tightly now. I'm suddenly struggling to control my emotions. 'We'd had a salad together in a café across the road and then I returned to her flat, desperate to sleep. That was the last time I ever saw her.'

I turn away. I have no desire for Tony to see my tears. After a few seconds, I am strong enough to face him and hold on to the bars again.

'I went to the police, of course. They investigated, added her to the long list of young people reported missing in Berlin, but she was never found.' I bow my head and take a deep breath, an anger inside me rising like nausea. 'No one knew then that you came into the café that day, sat at a corner table and watched us, looking for tiny flickers of recognition, traces of the night before.'

I can't restrain myself any longer. I open the cage door and walk over to him. 'Where did you take her?' I ask. 'What did you fucking do with her?' I'm shouting now and kick out uncontrollably at him, swinging my leg into his midriff. 'Take her to your sleazy studio? Where is it, Tony?'

He groans, clutching his stomach. I promised myself I wouldn't do this. Promised the monks. I would leave his punishment to the police.

Tony turns his head to face me. His eyes are still glazed, but for the first time he seems to have heard what I said.

'You have a studio, here in Berlin,' I say, my voice more measured now. 'I keep seeing images of it – us, you, seahorses. I need to know where it is.'

I will recognise the studio when I see it. My memory of the early part of the evening, coming here, is still an inky blackness, but isolated images of where he took us later that night have started to rise to the surface in recent months, like etiolated monsters from the deep. A large stencilled seahorse on a whitewashed brick wall. A bath. Tiled floor. Maybe a bed. A white coat. Medical instruments.

I squat down next to Tony again.

'Where the fuck is it?' I whisper, close to his ear.

After much searching, I eventually found his old website, but there was no contact address, just galleries of photos: nightclubs, DJs, a few women.

'My studio?' he says.
'Here in Berlin.'
'You want me to take your photo?'
'Just tell me the address.'
He looks confused.
'And give me the keys.'

IOI

Silas studies the image of the young Tibetan boy staring out at him from an A4 wanted-style poster. A headline reads: 'Help Find the Panchen Lama of Tibet.' Below the photo, details of a financial reward for information about his present whereabouts. Silas hopes the poster might give them the break they need. German police are struggling to trace Maddie's phone and he senses they are not taking their concerns seriously. He met a lot of Tibetan Buddhists when he went on holiday to Ladakh. Conor was young and it was the best family trip they ever had.

He looks up at Strover, on the phone to south India. Strover should travel to the subcontinent. It might improve her patience.

'I'd get a better line to Mars,' she says, dialling again. They've moved desks since the morning and are now by the window.

The poster was brought into the Parade Room a few minutes ago, found by forensics in the lining of Maddie's suitcase. Silas knew at once that he'd seen the face before, on his trip to Ladakh. It also reminded him about the recent online photo credit for Seahorse Photography, Tony's business name, that Strover came across. Tony had taken some press photos of a group of visiting Tibetan Buddhist monks. They were on a tour of English village halls, raising funds for a new kitchen in their monastery in south India, where they live in exile.

Silas has checked out their website: their original monastery, in central Tibet, was founded by the first Dalai Lama and is the traditional seat of successive Panchen Lamas. The photo in Maddie's suitcase is of the eleventh Panchen Lama, taken into political custody by the Chinese authorities in 1995, when he was six. He hasn't been seen since. Another unsolved misper.

He remembers his own attempts to explain the basics of Tibetan Buddhist history to Conor, sitting around a fire one starlit night in Ladakh. Neither of them were any the wiser at the end of it. He looks at the poster again. Why would Maddie carry around a photo like that? And why hide it, unless she was travelling to China?

All he knows is that it's another link to south India, where her mother is from. She returned there ten years ago after divorcing James Thurloe. Maddie seems to have followed a year later. They have been trying to trace them via the police in India – he has put in an urgent request, via Interpol, to the Criminal Investigation Bureau in Delhi – but so far no joy. Now at least they have a connection between Tony and Maddie, something that might help explain why she came to Wiltshire.

Strover gives a thumbs-up and starts to talk.

'Is that the Tashi Lhunpo Monastery in Bylakuppe?' she asks, struggling with the pronunciation. 'In Karnataka?'

A few uniforms look across at her. Why do people always talk in a strange way when they are speaking to foreigners? Silas knows he does. Loud and slowly, as if he's addressing a halfwit. Five minutes and several pages of notes later, Strover puts down the phone.

'OK, so Maddie and her mother are regular visitors to the monastery,' she says, coming over to Silas with her notepad. 'My man, "Lobsang Dorjee,"' she continues, glancing at her notes, 'described them as "kind friends" of their community who live in a nearby town – Kushalnagar? – where they both teach at a local school. Maddie's been up to the monastery's prayer hall a lot in the past six months, more than usual. Learning to meditate apparently.'

'You did say she'd become a nun,' Silas says.

'The monk wouldn't go into details, just that they were helping her to remember things from a long time ago.' Another glance at her notebook. '"Cleanse her mind." Ten days back, she left in a hurry, saying she was going to see a friend in the Gulf. They were all quite worried for her, particularly her mother. They've given me her mother's number – I'll call her now.'

102

Tony watches Maddie move the heavy sacks of cement, one by one, unable to stop her. It takes her a long while, but she doesn't seem to be in a rush. Or maybe it's just him. He knows she's slipped him a sedative of some sort. Until the effects start to wear off, there is nothing he can do. Nothing he wants to do. The lethargy is killing him, a complete deadener. He's just happy to lie down on the concrete floor of his cell and sleep. If only he could stop dancing to her tune. He has already given Maddie the keys to his studio – he watched himself do it with a mix of anger and complete indifference. He must stay awake, get himself out of here.

'If it was anyone else, I'd feel sorry for them,' Maddie says once she's finished constructing her barrier. She's standing in front of the bars, disdain in her eyes, sweat beading on her forehead from all the physical effort. 'Alzheimer's is a cruel disease. And in your case it can't kill you quick enough.'

She turns to go.

'How did you remember?' Tony calls out, his voice still

sloppy. The mental numbness is driving him crazy. 'After all this time?'

She hesitates for a moment, still with her back to him, and walks on, leaving him alone in the building.

'Hey, come back,' he shouts, hit by a sudden wave of paranoia. 'We should talk more.' Silence. Tony's frightened now. She's too in control.

After five minutes, he stands up, unsteady on his feet. The place is almost unrecognisable. GrünesTal was his best hunting ground in Berlin, favourite venue in Europe. Girls, boys, he wasn't fussy. Just had to be his type. He'd carved out a niche as a nightclub photographer and knew all the DJs who played here, taking their publicity shots as he followed them around Europe's top nightclubs, gaining backdoor access wherever he went. It proved the perfect cover. No one suspected a thing.

And when people asked why his business was called Seahorse Photography, he would say he couldn't remember. His private joke. He didn't tell them that seahorses share a name with the hippocampus, where memories are processed. Or that he was terrified that he would die of Alzheimer's, just like his father did. Or that, by inducing temporary amnesia in his victims, he got off on the knowledge that his synapses were superior to theirs, at least for a few hours. His hippocampus might have been rotting, but it was better than their benzo-soaked brains. He would remember everything, all that he did to them, and they would remember nothing. It didn't get much better than that. Not for a man who once harboured dreams of being a neurosurgeon. For a man whose cortex is atrophying.

Tony pushes against the bars. No give, nothing. Maddie has piled five sacks of cement on top of each other and stacked some old tyres next to them. The gate will move. Sooner or later. He just needs to regain some strength. A sense of purpose.

Maddie must have been one of the clubbers he brought back to the studio. It's why he stopped in the end. New country, a fresh start. Too many were beginning to remember, that was the problem, no matter where he sourced his pills. And when they remembered, he had to wipe their memories. Forever. Seven at the last count. Somehow she must have slipped through the net. And he was always very careful, took precautions. Why hasn't she rung the cops? No evidence, not yet. Distant memories don't stand up so well in court. Unreliable or false, Your Honour? Christ, he wants to sleep.

What's she playing at, arriving in the village like that? Did she come specially to seek him out? To seduce him back to Berlin? If so, she's playing the long game. Clever girl. He was right to be suspicious. *Someone to show me around Berlin.* Right to come out here with her, establish how much she knows about his old life. And make her forget if she knows too much. Except she's spiked his drink and thrown him in a frickin' cage. How come he didn't recognise her when she turned up that day on the doorstep? She looked familiar – he just didn't know why. And then he thought she was Jemma Huish. Wishful thinking. What a jerk. Too many plaques and neurofibrillary tangles.

He tries the bars again, more determined now. This time the sacks of cement move.

Half an inch.

103

Tony's studio is in Schillerkiez, a small neighbourhood in northern Neukölln that borders Tempelhof, the site of Berlin's old airport. I texted Luke the address as I left GrünesTal, told him to meet me at the studio in an hour. Built by the Nazis, the airport's hangars now house refugees, which somehow seems fitting. Graffiti is apparently banned on its buildings, unlike the surrounding streets, where the walls are covered in tags.

Fleur and I used to come here when it first opened as a park. It was a rougher neighbourhood in those days, full of edge and excitement. Fleur knew all the best places for Turkish coffee, which local artists were up and coming. We went to a lot of studio openings together, clutching bottles of Augustiner Pils as we nodded knowingly at conceptual art. The area has changed considerably in ten years, chichi cafés on most of the street corners, a boutique art gallery in what was once a laundry.

Today the airfield is full of families out in the summer sun. Teenagers skate past me on the former runway. A father flies a billowing pink kite on the grassy outfield with his son. Parents push prams, women practise yoga. I walk on in the direction of the address that Tony gave me. I don't think he was lying: the Xanax was still making him compliant. I could have asked him to do anything for me. That's what I find so terrifying.

It takes me time to locate the entrance to his studio, tucked away down an alley that's still to be discovered by the developers. No names on the intercom, just three buzzers. I look up at the old building: ground floor, two storeys above. Tony said his studio was in the basement. I walk around to the back where steps lead down to a garage, its rusting door covered in graffiti. Beside it is a small entrance with a lock and letterbox. I glance back up the alley and walk down the steps. One of the keys fits and I open the door, pushing against a mountain of leaflets and junk mail addressed to Seahorse Photography.

I peer down the dark, damp corridor, flicking at a light switch that doesn't work. Does any of this feel familiar? How did Tony get us from GrünesTal to here? By taxi? In his car? I don't recognise anything. Closing my eyes, I breathe in and think of the bodhi tree, letting its deep, reassuring roots help me to remember.

I switch on my phone – the battery is low so I've kept it off since texting Luke – and wait for it to power up. Using its torch, I walk down to a second door at the far end of the corridor. Tony gave me three keys and I insert the second one. My head spins as I shine the torch inside the room. I'm in the right place: a large studio space with whitewashed walls. A flicker of a memory. This is where it happened. I'm sure of it. On the wall in front of me a giant stencilled seahorse stares down in the darkness, its crenellated body reaching from the floor to the ceiling. A surge of adrenaline and I turn away, unable to look at the ugly, ossified creature. Its bulging eyes.

I remember. This is the image that started everything, stirred my memory, took me to a village in England, brought me to Berlin.

I force myself to look at the seahorse again, thinking back to how it all began. Our local monks in south India had just returned from their European fundraising tour, exhausted but elated. Rural England had been wowed by their Tibetan Buddhist workshops and sand mandalas. There was a big meal that night and we were invited up to the Tashi Lhunpo monastery to celebrate. Their tales of village halls in rural England made me homesick for the life I'd left behind. Photographs were passed around like holiday snaps, including one of an event at a village hall in Wiltshire. A row of young children, cross-legged and agog, watching the yellow-hatted monks as they chanted and danced.

I'm not sure why, but I turned the photo over and that's when I saw the logo for Seahorse Photography. The image triggered something so visceral that I struggled to control myself. I gave back the photo, my hand shaking, and ran outside into the courtyard to take some air. My mother followed close behind.

'What's wrong?' she asked.

'I remember.' That's all I said. I remember.

It wasn't much, but it was a start, a glimmer of light in the tranquillised darkness.

I had talked to my mother over the years about the end of my time in Berlin, how those carefree few months of my gap year were brought to a brutal halt by the disappearance of my best friend. I didn't go into details about the clubbing or the drugs. Or that Fleur and I were lovers. There's only so much a parent needs to know. The problem was that I couldn't remember anything about one night in particular. My last night with Fleur. Now, with a name, an image – Seahorse Photography – I had a key that might help me to unlock memories that were never meant to be found.

For the next six months, I worked closely with the monks, who taught me new ways to remember. I'm a teacher at the primary school in our town and I'd go up to the monastery before and after school, studying meditation on the top floor of the Tantric College. It used to be the monastery's original temple and I found it a good place to learn. Afterwards, we would walk outside to the courtyard, where a beautiful bodhi tree cast its cooling shade, just like it had done for the Buddha more than 2,500 years ago. I would sit beneath it, deep in meditation, for many hours at a time, joined by a succession of monks.

At first they thought I wanted to recall past lives, but they soon understood. They began to train my mind to feel its way into the past and retrieve unprocessed emotional memories. To recall what happened in Berlin that night. What happened to Fleur.

'When our minds are quiet, old memories rise to the surface,' one of the monks told me. 'We forget things when our souls are troubled.'

They detected a great fear inside me, dark and suppressed, and introduced me to the teachings of Machig Labdrön, an eleventh-century Tibetan Buddhist teacher and renowned yogini. Associated with enlightened female energy, she is most famous for her 'Chöd' prayer, a visionary practice that encourages you to confront your inner demons and detach yourself from the body and ego. It was scary at times but purging too and I eventually reached a state of clear, unattached awareness. My mind felt more subtle, my perception clearer, particularly of the past. But it wasn't enough. I still couldn't remember that night in Berlin.

It was then that a visiting monk suggested I try some powder, made from the fruit of the bodhi tree. I knew that the leaves and bark of the bodhi – also known as the peepal tree – are revered for their medicinal properties but I was unaware that its figs are said to improve memory. As well as being rich in amino acids, they contain high levels of serotonin and, as I soon discovered online, scientists in India have shown that the figs, in powder form, can reduce anterograde and retrograde amnesia by 'modulating serotonergic neurotransmission'. It was worth a shot.

One morning, when a light mist hung over the monastery courtyard, I had a breakthrough beneath the tree, unlocking a few words from the deepest vaults of my brain. I don't know if it was the powder or the meditation but I realised our strongest memories are wrapped up with emotions as much as images. And I suddenly remembered the feeling of revulsion in my stomach as Tony's voice echoed around the studio I'm now standing in.

'You know what really turns me on? Someone who forgets everything, *every* morning. Day after day. All nice and wholesome and chemical-free. Now that would be a fine thing.'

I'm sure his exact words were different – it was a long time ago – but I remember the appalling gist of it. *Someone who forgets everything, every morning.* It implied such evil. Not only was Tony turned on by the drug-induced blackouts of his victims, but he was seeking something else, a more permanent amnesia in them that would allow for indefinite abuse. *Day after day.*

I had enough to begin hatching a plan, spurred on by the fragments of memory that continued to surface beneath that fruitful bodhi tree. Frightening snapshots of Tony. Of Fleur. Slowly I pieced them together and worked out what I needed to do. It was a dark, devious plan, worthy of its target. Tony would struggle to resist me if I turned up on his doorstep in Wiltshire claiming to have lost my memory. I knew I was his type – I'd proved that once before. And this time there would be no need to slip me some Xanax. *All nice and wholesome and chemical-free.* A natural amnesiac. Organic. What was not to like?

I identified the address in Wiltshire easily enough, once I'd found his name on a new Seahorse Photography website and googled his career as a wedding photographer in the UK. He seemed to have moved recently from the Surrey Hills and I guessed he must have bought a house. I knew which Wiltshire village the monks had visited and the rest I found on Google Maps and the Land Registry website. An estate agent's online details gave me the house's floorplan – I thought it would help my story if I had distant memories of having lived in the property, knew the exact layout of the rooms, the downstairs bathroom, the garden office outside. Amnesiacs can often recall things from their childhood.

The one thing I couldn't have foreseen was being mistaken for Jemma Huish, or that my visit would coincide with the anniversary of her mother's death. I had no idea that Tony was obsessed with her. So much so that he even bought the house where she once lived, hoping she might return one day. As a boxer once famously said, everyone has a plan until they get punched in the mouth.

I look around the deserted studio, shining my light on old storage boxes. There's very little here now, no pictures.

He must have removed all the furniture and photographic equipment, taken it back to England. Just the hideous stencil on the wall. Another memory flickers into life. Fleur lying on a bed in the corner, staring at me with bewildered eyes as Tony does whatever he likes to her. I still can't remember what he did to me.

There's another door in the corner. I walk over and use the third key to unlock it, feeling dizzy as I shine the light around the walls. I've been here before too. I can feel it. The small room is empty except for a solid central surface, like a kitchen island. Or an operating table. And there's the rolltop bath in the corner, where Fleur sat sobbing, clutching her knees.

The floor is tiled, black and white, easy to wash down. I remember how cold it was. Another feeling. How clean it smelt. I walk around the island, running a finger across its smooth, marble-like surface. Tony would hate the dust. A flash of him in a white coat. Was it where he laid out his photos? He liked to print them up himself in the early years. A medical white coat. This wasn't for his photos. It's where he brought me later in the evening, prodded and poked my body like a surgeon sizing up a patient before an operation. Except that I was conscious. Sort of. What did he do to me? I hoped that by coming here I would complete the picture, but sometimes the brain protects us from our worst traumas, puts them beyond reach, even from Machig Labdrön and the serotonin-rich figs of the bodhi tree.

I walk around to the far side of the island, where there is a set of built-in drawers. I pull one open, shine my phone and gasp, barely able to look. A collection of medical tools and instruments. Hand drills, a few scalpels, a saw and surgical chisels. A small steel hammer. Clamps and forceps. What unspeakable things happened in here? I know I've seen them before, but I don't know why. The mere sight of them is making me shake, a deep, instinctive fear. I did well to keep it together at the surgery.

I try to tell myself they're just like the vintage tools my dad used to keep in his garden shed, but I know they're not. Another drawer. This time it is photos, A4 prints. More dried seahorses, like the image I found in Tony's loft. I lift up one of the prints and study it carefully, my hands trembling. A pair of desiccated seahorses photographed on the island surface in front of me. Except that they don't have eyes.

More than the price of silver. I look more closely at the photo. A drop of blood. I turn it over, fear swelling in the pit of my stomach. Anger too. I should have known. I'd read enough about them in India, that they shared the same Latin name as part of the human brain. They're not seahorses.

The writing is in pencil: 'In memory of Florence.'

I hear a noise outside.

104

Silas slams down his phone in the Parade Room. Old contacts have been crawling out of the Fleet Street woodwork all day, asking him for off-the-record comments about yesterday's shooting by the canal. He's got better things to do. Like trying to persuade the BKA in Wiesbaden to take his concerns more seriously. They still haven't managed to track Maddie's Indian phone and don't share his growing alarm that a serial killer might have just flown in to Berlin. His boss doesn't seem to believe him either, dismissing the '*Hippocampus madeleine*' file on Tony's computer as 'artist's whimsy'. Whatever that is.

'I've just got through to Maddie's mum,' Strover says, walking over to his desk. At least she's a believer.

'And...?'

'Beside herself. Had no idea Maddie was in Europe.'

'Did she say anything about the monastery? What Maddie's been trying to remember?'

'Berlin.'

Silas looks up.

'Something bad happened to Maddie there – ten years ago. Her mum wouldn't elaborate.'

His direct line rings. A German number. It's the officer he's been dealing with in the BKA in Wiesbaden.

'We've traced Maddie's phone,' he says, in shamingly good English. 'She switched it on half an hour ago – an old warehouse in Friedrichshain.' He gives the exact address, which Silas writes down. 'Does it mean anything to you?' the officer asks.

'Not yet,' Silas says, passing the address to Strover. She calls it up on her laptop.

'Our colleagues in Berlin have also just had a call from a taxi driver,' the German officer says. 'He was worried about two passengers he dropped off thirty minutes earlier at the same address.'

Strover passes Silas a piece of paper with 'GrünesTal nightclub – Detroit techno' written on it.

'Is that where GrünesTal used to be?' Silas says, glancing at Strover. 'You know, that Detroit techno club?'

'You are younger than you sound,' the officer says.

Silas rolls his eyes.

'It was an English-speaking woman and a man in a wheelchair,' the officer continues. 'He picked them up at Tegel Airport. We've checked with the airlines – Maddie Thurloe ordered a wheelchair.'

A wheelchair? 'What was the taxi driver's concern?'

'He was worried about the man. I think we can stand down. She is taking him sightseeing. "A trip down memory lane," I think you say in English.'

'With respect, I really don't think you can stand down,' Silas says, anger rising. He knows it's a lost cause.

'An interesting theory – about the seahorses and missing people. We must leave it with you now.'

105

I stop to listen. Silence. I should call the police now, tell them where to find Tony, what happened to Fleur. Abandon my plan. And yet I must know everything that happened here. Every last detail. That's why I came.

Tony said something else that night, another fragment: 'Tomorrow we will see each other again as strangers – if you are to live.'

I have thought about that long and hard, pieced it together with my other memories. He must have said it to us before he drove us back to Fleur's flat. A farewell warning to our drugged-up brains, an appeal to our unconscious not to recognise him if we bumped into each other in the street.

Tomorrow we will see each other again as strangers. It wasn't by chance we met the next day. It was a test to see if our amnesia was complete. If he was safe. When we went to a café across the road for a late lunch, still hungover and feeling sore, he must have come in and seen us, fixed us both in the eye. I didn't recognise him, but Fleur... My love, you were always so observant, so alert. Two hours later, she walked to the corner shop to get some soya milk and was never seen again.

I shine the phone around the room for one final time, the torchlight reflecting off the smooth island. I came here to see where Fleur's beautiful life was brought to an end. Pay my respects, purge some of the guilt. I feel close to her here. We shared everything when she was alive – hopes and dreams, headphones and baths. And now I want to share her death too, which I failed to prevent.

I take a deep breath and lie down on the cool island surface, turn off my phone and stare up into the darkness, stilling my mind. Five, maybe ten minutes pass before I see him peering over me, close to my face, wearing a surgical mask. He has some medical tools in his hand – I don't want to look too closely. A scalpel, I think. Maybe a drill. He doesn't do anything to me. He just explains. 'This is what happens to those who remember,' he whispers, close to my ear. 'All things considered, it's best you forget.'

And I did forget. Until now. Only dear Fleur remembered.

I finally feel at peace, here in the place where she spent her last waking moments. No pain, I hope, as the monster removed your memories. I will never forget you, my love. I hold my wrist up in the darkness and kiss the tattoo.

A click outside. Or was it my lips? Another sound, louder this time, like a steel shutter opening and then being closed. It came from behind another door off to my right, which must lead to the garage. Tony didn't give me a key for it. I try to listen, but my blood is beating too loudly in my ears. I feel in the darkness for the drawer by my side, careful not to make a sound.

The door to the garage opens. I turn my head to see the silhouette of a figure.

106

'I'm on my way to Neukölln,' Luke says on the phone to Strover. 'Maddie's texted me to meet there.'

He received her message after waiting half an hour at the airport.

'You might be on your own,' Strover says.

'How come?' Luke says, looking out of the taxi window. He's never been to Berlin before, wishes he wasn't here in these circumstances. His driver keeps pointing out landmarks – Charlottenburg Palace, International Congress Centre – but he's in no mood for sightseeing. He just wants to get to the address in Neukölln as fast as possible.

'Maddie was seen pushing Tony out of the airport in a wheelchair,' Strover says.

'A wheelchair?'

'Her phone was traced to a former nightclub in Friedrichshain before it was switched off. I'll pass your message on to our colleagues in Berlin, but don't hold your breath. What's the address?'

Luke reads out the details. He texted Maddie straight back,

but once again she hasn't replied. There's something very wrong. Is it her sending the messages or is someone else using her phone?

'Do you think she's in danger?' he asks, unable to disguise his mounting worry.

'My boss has passed on our serious concerns. There's not a lot we can do without more evidence. I'm so sorry.'

'And you really think this missing Freya Schmidt looks like Maddie?'

But the line's already gone dead.

107

'Maddie?'

It's Tony. I don't think he can see me yet, lying on the island in the darkness.

'Are you here?' he asks, still in the doorway.

I am barely able to breathe.

'That was so unfriendly,' he continues. 'Knocking me out on the plane like that.'

His voice is still slurred. He will soon be able to see me, once his eyes have adjusted. I can smell nail-varnish remover.

'You've got yourself nice and ready, I see,' he says. 'It's where they all lay. Those who remembered.'

'What did you do with her?' I ask, my voice barely a whisper.

'Normally I have to drug 'em up.'

'What did you do with Fleur?' I repeat. I feel so vulnerable lying down, but I don't want to make any sudden movement.

'Actually, maybe you did lie there. I sometimes gave little warnings. Like a verbal pre-med. You know, if I thought someone might remember.'

I was right. 'Her body?' I say. 'Where did you put her?'

He closes the door behind him and walks into the room. It's pitch black now. He stands there in silence, his breathing slow and steady, unlike mine. The medical smell is growing stronger, like alcohol. Antiseptic. Almost overpowering. I should have rung the police.

'And you did remember,' he continues. 'Jesus, you took your time though. Ten frickin' years.'

I should have found more bags of cement, stacked something else against his cage, taken extra precautions. Or did a part of me hope that Tony would follow me here? That I would share Fleur's fate?

'I thought you'd remember me,' I say, thinking back to that first day when I walked up from the station, limbs heavy with fear. 'When I arrived on your doorstep.'

'I recognised your face. Never forget a pretty face. Just didn't know who you were.'

He sounds drunk.

'You thought I was Jemma Huish,' I say. I need to keep him talking.

'For a while. I was confused.'

I can't help myself. 'How bad is it now? Your memory.'

'How bad?' He pauses. 'How bad?' His voice is mocking, angry. That's the irony. Bit by bit, he's becoming as forgetful as his victims. I know it's his worst fear. 'I can still remember what happened yesterday,' he continues. 'More than can be said for your dumb bitch of a friend Flo.'

'Fleur.' I close my eyes, trying to control my own anger now. How dare he? 'And she so wasn't dumb.'

'Told me her mom called her Florence. Just before I opened her up.'

I can't bear it, the last conversation that Fleur must have

had with him. Lying here on this table in terror, talking about her mother. She would have been brave to the end.

'I've always preferred formal names,' Tony continues. 'They look better on the pictures. More Latin-sounding somehow.'

'How many?' I ask.

Tony is closer now, to my right. I can just make out his outline. My hand is in the drawer on the left, feeling through the metal instruments.

'About to be eight. Each one's memories immortalised in art. I got your seahorse ready, just in case. Started to worry when you remembered your name. *"Hippocampus madeleine."* Never had you down as the lying sort though. You had me fooled there. One step ahead.'

My fingers move over the sharp edge of a chisel and slide down the shaft to grip the handle.

'Big frickin' gamble, that was,' he continues. 'Turning up on my doorstep.'

'Not really.' I pause. There was something else that I remembered in India, another piece of the puzzle that gave me the courage to pursue my plan, roll the dice and risk recognition on his doorstep. 'You said something that night: "My brain is dying." Those were your words. "My brain is dying." I calculated your decaying synapses might not recall my pretty little face. Or my tattoo. We both had one, Fleur and me, the night you took us. Matching flowers. Memorable. I watched you closely when I arrived at your house. The tattoo was my canary in the mine. If the sight of it triggered something, I'd have been out of there in a flash. But no. Nothing. Not even a flicker of recognition. Still forgetting what the car keys are for?'

'You bitch,' he says, lunging at me.

I feel a cloth on my face. A penetrating smell. Like overripe bananas. I grip the chisel tightly and arc my left arm towards his head in a vicious swing. As it makes contact, I roll off the table onto the floor, pulling the cloth from my face. Tony falls too, landing on his back. I don't want to look where the chisel is embedded.

He groans, reaches for the tool and pulls it out.

'That was a mistake,' he whispers.

I know I've hurt him. Blood is pooling on the tiled floor. The floor he kept so clean. What a mess he's made. I stand up, looking down on his helpless figure. Before I left our village, I promised the monks my demons had gone, leaving only compassion in my heart, just as Machig Labdrön wished. But I knew deep down what I had to do, why I was leaving in a hurry. I came here to complete the picture of what happened that night. And also to kill Tony. I hate him with a passion that I am unable to control. Hate him for what he did to Fleur. All the people he's taken or abused.

I reach for the drawer and pull out the small steel hammer.

'Kill me,' he says.

'Where did you hide Fleur's body?' I ask, surprised by the heaviness of the hammer. I need to know I've got it right.

'She shouldn't have glanced up at me.'

'Where?'

'In the café.'

My theory is correct.

'One glance, but that was enough. You can see it in their eyes. Recognition.'

I grip the hammer at my side. 'Tell me where,' I repeat.

'The Müggelsee,' he says. One of Berlin's lakes. Fleur took me there once. We walked the shore arm in arm in the spring sunshine before going to see *The Lives of Others* at a friend's flat. The bastard.

'All of them?' I ask.

'That would be telling.'

I can bear it no longer. I want to break Tony's head into tiny pieces, shatter the memories of all the pain he's ever inflicted, erase them from this earth for ever. I hold the hammer high, my eyes locked onto his.

'Do it,' he whispers.

'I will,' I say. 'Don't you worry.' And I know I will.

A moment later, I hear the sound of the garage shutter and the door is open and light is streaming into the room.

'Maddie!' Luke shouts out, rushing towards me. 'Stop! Put the hammer down. Please.'

The hammer is still poised above my head. I look at Tony, pathetic, dying, and let Luke take the hammer from me. My work here is done. Luke reaches for his phone, but the police are already on their way, sirens wailing ever closer from across the city.

ONE MONTH LATER

108

'Where's Milo?' Maddie asks.

'Round at Laura's.' Luke adjusts the iPad on his kitchen table so that he can still see Maddie on his screen while he pours himself a glass of water at the sink. 'She's teaching him yoga, would you believe it?' he calls out.

'That's great,' Maddie says, smiling, but Luke can tell she's making an effort to be cheerful. She's back in her mother's house in the town in south India with the name he can never remember. Kushalnagar?

'Something to take the stress out of his exams,' Luke continues, sitting back down at the table. 'He has two sessions a week with a couple of his female friends. I think he's just trying to impress them. Show them his feminine side.'

'How is Laura?' Maddie asks, her voice quieter now. They've been talking a lot on FaceTime in recent weeks. He needs it as much as she does as they both come to terms with what happened in Berlin.

'Doing pretty well. All things considered. We see quite a bit of each other.'

'I hope you can bring some happiness into her life.'

'Me too,' he says, pausing. Some days when they talk, Luke thinks Maddie's doing fine; at other times, like today, he worries for her. 'Are you OK?'

Maddie turns away from the screen. 'I'm fine,' she says. 'I think Mum's back. I better go.' She reaches forward to turn off the screen, a false smile on her lips.

'Wait,' Luke says.

Maddie hesitates, struggling to compose herself.

'Call me any time,' he continues. 'If you need to talk. You know, about anything.' On several occasions recently, he has felt that Maddie is on the point of telling him something important, but then she holds back.

'Thank you,' she says. 'I will.'

The screen goes blank. Luke turns off the iPad, hoping she's OK. She has told him her story, as she promised, first face to face in Berlin – they both had to stay on for a while to help the German police with their enquiries – and then online after she returned to India. He's decided not to write it up for the newspapers. She said he could if he wanted, but his life has moved on. What matters is that she isn't adopted, nor is her mother a Baha'i. And she is not Freya Schmidt, the woman on the missing persons list in Berlin.

As for the events of ten years earlier, Maddie followed her mother back to India after the trauma of being date-raped by Tony and the disappearance of her best friend. She hasn't exactly lived a monastic existence since, but she did choose to draw a line under her Western upbringing and realign herself with India and her mother's roots in the south of the country. It took ten years for her to start recalling what Tony did to her and Fleur in Berlin, prompted by one of his photos surfacing at her local monastery. What happened next has already been widely reported in the media and more is expected to come out at Tony's trial later in the year in Berlin, where Luke and Maddie will both be appearing for the prosecution.

After putting a couple of pies in the oven, Luke walks down School Road to see Laura. She's decided to stay on in the same house, despite its history.

'We've just finished,' she says, opening the door in her yoga kit. 'Come on in. They're having fresh elderflower juice in the garden.'

Luke follows her through to the low-ceilinged sitting room. He can see Milo and two girls out the back. Definitely chirpsing.

'Will you stay for a bit?' Laura asks, sitting down on a sofa.

'I'm on my way to the pub actually,' Luke says. DC Strover is visiting the village for a bit of community policing. A drink, in other words. She and Sean seem to have bonded and he's been invited along to join them. 'Maybe later?'

'That would be nice.' Laura doesn't like being in the house on her own and he's spent quite a few nights on the sofa she's sitting on. Milo's slept around here too a couple of times.

He watches Laura get up and walk over to the mantelpiece.

'Maddie's sent me a letter,' she says, holding up an airmail envelope. 'I haven't read it yet, but I will.'

They've done a lot of talking in recent weeks, about Tony, his victims, Maddie. Laura realises how brave Maddie was, but she's still struggling to come to terms with the method she chose to entrap her husband. The sheer cold-heartedness. The calculation.

Luke hopes the two women will one day meet up. He sees it as his mission to bring about a reconciliation between them. At least an understanding.

Down at the Slaughtered Lamb, Luke finds Sean and DC Strover huddled in a corner. He's still trying to get his head around their burgeoning relationship.

'My boss should be here any minute,' Strover says as Luke returns from the bar with a round of drinks.

'DI Hart?'

'On a date,' Strover says, making room for Luke to sit down. 'With your GP.'

'Villages, eh?' Sean says, taking the top off his pint of Guinness.

'Before the boss arrives, I need to share something with you and Luke,' Strover says, her voice quiet and conspiratorial. Luke and Sean lean in, listening closely. 'About Maddie Thurloe's DNA.'

'Sounds like you're about to contravene her human rights,' Sean says conspiratorially.

Luke feels genuinely uneasy about what might be coming, but he doesn't say anything. He hasn't told people in the village that he's been talking to Maddie on FaceTime.

'You didn't hear this from me,' Strover says.

'Honest to God, I swear we've never met,' Sean says.

Strover might have to take him home soon. His latest film script was bought last week by a studio and he's been celebrating in the pub ever since.

'It's been in all the papers that she had an Irish father and an Indian mother,' Strover says. 'What surprised forensics was evidence of Russian ancestry.'

Sean nearly chokes on his pint. 'What did I tell you?' he says, spilling his Guinness everywhere. 'Knew it all along. One of Moscow's finest, for sure.'

Luke looks at Strover, who winks at him. He'll tell Sean later, let him down gently.

Strover has gone out of her way since the events in Berlin to help Luke in his quest to find his daughter. She hasn't said as much, but there's a suggestion that Freya Schmidt is no longer technically a missing person in Germany and has simply chosen not to be in contact with her parents. The police in Berlin have been similarly cooperative, grateful for the help they received from Wiltshire Police in the capture of a serial killer. When Strover explained that she had an important message from someone for Freya Schmidt and could the German authorities please pass it on, no strings attached, they were more than happy to oblige. Luke is hopeful that she might one day choose to reply and get in touch with him. He is yet to establish if she is adopted but at least she is called Freya.

'Here's the boss,' Strover says.

Luke looks up to see DI Hart at the door. He's alone.

'Everyone alright for drinks?' Hart asks, coming over to their table, glancing at Luke. He looks slimmer than Luke remembers. It's not exactly friendship between them, but there's a mutual respect now. Hart called him in for a chat at Gablecross on his return from Berlin, thanked him personally for what he did.

The German police finally took Swindon CID's concerns seriously when Hart relayed the address of Tony's studio to them, sent by Luke. It promptly flagged up an old alert. A neighbour had reported suspicious behaviour at the address over the years – strange noises, the sound of a struggle, a car returning there late at night – but it was never investigated. Turns out Tony would carry the bodies through to the garage and then drive them over to the Müggelsee. Only three victims have been recovered from the lake to date – Fleur's has yet to be found – but it's more than enough for the case against Tony, who is expected to be sent down for life.

'Is there a doctor in the house?' Sean asks, tactless as ever.

'Dr Patterson's working late,' Hart says, catching Strover's eye.

'Let me get you a pint,' Luke says before things get any more awkward. 'What you having?'

'I'll come up with you,' Hart says.

Luke and Hart stand at the bar, unlikely drinking companions.

'Sorry about Sean,' Luke offers.

'I've heard worse.' Hart pauses. 'Not the first time I've been stood up either.'

'You look well,' Luke says.

'Vegan diet. Quit the fags. I've just read your witness statement, wanted to thank you. For what you wrote about the shooting by the canal.'

'It's what I saw.'

'I wish others had been so honest.' He takes his pint and drinks deeply from it. 'The heat's been taken off us, as you can imagine. Not every day Swindon CID catches an international serial killer.'

'Not since the Swindon strangler,' Luke says, glancing across the bar at Sean and Strover. Normally so demure, there's a bit of sparkle in her eyes tonight.

'That was the Major Crime Investigation Team – don't get me started on inter-force collaborations,' Hart says. 'Know anything about the eleventh Panchen Lama?'

'A bit.'

'Missing since he was six.' Hart pulls out a wanted poster and hands it to Luke. He studies the face of the young Tibetan boy.

'It was a promise Maddie made to the monks at her monastery,' Hart says. 'Before she left. To spread the word about him in the West. It would make a great story. You might even get to meet the Dalai Lama.'

'Thanks.'

Luke takes the sheet of paper, reads it and puts it away. Maddie has already told him all about the eleventh Panchen Lama, made him promise he'll write about him. He's planning to head out to that part of the world in the summer with Milo, call in on an old flame in Ludhiana before heading up to Ladakh. Maybe he'll invite Laura along too, if she's up to it.

'The German doctors are saying Tony Masters could be too ill to appear in court,' Hart says. 'A surgical chisel to the head wasn't great for his Alzheimer's.'

'I did what I could to save him.'

Luke thinks back to how he tried to staunch the flow of blood from Tony's wound, how Maddie has told him since that she wishes he'd died.

'Others might not have bothered,' Hart says. 'How's his wife doing – Laura?'

'Pretty good in the circumstances. Dr Patterson is proving an amazing friend and GP. Others in the village are helping her too.' He pauses. 'Maddie's just written her a long letter. I think it will help.'

'Collateral damage – that's how Maddie explained it to us in her interviews,' Hart says.

'She feels terrible,' Luke says.

'I'm sure she does.' Hart takes another sip of his pint and glances around the pub. 'Just so you know, our German colleagues called me tonight,' he continues. 'They've found another body in the Müggelsee.'

'Fleur's?'

'They think so. They're running tests now. You might want to warn Maddie. Prepare her.'

Luke has told Hart that he's in touch with Maddie in India. At least it will give her some closure. He could do with some himself. Fingers crossed about Freya Schmidt.

'What I'm still struggling to get my head around is the sheer audacity of her plan,' Hart says. 'Coming here to this village, playing the vulnerable woman in the home of a serial killer, knowing it was the only way to lure Tony back to Berlin. The only way she'd find out what really happened to Fleur.' He raises his pint glass towards Luke, as if toasting the absent Maddie, and fixes him in the eye. 'That takes balls of steel.'

109

I'm out of breath by the time I reach the top of the steps, but the view is worth it. Below me, the Kumaradhara river plunges two hundred feet into a gorge, the cascading waters throwing up a fine mist that drifts across the tropical forest. Indian rose chestnut, white dammar, mango, fragrant ashok – Mum taught me the names of all the trees when she brought me up here ten years ago, soon after I had returned from Berlin. They're alive with birds too – racket-tailed drongos and Malabar grey hornbills. I was damaged then, a silent, bewildered daughter, unable to understand what had happened to me, to Fleur.

Today I feel stronger, more at peace with the beauty of this place. The roar of the water was like a wounded animal when I last heard it. This time it sounds reassuring, empowering. I look up at the fertile, rolling hills of the Western Ghats in the distance and wonder why I would choose to live anywhere else.

It's been just over a month since I confronted Tony in Berlin. Mum's pleased to have me home again and I'm finding the routine of teaching in the school a great help. Children can be remarkably accepting, indifferent to the violent currents that wash through adults' lives. I spoke to Luke on FaceTime yesterday – he's become a good friend and I hope it's mutual. It would lessen the damage I have caused to Laura if they are able to move forward in life together, but let's see. There's no rush. First Luke wants to find his daughter – I nearly managed yesterday, but I still can't bring myself to tell him he is searching in vain. Perhaps because a part of me still hopes I might be wrong.

After a few more minutes, I walk back down the long flight of steps, passing breathless sightseers who are on their way up. The Mallalli Falls are not an easy place to reach. I came by bus from Kushalnagar and then had to share a jeep ride and walk the last two kilometres. The arrival of the monsoon has made the roads treacherous. It's also swollen the river magnificently and I'm determined to get closer to it.

Near the bottom of the path I turn off the tourist trail and head towards the thunderous waters. The air is almost opaque with river spray and my clothes are drenched. But it doesn't matter. Many people come here when it's not the rainy season to submerse themselves in the Kumaradhara. Further downstream, it forms a *sangam* with another river and the conjoined waters are considered to be holy.

I tread carefully on the big boulders, which are wet and slippery and covered in algae, but I'm soon close enough to the river for what I need to do. Someone high above me, a forest department official perhaps, calls down, warning of the danger. I'm more worried about the leeches.

I look around and take off my small rucksack, careful to keep my balance on the rock. On my way here, our jeep passed a row of shops selling souvenirs. I asked at one of them if they knew where I could find a lotus – the state flower of Karnataka – and he took me to a pond behind a nearby Hindu temple, where I was able to pick one (in return for baksheesh, of course). I take the purple lotus out of the box I brought to protect it and hold the flower out in front of me. Symbol of purity and beauty. Of Fleur.

I was devastated when the police failed to retrieve her body from the lake. They will find it soon and, if I'm right, there will be no need for me to tell Luke. Either way, the matter will be settled. He has convinced himself that a woman called Freya Schmidt is his daughter. I hope to God he is right.

My own suspicions started to gain a sickening momentum a few days ago, when I was up at the monastery. The recent events in Berlin seem to have unlocked more of the past and I'm working with the monks to retrieve further memories of what happened ten years ago. They are mostly vague, unformed recollections, but I am sure now that it was Fleur's idea to get the lotus tattoo that night, the night Tony took us back to his studio. The flower was a sign of our love for each other, but she said something else that subsequently got buried by Tony's benzodiazepines: the lotus was for her mum. I know that she'd run off to Berlin to rebel against her parents, but she clearly still loved them.

And I now believe Fleur's mum was a Baha'i.

I roll up my sleeve and look at the flower, just to be sure. For the umpteenth time I count the petals. Nine. When I first got back from Berlin, ten years ago, my own mother saw the tattoo on my wrist and asked about the 'extra' petal. In Buddhism, she said, the purple lotus usually has eight, symbolising the eightfold path to enlightenment. I thought nothing more about it until recently, when Luke told me that the woman who adopted his daughter was a Baha'i. Nine is important for Baha'is – the number of perfection. It's why their temple in Delhi, shaped like a lotus, has nine sides.

I know I should talk to Luke, be brave and share my fears with him. Everything that he has told me about his own daughter, the one he's looking for, makes me think he'll never find her now. It would certainly explain why I liked Luke from the start, when we met in the village surgery. There was an unusual connection. A familiarity. I will tell him soon.

I turn to look at the mighty waterfall above me, arms outstretched, and think of Fleur, of all the happy times we spent together, the laughter, the dancing, the long walks along the River Spree, drinking pilsner on the Island of Youth. I let the myriad droplets of water pass through my soaked salwar kameez, cleansing my soul of the evil Tony did to us in Berlin, washing away my tears. And then I throw the lotus high into the deafening roar and watch it fall into the white waters below, twisting and turning on its lonely way to the Arabian Sea and beyond.

Acknowledgements

Thank you to my superlative agent, Will Francis, and everyone at the London office of Janklow & Nebsit, particularly Kirsty Gordon, Rebecca Folland and Ellis Hazelgrove. Thanks too to Kirby Kim and Brenna English-Loeb in the New York office.

I am indebted to all the team at my UK publishers, Head of Zeus, particularly Laura Palmer, my excellent editor; Lauren Atherton, Maddy O'Shea, Chrissy Ryan, Blake Brooks and Suzanne Sangster. Thanks too to Lucy Ridout and Jon Appleton for the copy-editing and proofreading. At Park Row Books in America, I'd like to thank Liz Stein, Laura Brown and Erika Imranyi. Thanks too to Toby Ashworth, my Cornish publisher, for his unstinting encouragement and inside knowledge of hotel fire alarms.

A lot of people have helped with the subject of amnesia – apologies if I have forgotten anyone... Many thanks to Dr Angela Paddon, whose medical advice and expertise has been invaluable. Needless to say, her own village surgery is far more friendly, professional and efficient than the fictitious one depicted here. Thanks too to Dr Andy Beale and Mary Soellner.

Adam Zeman, Professor of Cognitive and Behavioural Neurology at Exeter University, gave a series of inspiring lectures on BBC Radio 3 entitled *The Strangeness of Memory*. Books that were helpful include Jules Montague's insightful *Lost and Found: Memory, Identity and Who We Become When We're No Longer Ourselves*, and *The Memory Illusion: Remembering, Forgetting, and the Science of False Memory* by Dr Julia Shaw.

Detective Superintendent Jeremy Carter of Wiltshire Police and Inspector Chris Ward of Thames Valley Police have been very generous with their knowledge and time. Thanks too to Daniel Webb, news editor of Wiltshire999s.co.uk and Clive Chamberlain (@MrCliveC), former village bobby and *Police Magazine* columnist.

Julian Hendy and his Hundred Families charity website (hundredfamilies.org) provided comprehensive and disturbing information about the number of mental health homicides in the UK – around 100 each year.

Jane Rasch, manager of the Tashi Lhunpo Monastery UK Trust (tashi-lhunpo.org.uk), introduced me to the teachings of Machig Labdrön, an eleventh century Tibetan Buddhist, and helped with other yellow hat queries too.

Professor Andrew Reynolds of the UCL Institute of Archaeology and Robbie Trevelyan answered all my earthy questions – apologies that the dig didn't make the cut.

Richard Castle shone an expert light on the airline industry and Jake Farman and Nick Holgate taught me the difference between classic and vintage cars. J.P. Sheerin's editorial feedback is always excellent, ditto his screenplays. Thanks too to Joanna Bridgeworth and the Abingdon writers for their encouragement; to Dr Stephen Gooder for his knowledge of maps. And to the late Len Heath, a much-missed friend, writer and inspiration.

Most of all I'd like to thank my family. Felix, for answering all my questions about Berlin and techno; Maya for talking things through in the early days; Jago for the teenage insights and lingo; and my ever patient and supportive wife Hilary, who continues to ride the highs and lows of being married to a writer with heroic stoicism, humour and love.